A HIGHLAND KNIGHT'S DESIRE

AMY JARECKI

All rights reserved.

No part of this publication may be sold, copied, distributed, reproduced or transmitted in any form or by any means, mechanical or digital, including photocopying and recording or by any information storage and retrieval system without the prior written permission of both the publisher, Oliver-Heber Books and the author, Amy Jarecki, except in the case of brief quotations embodied in critical articles and reviews.

PUBLISHER'S NOTE: This is a work of fiction. Names, characters, places, and incidents either are the product of the author's imagination or are used fictitiously. Any resemblance to actual persons, living or dead, business establishments, events, or locales is entirely coincidental.

Copyright © 2015, Amy Jarecki

Published by Oliver-Heber Books

0 9 8 7 6 5 4 3 2 1

Chapter One
MELROSE ABBEY, JANUARY, 1478

Before she knelt, Meg stole a glance behind her. A silent sigh slipped through pursed lips. As he'd promised, her tenacious guard wasn't standing at the rear of the nave watching. She had several things she wanted to accomplish on this pilgrimage—most importantly, gaining an audience with the abbot. After pleading nearly the entire two-day journey from Tantallon Castle, she'd convinced the guard to allow her a modicum of freedom—at least within the walls of Melrose Abbey.

Out of the corner of her eye, a bronze cross flickered. It sat atop an altar in a quiet aisle chapel. Meg tiptoed over. She'd have complete solitude there.

Kneeling, she folded her hands and gazed at the cross. She'd prayed endlessly for guidance, but presently her mind blanked. She closed her eyes. Ah, yes...

Firstly, thank you for our safe passage, and thank you for all my blessings...aside from my unruly red hair and my claw of a hand, but we've discussed that hundreds of times. I'm well aware Arthur will be unable to find me a suitable husband. I must take matters into my own hands...and give them over to you, God. That's where I belong—serving you. Please help me gain an audience with his holiness, the abbot, that I may make my wishes clear and take up the veil...

Someone tapped her shoulder. She glanced up. A pair of white-robed monks stood behind her.

"Come," one said.

Meg's heart fluttered. Had her prayers been answered so quickly? "Are you taking me to the abbot?"

They exchanged glances. "Aye," the tallest one clipped. A jagged scar etched the side of his cheek.

Meg eagerly stood and gestured for them to proceed. The corner of the shorter one's mouth smirked. They were an odd pair, indeed.

Single file, she walked between the two men. The tallest led her straight to the rood screen concealing the choir. Abruptly she stopped and clapped her hand to her chest.

The shorter one waved her forward with a flick of his wrist.

"I cannot." She kept her voice low. "I've not yet taken the veil."

The taller monk frowned, stretching his scar downward. He clamped his fingers around Meg's elbow, his grip a bit forceful for a monk. "You must pass this way to meet the abbot," he whispered, so softly Meg could hardly discern his words.

She withdrew her arm from his grasp and inclined her head toward the entry. If this was what God intended, then she'd proceed. Surely she would commit no sin by entering restricted holy ground for the purpose of declaring her wishes to become a novice.

Crossing through the ornately carved rood screen, Meg walked into the dim choir where only monks who had taken the vows of chastity, poverty and obedience were allowed to worship. The walls were lined with two tiers of choir stalls, where each monk would pray from lauds to compline. Their footfalls loudly echoed up to the vaulted ceiling.

A poke in the back caught her attention. The leader had already moved through and held open a thick wooden door. Meg understood the impatient look on the man's face. She'd seen the same expression from her brother a hundred times before. She hastened her pace. Why was there never enough time to stop and admire her surroundings?

Stepping outside into the frigid air, she used her hand to shield her eyes from the sun shining through the clouds. "I'm surprised the abbot is aware I'm here. I hadn't yet made a request to meet with him."

Neither man said a word. They'd just spoken to her, so they mustn't have taken a vow of silence. Was this an area of the abbey where no one was allowed to speak? Were they near the sacred tomb where Robert the Bruce's heart had been laid to rest—yet another relic to which Meg wanted to pay homage on this, her first pilgrimage.

She quickly scanned the surrounding garden. There were no graves at all. The monks sped their pace yet again. Arriving at a doorway leading through the cloister wall, the shorter monk stepped beside Meg and grasped her arm. "We'll be taking a detour, miss." This was the first time the stout monk had spoken.

Miss? The daughter of a Scottish earl, Meg's respectful courtesy was "my lady."

Something was awry.

Meg's mind clicked.

Her blood turned to ice. *English.* No mistaking it, this man had an English accent.

"Release me." Meg dug in her heels and yanked her arm away. Her heart flying to her throat, she shuffled backward and raised her skirts with trembling hands as she prepared to flee.

"Help!"

Gasping in short bursts, Meg sprinted toward the abbey.

Footsteps slapped the mud behind her. "Bloody hell, Isaac..."

A hand clapped over her mouth and another around her waist. Meg struggled, kicked, scratched—anything to break free. In the blink of an eye, the stocky monk hauled her outside the abbey curtain walls. With not a soul in sight, three horses stood tethered at the treeline edge.

Screaming through the brutal palm clamped over her lips, she kicked and thrashed her entire body until the imposter brutally slapped her across the face. Recoiling, Meg's feet touched the ground. She shrieked and tried to run. Fingers of iron held her in place. A gag filled her mouth while unforgiving hands bound her wrists.

The scarred monk grabbed Meg by the waist and hefted her onto the horse's back, belly first. Before she could right herself, the short one lashed another rope around her wrists and tied her hands to her legs under the horse's barrel.

Margaret cried out through the coarse cloth biting into her mouth. She jerked her arms, only to pull her legs under the horse. Her body slid sideways awkwardly. *God in heaven, why are they doing this?* Her gaze darted from side to side as she tried to scream louder, only to be muted by the foul-tasting gag.

The men mounted. One tugged her horse's lead and raced away at a gallop. Meg clamped onto the horse's short hair while her gut thumped into the unyielding gelding's back. Her heart raced faster than the hoofbeats. Her chin slammed into the steed's barrel repeatedly—until stars crossed her vision.

Chapter Two

Duncan Campbell followed the servant through the passageway of Tantallon Castle, his brother John at his elbow. The missive from Lord Arthur Douglas, the Earl of Angus, had been vague to say the least, but on one thing he'd been clear: Arthur's sister, Lady Meg Douglas, had been kidnapped by the English.

The servant held up his hand. "Please wait here and I'll announce your arrival." He opened the door and slipped inside a solar. "Sir Duncan Campbell and Sir John Campbell, m'lord."

Silence.

Duncan could picture the earl's frowning face, and he stood a little straighter. He'd come in his father's stead. Few men knew he'd taken up the Lord of Glenorchy's mantle—yet.

"Well, don't just stand there, show the *Highlanders* in." The earl's gruff voice filled the corridor, adding a deprecating inflection to "Highlanders," as if the Lowland earl believed himself superior.

The steward led them inside and made the requisite introductions. Sitting at a thick walnut table, the Earl of Angus appeared every bit as disagreeable as Duncan had envisioned. Arthur Douglas was only two years his senior. Duncan tipped up his chin. As heir to the

Campbell dynasty, they were peers. There was no cause to bow. John, however, bowed deeply. Blast him. Duncan swallowed his Highland pride and offered a courteous dip of his head. "We came as soon as we received word, m'lord."

"I expected the Black Knight, not a pair of wet-eared lads who've recently attained their majority."

"At three and twenty, my father had already returned from his first crusade." Duncan rested his palm on the pommel of his sword. If only he could draw it and slice that smirk off the earl's face. "I assure you, my men and I were trained under his critical eye. You'll not find another team better."

Licking his lips, the earl's gaze drifted to Duncan's hilt. "This matter is delicate. One wrong move and it could incite war between our borders and crush the truce the king has worked so hard to maintain." The earl swiped fingers, bejeweled with rings, across his mouth. "God forbid a Douglas is blamed for that."

"Your missive said your sister's been abducted," John said.

Duncan shot him a stern glare. They'd agreed he'd do the talking. He led his band of stealthy warriors, and Duncan would not have his authority undermined, not even by his younger brother, and especially not in front of a peer—one in possession of a vast sum of coin, at that.

The earl nodded and pulled a folded missive from beneath his surcoat. "Addressed to me, this was found at Melrose Abbey—in the pew where Lady Meg was praying. The bastards took her in broad daylight with no one the wiser. 'Tis almost as if she vanished into thin air."

Duncan grasped the note and read. "What rift have you with the Earl of Northumberland?"

Arthur spread his palms. "Me? None, but my father

sacked Alnwick Castle in '62. Da's the reason the Percy's lost the Northumberland earldom."

Duncan knitted his brows. "But Henry claimed it back."

"Aye." Arthur pointed at the vellum. "Now he's set his house to rights, it appears he's out for vengeance."

Duncan placed the missive on the table. The pieces of the puzzle were coming together. "And if you march an army across the border, you'll risk destroying the truce between England and Scotland."

"Exactly. Can you ferret her out quietly?"

"If anyone can, 'tis me brother," John said.

Duncan again glared at his younger sibling. "Sounds easy enough—spirit inside under disguise, find a weakness and slip her out."

"Do not underestimate Lord Percy. He's a slithering snake, that one—nothing about this mission is easy, else I'd have done it myself." Arthur leaned forward. "You've been to England?"

"Aye, let's say I've had my dealings with Queen Margaret and the Lancasters. I was there long enough to develop a foul taste for the Yorkists as well."

Arthur leaned back and drummed his fingers on his armrests, as if he were considering his options. "You're awfully confident, but then I'd expect that from a Campbell."

Duncan had no time for a pompous Lowlander or any slights against his kin. He crossed his arms. "Do you want your sister returned to Tantallon or nay?"

Arthur stood and moved to the sideboard. "She's a feisty one, Meg." He poured three tots of whisky. "She thinks she wants to take up the veil, but I've an alliance to make with her hand."

Duncan's gut twisted. "Do you believe Lord Percy would ruin her?" He could not abide any man who defiled a woman. The thought of it made the blood run hot beneath his skin.

7

Arthur paled. "If the bastard does, he'll break the truce for certain."

Duncan accepted the cup and sipped, savoring the oaken flavor. *I must spirit Lady Meg away quickly, lest she be ruined. Boar's ballocks, the entire country could go to war because of an earl's sister.*

The earl tossed his whisky back and cleared his throat. "Bring her home and I'll see you're rewarded for your trouble."

Duncan set his cup on the table and fingered it. Then he looked directly into the earl's eyes. "I'll need a quarter now."

Arthur gaped. "A quarter to an unproven pup?"

Duncan stepped close enough that the Earl of Angus was forced to crane his neck. "If it is credentials you're seeking, I'd be happy to give you a demonstration in the courtyard forthwith—else I'll be taking the quarter to cover my men's expenses and be on my way."

For a moment, Duncan thought Arthur might lead him outside, which he'd welcome. It never hurt to demonstrate one's abilities to a paying customer.

But the earl ran his finger around the inside of his cup and licked it. "Agreed."

Duncan let out a slow breath. Perhaps he should have negotiated for half.

Chapter Three

Meg paced across the wooden floor, her arms tightly hugged against her ribs to stave off the cold. Her misty breath billowed with every exhale. They'd locked her in a tower someplace in godforsaken England. Her tiny chamber had one arrow slit, from which she could see little. At least she'd discerned the room was higher than the battlements. Occasionally, a sentry passed on the wall-walk below. Opposite the courtyard sat a chapel with a cross atop a steeple, and that was all she could see.

Before she'd arrived, her captors had ridden for two long days. Fortunately, about three miles outside Melrose, they'd stopped and allowed her to sit astride the horse, though they'd kept her hands bound. She'd asked countless questions, until they gagged her again.

One day those two brutes would see justice, and so would anyone else a party to her kidnapping.

They'd approached this castle in the dark of night. Its enormous outline loomed in the moonlit sky. *The fortress of the devil.* The heavy black doors of the barbican opened for her like the mouth of a sea monster swallowing its quarry.

Pulled from her horse, there was no time to find her bearings while they'd bustled her up countless tower steps and thrust her inside this miserable chamber. Meg squeezed her arms tighter. The guard who brought her meals spoke in monosyllables. Sooner or later someone must come and explain why she'd been kidnapped from a place of sanctuary. She was the daughter of an earl. That also had to count for something.

The sound of iron keys clanked and scraped in the lock. Meg stood straight and faced the door. By all the saints, she would never allow a one of her captors to think her a coward. A tall and lanky man stepped inside with an appraising smirk. Well dressed in red velvet, he could have passed for a king, right up to his richly ornamented doublet and feathered cap.

Keeping her arms crossed, Meg balled her crippled hand into a fist and tucked it beneath her armpit.

He sauntered into the chamber. "Margaret Douglas."

"Lady Meg," she corrected. No one ever called her Margaret—that had been her grandmother's name.

He scoffed, his eyes trailing down her body as though he hadn't eaten in a week. "I'm shocked to see a repugnant chap like the fourth Earl of Angus could produce from his loins a creature so comely." He stepped closer.

"I demand some answers." Meg scooted backward. "Where am I and why was I stolen from the sanctity of holy ground, aside from being gagged, bound and wrestled into this abominable tower?" She tried to keep her voice from quavering, but the sneer stretching his lips unnerved her.

He took another step.

Meg's shoulder blades hit stone. Her heart hammered so forcefully, she feared it might thump out of her chest. She straightened her spine against the wall. "And you, sir, are *shameful* coming in here, eyeing me like roast mutton without so much as an introduction." She pursed her lips and tried to swallow. Her gaze darted to the door. He'd left it open, but a gauntleted hand grasped a poleax just beyond. *No chance to flee—yet.*

He stopped inches away. "I am Lord Percy, the Earl of Northumberland," he said with an air of arrogance. "And you are my prisoner."

She would not allow his English title to impress her. She'd lived in the castle of an earl her entire life. Meg willed herself to steel her nerves. "Why?"

"Let us just say your father had something to do with your unfortunate state of affairs."

That is madness. "My father has been deceased for fifteen years."

"Mercifully, he has."

How dare he be disrespectful? "You are a barbarian speaking of the dead with such disdain." She tried to slip aside, but his arms shot out and pinned her where she stood. "Where am I?" she demanded, staring at a ruby in the center of his medallion suspended from a heavy chain.

He pinched her chin and forced her to look up to his cold steel-blue eyes. His smug sneer made Meg shiver. She took an instant dislike to his gaunt face, made longer by a twisted English nose. "I beg to differ, my sweet. Scottish swine are not fit to dine at English tables."

She jerked her chin from his grasp and her head hit stone. Meg ignored the pain jarring her skull. Lord Percy hadn't answered a one of her questions. "Please." Perhaps being polite would gain her more information. "Will you at least tell me where we are?"

"Alnwick."

She gasped. She'd heard the stories. Her father sacked this castle in 1462. "Whatever it is you want, my brother can pay handsomely."

Lord Percy dropped his arms and laughed, not a warm laugh you might hear at a Yule feast, but a grating cackle, filled with scorn. "Do you think I'm seeking financial gain?"

Meg took advantage of the gap he'd opened, and scuttled toward the empty hearth. Dare she ask? "Then what is it you seek to gain by kidnapping a *woman*?"

He ambled toward her. "Ruination."

God, no. Ruined, she'd never be accepted as a novice. She'd be a burden to her brother for the rest of her days. Then the deadly glint in Lord Percy's eyes brought on another chill. "Do you aim to kill me?"

"Not yet. I'll use you first. 'Tis not *your* ruination I'm seeking—I want complete destruction of the Earl of Angus and George Douglas's spawn. I want to meet all of Scotland on the battlefield and watch them bleed. When your brother marches an army across the border, he'll break the truce and pull our nations into war." He spread his arms wide, with a sickly sneer on his face. "And it will all be blamed on him. The fool-born Earl of Angus will then know what it feels like to lose lands and title and have his name soiled throughout the kingdom."

She'd be the cause of a war? Her family's ruination? Meg's gut heaved, and she clamped a hand over her mouth to keep from vomiting all over his long, pointed leather shoes. "You're mad."

"I'll have my revenge. My title was stripped because of your father. Do you have any idea what it cost me to have it reinstated?"

Meg could only imagine the cost, but groveling to his peers would have been involved. Humiliated men would stop at nothing for vengeance. What if Arthur *did* lead an army across the border? *He won't*. Her brother was as shrewd as he was the Earl of Angus. Besides, she could not be the cause of war.

Her own death would be preferable to the senseless slaughter of Scotland's fighting men. If she could convince Lord Percy his tactics were in vain, he might just kill her now and be done with it.

Boldly, she held out her left hand—*the claw*—a cleft consisting of a healthy thumb and a pointer finger fused to a stumpy malformed nub. "Do you honestly believe my brother would risk leading an army against England merely to rescue a deformed sister?"

She didn't miss the flash of doubt in his eyes, quickly covered by a frown. "He'll come."

She squared her shoulders and stepped into him, an aggressive move. "What makes you so certain?"

Lord Percy crossed his arms. "I left my calling card. No hot-blooded Scot can resist a challenge, especially a Douglas."

Meg whipped around and faced the empty hearth. The earl did know her family well. For centuries, all factions of Clan Douglas had earned their reputation for hot temper and hot blood. Though she fought to control it, she was woven from the same cloth—but she wouldn't give him the satisfaction of seeing it now.

Who knew how long she'd suffer the hospitality in Northumberland's dank tower? "I may be your prisoner, but I'm no criminal." She pointed at the hearth and faced him. "I need wood for the fire to take the edge off the cold, and I insist upon being granted leave to visit the chapel."

He stepped into her, his hot breath on her neck. "How is it you see fit to make demands when I hold your life in my grasp?"

"You said you need me alive." She narrowed her eyes in challenge. He'd said he would use her for leverage—that gave her some room to make a few small requests. "What good would I be if I succumbed to the cold—froze in the night? Must I remind you 'tis the dead of winter?"

His gaze dipped to her breasts. "I'll allow a fire, but you can pray on your knees in this very room."

Meg crossed her arms and opened her mouth for a rebuttal, but Lord Percy spun on his heel and marched out the door. Before she could dash across the floor, the hinges creaked and it slammed with a boom that shook the chamber. She pounded her fist on the hard wood. "Are you afraid to keep me, a mere woman, from Sunday mass—from compline, from vespers? Have you no decency? Are you to be damned to the fires of hell?" With every word her voice rose and echoed through the tower. "I thought the English prided themselves on their manners, *my lord*."

She took a deep breath and leaned against the door. With any luck, her shouts were loud enough to be heard all the way down the tower stairs. Heaven help her, he'd disgustingly stared at her breasts. She shuddered down to her toes. If he tried to take her virtue, Arthur would seek vengeance for certain. She could never allow that to happen.

What chance of escape would there be? If she could convince Lord Percy to allow her to the chapel and perhaps a turn on the wall-walk, she'd devise her escape. Could she take a guard into her confidence? Meg paced. There had to be a way out. She must keep her wits and think.

LISTENING TO THE WOMAN'S TIRADE, HENRY PERCY'S neck prickled. He'd nearly drawn his dagger and slit the vixen's throat when she showed him her hand. In no way had he expected a cripple. Was she a witch? She certainly spoke bile. Did the Earl of Angus want to be rid of her? No. All Douglas spawn had a sharp tongue. Obviously, Lady Meg was no different. He would not allow doubt to sicken his mind. His plan was sound. Meg's beauty far outshone her deformity.

Henry trusted his spies. He'd spent months waiting

for his chance to steal the Earl of Angus's youngest and, according to his informant, most beloved sister. Henry's trusted men had followed discreetly while she made her pilgrimage to Melrose. Half the distance to Alnwick, the opportunity was too fortuitous to let pass.

Isaac, his scar-faced man-at-arms, followed Henry down the winding tower stairs.

"See to it she has wood for her fire. If she dies and word gets out, our cause will be lost."

"Yes, my lord."

"Escort her to the chapel each night after compline. I'll not be judged by God because I refused to allow the wench to pray."

"As you wish."

Henry stopped and shook his finger under the guard's nose. "Do not allow her out of your sight."

Isaac chuckled, stretching the jagged scar on his right cheek. "My men will guard the slip of a girl with weapons drawn."

The earl held up his fist. "Do not mock me."

"Never, my lord." Isaac held up his palms. "Where would she hide within these walls? There's no escape."

"Women are conniving enigmas. One never knows what their little minds are scheming. I bid you keep a tight rein on her, and *never* allow Lady Maud to see her. The last thing I need is for my wife to become involved. She might sympathize with the guttersnipe."

Again Isaac chuckled.

Henry slid his hand over the pommel of his sword. Isaac's grey eyes always made him uneasy. "You find me amusing?"

"Pardon, my lord, but *guttersnipe* is the last word I'd use to describe Lady Meg. She's anything but a wastrel."

A ping of desire shot through the tip of Henry's cock, followed by a flame of hatred blasting in his chest. "Keep your mind out of your braies. If anyone lays a hand on the woman, it will be me. I'll tug up her skirts, bend her over and defile her in front of Angus—and not before. I want her brother to hear the virgin scream when I tear through her maidenhead whilst he watches."

Isaac's jaw twitched.

"Not to worry. You'll see it all, standing beside me while you hold a dagger to the bastard's neck."

🐾

ALONG THEIR JOURNEY SOUTH, DUNCAN HAD TWO days to think about how they'd slip inside Alnwick Castle. They stopped on the bank of the River Aln, about a mile west of the village. He eyed his men, the best fighting warriors in the Highlands—in all of Scotland, truth be told. Each man had been handpicked by his father and trained since the age of four and ten.

His brother, John, had the sharpest mind but abhorred fighting. He had a daft dream to enter the priesthood. *Damned waste of a stealth warrior*.

Robert and James Robinson were cousins on his mother's side, allied with the Struan dynasty. Archibald Campbell, a cousin, heir to the Earl of Argyll. Sean MacDougall and Eoin MacGregor were both heirs to neighboring lairdships.

Together, this band of six noble knights made up the renowned Highland Enforcers, continuing the legacy of Black Colin, Lord of Glenorchy, Duncan's legendary father.

Robert trotted his horse toward them, returning from surveillance in the village. A frown turned down the knight's mouth. "It isn't going to be easy to enter. The castle gates are kept closed all hours. Word is the earl has refused to hear supplications."

Duncan glanced at his brother. "Looks like we'll need to pay Alnwick Abbey a visit."

John arched a brow. "Oh? That's not like you. Planning to pray our way through the curtain walls?"

Duncan never prayed his way through anything. "We'll borrow some vestments."

John ran his fingers down his brown beard. "I didn't think there was any hope for your soul."

"There'll be time enough to pray for me after you take up the cowl."

"Aye. If I should live so long."

"You've nothing to worry about—especially if we can discover the name of the castle's priest." Duncan drew his dirk and dropped to one knee, the others following suit. "John and I will walk in through the front gate—tell the guard we've business with the priest." He drew a circle in the dirt. "In the town square stands the Alnwick Market Cross. There's enough trade going on there, you lot can blend in without causing suspicion."

"Four knights won't create a stir?" Archie asked.

Duncan shook his dirk at him. "You'll hide our armor first. Then I want you milling about, learning all you can about Lord Percy without making yourselves suspicious."

"How are we supposed to do that?" For an intelligent man, Archie asked too many questions.

Duncan flicked the tip of his dirk into the dirt. "Stay sober at the alehouse. Listen. Guaranteed, Percy's men will be on our trail before we make it to the town's border." Duncan skimmed his hand through the air. "Who is Percy's man-at-arms? How powerful is his army? Will they follow us into Scotland—or will Percy send a mob of heathens like us to sniff out our trail?"

"How do you plan to spirit Lady Meg out?" Sean asked.

"I'll figure a way." Duncan pointed to the MacDougall heir. "Purchase another mount for her."

The big man spread his palms. "With what?"

Duncan flipped him a gold sovereign. "This should more than take care of it." He then turned to Eoin. "Watch the castle gate. Keep the horses nearby, but out of sight."

"Aye? Ye aiming to take a Sunday stroll out the barbican with Lady Meg on your arm?" Archie asked.

"Something like that. Have the horses waiting when we need them."

Eoin smirked. "I'll summon a bolt of lightning to strike down the bastards on your tail."

Duncan had more faith in Eoin's intuition than the MacGregor heir did himself. "Just have them saddled and ready to ride." He eyed them all. "The rest of you, too. Gather what information you can and be at the edge of the tree line by dark."

※

DRESSED IN A BROWN MONK'S HABIT, CINCHED around his waist with a rope, John grumbled, "You should have let me wear the priest's vestments. Did you ever even read your Bible passages?"

Duncan smoothed his hands over his black priest's robes—hardly more lavish than John's. "You know I did. Besides, I'm leading this charade. Put up your hood." He walked with his brother through the wooded path linking the abbey to Alnwick Castle.

"I'll be glad when we finish with this task." John ran his fingers along the inside of his collar and stretched his neck. "England doesn't agree with me."

A tic twitched above Duncan's eye, as it always did before he stepped into peril. "Nor me."

It was dusk after they passed through the barbican and neared the gateway of the castle. With two octagonal towers on either side, Duncan studied the fortifications. Four guards stood at the top of the towers, armed with arrows and pikes. The curtain itself was immense. Twice the size of Kilchurn Castle, the fortress sprawled in every direction like a mountain range. Cannons lined the curtain walls—must have cost the earl a year's worth of income. Three arrow slits loomed as dark caverns on each side of the gatehouse.

An impressive stronghold in anyone's eyes, yet a Scottish army had laid siege to it only sixteen years past.

Duncan and John wore only hauberks and chausses beneath their robes. His armor left tied to Archie's saddle, Duncan felt naked without his claymore strapped to his back. He wasn't walking into Alnwick unarmed, however. His dirk was hidden beneath his vestments, though all Duncan had to do was reach through an opening at his waist to grasp it. As always, for added protection, he and John both wore daggers lashed to their calves and arms.

As they approached the gate, the sentry lowered his pike across his body, pointing the razor-sharp lance at them.

Duncan leaned into John. "Let me do the talking."

"Do I not always?"

The tic above his eye twitched again. "Nay."

John emitted an exasperated cough as they stepped up to the guard.

"Stay back." The man trained his pike between them. "State your business."

"We've a meeting with Father Chamberlain," Duncan said in a practiced English accent. He'd "borrowed" the robes while John chatted with a monk and learned the name of Alnwick's resident priest.

The guard eyed them both from beneath his conical helm and raised his chin. "The priest didn't notify me visitors would attend him."

"How could he?" Duncan asked. "We've been sent with a message from the abbot."

The guard hesitated and glanced over his shoulder. "Have you any weapons?"

Duncan spread his palms to his sides. "We're men of God."

The guard inclined his helmed head toward John. "What about you?"

Duncan made a show of speaking in Latin to ask John to hold up his hands. Only then did he obey. His younger brother couldn't affect an English accent for his life—sounded as Scottish as the Highlands, even when he spoke Latin.

Duncan offered a thin-lipped smile. "Brother Julius has taken a vow of silence."

The guard upended his pike and tapped the staff on the cobblestones. "I'll allow you to pass this once."

"My thanks," Duncan said. He grasped John's elbow and pushed ahead—straight through the gates of hell.

Chapter Four

❦

"Slow your pace," Duncan whispered. Without his armor, he could have floated through the castle grounds.

Entering the inner courtyard, he quickly took in their surroundings. A five-story keep to the east. The grey stone walls of the chapel loomed directly across. Once they found her, the direst part of their escape would be exiting the gateway and the long trail within the walls to the outer barbican.

"Now we're inside, how do you plan to leave?" John asked.

Duncan headed toward the chapel. "The same way we always do."

"Fight?"

"Brother, for a religious man, you have little faith. I aim to walk." Duncan elbowed John's arm. "Why are you doubting me?"

John slid his hands inside his sleeves—checking his weapons, no doubt. "I've never seen you in a priest's robe or without your sword. God will strike us dead for our deception, as sure as I'm standing."

Duncan cared not for a naysayer, even if he was blood kin. "Remember your vow of silence, Brother *Julius*." He didn't like dressing in holy garments either, but this was war. Besides, so far his ploy had proved brilliant. How else would they gain entry to the fortress without causing a stir?

He grasped the cold iron latch and quietly opened the heavy door—until the hinges screeched. The priest paused his Latin incantation. Duncan tugged John into the shadows of the vestibule. On his knees, a richly dressed man turned and frowned—undoubtedly Lord Percy kneeling beside his wife. Unfortunate, Duncan would have preferred to avoid the Earl of Northumberland altogether.

They waited until compline ended. With his wife on his arm, Lord Percy sauntered toward them. "What is so urgent, you intrude on my worship?"

Duncan bowed deeply. "Forgive me, my lord. We've a matter of the cloth to discuss with Father Chamberlain. I heard not the mass until I opened the door."

Lord Percy sniffed, a distrustful glint in his eye. "Where do you hail from?"

"Sent from Rome," Duncan improvised. "Meeting priests to ensure no heresy pervades Catholic walls."

"I assure you, there is no false doctrine practiced here."

Duncan smirked, thankful Father Chamberlain hadn't followed Percy into the vestibule. "With all due respect, that is yet to be determined, my lord."

The earl glared down his inordinately long nose. "State your business with Father Chamberlain and begone. I'm sure the abbot can provide you with suitable accommodations at the abbey."

"As you wish." Duncan bowed toward the Lady of Northumberland. "Good evening, my lady."

Silently, John followed suit and watched them take their leave. "Now what?" he growled under his breath.

"Come." Duncan led him to the sacristy behind the altar. "We shall ask Father Chamberlain a few questions."

"You cannot harm a priest," John whispered loudly.

"Did I say anything about harming him?" Duncan tapped on the door and walked inside. "Father, I bid you good eve."

The gaunt priest quickly stood from his writing table. "Excuse me. Do I know you?"

Duncan's eye twitched three times. "Are you a man of God?"

He gestured to his vestments. "Obviously, I am."

"Then you follow the commandment, 'Thou shalt not bear false witness'?"

"You best state the reason for your visit quickly." Chamberlain's gaze darted between John and Duncan. "I've another mass to give, and I'll not be affronted by your insolence."

"Apologies. I've a matter to discuss that's rather surreptitious." Duncan hesitated, his mind racing ahead. "Compline has ended, the lord and lady have left to dine and yet you have another mass to pray?"

"Yes. For one."

Och aye? "And who might that be?"

The priest hastily gestured toward the sacristy door. "You have not yet told me your name, nor have you removed your hood or bowed your head. How could I possibly take you into my confidence?"

He keeps a secret.

The chapel door screeched open. Fast as a bullwhip, Duncan spun the priest around and snapped a hand over his mouth while shoving a knife against his neck. "I do not want to kill you, but one word and I'll spill your blood across this very floor."

Father Chamberlain nodded, his breathing shallow.

Holding the knife firm to the priest's neck, Duncan eyed John. "Bind his hands and legs."

"Brother Julius" worked quickly, then shoved a wad of cloth in the priest's mouth and used a clergy's stole to gag him.

John frowned. "We bound a man wearing holy vestments?"

"Wheesht." Duncan's eye wouldn't stop twitching. "I've a mass to chant."

John clapped his hand to his forehead. "Heaven help us, you should have let me dress as the priest."

"Aye? If I had, Father Chamberlain would be blasting his gob to the rafters about now."

John paced. "We're all headed for hell."

"Not before we finish this mission." Duncan straightened his robes. "Stay here and make sure the bastard doesn't make a sound."

John cringed. "Do ye have any idea what you're doing?"

"I've listened to mass enough. How hard can it be?"

The naysayer crossed himself. "God save us."

Duncan stepped into the nave and cleared his throat. A petite woman sat in the front pew, a blue woolen veil covering her head. Red curls framed her face, almost bouncing as if they wanted to spring from the confines of her veil.

A guard at the back of the chapel stepped into the light. "Where's Father Chamberlain?"

Duncan swiped a hand across his mouth. "He was called to the abbey on short notice." He then cast his gaze to the woman—it had to be Lady Meg. She kept her eyes downcast. He launched into the only Latin litany he knew. Thanks to the tutelage of his stepmother, he could recite Sunday mass almost error free.

The lady's eyes snapped open when Duncan's voice filled the chapel. God in heaven, her eyes were bluer than the veil she wore. They assessed him critically. Was he too loud? Had he mispronounced something? He quickly made the sign of the cross and sped his delivery.

Moving to her knees, Lady Meg mouthed the words, crossing herself over and over. Had he not done that enough? Duncan crossed himself hastily while he willed away the relentless tic above his eye.

When she drew her eyebrows together, he turned his back and proceeded to chant the communion prayer, blessing the wine and the bread. The heat of her gaze blazed into his back. He could still picture the vibrant blue of her eyes contrasting with her red curls. Jesus, her iridescent ivory skin made them appear all the more intense. God's teeth, Arthur Douglas hadn't mentioned a word about his sister's beauty.

Duncan picked up the plate and walked to the rail. She stepped out of her pew and knelt before him, holding up only one hand. Odd. He would have thought she knew to cross her right palm atop her left. He blinked. This was no time to think of formalities. "*Am bheil thu Meg?*" he asked in Gaelic.

Again she knitted her brows. "*Tu es sacerdos?*" she whispered in Latin.

He could have kicked himself. Obviously, a Lowlander wouldn't understand Gaelic. But his charade hadn't fooled her. "*Fortis*—a warrior." He placed the host in her palm.

"What are you talking about, priest?" the guard shouted while marching forward. "I may not be able to speak Latin, but I know you're saying things you oughtn't."

Meg crossed herself yet again. "Dear Lord, please deliver me from my oppressors," she said.

Stopping at the rail, the guard glared and pounded the shaft of his poleax into the flagstone floor.

Duncan stole a quick glance at Lady Meg. "As you wish, m'lady." He flung the silver plate at the guard and snatched a knife from his left sleeve.

Smacked between the eyes, the sentry flinched and stumbled backward.

With a flick of his wrist, Duncan threw the dagger.

The guard scarcely blinked as it hit him in the neck.

"Help!" he croaked. Falling to his knees, he clutched the knife while blood poured down his hauberk. "Our walls have been brea—" He fell flat on his face, his body convulsing in the throes of death.

Though Duncan's heart thundered in his ears, he paused to listen for the creaking hinges of the chapel doors. With any luck, the guard's voice hadn't carried outside the thick walls.

Meg clasped her hand over her mouth.

"Do not scream." Duncan held up a hand. "How many are guarding the chapel?"

"One, I believe. Two escorted me."

John stepped out from the sacristy. "You killed a man in God's holy church?"

Duncan glanced at the misfortunate guard, a river of blood streaming toward the altar. "He gave me no choice."

"Who are you?" Meg asked, and stood.

He bowed. "Sir Duncan and Sir John Campbell at your service."

"They'll know you killed the guard as soon as you open the door." John stepped beside him. "How to you expect to walk out now?"

Duncan eyed Meg and winked. "Have faith. We shall take a wee stroll the same way we came in."

John snorted. "Have you lost your mind?"

"You must excuse my brother, m'lady. He's the grandest naysayer in all of Glen Orchy." Duncan smacked John's shoulder. "Give her your robe."

John stepped back. "What?"

"Do it quickly, then put on the priest's vestments."

"But she's at least two hands shorter than I."

"Aye, and I'm banking they'll figure that out after we've passed through the barbican. Hurry." Duncan yanked the knife from the dead guard's neck and wiped it clean on the man's chausses.

John shrugged out of the brown habit and handed it

to Meg. She blinked twice at the knives strapped to his arms and legs before he sped back to the sacristy.

She hastily wrapped the oversized garment around her petite frame and tied it at the waist. "Who sent you?"

"The Earl of Angus. Who else?" Duncan eyed her baggy habit and tugged it up over her rope belt.

She swatted his hands away and gasped. "Arthur? Why did he not send the Douglas guard?"

Duncan shrugged. "My reputation, I suppose. Now hide your tresses beneath your hood and stay close behind me."

&

MEG SHOVED HER VEIL BACK FROM HER CROWN AND pulled the brown hood low over her brow. Though the audacious knight had tugged it up, the robe still dragged on the floor. She held up the hem as they crept to the chapel door. Standing between Duncan and John, she prayed they would escape alive.

Aye, she'd known the big man was no priest as soon as he stepped into the nave. Not only was his head unshaven, he recited the mass like he was auctioning a herd of cattle. But she didn't laugh—not when he looked at her with eyes so intense they could claim her soul. Never in her life had she seen a man so virile. Jaw set, she had no doubt he could exude complete command over anything he desired. His fingers had brushed hers when he placed the host in her hand. She'd nearly gasped at the tingling sensation shivering up her arm.

But Arthur had sent him as her deliverer, and she thanked the stars he was powerfully built. If anyone could spirit her from Lord Percy's grasp, this Highlander might have a good chance—if his brash confidence was any indication. *My stars, he killed the guard without a modicum of hesitation.*

Duncan placed his hand on the latch and turned—his dark eyes almost black, deadlier than nightshade. "Stay back. I'll take care of the guard first."

Cracking open the door, Duncan grasped the sentry by the neck and yanked him inside. "Sorry," he said with a growl.

Before she could blink, he grabbed the guard's chin and yanked his head sideways. A sickly crack of bone echoed off the stone chapel walls. It happened so fast, Meg wasn't sure if the man was dead or had fallen. One look at his twisted head and stunned eyes confirmed it. "My God. Why did you kill him?"

"Better than the other way around." Those nightshade eyes grew darker.

And why did Duncan's voice have to sound so deep? So utterly dangerous? Her savior could be more devil than saint.

John pulled the priest's hood over his head. "My brother would never settle with words that which he can accomplish with a claymore."

Duncan held up his palms. "I used my hands, for Christ's sake."

Meg cringed at his vulgar language, especially in a church. "Mind your mouth."

Smirking, the knight appeared impervious to his crudeness and gathered them at the door. "We're going to attempt to walk out of here." His gaze met hers. "If there's a skirmish, move your arse out of the way and hide. Understood?"

She nodded, positive her shocked eyes were about to spring from their sockets. "Aye."

"Walk with purpose and let me do the talking."

John coughed. "He always insists on talking."

"Only because you sound like a Highland sheep herder bleating after the flock." Duncan turned and poked John's shoulder. "I mean it. Our very lives are in peril. One misspoken word could see us all killed."

He focused his gaze on Meg. "Act like a monk and you just might live, m'lady."

She shuddered down to the tips of her slippers. "You'd best know what you're doing, sir." Meg wasn't sure if Sir Duncan would kill her or if Percy's guard would, but she absolutely planned to walk through the barbican doing her best impression of a monk.

Folding her hands, she clasped the robe in her palms and held it up as inconspicuously as possible. No self-respecting monk would shuffle out the gates whilst tripping over his habit. Duncan opened the door and stepped outside.

Head bowed so the hood hid her face, she followed the gruff Highlander, with Sir John close behind.

Thank the stars it was dark. No one noticed while they made their way to the gatehouse.

But once there, Meg's stomach flew to her throat when a guard sauntered up to Duncan. "Your business accomplished, I see."

The knight continued walking. "Yes."

The guard stepped toward John. "Where are you off to, Father Chamberlain?"

Duncan stopped. Meg almost stumbled into him. "His presence has been requested by the abbot."

The guard turned. "Is that so?" Then he sauntered to Meg. Her heart now pummeling her chest, she squeezed her trembling hands against her stomach while she kept her head down and watched his booted feet step toward her. "What? Did they cut you off at the knees?" He plucked her robe with his fingers. "It looks like two monks could fit inside all that wool." He tried to push back her hood.

Meg clapped her hands to her head and jerked away. "No." Her high-pitched voice pierced through the air.

"Christ." Duncan shoved her aside. Baring his teeth, he pounced like a feral cat. Before the guard could move, Duncan snatched the pike and plunged it into the man's heart. Stunned, the guard grasped the shaft and tottered backward before he crashed to the ground.

Shocked at more blood spreading across the cobblestones, Meg froze.

"Run!" Duncan boomed.

Without thought, she took two steps. Her slippers caught in her robe. She tried to tug the heavy folds aside, but they twisted around her legs. Toppling out of control, she fell face first. Her hands slapped the stone as an arrow skimmed past her ear. Ignoring the pain jarring her wrists, Meg covered her head with her arms.

This was the end. She was going to die.

Chapter Five

Duncan glanced over his shoulder. *Bloody hell*. Lady Meg sprawled facedown on the cobblestones, protecting her head with her arms. Rescuing a woman brought more trouble than it was worth. In two bounds, he crouched at her side and hefted her into his arms.

He'd expected the lass to carry a bit of bulk, but she weighed no more than eight stone. Speeding ahead, he cradled her in his left arm and fished for his dirk beneath his cumbersome robes. John raced beyond, nearly to the barbican. Towering battlements surrounded them. Duncan didn't need to look. From the shouts above, sentries were amassing toward the outer gateway along the wall-walk. His only hope was to outrun them.

An arrow hissed over his head. Meg latched her arms around his neck and crushed into him. Instinctively, he crouched over her body to shield her from being shot.

"They're gaining on us. Put me down. I can run."

"Robes...too...long."

"Then run faster!" she yelled.

Easy for her to say. "Aye," Duncan huffed. He would have liked to ask her if she preferred to use a crop to lash his backside, but hadn't the wind for sarcasm.

Ahead, John made quick work of the next guard. Picking up the dead man's sword, he slipped under the protection of the barbican, waving his arms like a spectator at a finish line.

Duncan's thighs burned. He couldn't keep this pace much longer. Meg might be light, but she still weighed more than his armor—which would have come in handy about now. Another arrow whooshed. The feathers brushed his shoulder.

Only a few more paces and he'd reach the shelter of the barbican.

Swords clashed in the dark shadows. More arrows flew past and clattered on the cobblestones. Duncan clenched his teeth and kept running.

Sprinting under the protection of the stone archway, Duncan counted five dead Northumberland guards. Eoin held the horses on the far side.

Duncan rushed to him and set Meg on her feet. "I can always count on you, MacGregor." He stooped to give her a leg up. "Where are the others?"

"At the tree line—archers poised to give us cover."

His men were the only thing in this world Duncan could count on. "John, ride out with Lady Meg first. Eoin and I'll take up the rear." Tearing off the cumbersome priest's vestments, Duncan bellowed his war cry to alert his men.

Defensive arrows flew from the forest.

"Now!"

Meg crouched over her mount's head, racing beside John like a well-trained cavalryman. No lad could have ridden harder or more sure-seated.

Duncan glanced at Eoin. "Ready?"

"Aye."

With a roar ripping from his lungs, Duncan slammed his heels into his stallion's barrel. A cold wind bit his face. Lady Meg and John disappeared into the shadows of the trees. Thank God they were safe.

Duncan slapped his reins, arrows hissing around him. His heart hammered in his throat.

Nearly there.

His horse whinnied and dipped his rear. Sliding out of control, the warhorse listed, snorting in agony. Flying through the air, Duncan released the reins and readied himself for a jarring thud. As he slammed into the earth, a rumbling grunt ripped from his throat. Something sliced open his buttock.

He craned his neck. The trees were only paces away.

Eoin rounded his horse. "Hurry!"

Duncan tried to stand—groused through his teeth at the sharp pain. He clenched his gut. The big horse lay on its side, snorting—no time to save him.

Springing to his feet, Duncan grabbed Eoin's hand and launched himself behind the warrior's saddle.

"You all right?" Eoin asked.

Duncan swiped his hand over his hip. Hot blood oozed through his fingers. "Ride!"

Together they sped through the darkness, deep into the shelter of the forest.

※

LORD PERCY SAT BY THE HEARTH AND SIPPED HOT mulled wine. He hated winter. The castle was always miserably cold. It didn't seem to matter how much wood the servants piled on the fire, it was still too bloody cold.

Isaac burst into the room, his face white as the frost outside. "My lord."

Henry set his goblet on the side table and stood. "What the devil? How dare you barge into my rooms like a blustery north wind?"

The guardsman spread his palms and opened his mouth, but uttered nothing but a glottal grunt.

"What is it, man? Out with it."

"She's gone."

The warm wine roiled in Henry's gut. "It best not be Lady Meg to whom you are referring."

Isaac combed his fingers through his hair. "It is."

"Imbecile!" Henry stomped in a circle, smacked the goblet from the table and sent it smashing into the hearth. "I told you to guard her at all times." He jabbed his finger forward. "This is your fault."

The man-at-arms blinked rapidly. "I thought she'd be safe in the chapel, blast it all. I left to eat my supper. After which I discovered the guardsman allowed a priest and a monk through the gates."

"It gets worse." Percy balled his fist. He knew he shouldn't have trusted the large priest at the chapel. He'd sensed something amiss straight away. Damn it all, the man had the look of a killer. Henry should have thrown him and that bumbling monk in the pit the moment he'd seen them. "Who were these men?"

"We know not. Everyone who spoke to them is dead."

"Scottish heathens, no doubt." Percy paced. God, he hated the Scots. "Bloody Angus sent in a pair of holy men rather than an army? The bastard is smarter than I thought."

"Those were no holy men. The way they took down my guards, they're highly trained assassins. And they had help waiting on the outside. Sped away—though our arrows injured a horse."

"You mean to tell me two men walked into my castle, abducted my hostage, and my vast army only managed to maim a horse?"

Isaac took a step toward the door. "Yes, my lord. My men are preparing to follow them now."

Lord Percy clenched his fists. "I should strip you of your rank for this."

A thin line formed across the soldier's lips.

Henry sauntered up to the miserable wretch and

stared him in the eye. "Send the army after the milk-livered swine. Make sure you kill them all before they cross the border—all except Lady Meg."

"Straight away, my lord." Isaac turned on his heel.

Percy drew his dagger with a scrape of metal. "And if you *do not* beat them to the border..."

The soldier stopped.

"I do not want to see your face until you can bring me dirt. Track their leader. I want to know everything about him—where he lives, what he eats, for whom he cares." Percy stepped in and ran his dagger along Isaac's jaw. "Because I'm going to rain fire and brimstone upon *his* family. He'll rue the day he accepted his first farthing from the Earl of Angus. And when he's on his knees praying for mercy, he'll lead us straight into Arthur Douglas's lair. If we cannot lure them into a full-out war, we'll beat them at their own game."

a⃝

DUNCAN HADN'T BOTCHED A MISSION THIS BADLY—not ever. They were supposed to quietly walk through the gates of Alnwick Castle, mount up and ride away *before* Henry Percy's guard raised the alarm. Now the enemy would be on their trail before they rode out of the shire.

He grunted when a sharp pain in his buttock stabbed him.

"You're not dying, are you?" Eoin asked over his shoulder.

"Nay." Duncan arched his back and grimaced. "Something cut my arse when I was thrown from my horse."

Eoin slapped his reins, demanding more speed. "Better your arse than that bonny face of yours."

"Wheesht and keep pace. We're lagging behind the others." Duncan needed to be up ahead leading the knights, not riding double, bringing up the rear, for Christ's sake.

"My mount is a warhorse, but he'll not last long carrying the both of us."

"We need to put some distance between us and Northumberland." Duncan peered through the darkness and raised his voice loud enough for all to hear. "Pull up atop the outcropping ahead."

John and Meg were the first to arrive. She spun her mount to face them, the whites of her eyes glowing through the darkness. "Why are we stopping? They're after us for certain. We must ride."

Duncan would not be taking any quip from a wee lassie. "I'll be riding with *you*."

She was a feisty one. He'd seen it in her eyes in the chapel when she'd looked at him. He slid down from Eoin's horse; the stabbing pain made his knees buckle. Stumbling forward, he bellowed like a bull. "Bloody oath, that hurts."

Meg sat erect. "If you'll be sharing my mount, I'd appreciate it if you'd curb your tongue."

Curb my tongue? No one besides him issued the orders, especially not a half-pint, outspoken, spoilt Lowland lass. "Let me set this straight—"

"God's teeth, Duncan, you're bleeding like a stuck pig," Archie said.

"What happened?" Robert asked.

"Would you all stop acting like a gaggle of old women?" Duncan straightened and strode to Meg's mount. "Scoot forward, m'lady. I'll return your reins as soon as we find another horse."

"This is untoward," she clipped, moving forward as asked. "I'll be requiring a fresh horse to myself at the very first opportunity."

"Aye, lady, that's the plan." Duncan mounted the gelding, grinding his teeth against his bellow this time. He reached around her and gathered the reins. "Sean, circle back and scout out what's behind us. I want not a mob of English soldiers taking a shortcut and cutting us off."

"Aye, m'lord."

By God, Sean was a good man. Duncan could count on him for anything—count on all of them, really.

Her teeth chattering, Meg wriggled against him. "How far are we going?"

Duncan shoved his feet in the stirrups and cued the horse to a fast trot. "As far as we can manage until dawn —with any luck we'll make it across the border."

She adjusted again. Holy Mother, her bottom settled against his cock like that of an alehouse tart begging to lose her maidenhead. Duncan grimaced and tried to push his hips further back in the saddle, only to slide forward, right between those two soft cheeks. He groaned. With a throbbing wound in his backside combined with a growing ache in his crotch, this was going to be a long night.

&

Sir Duncan nearly touched her claw when he took the reins from Meg's grasp. Thank heavens it was dark. Something about the big man unsettled her. Of course he swore like a heathen. Nearly every sentence he uttered was laced with something blasphemous.

Yet it didn't bother her. Not really—though she'd never admit it. Meg couldn't quite put her finger on it, but something about his air, his powerful presence, made her trust him...and fear him. In the chapel, all it took to twist her stomach in a knot was a glance from his lignite eyes and a slight smile, which produced two boyish dimples. No, from his striking black hair framing his chiseled features, Duncan looked nothing like a lad, but if Meg must trust anyone outside her own kin, it would be he. In the blink of an eye, he'd come to her rescue and killed two men to protect her.

When he announced he was going to share her mount, she should have put up more of a fuss. Surely it wasn't proper. But the butterflies in her stomach were too busy flitting about as if she'd never seen a warrior before. Even if she was the smallest in their party, Meg needed to regain her senses and be assertive. Sir Duncan Campbell was a Highlander—a man bred of rugged stock, fabled to beat their wives and survive the winters chest deep in snow.

She'd simply become overly excited at the prospect of being rescued. *My stars, watching Sir Duncan and Sir John fight those men, 'tis a wonder I've not completely lost my faculties for the shock of it.* Soon she'd be back behind the walls of Tantallon Castle. She'd be bolder with Arthur when she faced him. He'd see the need for her to take the veil. She had been kidnapped because he wouldn't listen to her reason. Arthur would pay attention to her now, she was certain of it.

Meg let out a long sigh. Her back accidentally pressed against Duncan's chest. She quickly sat forward. "Pardon me."

"You may as well relax, lass. Besides, you'll be a mite warmer if you do."

Heaven help her, the deep bass of his voice rumbled through her whole body and made her insides quaver. Meg nervously adjusted her hips. Did Duncan have a weapon hidden in his braies? Something solid rubbed between her buttocks. Oddly, it made her tingle when she moved. She did it again.

"I meant you might want to rest against my chest, not tempt me with your taut little arse." The devil himself could have recited those words.

Meg jolted upright.

"Aye, that's what I'm talking about. You keep

squirming around like that and I'll be itching to lead you off into the glade and have my way with you."

She knew enough of men to realize there was no weapon lodged between her buttocks. The brute was a flesh-and-blood stallion. Her mind blanked. What should she do? There was no other horse to ride. She glanced at John. He seemed a tad more genteel. Meg tapped her pointer finger to the thumb of her claw—something she did when nervous. She'd further hold them up if she demanded to ride with another.

Duncan placed his palm on her belly and encouraged her to rest against his chest. She fought his tug at first, but heaven help her, he was incredibly warm compared to the icy cold of the winter's night air. She surrendered to the demands of his hand. The tension in her shoulders eased a bit.

"That's better, lass," he purred. "We'll both have a smoother ride if we settle into the horse's motion."

The pressure needling her bottom eased too. "How is your wound?"

"'Tis coming good."

"You should have it seen to by a healer."

"Aye? I'm a bit occupied at the moment."

She couldn't argue with him there. Besides, she wouldn't trust an English healer with *her* life, let alone anyone else's.

Chapter Six

※※※

Meg's head bobbed forward as she jolted awake. She reached out and grasped Duncan's arms.

"Good morn, m'lady."

Holy fairy feathers, had his voice become even deeper through the night? She realized the pincer fingers of her claw clamped his arm, and she quickly released, hiding the crippled hand inside her long sleeve. She shivered. Bitter cold, a snowflake landed on her nose. She peered through the dense forest. "Where are we?"

"Scotland borders—though we've yet to cross the River Tweed."

"The snow's getting heavier," Eoin said.

Meg looked up. Before she could open her mouth, her face was covered. Again she shivered. "I'm freezing."

Duncan molded his arms around her. "We all are, lass."

She nestled into him—purely to stay warm. In no way would she allow herself to be allured by his masculine scent or the muscles enveloping her.

"There's a farm up ahead." Archie pointed. "Mayhap they'll let us see out the storm in the stable."

Duncan's chest rumbled against Meg's back with his hum. "We need to keep going."

John arched an icy brow. "Aye, but the horses must be rested."

"Bloody Christmas," Duncan groused.

Meg stifled her laugh. Was he attempting to keep his foul mouth in check?

He tapped his heels against the horse. "All right, then," he said, as if everyone had been arguing with him. "'Tis snowing hard enough to cover our tracks. We'll ask the farmer for a lend of his barn."

Watching Duncan pound on the door, daylight was hardy discernible through the thick covering of clouds. Still wrapped in the oversized monk's habit, Meg shivered on the horse. Her teeth chattered, her fingers numb, hidden in the folds of the wool. How cold would she be if she weren't covered with the woolen robe? She couldn't imagine being any colder.

Duncan had to pound on the door three times before the crofter opened it, wearing a plaid draped over his head, clutched at the neck. That put Meg at ease—she doubted she'd see plaid on the English side of the border. He nodded and gestured toward the stable then closed the door in Duncan's face.

Limping, Duncan led them all inside the crude shelter. Though Meg could see her breath, it was a fair bit more comfortable than being out in the snow. She brushed the icy white fluff from her shoulders.

Duncan reached up to help her dismount.

She grasped the pommel and leaned back. "I can do it."

Those dark eyes narrowed. "I'm sure you are quite able, but I'd be no gentleman to stand aside and watch."

So he was a *gentleman* now? Meg bit her bottom lip. He put a hand on her waist. Tingles skittered up her side through the top of her head. What harm was there in letting him help? She'd been pressed against his body for hours. Ensuring her sleeve covered the claw, she placed her hands on his shoulders.

He lifted her with such ease, she completely forgot about his wound until a slight grunt escaped his lips.

"Are you all right?"

He drew her into his body and slid her down. "Aye." His deep voice was barely perceptible.

Meg's breasts rubbed along his solid chest. Her breath caught. He held her there for a moment. She dared look at his face, and her breathing completely stopped. His dark features were both wickedly handsome and terrifying. A longing smoldered in his eyes—as if he were starved. He probably was. Meg forced a swallow. "Another inch or two and you can release me."

He blinked as if she'd slapped him. "A-apologies." He set her down.

Her sleeve dropped back and exposed the claw. She snapped it away. But Duncan's brow furrowed. He'd seen it.

She steeled herself for a sharp remark, but he turned to the men. "Put the horses in the stalls and heap the straw into a pile. We cannot light a fire in here, but we'll huddle together to stay warm."

Meg frowned. "Having already done enough huddling, I'd prefer a fire."

John used a pitchfork to amass the hay. "No need to worry, Lady Meg. We're all knights. Your virtue's safe with us."

Now Duncan had seen her claw, he'd probably give her a wide berth. She doubted he'd be riding with her again. He'd most likely ask her to ride with John. The younger brother seemed quieter, better mannered and unquestionably not as devilish or handsome. "I thought no less." She stepped forward. "I'm afraid we all haven't been properly introduced."

John bowed deeply. "My brother and I are sons of

the Lord of Glenorchy—hail from Glen Orchy in Argyllshire."

Duncan removed the bridle, but left the saddle on the horse and closed the stall gate. "Apologies, m'lady. I'm afraid there wasn't time with arrows flying past our ears." He gestured to each man. "Robert and James Robinson are cousins from Loch Rannoch. Archibald Campbell, my second cousin—heir to the Earl of Argyll. My closest friends, Eoin MacGregor, one day to be laird, as well as Sean MacDougall who's scouting behind us."

Meg rubbed her shoulders. Every single one of them was enormous. "Are all Highlanders as large as you?"

"No bigger than your Lowland kin, I'd reckon." Duncan chuckled. "These men were handpicked by me and my father. After Da returned from the Crusades, the king tasked him with keeping order in the Highlands."

"Campbell?" Meg mused. "Is your father the Black Knight of Rome?"

"Aye," John said.

King's men. Now answers were coming together. "Are you men the fabled Highland Enforcers?"

Eoin tossed a blanket on the hay. "Flesh and blood."

She snapped a hand over her mouth. *Heaven's stars*. "Why are such important knights riding into England and rescuing an insignificant woman like me?"

"Your brother doesn't think you're unimportant." Duncan gave her a lopsided grin. "I daresay he's right."

"You going soft on us?" Archie asked.

Duncan batted the air. "Never." He held up a blanket. "Come, Lady Meg, you can lie down between me and Sir John. We'll keep your bones from freezing."

"Oh no." Meg turned in a circle. "There absolutely must be someplace else for me to bed down. I cannot possibly sleep beside you men. My reputation would be as good as ruined."

Duncan looked to the others and spread his palms to his sides. "You want to sleep with the horses?"

Meg peered through the crude shelter. Aside from where they stood, there wasn't a spare stall or crevice. She wrung her hands. "This is highly improper."

"What did you expect on the run from the English, a toasty inn and a chambermaid to tend your needs?" The big man looked as if she'd slapped him. "Do you have a better idea?"

Her gaze swept across inquisitive faces, and she shivered. "Ah." *My stars, I'd freeze to my death by morning, even if there were an open stall. But must Sir Duncan be so smug about it? What about his male parts and his comments when we were riding together?*

Duncan plopped down on the mound of straw and beckoned her. "Do not be shy. As Sir John said, we're all knights, bound by an oath of chivalry."

Meg couldn't remember ever being this cold in her life. Things had been warmer surrounded by his arms when they were in the saddle. "Since I have no other choice in the matter, I shall this once." She shook her finger at the lot of gaping knighted faces. "Not a one of you will ever mention this to a soul. Do you understand me?"

"Aye, m'lady," they chorused with nods. Thank heavens no one laughed, else she would have been forced to further assert herself.

She turned her attention to Duncan and John. "You both must keep your backs to me."

Duncan shrugged. "As you wish." He nestled into the straw and spread the blanket, holding up one side. "Come on, then."

She clutched her arms tight to her chest and scooted under the woolen plaid. At least he hadn't been so put off by the claw he'd opted to make her sleep with the livestock. She curled as close to him as possible without touching. John lay on the other side, presenting his back, as she'd requested. Duncan pushed against her. Meg rose up on her elbow and glanced at his face. His eyes were already closed, his breathing slow.

It was warmer with his body touching hers. She lay back and nestled into him. She wasn't exactly toasty, but comfortable enough to sleep. Thank heavens Duncan had no improper feelings for her. Now he knew the truth about the claw, she could relax sleeping beside him—and his brother, for that matter.

*

Duncan grinned when Meg snuggled her backside into his. He couldn't remember ever resting beside a woman whom he hadn't ravished—and usually, he didn't linger long. This was definitely new and interestingly erotic territory for him. Touching Meg with every part of his body before he'd even kissed the lass was arousing. His only problem? In no way could he act on his desires.

When they were riding, he'd wondered why she constantly pulled the sleeve over her left hand. After he'd helped her dismount, he caught sight of her crippled appendage. In that moment, he'd wanted to examine it, but she'd seemed embarrassed.

Duncan didn't care. The hand did nothing to detract from her beauty. And heaven help him, she was prettier than a white rose in full bloom. Her wide-set, azure eyes reminded him of the sky on a winter's day with not a cloud above. Feminine, coppery eyebrows arched over her eyes as if in a constant state of amusement, taking in every detail. Her face flawless like the white rose petal, kissed by an ever-present pink-rose blush. A pert nose suited her face. But gazing upon her red-rose lips brought on unholy stirrings beneath his braies.

Those urgings intensified when he'd cradled her buttocks between his thighs through the entire night's journey. He'd not deny that her scent nearly drove him mad. Meg wore no perfumed oils. She didn't need any. Her own bouquet reminded him of honeysuckle warmed by summer's heat, and it had filled his nostrils with each breath.

When on horseback she'd fallen asleep, and a lock of beautifully curled hair caught the breeze, caressing his face. He'd snatched it between his fingers. Surprised at her hair's silken softness, he raised it to his nose. Her scent ravished him. He'd clenched his bum cheeks to dispel his longing.

In no way could he fondle, kiss or lust after the Earl of Angus's sister. Any errant move on Duncan's part would most definitely result in the earl withholding payment, or worse, sullying his reputation as the king's enforcer.

Unfortunately, the lady was forbidden fruit.

Duncan adjusted so his backside wasn't touching Meg intimately. He'd control his errant thoughts if it killed him.

Meg's bottom angled into his with her soft moan. Duncan's entire body tensed—including the damned part that shouldn't. He rose up on his elbow and glanced over his shoulder. Lips slightly parted, she was fast asleep. God help him, she looked like an angel.

He lay back down and closed his eyes. He didn't even like angelic women, for Christ's sake. He preferred the brazen women from the alehouse—women with large breasts and hearty behinds. Meg's scent had forced his mind to run amuck. Yes, that was it. 'Twas time to snuff her from his mind. Besides, if he didn't sleep, he'd be of little use when the time came to ride.

Meg jolted at the deafening sound of rapid hammering on wood. Her eyes flashed open, only to be stung by thick smoke. Horses whinnied. Their hooves pummeled at the stall walls.

Springing to her knees, she shook Duncan's shoulder with all her might. "The stable's on fire!"

Everyone sprang into motion.

Archie and Eoin raced toward the horse stall.

Duncan jerked up, brandishing his sword. "Bloody hell. Where's Sean?" He glared at Meg as if she should know.

She spread her palms to her sides. "Do you think they caught him?"

Duncan grasped her elbow and pulled her up. "Not Sean. He's a ghost."

Running through the foggy smoke, Eoin lead two horses. "The fire's spreading fast."

"Mount up." Duncan beckoned Meg with his hand, grasped her by the waist and tossed her onto the saddle like she weighed no more than a sack of oats. Then he effortlessly slipped into the saddle behind her.

Meg's eyes burned. She fanned her face and coughed.

John rode beside them. "What's the plan?"

"They'll be waiting for us for certain." Duncan pulled a dagger from his sleeve and handed it to Meg. "Do you know how to use this?"

Holding one arm across her stinging nose, she grasped it. "Aye."

Duncan picked up the reins. "Run for the trees!"

James drew his sword. "Their horses will be spent."

"God, I hope so." Duncan leaned forward and kicked his heels.

Archie removed the crossbar just as Duncan and Meg crashed through the door.

Meg clung to Duncan and closed her eyes. Swinging his sword, he barreled into the open lea. Men screamed;

arrows hissed. Meg prayed. Hooves slapped the sloppy snow. The wind beat her face, and her nose ran.

She dared open her eyes. The tree line swiftly approached. She glanced behind. English soldiers were on their heels, keeping pace. Black smoke from the barn billowed into the heavy clouds above. Flames engulfed the door they'd just ridden through.

The English charged after them, but as James said, their horses were spent. With every step, the Highlanders raced further from their pursuers. Meg looked to the sky. It was still morning. They'd perhaps gained two hours of sleep, mayhap three.

Who knew when they'd be able to stop again? Though she felt inordinately tired, Meg's excitement thrummed hot through her blood. For the first time in her life, she was in danger and on the run. She clutched the dagger and fingered the grip. She'd use it if left with no other choice. The idea made her heart beat faster. She'd never guessed danger would ignite a fire deep within. The chill biting her face and the wind in her hair invigorated her. She was on an adventure far away from the protection of Tantallon Castle, and she'd never felt so alive. Meg slid the dagger into her rope belt and patted it.

When the sun reached the noon hour, Duncan finally slowed their mount to a fast walk.

"I knew we shouldn't have stopped before we crossed the Tweed," John said.

The hackles on Meg's neck stood on end. "If we hadn't stopped, the horses would be worthless." She hated it when someone suddenly became an expert because of circumstances past.

"Aye," Duncan rumbled against her back.

Something moved in the shadows. Meg tensed.

He tugged the horse's reins and drew his sword. Meg brushed her fingers over the dagger in her belt.

Metal hissed, drawn from the five other men's scabbards.

A lone horse and rider walked out from the scrub, hands held high. "Thank God you got out..."

Duncan sheathed his sword. "Sean? Could you not give us fair warning? The fire in the stable nearly cooked us alive."

Meg swiped an errant strand of hair from her face while the others rode alongside them.

"I rounded back, but they cut me off. I nearly killed my horse trying to beat them." Sean steered his mount west and led onward. "It gets worse. Northumberland's men fanned out. They're everywhere."

Duncan cued his horse to a fast trot. "Expecting us to ride straight to Tantallon..."

"I'd reckon so. I'll wager he's setting traps all the way from Melrose to North Berwick."

"There's a lookout yonder." Duncan pointed. "We should have a good view from there—hopefully see how far behind us the English are."

They rode up the steep incline, the horses snorting with exertion. Holding tight to the pommel, Meg surveyed the view behind. If she could see the enemy, they'd be spotted for certain. Fortunately, all remained quiet.

They crested the hill and Duncan circled the horses. "We must split up."

Everyone nodded in agreement.

"Robert and James, head to Roxburgh and then cut north. The rest of you, spread out—lead them north. Sean, take a message to the Earl of Angus that his sister's alive and will be returned as soon as 'tis safe."

Sean gave a clipped nod with his helmed head.

Archie pointed his thumb at the coat of blackened armor tied behind him. "You'd best set to arming yourself."

"Nay," Duncan said. "This gelding is already overburdened carrying the both of us. Keep it safe for me."

John patted his horse's neck. "And where are you heading, brother?"

Meg's ears pricked. Exactly where would this big Highlander take her now?

"West." Duncan steered the horse to the far slope of the outcropping. "I'll see you all at Kilchurn in a sennight's time." He tugged the reins and regarded his men over his shoulder. "God's speed."

Chapter Seven

As soon as the others were out of sight, Meg couldn't shake the eerie sense of being watched. Her gaze darted through the trees, and she leaned forward to peer around Duncan's enormous frame to gain a glimpse behind them. "Why did we separate from the others?"

He swayed in the saddle in concert with the horse's movement, and seemed unusually calm, as if running from the English were a daily occurrence for him. "They won't expect us to head west."

Meg refused to allow his serenity to put her at ease. "But is it not more dangerous without your men-at-arms?"

"Everything we do is dangerous, m'lady." His gruff voice rumbled and filled her with disquiet. At least she told herself as much. The gooseflesh rising upon her arms could be caused by nothing other than unease. Heavens, Duncan's voice alone *sounded* dangerous.

"How is your...uh...your injury?" Surely it wasn't improper to speak of a man's backside when she referred to it with concern for his well-being.

"It bloody hurts."

She cringed. "Someone should tend it."

"Do not worry about me. It'll come good in a sennight or two."

Meg sat quietly for a moment, but Duncan's every breath filled her ears like the roaring of the sea. Tapping the claw's pincers, she tried not to think of his incredibly warm thighs cradling her buttocks, or the protective chest pressed against her back. If she kept talking, surely these things would stop muddling her mind. "Do you know where we are?"

"Still in the borderlands, I'd reckon."

Meg clapped her hand to her chest. "You're not certain?"

"Aye, m'lady, I'm well aware that we're between Melrose and the Firth of Clyde—where you Lowlanders draw the line between borderlands and lowlands is a quandary to me."

Meg groaned. Sir Duncan could be maddening. "Since I hail from the lowlands, you probably think me snobbish and daft."

"I did not say that, but now that you mention it, Lowlanders can come across as believing themselves to be superior."

Meg straightened her spine. "I most certainly do not believe myself superior to anyone."

"Nay?" His chuckle rolled through her insides. "You're the daughter of an earl—born into nobility and a life of great comfort. Tell me, do you believe your chambermaid to be your equal?"

"You're preposterous." Meg ground her molars. "How about your groom? Your servants? *Your* valet? You are nearly as nobly born as I."

His devilish chuckle rumbled again, making her heart flit about like a finch. "Ah, m'lady, but you were the first to mention snobbery."

She glanced at Duncan's face over her shoulder. Why did he have to be so wickedly handsome? "You're insufferable."

"Am I?" He ran the reins through his fingers, as if she hadn't insulted him in the slightest.

Meg adjusted her seat and cringed. Blast him. Riding double with Duncan was far too intimate—scandalous, even. The sooner they could find her a mount, the better. "Do you think Lord Percy's men will follow us?"

"I hope not."

His response was no answer. And why on earth were they traveling west? Presently they were moving farther away from North Berwick with every step. Did he have a plan? Meg cared not to be used as a pawn. Nor did she care to be taken around the countryside without a clue as to her whereabouts. "Where is this Kilchurn you spoke of?"

"'Tis the seat of the Lord of Glenorchy. My family's keep. You'll be safe there until I can spirit you to Tantallon."

"Is it in the Highlands?"

"Aye, on Loch Awe." From the reverence in his voice, one would think it the most idyllic place in Scotland.

Still trying to peer through the trees, Meg adjusted herself in the saddle, her buttocks flush against Duncan's thighs. He grunted. She ignored his protest. "What is it like?"

"*Och*, you ask too many questions, just like Archibald."

"Honestly?" She tried to sound astounded. "You're as overbearing as I envisioned a Highland barbarian to be. Besides, what else is there to do? Sit atop this poor gelding and ride all the way to the western shore as if we are taciturn?"

He grumbled and remained silent for several uncomfortable paces. "'Tis the solace."

Meg gave up watching for the English. Surely they

wouldn't be lying in wait ahead of them. "Whatever do you mean?"

"You asked me what I like about Kilchurn." He shifted his hips. "The keep sits at the base of Ben Cruachan and overlooks the bluest loch in all of Scotland. I love to stand atop the battlements at sunset and watch the sun reflect oranges and violets off the water. When all's quiet, it puts my soul to rest."

That got her attention. Now the rugged knight spoke like a poet? Meg sighed and reclined against Duncan's chest. Just when she'd begun to think him a complete brute, he blurted out prose from the heart. No matter how hard he tried to portray the gruff warrior, Meg suspected a softness simmered at his core— one he guarded fiercely.

"Are you the eldest?" she asked.

"Aye."

Are we back to monosyllables now? "I've met John—do you have other siblings?"

"Aside from John, I've a younger brother, Iain, who's fostering with the Earl of Argyll." He eyed her. "Then I've four sisters, and they're all as chatty as you."

She chose to ignore his jibe. "Aside from Arthur, I have four sisters as well—all married but me."

"Yet, lass. You'll be a fine match for any nobleman."

"Nay." Meg held up her left hand. He'd already seen it, after all. "'Tis the claw."

"A wee crippled hand shouldn't make any difference. Especially when you have..."

"What?"

"Never mind."

Meg wasn't about to allow that comment to pass without an explanation. "No, tell me."

His hand slipped from his reins and pressed against her abdomen while he shifted his hips again. "Eyes that can claim a man's soul and hair of fire."

Heaven help her thundering heart. Thankfully, he

resumed his grasp on the reins. Meg emitted a nervous chuckle. *Bah. He couldn't possibly mean a single word.* She swiped her hand over her tresses. "I cannot abide my hair. 'Tis as unmanageable as a gnarled stack of straw."

"I wouldn't say that—your curls are a bit profuse, but I like a wild mane of locks on a woman."

He had the most vexing way of making her feel self-conscious. How was she supposed to respond? No man had ever thus complimented her, especially after a glimpse at the claw.

"What happened to your hand, if you don't mind my asking?" His voice took on that deep burr again.

But Meg considered this a more suitable conversation. "Has always been this way—born with it." She tapped her pointer finger to her thumb. "The pincers work fine."

"Is it a family trait?"

"Nay, just a feature of Meg, thank heavens. However, I did inherit a number of Douglas vices, like impatience and an awful temper."

"I'll have to keep that in mind." He ran the reins through his fingers. "But if being quick to anger is a vice, then I think all of Scotland is afflicted."

Meg hummed. "You do have a sense of humor, aye, Sir Duncan?" She craned her neck and looked at him. A flutter stirred deep inside. She could study the dark angles of his handsome face all day.

Dipping his chin, his gaze met her eyes. Alluring, deep mahogany rimmed by black. Everything about his eyes screamed danger. Meg's heart skipped a beat. Her stare trailed to his lips. The bottom one was fuller— pouted a bit. Her tongue shot out and moistened hers. Duncan's mouth was so close, all she had to do was rise up a few inches and their lips would touch.

His eyelashes lowered with his gaze. She hadn't noticed before, but his black lashes were inordinately long. Something inside her breasts swelled. It was unholy for a man to be so indescribably beautiful, yet rugged as the Highlands.

Without thinking, she ran a finger along the angular line of his stubbled jaw. He'd appeared clean shaven in the chapel, but now, a beard shadowed his face. When it prickled her finger, she gasped, not expecting the stubble to be so coarse.

"You keep looking at me like that and we'll not make it to Peebles," he said with the growl of a devil.

Meg shook her shoulders and adjusted her bottom in the saddle—right against his crotch. *Lord have mercy*. She needed her own mount. Being this close to a barbarian toyed with her sensibilities. "Your beard has grown in since we met. I simply found so much unruly growth strange." *There. That should prove I'm not to be trifled with.*

"As I recall, your brother had an impressive beard. Surely a man's facial hair isn't foreign to you."

Generally speaking, men's facial hair had never fascinated her in the least. But something about Duncan's black beard had wee fairies flitting about her stomach. She mustn't tempt him. He'd already alluded to his improper thoughts before. "I apologize." She shifted her hips before she could stop herself. *I must stop moving.* "Sharing a saddle with you is rather disconcerting. I do hope we can acquire another horse in the next town."

He tugged her closer. "As do I, lass. As do I."

🐾

ISAAC STOOD AT THE TOP OF THE CRAG AND TURNED full circle. Hoof prints scattered in every direction except south. Miserable heathens; they'd made his task near impossible. He'd never be able to return to Alnwick. His wife and newborn daughter would starve. Not that it concerned Lord Percy in any way. Isaac clenched his jaw. He bore the earl's harsh treatment only to support his family. If it weren't for his girls, he'd have walked away from Northumberland a long time ago.

Lusting for revenge, the earl walked a thin line between madness and sanity. He had his title reinstated, his riches—what more did he need? Northumberland should leave well enough alone and move on with his wretched life.

Isaac stared at the long faces of his remaining men. After they'd crossed into Scotland, he'd sent groups of five all along the eastern lowlands. If they'd caught the marauders on the border, he would have been able to cut them down without creating too much of a stir. But now they were a few miles outside Melrose. He'd missed his opportunity to end this swiftly.

He'd nearly had them in his grasp at the old stable. He could have killed the men in his company. Not a single soldier could fire a straight arrow. He kicked a rock and watched it tumble down the crag. If they'd injured even one of the bastards, he could have returned to Alnwick with his pride intact.

Now the only thing he could do to protect his wages was travel into bloody Scotland in the dead of winter, trailing a phantom. He walked to the western slope and stopped. Only one horse descended there. Meg had doubled with a big Scot when they'd fled the burning barn. *Hmm. Perhaps all isn't lost.*

He glanced at his second in command. "Split up. Follow each pair of tracks and report back to Alnwick. We're too far past the border to fight them now. Find out who the bastards are and head for home."

"You mean we're just going to let them go, sir?"

"No. We'll be smart about it—hit them when the time is right, and in a way to avoid breaking the truce."

The soldier scratched his head. "All right. We'll see you back at Alnwick, then."

Isaac mounted his horse and followed the lone set of prints, praying his gut was right.

❧

THE SUN HAD SET BY THE TIME THEY CROSSED THE River Tweed and rode into Peebles. Duncan tried to keep Lady Meg warm between his arms, yet her delicate frame still shivered. "We'll find an inn and you can warm yourself by the hearth."

"I'm so cold, I cannot imagine ever being warm again."

He dipped his head until his nose skimmed her tresses and inhaled. Meg's scent was as intoxicating as a cup of fine whisky. "I ken, lass, but we couldn't ride into town with you wearing monks vestments. We'd be spotted for certain." He'd made her remove the woolen robe in the forest, and then he'd doused it in the river. After it was soaked through, they stood on the shore and watched the habit disappear under the icy torrent.

"It would have been nice if we'd had something to replace it with first. I swear, men think nothing of freezing a lass to the bone. Lord Percy locked me in a chilly chamber, and now you expect me to ride through the snow without so much as a cloak. 'Tis as if you both would like to see me meet my end."

Duncan clenched his teeth and fought back his ire. He didn't appreciate being compared to a murdering English bastard. The horse clambered over the bridge, crossing the River Tweed. "Enough. You'll be toasty warm in no time."

Peebles was a typical Lowland village, with whitewashed stone cottages and buildings. Duncan stopped the horse on the edge of town and looked to his right. A short distance from the main road stood a two-story building with a shingle out front that read, BIGGIESKNOWE INN.

He pointed. "Looks like we're in luck, lassie."

Meg followed his finger. "Thank the Lord for small mercies."

He led the gelding to the stable around back. After he hopped down, he held up his hands and grasped her waist. "M'lady."

He didn't miss the disquiet reflected in her gaze, but she said nothing and placed her fine-boned hands on his shoulders. "You have a firm grip."

"Am I hurting you?" With the momentum of the lift, he held her against his body and tried to ease his fingers.

Her breath caught.

Level with his face, he stared directly into her eyes. He parted his lips and his tongue grew dry. Then he focused on her ruby-red mouth. He'd never seen lips draw into a taut cupid's bow as hers did—so perfectly shaped, they begged to be kissed. He tilted his head to the side. She closed her eyes and pursed those delightful lips, her breasts still flush against his chest. Duncan's tongue shot to the corner of his mouth. If he kissed Lady Meg now, he might not be able to restrain himself once they found a room. With a muffled groan, he slowly lowered her to the ground.

She looked up at him and blinked rapidly, then fanned her face. "Perhaps in the future I should dismount on my own."

Duncan turned toward the horse and loosened its girth, needing a distraction to allay his inappropriate urges. "Perhaps I shall find you a mount on the morrow."

After paying the groom to care for his horse, Duncan pressed his hand in the small of Lady Meg's back. "Pull your veil over your tresses and let me do the talking."

She gaped at him. "You do not believe me capable of speaking for myself?"

"'Tisn't that at all—but we've a mob of angry Englishmen scouring the countryside looking for a maiden with a mane of fiery red hair. We cannot let on who we are. For tonight, you shall be Mrs. Armstrong."

She tugged the blue silk tight over her spiral curls. "Mrs.? Isn't that a sacrilege?"

Duncan hurried her along. "Not when you're running from the devil."

"I knew you didn't like my hair."

Ignoring her ludicrous remark, he opened the door to a rush of warm air accompanied by noisy barroom banter. "Remember what I said. I'll do the talking."

Meg rolled her eyes and stepped inside with a huff.

A buxom woman strode toward them holding a pint of ale in one hand, a pitcher in the other. "Look what blew in with the north wind." At least she didn't say south.

"Mr. Armstrong, here." Duncan wrapped an arm around Meg's shivering shoulder. "My wife and I need a room for the night."

"What are you doing taking this lovely little creature out in weather like this?" The matron studied Meg, a concerned pinch to her brows. "With not even a cloak—the poor lassie is blue."

Meg pursed her lips and gave him a sideways glare.

The woman set the ale on a nearby table. "Come with me. We'll set you to rights." She tugged Meg from Duncan's grasp and marched up the stairs.

"Och, where's me pint?" hollered a voice from the pub.

"You'll have it soon enough," the matron yelled over her shoulder. "Bloody tinker's already in his cups."

Duncan followed, none too appreciative of the matron's vulgar language in Lady Meg's presence. He'd been consciously trying to curb his tongue, and especially did not appreciate hearing "bloody" coming from an innkeeper's wife.

At the top of the stairs, the woman led them down the hall and slid a key into a door at the end. "Fortunately, we have just the room." She beamed and pushed open the door. "If this meets with your approval, I'll have the lad come up and light the fire."

Duncan stepped inside and gave the modest chamber a cursory glance. "This will be fine."

"Two shillings for the night, plus a shilling if you want your meals."

Duncan fished in the leather purse that hung from his belt. "You drive a hard bargain."

She held out her hand. "An innkeeper's got to live."

The three coins clinked as he dropped them into her palm. "There'll be an added three pennies if you bring our meals up."

The woman's eyebrows arched. "Newlyweds, aye?"

Meg clapped her hand over her mouth and coughed.

"Aye." Duncan grasped the innkeeper's elbow. "We'd be much obliged if you'd send up the lad with an armful of wood and his flint forthwith."

Her fingers closed around the coins. "Straight away, Mr. Armstrong. And I've got a nice lamb pottage to warm your insides as well."

"Ever so kind, matron." Duncan held the door. "A hot meal is exactly what we need."

He grinned at Meg. Her cheeks flushed red, and she looked as if she could blow steam from the top of her head. If only he could pull the feisty woman into his arms and smother her with kisses—give her a sampling of what it would be like to be newlyweds.

❧

As soon as the door closed, Meg folded her arms. "Only one room?" She gestured toward the narrow bed shoved against the wall. "Exactly where do *you* intend to sleep?"

Duncan tapped the threadbare rug with his toe. "I can make do with the floor."

"In this chamber? Pray tell, where *I* will be sleeping?"

"You slept beside me last eve and didn't complain overmuch."

Meg wrapped her arms around her middle. Share a room with Duncan when there were other people around—when she'd all but swooned in his arms when she'd dismounted this eve? "But that was in a stable," she objected. "With no other alternative."

"I do not see much choice here, either. Would you prefer to be in a stable?"

"You, sir, are exasperating." She shook her finger at the door. "You could have at least asked the woman if she had two rooms."

"How would that look?" He spread his palms to his sides, his eyes growing dark as a stormy sky. "We are *supposed* to be married."

Meg cradled her head in her hands. "Och, what will my brother think to know I'm staying in an inn with a man? Moreover, I'll never be admitted as a novice."

"I'll not tell anyone." He shrugged like a big oaf. "Your virtue's safe with me, m'lady."

Meg wrung her hands. She'd been "safe" with him for two days now. No, he hadn't done anything to compromise her virtue, but he'd alluded to it enough. "This isn't right."

"Dammit, woman." Duncan plodded to the door and grasped the latch. "I've tried to hold my tongue, but you have the most annoying way of pulling out the ogre in me."

Meg clutched her fists to her chest and took a step back. His brows angled down over his eyes, like he was about to hit something...or her. "I merely wanted to point out the impropriety of"—she gestured with her arms, encompassing the miniscule room—"this."

"Do you not think I ken? If it were not for the English spies fanning out across the borderlands, I'd have delivered you back to your brother by now and you'd never have the displeasure of laying eyes on me again."

"I don't—"

Duncan sliced a hand though the air to silence her, then opened the door. "Stay here. I'm off to find another horse and something to keep us from freezing to death before we reach Kilchurn." He held up his palm. "I repeat, do not leave this chamber. Keep the door locked. Only open it for me." He started out.

"What about the lad with the flint?"

Duncan stopped. "Aye, you can open it for the lad if his voice hasn't yet changed."

Meg stepped toward him, shoving her fists upon her hips. "And the matron with our supper?"

"Och, I'll be back afore she brings the food." He slammed the door before Meg could utter another word.

She stomped her foot. *Curses to him.* If Duncan weren't so overbearing, she might care for the enormous knight. But no, he continually chose to act like a brute. Presently, she could not wait to return to Tantallon Castle and resume her life as quickly as possible.

&.

WHEN DUNCAN FINALLY RETURNED, MEG SAT wrapped in a plaid, warmed by the fire—and thank heavens she hadn't heeded his commands. She'd opened the door wide and allowed the matron to bring in a trencher of food, else she would have starved.

He limped into the chamber with a bundle under his arm, frowning like a lout. "I thought I said to not allow anyone in."

A dozen quick-tongued responses came to mind, but she simply gave him a look—the same one she used when her brother said something entirely exasperating. Then he stumbled. Meg jumped up. "You're hurt."

"I'm fine." He pushed past her and set his bundle on the table. "Not to worry, 'tis coming good."

"Someone should have a look at it."

"Whom do you suggest when we're trying to keep our identities hidden?" He opened the parcel. "Besides, I purchased a few things from a kindly Gypsy." He held up a stoppered stoneware pot and a jar filled with dirty water. "A salve and a handful of leeches."

Meg walked to the table and peered into the jar. "A Gypsy? I'm surprised he didn't rob you blind."

Duncan chuckled. "Me? He wouldn't have survived the night."

She tapped her top lip with her tongue. "I suppose a knight as large as you can move within many unsavory circles without fear."

He grinned and picked up the vessel containing four ugly bloodsuckers. "I could put these on myself...if I had a twist-around spine."

Meg couldn't look him in the eye. "You want me to do it?" She clapped her good hand to her chest. "I-I don't know much about healing."

"Aye? Well, 'tis time you learned—I've no intension of being waylaid with a fever."

Meg eyed the jar, then glanced at Duncan's backside. A tempest of butterflies swarmed in her stomach. She'd never seen a man's flesh—never even seen Arthur without him being fully clothed. "Do you think I can place the leeches through the wee hole in your chausses?"

Duncan unclasped his belt. "If only the hole was directly over my wound." He chuckled. "Do not worry yourself. I'll keep my back turned." He pointed at the jar. "Put two leeches either side then swipe the salve right down the middle."

Before Meg could blink, he dropped his chausses

and lowered his braies. Her mouth went completely dry. His chiseled, naked bottom peeked from under his linen shirt. She gaped at the hard lines and smooth, rounded buttocks. The backs of his thighs were long, yet they bulged with sinew and muscle, peppered with black curls.

He twisted around. "Lady Meg?"

Blinking, she jolted and met his gaze.

He pointed to his right buttock. "My wound's over here."

Her eyes popped wide. Yes, indeed. It was a huge mass of purple, black and yellow, with an angry, jagged red cut down the center of the mess. She hissed. "That looks awful."

"'Bout the same as it feels."

Meg tried not to ogle the male flesh presenting to her, and focused on Duncan's wound. She reached out her hand then quickly snapped it back. It would be ever so improper to touch him.

"I don't reckon staring at it'll help me heal."

She stepped back. "True." She fumbled with the stopper on the jar of leeches. "Two on each side, you say?"

"Aye."

Leeches were such slimy, vile creatures. Meg gritted her teeth. Clearly, Duncan needed their medicinal magic. Even she knew leeches were one of the best options to keep infection away. She squeezed one gently and pulled it from the glass. Her stomach turned over. Fingers trembling, with a grimace she put the squirming black glob of slime beside Duncan's wound. Her fingers brushed his flesh. Unexpectedly soft, she stilled her hand as if she'd just avoided being burned.

He grunted.

The cut oozed yellow. Meg balled her fists so she wouldn't touch him and peered closer. "It looks awfully bad."

"You'd best apply the other leeches, then."

Meg did as asked until four unsightly blobs hung from his bruised bottom. "Now what?"

"They'll feast until they fall off." Duncan glanced at her over his shoulder. "Spread on the salve."

Meg swallowed. For a moment, she'd forgotten a rugged warrior stood bare arsed in front of her. She mustn't pay heed to the softness of his skin. The wound looked horrid. If she didn't tend him properly, he could succumb to a fever—even an enormous, strapping man like Duncan wasn't hewn of iron. "The cut needs to be properly cleansed first." She slid her hand over her mouth—now she'd have to bathe him too.

"Very well." Duncan shifted, sounding unflappable. "Douse a cloth in the bowl. That'll fix me right up."

Meg exhaled. When he'd moved, she feared he might turn around, mayhap call for a bath. Oh, God in heaven, what if she saw him from the front? She'd die. Heat pooled in the crux of her legs while her knees turned to wobbly mush.

"You want me to fetch it?" His gruff voice took on an air of impatience.

She crossed to the bowl. "Sorry. I'll do it." She poured some water from the ewer and dunked the cloth.

"Are you nervous, lass?"

She nearly dropped the cloth. "No...yes. 'Tis just your injury isn't in the most *genteel* location."

"Apologies. If I could transfer it to my elbow to appeal to your sensibilities, I'd do so in an instant."

"How you can jest at a time like this, I cannot fathom."

She stole a glance at the well-formed male specimen across the room. Honestly, she shouldn't gawk. The poor man was in pain. He merely needed her to tend his vicious wound—and the sooner she did so, the sooner he'd cover up his backside, and her ridiculous desire to stare at it would go away.

Meg held the claw in front of her nose and frowned. *Remember? No man wants a woman with such a grotesque deformity.*

She wrung out the cloth and boldly strode to him. As soon as she bent down, her hand started shaking again. She clutched the cloth tighter. "Just a few quick swipes."

Duncan hissed. "Bloody oath, are you washing me with sackcloth?"

"'Tis linen." Meg tossed the cloth on the table and reached for the stoneware pot. One of the leeches dropped to the floor. She quickly glopped the ointment on two fingers and spread it over the gash. Two more leeches dropped and writhed.

Duncan looked back. "I'll fetch them in a moment."

Meg looked at her handiwork. "You could use a few stitches."

"Do you have a needle and thread?"

"Nay."

He shifted his weight. "Feels better already."

Meg held the pot of salve to her nose and sniffed—leek for certain, combined with something that made her eyes water. "What's in it?"

After the fourth leech dropped, Duncan pulled up his braies and bent down for his chausses. "Gypsy magic. They may be an odd lot, but they have potent medicine."

She stoppered the pot and rested it on the table. "I hope it helps. I can hardly believe you can sit a horse. Half your bum is bruised."

He faced her, his grin halfcocked. "Wheesht. I cannot believe a delicate lassie is speaking about my arse with such recklessness."

"I..." Meg clapped her hands over her burning

cheeks. He was right. She should not speak of a man's backside. Not ever. "Forgive me."

His white teeth flashed with his grin. "Aye, lassie. With four older sisters and the Earl of Angus for a brother, I'd think you'd ken when someone is teasing you."

Meg clenched her claw and covered it with her good hand. *Goodness gracious*, Sir Duncan had a way of making her self-conscious like no one she'd ever met. He sauntered toward her and placed his hands on Meg's shoulders. His dark chestnut eyes bored into hers, as if he'd never gazed upon a woman before.

His tongue flicked out and moistened his lips. "Thank you, m'lady."

She swallowed, her heart thumping out of rhythm. "I…" Goodness, his mouth was ever so close to hers. She gasped. His gaze trailed from her eyes to her lips. *Was he…?*

Without thinking, Meg lifted her chin, her skin alive with tingling. The scent of spice and male filled her senses. Duncan's lips met hers ever so softly. Such a rugged man, yet his lips were softer than silk. He slid his hands down her back, and Meg's insides swirled in a fluttering torrent. Closing her eyes, she could stand there and kiss him until the sun rose anew.

Duncan pulled her closer, his tongue brushing her lips. Meg startled, but his hand caressed up the back of her neck. Her skin came alive with gooseflesh. She couldn't pull away from him even if she'd tried. For years, she'd wanted to know what it was like to kiss a man—not a peck on the cheek, but a deep, longing kiss —one intended only for her.

She molded into his chest. He tasted like whisky and rain while his tongue swirled with hers in an intoxicating dance. Meg prayed he'd hold her in his arms forever. If he released now, she'd swoon for certain.

Chapter Eight

Holding Meg Douglas in his arms, Duncan's pain melted into oblivion. God forgive him, he'd needed to kiss the lass ever since her long red lashes unveiled her eyes in the chapel. The way she came undone in his arms, she felt the same, whether Lady Meg knew it or not. Aye, initially she may have been a wee bit resistant, but once Duncan showed her how a man kisses a woman, she'd melted like butter in the sun.

Bless the sweet smell of wildflowers that wafted from every crevice of her body. He couldn't recall a woman ever tasting so sweet. And her soft curves molded into his chest so well.

Only one kiss and I'll be able to push her from my thoughts.

Closing his eyes, he swirled his tongue down her neck. A smoldering moan escaped her throat. "Sir Duncan." Her voice had turned husky. "I cannot ..."

The muscles in his arms clenched. God on the cross, ever since he met the lass he'd done nothing but tell himself Lady Douglas was forbidden fruit. As soon as they were shut in a chamber alone, his lustful Campbell urges surged straight through the tip of his cock. Of course, lowering his braies while Meg tended his naked arse did nothing to quash his yearnings. Bloody hell, he couldn't be trusted—aye, he, a knight who'd taken an oath of chivalry, got a maid alone in a chamber, bared his bum and then proceeded to ravish her. Heaven help him, if she hadn't stopped them, he'd have deflowered her before the fire needed another stick of wood.

His payment for her rescue wouldn't be the only thing forfeited. Blast the English to hell for their dimwitted chase. Now only God knew how long he'd be forced to endure Meg's presence. How complicated and awkward he'd just made things.

Duncan grasped her shoulders and stared at her nose. He couldn't bring himself to look into those crystal blues. Not now. "Apologies. I do not ken what came over me."

Meg covered her mouth with her hand and stomped her little foot. "I'll...I'll not have you taking advantage of me because of my deformity. I have a sharp mind in spite of my hand."

Duncan furrowed his brow. "You think yourself unappealing because of a wee bent hand?"

Meg whipped around and turned her back. "I saw the fear in your eyes when you first saw it. But allow me to say, I know my languages and I can read better than Arthur, calculate sums, and I can ride a horse as fast as any man."

He stared at her slender shoulders dumbly. "Aye, you do have an impressive seat." *I'm sure that appeased her worries, ye big oaf.* If only he could reach out and caress her wild locks—show her how extraordinary he believed her to be.

Those red tresses shook. "Nay. You're just saying that to soothe my feelings."

He placed a hand on her shoulder. After all, it was only a hand. Her body tensed. So did his. "One thing you must know, Lady Meg. I never pay a compliment which isn't due. If I say you have a talent, I mean it." *Better.*

She stood motionless for a moment and then regarded his hand, still resting on her shoulder. "You're not put off by the...my hand?"

"Nay. I can see no reason to fear it."

She sidestepped out from under his grasp, and looked him in the eye. "Why did you kiss me?"

Because you're more wily than a devil cat. Duncan swiped his hand across his mouth. Lordy, what should he tell her? He abhorred lying. "Forgive me. I was hired by your brother to rescue you from the Earl of Northumberland and return you safely to your kin. I had no right to take liberties."

She narrowed her gaze, her fingers lightly tapping her lips. "Did you enjoy...ah...it?"

She lowered her hand, her bow-shaped mouth pouted, crimson—begging for another wee kiss. Lord have mercy, he could ruin everything for him and his men. Duncan ground his back molars and bowed deeply. "My personal happiness is not your concern, m'lady. I am your servant. I promised your brother to return you to Tantallon unharmed and untouched. That vow I will honor."

Her cheeks flushed, and she cast her gaze to the hearth whilst wringing her hands. "I thank you."

Duncan resisted the urge to drop to a knee and apologize. He needed to ask forgiveness for nothing. He'd kissed the lass. That was all. He would put it behind him and carry on with his mission.

She gestured toward the table. "You'd best eat something."

His mouth watered—he hadn't thought about food since entering the chamber. "I'm starved."

"'Tis most likely cold."

"Not to worry." Duncan sat, wincing at the jab of pain that shot from his arse up his spine. "I could eat dirt with a bit of seasoning if I had nay other choice."

She chuckled. Good. The lass must have let the ludicrous kiss go, too. It would be easier for them both if they blocked it from their minds. Meg sat in the wooden chair across from him. "Did you find another horse?"

Duncan tore a piece of bread with his teeth and shoved it to the side of his mouth. "Nay, but I sold the gelding."

She jolted straight up. "You did what?"

He picked up a spoon and pointed it at her. "Sold him in payment for a wagon ride to Glasgow. We'll be a mite less suspicious if we look like a pair of tinkers—and then we can hire a transport on the River Clyde." He gestured to the bundle he'd tossed on the bed. "Found us a couple of used cloaks as well."

After crossing the floor, Meg untied the bundle and unrolled it. She held up a grey cloak. "This moth-eaten blanket has so many holes I doubt it could provide warmth for anyone."

"Ah, m'lady, I daresay most poor souls would be grateful to have such a woolen garment to keep the north wind at bay."

She held up the other. "I suppose I shouldn't complain. I could very well end up in garments such as these."

"Why would you say that?"

She shrugged. "When I take up the veil, I'll be relying on the church for support."

He didn't like the idea of Lady Meg becoming a nun, but then he had no say in the matter. "Surely your brother would provide your dowry to the abbey."

"Aye, but those riches will be used to help others, not for me."

He doused the end piece of bread in the stew. "They'll be used to feather the abbess's bed, no doubt."

Meg pursed her lips and looked away.

He stuffed the whole thing in his mouth. "Why are you so hell-bent on becoming a nun?"

"Why are you taking up your father's mantle?" she

retorted without answering. "The Black Knight has a notorious reputation."

"Someone's got to do the king's bidding. Besides, I believe in law and order. The lawlessness that pervades the Highlands must stop. Innocent women and children must be protected—lands tilled and not burned."

"Do you fancy yourself a savior of innocents, Sir Duncan?"

Was she toying with him? He glared across the table. Damn it all, the fire danced in her sparkling blue eyes. They challenged him in a way no other woman had ever done. He scooped another bite of stew. "I uphold the decrees of Scotland and support the king. That is all."

Meg moved to the edge of the bed and sat. "We'll be taking a sea transport from Glasgow?"

Damn, she changed the bloody subject again. He nodded her way. "Aye."

"It seems like you're taking me farther and farther away from my home."

Duncan scooped the last bite of stew. "'Tis just a roundabout route to keep you safe."

"If you must." She pulled one of the cloaks over her lap and thoughtfully smoothed her good hand across it. Duncan had hardly seen her use the crippled hand. "I think I should like to see the Highlands before I take my vows and live within cloistered walls."

"There's no place more beautiful."

"What's it like?"

"I could tell you, but words would not do it justice. There are mountains and lakes aplenty..." He winced at a sharp stab of pain in his backside. "And the weather cannot be predicted—could be sunny and warm in the morning and snowing by midafternoon."

"Ah." She smiled. "I do not think there's a place in all of Scotland where one could predict the weather."

He pushed his chair back and grunted with the twist of pain.

She jumped to her feet. "How is your wound?"

"It hurts like a bloody venomed rat sank its fangs into my arse." He didn't care a lick about cursing—perhaps she'd keep her distance if he reverted to using a vulgar tongue.

Meg crossed the floor and reached for the pot of salve. "Should I apply more ointment?"

Duncan grasped it from her. "I'll rub in my own salve. Having your fingers upon me fills my mind with all sorts of untoward ideas."

"What kind of ideas?" The innocence filling her eyes made his heart twist into a knot.

Duncan gave her a stern look—the one he used with his sisters when they asked too many questions. "You'd better take your rest. We've a long day's journey on the morrow."

###

MEG BIT THE INSIDE OF HER CHEEK. IF ONLY DUNCAN would tell her how *he* felt when she touched him. She certainly would never forget the moment when he'd kissed her. Her fingers still trembled. She returned to the bed and slipped off her shoes. "It doesn't seem right that I should have the bed when you're wounded and in pain."

She stole a glance at him over her shoulder. For a fleeting moment their eyes met. Something in the intensity of his stare caused a stirring in her stomach so violent, she clutched her hands to her midsection to quash it.

Then he cast his gaze to the fire. "You needn't worry about me. I've been in far worse pain and slept in far less comfortable accommodations." He held his palms up. "'Tisn't even raining."

He smiled with a boyish charm, though she knew he was just being friendly. Why would a warrior like Duncan Campbell, the future Lord of Glenorchy, go out of his way to be nice to her?

Since they'd kissed, he'd changed. He was more formal in his address toward her, yet the coarse language he'd used when they first met had returned. Meg touched her mouth. Who knew kissing a man could be so invigorating?

She climbed into the bed and tugged the bedclothes over her shoulders. The soft, downy mattress enveloped her in heavenly comfort. The floorboards creaked. Meg stiffened. What was he doing now? Wood clunked and the fire crackled. Meg sighed—*stoking the fire for the night*.

With a whoosh of air, he snuffed the candles. The floorboards creaked again. "Goodnight m'lady." His voice was soft and buttery—not nearly as gruff as before.

"Goodnight."

Meg rolled to her back. Turning her head to the side, she could see him now. He lay on his unwounded side, facing the fire, his head cradled in the crux of his arm. Duncan's shoulders were so broad, there was no question as to why he was the leader of the king's enforcers. He made an imposing knight—one to make an enemy quake just because of his size. The fluttering in her midsection started again.

Sighing, Meg picked up the pillow beside hers and tiptoed toward him. "This should help make you a wee bit more comfortable."

His head jerked toward her. He reached out, grabbed it and stuffed the pillow under his head. "*Ta.*"

She watched him for a moment. He ignored her, or pretended she didn't exist. Was he upset about the kiss? Was there something else? She returned to the bed.

"Are you married?" The question had been needling at her mind for days.

"Me?" His silhouetted hand batted the air. "I've no time for that."

Meg slipped between the linens again. "Why not?"

"I'm hardly ever home, for one. My duty is to keep order in the Highlands—and since Denmark ceded Orkney and Shetland, the task has been all the more challenging."

"Sounds dreary to me, always sleeping on the trail or in drafty inns. Since I've been abducted, I've decided I like the feel of my bed, and would be quite content to sleep there for the rest of my days."

His deep chuckle made the floorboards rumble. "Would you now?"

Meg tugged the bedclothes to her chin, determined to quash the fluttering caused by his voice. "Aye."

"What about joining an order?" he asked. "You'd be sleeping in a cell or an open dormitory—possibly with no walls—especially as a novice."

Meg tried to burrow into a comfortable spot for her head in the old pillow. "It wouldn't be all that bad, as long as I slept in the same place."

"Well, I wish you luck with it."

Meg rolled to her side to better study his outline. She sighed loudly then slapped her hand over her mouth. Had he heard her? What would he think if he knew she admired him? Here she was, only one step away from giving herself to the church, and her eyes couldn't drink in enough of the Highlander. She flopped to her back. She would stop ogling him this instant.

She closed her lids and willed sleep to come. Duncan's chiseled, bare behind flashed though her mind. It was as if he'd been hewn from pure white marble—just like Roman statuary. She pressed the heels of her hands to her eyes. She must fixate upon something else—something pure and holy.

Recalling the shiny brass cross at Melrose Abbey, she folded her hands to her chest and prayed. There were a great many things needing care—Duncan's men, Arthur, and her sisters. Meg prayed she and Duncan would safely make it to Glasgow and board a transport without being discovered. She even asked forgiveness for Lord Percy, that he might find compassion in his heart and cast aside his ill will for her family. Praying for the injured and oppressed, somehow her final words were: *Please heal your servant, Duncan*. With that, the image of his naked bottom filled her mind once again. Heaven help her, would she be plagued by inappropriate imaginings for the rest of her days?

Chapter Nine

Meg harrumphed. Last eve Duncan had conveniently failed to mention he'd arranged for them to ride in a *Gypsy* wagon. She sat on the hay-lined floor in the wagon and clutched Duncan's arm. She had never heard a good word about Gypsies. Honestly, she'd never been within a stone's throw of one, but the man sitting opposite her hadn't shifted his gaze from her face since she'd climbed into the back of the wagon. His intense, dark eyes made her uncomfortable, and she kept the claw hidden beneath her moth-eaten cloak. If only Duncan would have sat closer to the back end of the canvas-covered wagon in case they needed to make a quick escape. Over and over her mind recited how she would shield herself behind Duncan if the Gypsy tried to grab her. The man's eyes made him look like a wolf ready to pounce. She squeezed Duncan's arm tighter.

What gave the Gypsy cause to stare? Had her hair come loose from her veil? Most likely, yes—the unruly mop of curls. Meg tried to focus on the three children sitting beside him, all wearing linen scarves tied over their black locks. They smiled and appeared friendly enough, though their brilliantly colored clothing was like nothing she'd ever seen before. The two boys wore breeches striped with purples and golds. The lass too, aside from the bright orange skirt she wore atop. Interesting attire, though Meg could understand its practicality in keeping the lass warm.

Meg took pity on the youths. What chance did they have of growing up and gaining a trade? If the rumors she'd heard were true, even Gypsy children could steal a coin purse and vanish before the owner was the wiser.

Duncan sat rigid beside Meg. She couldn't tell if his severe posture was caused by the injury in his backside or if the Gypsy gave him pause. Before they left the inn, she'd inquired as to his pain, and he'd grunted a dismissive mumble akin to what she'd come to expect from the rugged Highlander.

She looked up at him. His gaze slanted toward her, and then shot back to the Gypsy man. Sir Duncan didn't appear to trust the fellow either.

The old wagon creaked and groaned as it ambled. Completely enclosed by canvas pulled taut over pole branches bent in arcing supports, Meg didn't like that she had no view of the landscape passing by. But at least they were hidden from the English. With colorful pillows and blankets folded at the front, Meg assumed the family slept there. The relentless clanging of cast-iron pots above nearly drove her mad and caused a painful ringing in her ears.

A Gypsy couple had met them that morning. Presently, the pair was out front, driving the team of oxen—the gelding Duncan had traded was tethered and trotted along behind.

The steady clang of pots eased, and the three children jumped to their feet, grinning as if they knew something was about to happen. Meg arched her brow at Duncan. "Are we stopping?"

"Most likely. My stomach's telling me 'tis time for our nooning."

Meg stretched out her legs and rubbed them awake while the children jumped out the back.

The beady-eyed man across the wagon still hadn't moved.

If Meg had a choice, she would prefer to continue on to Glasgow sharing the horse with Duncan. The wagon jostled and stopped. Squeezing Duncan's arm, she turned her lips up to his ear. "May I have a word in private?"

Duncan grunted and stood. "Do you need to relieve yourself?" He offered his hand and helped Meg up.

The man stretched and hopped out the back.

"I do." She looked through the gap in the canvas to ensure the Gypsies were out of earshot. "But not with that vile man about."

"Who?" Duncan hopped down, and before she could blink, he'd lifted her to the ground.

She led him away from the wagon, toward the trees. "The man who's been staring at me from across the wagon the entire journey. We're in Scotland, yet he gaped at me as if he'd never seen a Scottish woman before."

"Most likely he's never seen a ginger-haired lassie in the back of his cart." Duncan ran his palm over his sword's pommel. "But you ken you're safe with me. Any man must go through me before laying a finger on you."

Meg frowned. "He looks disagreeable, that one."

"Aye, but I can take the likes of him with one hand tied behind my back."

Meg looked to the heavens. She didn't want Duncan to fight the Gypsy. "Must everything be about violence with you?"

"I thought the miserable sop made you feel uncomfortable?"

"Aye, but I'd rather take the horse and ride with you the rest of the route to Glasgow. Sitting in the back of their house-wagon seems as if we're intruding."

Duncan scratched his head. "We shall be in Glasgow

before dark, then you'll never see them again. Riding in the back of the wagon keeps us out of sight. You ken?"

"Aye, but I do not like it."

"There, there." Duncan patted her shoulder as if she were a wee lass. "I'll stand guard while you take care of your necessities, we'll eat a meal and you'll feel better."

Meg groaned. "Do not placate me. I'll not stand for you treating me like a child."

One corner of his mouth ticked up and he bowed. "Very well, m'lady." Blast him, he was insufferable.

He turned his back while Meg slipped behind a hearty clump of broom and made quick work of her business. Brushing her hands, she stepped beside him. "Now you."

He blinked and opened his eyes wide. "Are you planning to stand guard for me now, lassie?"

"Nay, but I'm not going back to the wagon without you."

He stepped behind the same clump of broom. "There's a good lass. Remember that. You stay close to me until I can spirit you back to Tantallon, and no harm will come to you."

"You do have a rather inflated opinion of yourself, do you not?"

His water splattered the ground, and Meg held her hand over her eyes to keep herself from inadvertently looking.

"I wouldn't say that," he said as if he weren't taking care of his needs. "I know my limitations as well as the next man."

"It's just you can usually fight your way out of most predicaments."

"Aye."

She inadvertently lowered her hand and glanced in his direction. "Have you ever met a man who could best you?"

He grinned, though she could only see him from the shoulders up. "One."

"Perhaps I should go find him and see if he can return me home a mite faster than you."

Clothing rustled behind the thicket. "You can ask. You'll see him when we arrive at Kilchurn."

"Will I now? I cannot wait to see this behemoth. I'll wager he's taller than a pine and broader than a stallion's hindquarters. Pray, what is his name?"

Duncan stepped from behind the broom. Meg could scarcely imagine a man larger than he. He smiled at her, as if he'd enjoyed her ribbing. "Colin Campbell, Lord of Glenorchy, my da."

"You mean there are two of you?"

He chuckled. "Da isn't quite as tall as me, but I'd wager you were right about his shoulders."

She fanned herself. "Lord have mercy."

Duncan placed his hand in the small of her back and gestured forward. "Let us see what the heathens have prepared for us to eat."

Meg started forward. Ahead, movement made a warning prick the back of her neck. She abruptly stopped. Grunting, Duncan tripped over her and grasped her shoulders before she could fall.

"What the blazes?" he grumbled.

"Wheesht." She held up her palm while her heart hammered.

His fingers wrapped around his sword. Slowly, he pulled it from the scabbard with a soft hiss. "How many?"

She shrugged.

He placed a hand on Meg's shoulder and moved her behind him.

Voices carried from the wagon. She recognized an English accent and stood on her toes. No use; she couldn't see.

Duncan crept forward and gazed out through the

trees. "Only one," he whispered, beckoning her. "Do you recognize him?"

Meg peered through the crook in Duncan's arm, but the mounted man cantered his horse away before she could glimpse a good look. "Did you see his face?" she asked.

"Nay, he had his back to me."

"That's a good thing, is it not? You didn't want us to be seen."

Duncan sheathed his sword. "I suppose it is. No one would ever suspect us of riding with a mob of unsavory Gypsies."

Meg looked toward the beady-eyed man who'd been staring at her all day. "I can understand why."

&

IT APPEARED ISAAC HAD LOST THE TRAIL IN PEEBLES. Though it was a guess, he'd been fairly certain they had stopped to spend the night in the village. If they had continued on, they would have needed a fresh horse. And only God knew how they would have stayed awake all night.

They. Though he'd seen only one set of tracks, Isaac felt confident the single horse was the one with Lady Meg and her knight. Did the maid already know the man with whom she was riding? Was there some other skullduggery at work here? Was the bastard aiming to profit from kidnapping Lady Meg himself? Isaac pinched the bridge of his nose. None of his misgivings mattered. Lord Percy had tasked him with uncovering the identity of the interloper, and that was all.

Isaac could barely feel his toes, and he continually blew on his fingers to keep them from turning to ice. What he wouldn't give for a steaming bowl of pottage or a tankard of hot cider. He'd camped in a copse of trees outside Peebles, not far from the main road. He'd nearly frozen his cods during the night, but he couldn't risk letting a room in town. If Lady Meg recognized his face, he'd have little chance of trailing the maid and her bloody accomplice.

This Scotsman had been heading west. Riding his horse in a zigzag tracking pattern, Isaac puzzled at the lack of new tracks. Had the blighter doubled back? That was a possibility, especially if he had Lady Meg in tow. Doubtless she'd need to return to her brother in North Berwick. Taking the road to Glasgow made no sense at all, but Isaac's instincts told him to keep heading west.

Now the trail had gone cold. The bloody Gypsies he'd just encountered spoke broken English at best. Hell, he had no idea if they'd seen a man and a woman on horseback or not. Isaac pulled his cloak tighter around his shoulders. If he'd misjudged and chosen the wrong trail, perhaps one of his other men had been successful.

But there was no turning back now. He may as well see out his plan. At least he'd let a room and treat himself to a warm meal in Glasgow. Isaac sighed. After that, he'd need to come up with a plan. Perhaps he'd take a detour through Carlisle on his way home to see if he could find employment there. Lord Percy would surely torture him if he returned with nothing.

Chapter Ten

The wagon shifted from a rocking motion to a steady rattle when the wheels hit the cobblestones of Glasgow. Duncan had never been so relieved to be rattled. The sooner he stepped out of the carriage, the better. However, considering the throbbing pain in his arse, there might not be any place he'd be able to find comfort.

For the past hour or so, he'd been shivering from the cold. Christ, he never shivered. This whole mission was bungled from the outset.

Fortunately, when the wagon rolled to a stop, daylight still shone through the canvas. Duncan stretched and stood, crouching under the low roof. He pushed open the rear flap and shaded his eyes. The sun shone low in the western sky. *'Tis nearly sunset.* The smell of fish and stagnant water wafted into the wagon. They'd stopped alongside Clyde Street, which meant he and Lady Meg wouldn't have far to go to find a transport.

He hopped down and grunted. Ballocks, the pain in his backside was worse than a cut with a blade. He didn't care to be tended, but he'd send for the healer once they reached Kilchurn if it hadn't improved.

Straightening, he reached up to Meg. "M'lady."

She allowed him to lift her down without so much

as a purse to her lips. Perhaps she was growing accustomed to him.

When he again grunted, Meg gave him a concerned look. "Are you well?"

Duncan tried not to grimace. "Never better."

"I do not believe you."

He offered her his elbow. "Complaining never did anyone a lick of good." He nodded his thanks to the Gypsy family and led Meg toward the bustling pier, the odor of fish strong on the air. There were only a few small boats moored. Large ships couldn't sail up the River Clyde, but they only needed to find a *birlinn* headed north, preferably to Inverary. There he could borrow his uncle's horses and ride to Glen Orchy.

"Come." He inclined his head toward a galley being loaded with barrels. "Let us see who's sailing north this eve."

The bell from Glasgow Cathedral knolled the hour as Duncan led Meg through the crowd of busy laborers, all smelling of sweat and seaweed. They stopped to allow a sailor to pass as he rolled a barrel up the gangway. Duncan pulled Meg behind him. "Ahoy there, mate."

The man rolling the barrel mumbled and continued on. A Highlander draped in red plaid stood upright from the deck and gave Duncan a deprecating onceover. "What is your business?"

Duncan had forgotten about his shabby cloak. He looked far more like a peasant than the heir to a baronial estate—not that his appearance bothered him. "My wife and I are looking for a transport to Inverary. Would you be headed north?"

Meg cleared her throat behind him. She'd made it clear she didn't care to be passed off as his missus, but presently it was the best way to ensure her safety.

The sailor squinted. "Aye, but we're heading to Mull. Inverary would take us too far off course."

Duncan scanned up and down the pier and saw no other seaworthy boats moored, blast it all. "Are there any transports heading up Loch Fyne?"

"Not certain. Even if there were, you'd not find any sailing until the morrow."

"I'd be willing to pay handsomely if you'd take us to Inverary."

"Cannot do it. This shipment is heading straight to Durart Castle. I could take you to Dunollie or Dunstaffnage."

Duncan scratched his chin. He could gain a pair of horses at Dunstaffnage Castle as well—another keep governed by his family. That option wouldn't add more than an hour to their ride. "Can you leave now?"

The man shook his head and pointed to the sunset, glowing bright orange. "Sail out of the Clyde in the dark? Only a fool-born captain would make such a blunder."

Duncan frowned at Meg. "It looks like we'll need to spend the night here."

"Unfortunate." She cringed. Did she find the prospect of posing as his wife entirely distasteful?

He'd prefer to set sail as well, but there was no other choice. "Very well. How much would you charge for two passengers to the Dunstaffnage pier?"

"A crown ought to cover it. I'm supposing you'll want to be fed."

Bloody hell, the man was akin to a thief. "By the looks of your plaid, I thought you were a Highlander."

"Aye, but a sea captain's got to make a living." He reached his hand over the hull. "And I'd like payment now."

Duncan itched to grab the bastard by the neck and yank him over the side. Overcharging, and now asking for payment in full before the galley cast off? "How will I know you won't sail without me?"

The man squinted with a seedy grin. "I will if you're

no' here by dawn."

"I'll give you a shilling now and the balance when we sail."

The captain hesitated and glanced toward another barrel being rolled up the gangway. "Och, you drive a hard bargain."

Duncan fished in the leather purse tied to his belt, pulled out a single shilling and placed it in the man's outstretched palm. "Do you know of an inn where we can find a meal and a bed?"

He pointed. "The George Inn across the way, but it'll cost you a half-crown for certain." The captain slipped the coin into his sporran. "Where do you hail from? And what's at Inverary?"

Duncan winked. "My uncle." He didn't trust the captain. Besides, it was best to omit as many details as possible. "I'll see you on the morrow."

🙦

Meg stood when Duncan pushed through the chamber door carrying a trencher of food and a ewer of ale. "Boiled meat and turnips," he said, limping toward the table.

She wrung her hands. "The hitch in your step is getting worse."

He set the trencher on the table. "Just a bit stiff from riding in the back of the wagon." A sallow sheen covered his face, even paler than before.

He didn't fool Meg. He was too tall for her to reach his forehead, so she placed the back of her hand to his cheek. Just as she thought, he was burning up. "You're fevered."

Duncan gestured to the chair then pulled a flagon and a loaf of bread from beneath his cloak. "Sit and eat. 'Tis nothing a good meal and a few tots of whisky will not cure."

"Aye, food and drink will help, but you need rest and more of the Gypsy salve." She grimaced, wishing she knew for certain what herbal remedies it contained. Breaking the loaf of bread, she watched Duncan take a healthy swig from the flagon. "You'd best put some food in your belly before you drink too much of that."

He removed his cloak then took another swig. "Not hungry."

"Must you be pigheaded?" She crossed her arms. "You could try to listen to reason for once on this misbegotten adventure. Besides, not wanting to eat is another sign the wound's turning bad."

His eyes darkened with his angry glare, but he reached for the eating knife and cut himself a piece of meat. Shoving the bite in his mouth, his color turned paler.

Meg averted her eyes and concentrated on her meal. Duncan washed his food down with another tot of whisky. At this rate, he'd be in his cups before she finished eating. She glanced toward the bed. Yes, she'd been alone with Duncan the night before, but would he respect her virtue when intoxicated? Her flesh tingled and she rubbed her hands over her arms.

"Are you feeling chilled?" he asked.

"Mayhap a bit." She wasn't cold in the slightest. Her gaze drifted from his shoulders down his well-muscled frame, all the way to his toes. Heaven help her, she admired his form.

Duncan's breathing stuttered, and he also rubbed his arms. "I'll stoke the fire." He stood and took one step before he clattered to the floor.

Meg leapt to her feet. "Duncan!"

Grunting, he tried to push up. "Boar's ballocks, blast my human weakness."

Meg grasped his shoulders, leveraging all her strength to pull him to a sitting position. "We're getting you to the bed."

"Nay," he slurred. "The bed's for your ladyship."

"Enough! You shall not argue with me any longer." She braced her hands under his armpits and planted her feet square. "Now help me lift you to your feet."

He sat like a burlap sack of oats. "Damn it all, for the love of Christ, I cannot believe I'm allowing a tiny wisp of a lass to order me about. Jesus spare me."

Meg giggled.

His face fell. "God's teeth, what are you on about, woman? Laughing at a man when he's injured?"

She tugged up without a modicum of success. "I'm chuckling at your string of blasphemous curses, and I'll be saying Hail Marys all night, begging a pardon for your soul."

He glanced up with a sober expression. "You'd pray for me?"

Her shoulder ticked up. "Why should I not? You've done a great service, rescuing me from the Earl of Northumberland. Though your tactics of keeping me safe are a wee bit untoward, I owe you a debt of gratitude." She tugged again. "Now help me tug you to your feet so I can tend your wound."

It was Duncan's turn for a chuckle. Shaking his head, he leaned into her pull. After a great deal of straining, she somehow managed to lever him up. She scooted her body alongside him and draped his arm over her shoulder. "Now walk with me. 'Tis only a few paces."

Grimacing, he nodded. Together they shuffled across the floor, Duncan's face ever so white. He grunted, though the sound was barely audible. Meg guessed all this time he had been in more pain that he'd let on. *Silly man.* If she were planning to join a nunnery, she'd surely be required to tend the sick. With no better time to start than now, she moved her grasp to his arm and pulled him to the mattress. "Lie here and I'll fetch the salve."

Duncan grumbled something that sounded like "thank you." She couldn't be sure, but chose to believe he'd thanked her. Sliding the pillow under his head, he moaned. The poor Highlander needed a soft bed and a good sleep.

She retrieved the satchel with the salve and bandages. Fortunately, the inn supplied a bowl and ewer of water. After arranging these items on the bedside table, Meg stood back and observed Duncan. She clasped her hands together and rubbed them. He lay on his side with his back to her. From the slow cadence of his breathing, Meg thought he might have fallen asleep. *I don't know if that's a good thing or bad.*

She eyed his belt. *A pious sister wouldn't pay a mind to his physique.* Duncan needed her help and that was the end of it. She gently placed her hand on his hip and leaned over so she could see his face. "Duncan?"

"Mm."

"Are you awake?"

"Aye," he said without moving, keeping his eyes closed.

"I need to lower your chausses." Her hands trembled.

One eye opened. "'Tis music to a knight's ears."

"I cannot believe you're jesting—fevered and all." She drew in a steadying breath, reached in and unclasped his belt. The moan that escaped his throat made her insides erupt with uncontrollable butterflies. She pressed a hand against her chest to calm her heartbeat. *Bring yourself under control, Meg. It isn't as if you have not seen him before.*

She loosened the ties on his waistband and tugged. Duncan had the wherewithal to raise his hips slightly. Not wanting this process to take an eternity, Meg clenched her teeth and bore down with all her strength. In one motion, she had him completely bare all the way to his knees. Scooting back, she clapped her hands over her mouth. *Heaven help me, his braies must have been untied.* "Forgive me."

Duncan peered over his shoulder. "Do not worry, lass," he said in a slow, lilting burr. "Apply the salve and I'll be fit as a wee bairn come morn."

She couldn't help her cursory glance over the masculine flesh presented to her. He had a long, puckered white scar on his hip, as if he'd been cut open. Curious, she examined the old wound closer, gently stroking her finger along the length of it. "Were you in a battle?"

"Mm. More than one."

By the dreamy tenor of his voice, he must be close to sleep. Meg leaned over to look at his face. Yes, his eyes were still closed. She sighed while her bosom filled with yearning.

He moved his hips. Glancing down, she gasped. Oh heaven help her, she shouldn't have looked. Extending from a patch of tight black curls, his manhood was far more sizeable than Meg imagined a man's member would be. Her tongue snuck out and tapped her top lip. Her palms perspired. What if she had touched him there?

Her knees buckled. She almost reached out and ran her fingers along his length before her sensibilities reminded that she was to become a nun, and in no way should she ever allow her gaze to so much as flicker to any man's...

Forcing her mouth closed, Meg stood upright and clapped her hands over her eyes. Had she honestly just ogled Duncan's unmentionables? Who knew how many sins she'd committed in that single moment? Fanning her face, she vowed not to bend over him again and turned toward the bowl. She doused a cloth and wrung it. "I'll cleanse the wound first."

"Mm."

Perhaps the whisky did him some good. Meg examined the gash in his backside and hissed. White pus congealed in the center, with angry red flesh surrounding it. It had definitely turned putrid. She sniffed. The smell wasn't sour yet. She grimaced, ever so mindful of causing more pain. Carefully, she touched the cloth to it.

Duncan jolted with a grunt. Meg pulled her hands away. She'd tried so hard not to hurt him. "Are you all right?"

"Aye." He must have lied, because the word was clipped and strained.

"I'll try to hold the compress to it rather than rub."

He nodded slightly, but she dared not lean over him again to see if his eyes were open. No, she wouldn't make that mistake again. What did it matter if they were opened or closed, anyway? She doused the cloth again and gingerly held it against his backside. A shiver coursed through him, and while she held her hands in place, the compress warmed. Three times Meg rinsed the cloth and reapplied it.

"I shall rub in the salve now."

"Aye." The word now rolled across his tongue like honey.

Meg would have preferred it if Duncan had uttered more than one word at a time, but then, he was fevered.

She picked up the pot and froze. What if he lost consciousness altogether? What would she do if discovered sharing a chamber with a man in Glasgow? In no way could she send word to Arthur.

Oh, heaven help. I had enough difficulty helping Duncan to the bed. If his fever doesn't improve, we will not make it to the pier on the morrow.

What more can I do?

She pulled the cork stopper and dipped her fingers into the goo. "You must have plenty of rest this night. I'll pray your strength returns by dawn."

"Strength. Must." He jerked and grunted when the ointment touched his wound. "Return," he growled.

Meg continued to dab, trying to smooth in the liniment. "Pray the Gypsies know a thing or two about healing, else this salve will be for naught."

"Mm."

With a deep sigh, Duncan appeared to relax. Evidently, the ointment soothed after its initial application. Meg pushed in the cork and studied Duncan's bare-bottomed form. Heaven strike her dead, this view ignited a spark deep inside she'd never before experienced. She yearned to cup his buttocks and dig her fingers into the chiseled flesh. She clapped a palm to her head as if she were daft. From where on earth had her entirely disgraceful thoughts come? Meg was a well-bred, pious woman who wanted nothing to do with men. Even her sisters had supported this certainty. Who could fall in love with the claw?

Deciding it best to leave Duncan's wound to air, she pulled a plaid from the end of the bed and draped it over him. After stoking the fire, Meg took the candle and crossed to the other side of the bed where she'd be able to see his face without jostling him. As she thought, his eyes were closed, his breathing deep and steady. The candlelight flickered amber shadows across his face. He had not a blemish, though he hadn't shaved since her rescue. His short beard gave him the look of a pirate. If she didn't already know his kindhearted nature, she might fear a man as large as he, dark features and all. His lips parted and he sighed with a deep rumble.

In that moment, Meg wanted to climb onto the bed and kiss him. He'd let his guard down and kissed her once. She'd never forget how his lips felt when they touched hers—soft, gentle, spicy. Yes, she would kiss him again if she believed he'd want her to. But a man like Sir Duncan Campbell would never desire a cripple like Meg Douglas. Aye, such a brawny knight could most likely win any fair lassie to whom he took a fancy.

Chapter Eleven

❦

Something heavy draped across her waist. From the warmth radiating along her back, Meg needed no coverlet. A balmy puff of air caressed her neck. She sighed, not wanting to move. Cradled in the folds of a featherbed, she snuggled into the warmth, and her mind hovered in that dreamy place on the precipice of sleep.

Behind her, a deep voice moaned. "*Mo leannan.*"

Meg's eyes flew open. Adjusting to the dim light, her breathing sped. She remembered climbing into the far side of the bed late last eve. The bed was large enough for three or four people, and with Duncan fast asleep, she'd seen no harm in it if she kept to her side.

She ran her fingers over the mattress and met the edge. Thank heavens she hadn't scooted all the way across in her sleep. But Duncan must have.

He'd uttered a Gaelic endearment. Was he delirious? Praying he was not, she took a chance and rose slightly on her elbow. She looked over her shoulder; his eyes were closed and the slow cadence of his breathing indicated he was deep in slumber. Beyond him, the coals in the hearth smoldered with their last embers.

His arm tugged Meg to his chest, and he pressed his hips against her buttocks. Closing her eyes, her hips moved in concert with his. Never in her life had a hot, fire-like yearning inflamed her insides. She arched into him. The driving desire to touch her flesh to his made her wish her skirts and the bedclothes weren't obstructing her so much, on the one hand—on the other, grateful they were. An image of Duncan's manhood appeared in her mind. Oh dear—would she now be plagued with the constant memory of his sex? Inhaling, she conjured another image, not so erotic, but ever so moving. Picturing his beautiful backside made her breasts grow heavy, and the stirring between her hips swirled into a maelstrom of desire.

I cannot allow these thoughts to consume me.

Abruptly, Meg sat up. A hint of light peeked beneath the window coverings. *Is it past dawn?* Beside her, Duncan stirred.

She quickly jumped off the bed. What on earth would he think if he roused with her lying in his arms? She smoothed her hands over her hair and cleared her throat. "Duncan. You must wake. The captain told us to be on the pier at dawn."

He didn't stir. Meg skipped around the bed and shook his shoulder. "Duncan?"

He rolled to his backside and groaned, his entire body stiffening. "Jesus strike me dead, that hurts."

"We must make haste if we're to meet the ship."

He opened his eyes and looked at her. When he cast his gaze to the streaming light, he bolted upright. "Bloody hell, how could you have let me sleep until daybreak?"

She wrung her hands. "I only just awoke myself. Surely 'tis not too late to meet the sea galley."

Stiffly, he swung his legs over the edge of the bed. The plaid shifted, exposing his hip. Quick as lightning, his hand swooped down and caught it before it dropped. He glanced down, eyebrows arching. "Ah." He cleared his throat.

Meg turned away and shielded her eyes. "Forgive me. After I applied the salve, I thought it best to let your bot—ah...your injury air."

He mumbled something that sounded like, "Bleating bloody hell, I had my bare arse hanging out of me braies all night."

Meg most definitely would not ask him to repeat it.

The floorboards creaked. Cloth rustled then stopped. "As long as I'm in a state of undress, would you be so kind as to apply the ointment?" he said politely. "Then we'll need to head out straight away."

"Is your back turned?"

"Aye, lass."

She reached for the pot. "Very well." She made quick work, rubbing in a bit of salve and corking the pot. "That should put you to rights."

He bent down and tugged up his braies and chausses with another grunt.

"How are you feeling?"

"I've been better."

"You're still too pale." She felt for a fever. "And too hot to the touch."

He drew away from her touch. "I'll be right as soon as we make it to Kilchurn."

"The question is, can you make it to the boat?"

He grabbed the flagon of whisky and took a swig. "With this I can withstand anything."

Meg shoved the salve and bandages in the satchel. "Aye? You didn't appear all that impervious to the pain last eve."

He dragged his cloak over his shoulders. "'Twas because I didn't have to be. Now let's be off afore we miss the transport."

After snatching the leftover bread, Meg followed him down the stairs and out into the street. The scene alive with activity, horses pulled carts and people scurried past, bundled under heavy cloaks. Against the wall, a beggar held up a tin cup. "Alms."

Meg's heart squeezed. If only she had time to help the indigent, but Duncan reached back and tugged her arm. "They're casting off, hurry!"

Though she sensed the knight was trying to make a show of robust strength, he still limped. Ahead, a sailor started pulling in the gangway.

Duncan hobbled faster. "Och, what the blazes are you doing? We're paying passengers here." He raced for the wooden plank and bellowed in pain.

The captain popped his head over the side and motioned for the man to push the gangway back out. "What? Did ye and the missus have a romp afore crossing the street? Another knell of the bell from the cathedral and you would have missed us."

Duncan ushered Meg onto the gangway. "A decent man would have sent someone across the road to fetch us."

She agreed with him—the captain knew where they were staying. How difficult would it have been to send a cabin boy over to knock on their door? A sailor offered his hand, and Meg climbed down the three steps into the galley. She turned back to see how Duncan was faring, and movement across the road caught her eye. The beggar was no longer there, but she stared right into the grey eyes of Isaac, Lord Percy's man-at-arms. She'd never mistake that man's face or its jagged scar.

"Cast off," the captain hollered as the sailor pulled the plank into the boat.

Meg swiftly hid behind Duncan's large frame. Had Isaac recognized her? She chanced a glimpse around the Highlander's shoulder. Northumberland's man-at-arms started to run across the cobbled road. But his anxious expression was blocked by a horse and cart trotting across his path.

Meg's gaze shot to the captain. "Hurry!"

"What's the sudden rush?" He sauntered toward them and held out his palm. "Besides, you owe me a half-crown."

She crouched below the hull.

Fishing in his purse, Duncan eyed her as if she were daft. He held out the coin to the captain. "For this outrageous sum I expect to disembark at the pier on Loch Etive."

The man snatched it. "With a good wind, we'll be there before sunset."

Duncan's face took on a sallow pall, and he motioned for Meg to sit on the bench beside him. She was only too happy to remain below the ship's rail and sit. He pressed his lips to her ear. "Tell me, why were you so anxious for us to cast off?"

She warily glanced around them. "I saw Lord Percy's man-at-arms standing exactly in the spot where the beggar had been."

He glanced over his shoulder as if Isaac were in the boat. "Bull's ballocks." Duncan grasped her arm. "Did he see you?"

"He looked straight at me."

Duncan jumped onto a rowing bench and peered over the rail. "I'll be the son of a tit-sucking swine."

"Pardon me?"

Duncan swayed in place. "What does the bastard look like?"

Meg drummed her fingers on her lips. "He has an ugly scar on his right cheek. He's tall, with darkish hair, I think."

"You think?" He leaned into the rail and continued scanning. "Are you certain it was he?"

"Aye. I'd never mistake that scar." Meg took a chance and straightened enough to peek over the hull. "He's not there now." She resumed her seat.

Duncan plopped beside her. "Ballocks."

By the increase in his cursing, Meg figured he was in

a lot of pain. "I doubt he'll find us unless he can commandeer a boat quickly."

"It won't be difficult for him to find out where we're headed. All he needs to do is ask a laborer."

Meg thought Duncan might be growing delirious. "But this boat is destined for Mull."

"Aye, as long as no one from the ship mentioned they'd be ferrying a pair of paying passengers to Dunstaffnage."

"But no one knows we're"—she leaned in to ensure only Duncan could hear—"heading to...you know."

"We'll not tarry at Dunstaffnage, for certain." He pursed his lips and offered a stiff nod. "Sit back and enjoy the voyage. Once we sail into the Firth of Clyde, the seas could become rough. We'll feel it in a boat this small."

Meg smoothed her hand over the space on the bench beside her. The old vessel was worn. Living on the Firth of Forth, she'd seen hundreds like it—fishing galleys, for the most part, owned by local fishermen. Smaller galleys like this one never went far out to sea or crossed the channel to France. They weren't robust enough.

Beside her, Duncan's head hit the hull with a bang. He looked like death.

"Are you well?" she asked.

"Aye, just resting my eyes."

Of course. Everyone smashes their head into the hull of a ship when they want to close their eyes. She wagered he was still fevered, not that he'd admit it. Presently, Meg had more to worry about than Percy's guard. At least they'd left Isaac standing on the pier. She steepled her fingers to her mouth and offered up a silent prayer that Duncan would keep his wits at least until they reached the shore—else she'd be at the mercy of the captain and the vast Highlands.

Speaking of the leader of the ship, he stood at the

rudder and eyed her, just like the Gypsy had done in the back of the wagon. Meg crossed her arms and studied the galley's timbers. *My, how barbaric and dangerous the world is away from Tantallon Castle.*

🌿

DUNCAN HAD NEVER BEEN SO COLD. IT DIDN'T matter how tightly he clamped his arms to his body—he couldn't get warm, and the gusts of wind blowing in from the north only served to make his chills worse. He could not allow himself to succumb to a simple scrape on his arse. Surely he'd come through the worst of it.

In no way could he collapse and leave Lady Meg to fend for herself. Christ, the sailors on the galley all looked at her with lecherous grins. He ground his teeth and squinted through his lowered lashes. Meg was too naive to notice the blighters all drooling over her lovely face.

But a mob of lusty sailors was only half his worries. Percy's man had tracked them all the way to Glasgow? A bead of sweat slid down Duncan's temple. There he sat, colder than midwinter without a fire, so fevered, sweat poured off him. God bless it, he hadn't outsmarted the English bastards. What the blazes were they doing in Glasgow, and how far did they intend to go?

When he and Lady Meg reached Dunstaffnage, they'd be on Campbell lands, and safer. It would be suicide for an English army to trespass into Argyllshire. Duncan's eyes rolled back, and he shook his head. This damnable fever couldn't get the better of him. He must send out spies and alert the guard as soon as he reached the shore.

Bless it, God would strike him dead before he allowed anything to happen to Lady Meg.

She grasped his hand, and Duncan's lids opened. "I'm concerned about you."

Her blue eyes sparkled in the sunlight and reflected the color of the sky. This was the first day the sun had made an appearance since he'd met Meg. Her intelligent brows arched in question. Duncan cleared his throat. "I'm well enough. You needn't worry overmuch."

She offered an anxious smile and tried to pull her hand away, but Duncan tightened his grasp. He liked the silken smoothness of her fingers in his rough palm. "Your hands are cold."

A lovely blush crawled up her cheeks, her eyes nowhere near as happy as her demeanor. "Aye."

He studied her face. How she could be wise yet so innocent perplexed him. "Do you have any clue how beautiful you are?"

"I beg your pardon?" Again she tugged her hand, but he held it fast. "You must be horribly fevered." Her eyes drifted to the appendage she'd ashamedly named "the claw." He'd never understand how a woman so incredible could consider herself ruined because of a minor deformity. Aside from her hand, Meg possessed everything a man desired—eyes that could see through to his soul, a full mane of wild tresses with natural curls, a figure that was not too slight and not too round.

A satisfied moan rumbled from Duncan's chest. The dip in her waist had cradled his arm perfectly in the wee hours last eve. He lowered his chin and pressed his lips against her ear. "*Mo leannan.*" He knew he'd uttered the endearment in the wee hours as well, though he hadn't really been awake.

Meg gasped, her cherry-red lips tempting him.

"Aye." He grinned—swaying as if drunk. "I did say it, and I wish it could be so."

The deep pools of blue stared into his eyes, as if she read his every thought. "I couldn't dare to dream…"

His mind a wee bit blurry, all he focused on was

Meg. He leaned closer to inhale the wildflower scent of her hair. "Only in my dreams have I ever held a woman as ravishing and desirable as you."

She pushed her hair under her veil with her claw as though it were a nervous habit.

"I like to see your tresses peek from beneath your headpiece."

Meg rolled her eyes. "My sister Elizabeth says they're wild as Scotland."

"Aye? I like that." Duncan swirled his palm over her hand in his lap. "What else does your sister say?"

"She agrees I should join a nunnery—says I'm too headstrong." Meg hid the claw under her cloak. "She knows my deformity isn't the devil's work, but she—the whole family—fears it might be taken that way outside of Tantallon's walls, except in a place of worship, of course."

"You're serious?" Duncan blinked. "Your family agrees you should be hidden?"

"All except Arthur. He'd prefer to arrange my marriage to some unsuspecting baron to strengthen the family alliances."

Duncan wiped the clammy sweat from his forehead with the crook of his elbow. "So, Arthur doesn't fear your hand?"

"No, but the family is torn about what should be done with me. I suppose that's what happens when both your parents die when you're very young. Your elder siblings argue about what is to become of the 'misshapen black sheep.'"

Duncan raised her hand to his lips and kissed. Catching a whiff of a meadow in spring, his heart stuttered. Why did everything about Meg tug on his sensibilities? "I think you're entirely too hard on yourself." He shivered. Lordy, his bones ached with fatigue—he could scarcely keep his eyes open.

"What would you do if you were in my place?"

He leaned into her, wishing he could rest his head on her shoulder. "Me?"

"Aye?"

First of all, as a man and heir to a considerable dynasty, Duncan would never be in her situation. He gazed at her red lips, pursed in challenge, and his daft head spun like juggler's clubs. "I'd not allow a one of them to make me feel any less a person."

"I'm certain 'tis easy for you to say. You are a brawny knight, after all."

"Aye, but I've four sis...ters." His words slurred. "I wouldn't want a one of them to feel less...less of a woman because of something she cannot change."

Meg studied his face again with those irresistible eyes. "You are an odd sort, Sir Duncan. Perhaps that's why I like you so much."

He held her hand to his cheek and closed his heavy eyelids. "I like you as...well, Lady Meg."

"Passing the Mull of Kintyre," the navigator yelled and pointed.

The galley had entered the Irish Sea. Depending on the wind, there were several hours remaining in this journey. Duncan leaned his head against the hull and closed his eyes. Perhaps a few moments of sleep would do him good. Undoubtedly, he'd need his strength when the ship moored.

Chapter Twelve

※

Duncan slept holding Meg's hand until her fingers fell asleep. In all honesty, she reveled in his touch, wanted his palm to warm her hand into eternity, but soon her entire arm would be asleep, too. Gradually, Meg slipped her fingers away and rubbed them awake.

Once the boat entered open seas, the sail billowed with the wind and sped their pace. Meg's head swooned a bit while the swells rocked the galley as it climbed and fell in time with the white-capped waves.

Duncan's shoulder leaned into her.

She'd meant it when she told the knight she liked him. No man had ever paid much attention to her—not that she'd had much experience with men who were peers. At the age of five and ten she'd thought she fancied the farrier's son, but quickly discovered a highborn Douglas daughter could fancy no one of her own choosing. Arthur had fired the farrier as soon as she'd mentioned her attraction to her sister Elizabeth.

Meg took a moment to study the hard lines of Duncan's face. His beard had grown even longer now. Starting to curl, it almost hid his square jaw. He had called her beautiful more than once. *Mo leannan*—he'd uttered the Gaelic endearment for "sweetheart," but he'd also repeated that he must return her to Tantallon where she belonged...that her brother had paid him to rescue her. As a man of honor, Duncan must fulfill his contract. Soon she would return to her life as if nothing had ever happened, and it would be highly unlikely their paths would ever cross again.

Meg sighed at the emptiness stretching throughout her chest. Perhaps one day she'd spy Sir Duncan across the nave at Dunfirmline Abbey during a king's coronation or at the baptism of a royal bairn. Would he be married by then? Would she be draped in the robes of a nun?

She again watched his face; curiously angelic in slumber. Her insides fluttered. How could she take up the veil now she'd lain beside a man and enjoyed it so? Would she ever be forgiven for such a sin? So many things confused her, but on one thing she was absolutely certain—there was no other man in the world like Duncan Campbell. He accepted her, flaws and all, and considered her beautiful. Even if she never again kissed another man in her lifetime, she would lock away the tenderness they'd shared in her heart.

"Entering the Firth of Lorn," hollered the navigator.

With calmer seas, the boat eased into a steady sway. Meg sprang to her feet and scanned the shoreline. In the distance a massive grey castle presided over the loch, its bailey walls rising from a craggy outcrop. She'd heard tales of Dunstaffnage, captured from the Mac-Dougals during the time of Robert the Bruce. "Campbell lands," she whispered under her breath.

Forested and wild, she could only imagine what lay beyond the shore. "Duncan." She shook his shoulder. "We're nearly there. You must wake."

Duncan didn't move. Meg held her hand to his forehead. As she feared, he was afire. Glancing over her shoulder, the sailors looked at her like salivating dogs. Who knew what they would do if she couldn't rouse

Duncan? She grasped both of his shoulders and gave him a firm shake. "Sir Duncan!"

"Sir?" the captain asked from across the deck.

Meg ignored him and slapped Duncan's cheeks. "'Tis nearly time to disembark."

Duncan stirred.

Thank you, Lord Jesus.

The captain sauntered up behind her. "Odd you call your husband sir."

"Oh?" Meg faced him. "Why? He is a knight of the Order of St. John."

"And a nephew to the Earl of Argyll?"

Meg shot Duncan a sideways look, hoping he'd be alert enough to answer. His eyes rolled back. She opted for the middle ground. "Sir Duncan Campbell is his name."

The captain narrowed his eyes. "And why is a knight dressed in a ragged cloak?"

Pulling on her inner strength, she muttered an apology and walloped Duncan across the face. "That, captain, is none of your concern." *Please wake. This man is up to no good. I can feel it in my bones.*

Stretching his jaw to the side and rubbing it, Duncan cleared his throat and wobbled to a stand. His cloak parted and he brushed his fingers over the hilt of his sword. "Is all well, my...la...Meg?" He sounded as if he'd been in his cups.

"Yes, dearest." Meg feigned an adoring smile. "The captain was questioning your knighthood and family name."

Duncan glared at the man, who was a good two hands shorter. "Is that so?"

The captain planted his fists on his hips. "Why would a knight and his missus be dressed in rags?"

"Why would a galley captain give a rat's arse how we're dressed?"

The man folded his arms.

Duncan swayed and pulled Meg under his arm, she thought more as a crutch than to protect her. "If you must know, I was down on my luck. Lost at cards."

Surely Duncan will be forgiven for a necessary fib.

"Heading home to da, are you?" the captain asked.

"Aye."

He flicked a dismissive wrist. "Spoilt nobility."

The captain turned his attention to the mooring, and Meg pulled Duncan aside. "Will you be able to make it off the boat?"

"Bloody oath I will." He turned a shade of yellow and clamped his hand on to the rail. "What did you tell them?"

"Only that you are a knight and your family name is Campbell."

He swiped a hand across his mouth. "'Tis enough. When they return to Glasgow, Percy's man will be asking questions, that is a certainty."

Once the ship had been tied off, Meg helped Duncan down the gangway and onto the pier.

He pulled away from her. "I do not need your help."

She grasped his arm and tugged it over her shoulder. "Nay? You're swaying as if you were still at sea. Just let me steady you until we can find a pair of horses."

Peering over her shoulder, she noted the captain watching them from the deck while the galley cast off. At least they were out from under *his* scrutiny.

Duncan stumbled. Meg tried to steady him, but he crashed to the ground.

"Sir Duncan!" She dropped to her knees and gave him a good shake.

His body remained flaccid.

She crouched beside him. The world spun in a panic. Alone in a foreign place, where could she find help? Ahead, she scanned the pathway that led up to the stronghold. Three guards marched in formation, paying her no mind. She pulled on Duncan's arm, but he didn't respond. Making a decision, Meg sprinted for the soldiers. "Help! Please, stop." If there were a time to be an assertive noblewoman, it was nigh.

The lead man gave her a deprecating once-over. "And who might you be?"

Clenching her fists, she raised her chin. "I am *Lady Douglas*, daughter of the fourth Earl of Angus." She turned and pointed. "And that injured soul is *Sir* Duncan Campbell, heir to the Lordship of Glenorchy."

The man apprised Meg incredulously. "But—"

"What?" She stepped toward him and fisted her hips. "Have you not seen nobles dressed in rags to conceal their identity?" She again pointed at Duncan. "Do you not recognize the *Lord of Glenorchy's* son?"

The man looked to Duncan and paled.

"Looks like Sir Duncan to me," one said. "There's nary a black-haired man in all of Argyllshire as large as he."

"M-m'lady. Why did you not say something sooner?" The leader motioned to his men. "Quickly, take him into the keep."

"No." Meg stood her ground. Finally being able to reveal her identity emboldened her. "Sir Duncan wishes to be taken to Kilchurn with haste."

One of the soldiers stepped forward and shook his head. "He's in no state to travel."

"I beg your pardon, but he's just traveled here from Northumberland." She pointed at the man's sternum and looked him in the eye. "I command you. Fetch a team and cart, and bring it forthwith."

Lips thinning, the sentry offered a clipped bow. "Yes, m'lady."

If Meg weren't so worried for Duncan's well-being, her chest would have swelled with pride, but this was no time for self-accolades. She dashed back to Duncan's side and knelt. "The guard is bringing a cart with a team of horses." She smoothed a hand over his head. "Can you hear me? As you desired, we shall be at Kilchurn this eve."

Meg slid Duncan's head into her lap. It was the least she could do until the guards returned. Gently, she swirled her fingers around his temples. "Hold on, my love. I shall have you to your home in no time. You'll see. Everything will be fine once we reach your family." *I should have paid more attention to Hubert and his herbs at Tantallon. If only there was more I could do to help you, Duncan. Please, please, please do not succumb to your wound.*

When the men returned, they made quick work of hoisting Duncan into the cart.

Meg faced them. "I'll need you to accompany us to Kilchurn."

The man-at-arms frowned. "I do not understand why we cannot spirit him up to one of the chambers here at Dunstaffnage."

"'Tis Sir Duncan's wish." Meg wanted to tell them all that had happened, but with no idea who she could trust, she held her tongue. She climbed into the back of the wagon with Duncan. "How long will it take to reach the castle?"

"If we travel at a steady trot, we should make it by nightfall."

She pulled the moth-eaten cloak taut around Duncan's body and looked to the sky. His teeth chattered. It was even colder here than it had been in Glasgow. "Fetch some blankets before we set out. Sir Duncan is fevered. I'll not have him catch his death on this journey."

"Very well, m'lady," the man-at-arms said, motioning for a soldier to ride back to the castle. He turned to the cart driver. "Lead on. The guard will catch up in no time."

THE SENTRY HAD BEEN RIGHT. THE GUARD CAUGHT UP with the plaids before they'd traversed a mile. Gratefully, Meg took them and spread the woolens over Duncan, tucking the edges in at his sides.

"One of those plaids is for you, m'lady," the guard said. "Your cloak would hardly withstand a summer's breeze, let alone a February gale."

"I thank you, but I daresay Sir Duncan needs them more than I." Once content she'd made him as comfortable as possible, she again moved to his head and cradled it in her lap. The jerking motion of the cart was nearly enough to rattle Meg's brain. She hated to think what it was doing to Duncan, and she held his head as if he were a wee bairn.

True to his word, the man-at-arms led the procession at a trot, with four horses hitched to the cart. The only bad thing was, with no hay lining its bed, the old cart was nothing but a flatbed of planks. Duncan couldn't be comfortable. Meg most certainly was not.

The sky had taken on a violet hue by the time the guard hollered, "Kilchurn straight ahead."

A long sigh slipped past Meg's lips. She cast her gaze eastward. The sun reflected brilliantly against the battlement walls, further illuminating the great stone keep rising above. A deep blue loch surrounded three sides. Indeed, everything about Kilchurn was as Duncan described. With verdant mountains surrounding the castle, Meg imagined no force would ever be powerful enough to breach its walls.

"Open the gate!" bellowed the guard.

The driver slowed the horses while the portcullis chains groaned.

At a walk, they passed through the guardhouse and into the busy outer bailey. Not unlike Tantallon, the smithy's shack rang with the sound of pounding iron, accompanied by the hammer of a farrier shoeing a horse, and chickens squawking.

The men stopped the procession just outside the inner bailey gate—more like an enormous door with square blackened nails in vertical lines.

The door creaked open. "What the devil?" Duncan's voice boomed from the blackness.

Still cradling his head in her lap, Meg snapped her head around. A much older, grey-haired form of Duncan glared at her, eyebrows knitted.

"Lord Campbell?" she asked.

The man scowled. "Aye." He wore a dark green doublet, leather breeks on his legs and a feathered bonnet. "And what have you done to my son?"

The power of his menacing stare could have made Meg shrivel into a prune, but she squeezed her bottom cheeks and sat tall. "Sir Duncan was injured coming to my rescue. He managed to spirit me to Dunstaffnage, but as soon as we arrived, he succumbed to fever."

Lord Campbell appraised her quickly, stepping in as if his eyesight were failing. "You're Lady Douglas?"

Meg followed his much-too-close gaze to her moth-eaten cloak. "Aye."

Lord Glenorchy motioned to his sentries. "We must take him inside at once."

"Sooner, if possible." Meg steadied Duncan's head while four men each grasped an arm or leg.

"Where is he wounded?" Lord Glenorchy asked.

Meg bit her lip. "'Tis best I tell you behind closed doors."

By his frown, he didn't care for her response, but he gestured toward the keep. "Send the healer up to my son's chamber at once."

As Meg neared the entrance, the mouth-watering smell of baking bread made her knees weak. The miserly captain had given her a piece of bully beef on the ship. That and a bit of bread was all she'd had to eat since last evening's meal. They walked past the kitchens, with a typical flurry of activity outside the door. But Meg kept her gaze ahead and stayed close behind the entourage. In no way would she be separated from Duncan.

Once inside, Lord Campbell grasped her arm. "I believe you owe me an explanation."

She tugged against him and watched the men turn into a stairwell. "I must follow Sir Duncan, m'lord."

"Come." He pulled her into a solar and closed the door. "You must tell me what happened first."

Clenching her teeth, she pulled her arm away and started for the door. "I cannot leave Sir Duncan's side—not until he wakes."

Lord Campbell placed his rather large palm on the oaken door. "This shan't take long, but I am the lord of this castle, and Duncan is my son. I believe that entitles me to an explanation."

With a nod, Meg cast one last gaze at the door and launched into a hurried account of how Duncan fell from his horse and injured his backside. "Please. I have tended him all this while. I will not rest until he is set to rights."

"I've called for the healer. He will be in good hands now." Lord Campbell gestured for her to sit. "If you please, Lady Douglas."

A healer? Another cannot assume Duncan's care. After she sat, Meg tapped the pincers of the claw and shook her foot. "Please, call me Lady Meg. Now—"

He drew his eyebrows together, looking so much like Duncan, though his face was etched and weathered with deep lines. "Why the blazes did he bring you here?"

Must she relay the whole adventure? As swiftly as she could, Meg told him everything she thought pertinent about their journey, leaving out certain details, like kissing Duncan and pretending to be his wife. Divulging that wee tidbit of information could find her in a world of trouble, if not completely ruined.

"It seems you've had quite a harrowing adventure." His harsh features softened. "You are welcome at Kilchurn, m'lady. I shall have my wife appoint you with a suitable chamber straight away."

"Oh, no." Meg stood. "I need to see to Sir Duncan's healing."

"Are you an herbalist, a healer?" he asked.

She hated to lie. "Aye, of sorts." She'd applied Duncan's ointment and helped him with the leeches. That had to count for something.

He scratched his grey beard. "'Tis a bit untoward..."

"Please. He saved my life. And I...I'm in training to be a nun." She stood and clasped her palms together. "We've been traveling together for days. He is unconscious. What harm could befall me?"

Lord Campbell had immediately stood when Meg rose, as was courteous, but worry now etched his weathered face. "How long has he had the sweat?"

"A day."

"And you've been applying a Gypsy salve?"

"One purchased by Duncan himself." Her mind rifled through the list of herbs Hubert, the healer at Tantallon, kept on hand. "He needs an astringent for certain. Ah..." She held up her finger. "St. John's wort." She sounded like a sheep-brained simpleton, but Lord Campbell couldn't keep her from Duncan's side.

"We must do everything possible to see my son survives this."

Meg crossed herself. "I've been praying to the Holy Mother ceaselessly."

He gave her a grim nod. "If you desire to assist the healer, I see no harm in it."

She could have thrown her arms around Lord Glenorchy's neck and hugged him. "Thank—"

He held up a finger. "But as soon as he rouses, I shall have a retinue to accompany you home. Duncan sent your brother a missive?"

"Aye."

"Thank heavens for that. I wouldn't want the Earl of Angus in a rage because he thinks the Campbells have absconded with his sister." Lord Glenorchy shook his head. "We've enough troubles without creating them for naught."

A heavyset woman opened the door and bustled into the solar. She carried a basket, and panted heavily as if she'd just run a distance. "M'lord. I came...as soon...as I received word."

Lord Campbell gestured with an outstretched palm. "Mistress Alana. This is Lady Meg. She has been tending Duncan's wounds whilst they traveled from Northumberland. Between the pair of you, I trust you can set my heir to rights."

The matron frowned in Meg's direction, but bowed her head respectfully. "Very well, m'lady. We've no time to waste."

Meg stepped beside her. "Agreed."

Following the healer up the winding tower stairs, Alana glanced at Meg over her shoulder. "What happened to the lad?"

Meg hardly regarded Duncan as a lad, but relayed the same story she'd given to his father.

"Gypsy salve?" the healer asked. "'Tis a wonder he survived."

"Sir Duncan said Gypsies put all sorts of mysterious essences in their healing ointments."

Mistress Alana grimaced. "Aye, like sheep's piss."

Meg covered her mouth to hide her gasp. "I pray not."

"Well, we shall have a look. We cannot have Sir Duncan succumbing to the sweat." She exited at the third landing and pushed through a chamber door.

Duncan rested on the bed, lying on his side. He didn't appear to be awake.

Meg hid the claw behind her back. She recognized

Duncan's brother standing with five other women. "Sir John? You've returned."

"I arrived but moments behind you." Striding forward, John clasped her hand. "I feared this would happen, given his fall."

She glanced past him to five women, all staring at her with exasperated expressions, as if she were personally responsible for Duncan's state of health. "Sir Duncan held on right until the last. As soon as we docked at the Dunstaffnage pier, the fever got the better of him."

"Using Gypsy salve, he was," Alana said, frowning and arching her brow toward Meg.

Everyone in the room gasped.

Meg suddenly wished she'd taken the soldier's advice and stayed at Dunstaffnage until Duncan's fever broke.

John regarded the women over his shoulder. "Forgive me. These are my sisters, Helen, Gyllis, Marion and Alice." He gestured to a lovely older woman wearing a grey wimple. "And my mother, Lady Margaret."

Meg curtsied. "I wish we could be making our acquaintance under less dire circumstances."

"Aye," Alana said. "Everyone out and let me work. You too, Lady Meg."

No. Meg planted her feet firmly. Lord Glenorchy had given her a direct order to work beside the healer. "I will not leave Duncan's side."

"I, too, would like to stay," Lady Margaret said. "Though he did not come from my womb, Duncan is my son."

Alana knitted her brows. "Very well. You'll need a strong stomach. His wound is on his arse."

Lady Margaret arched a dour eyebrow at Meg. "Well then, 'tis not proper for you to be here."

Must everyone stand in her way? Did no one understand that she would *not* leave Duncan's side? "I have been tending his tender behind for days." She stood a wee bit taller and clenched her fist. "I intend to take up the veil after I return to Tantallon. Besides, Duncan was injured during my rescue. I am *personally* responsible for his recovery."

Alana set her basket on the table and moved to the bed. "If you're both staying, you can help me remove his chausses."

Lady Margaret picked up a folded plaid from the footboard. "Drape this across him for modesty's sake."

Meg chewed her bottom lip. She should have thought to do that at the inn. She wouldn't have seen quite so much of him if she had.

Once Duncan's sleeping form was covered, Lady Margaret turned to Meg. "You hold the blanket down while we take care of the rest."

She nodded. At least they had allowed her to stay.

The two women quickly removed his shoes, chausses, and braies. Alana lifted the blanket and hissed. "'Tis angry red and filled with pus."

Meg peered around the plaid. "As I feared, 'tis worse than this morning."

Alana leaned near the wound and sniffed. "I need hot water and bandages."

Lady Margaret hastened to the door. "I shall have them sent up straight away."

"And some willow bark tea. We'll spoon it into him." Fishing in her basket, Alana pulled out a stoppered vial and held it up. "This is my own concoction. 'Twill hurt like the devil, but drastic measures are needed. We cannot have the heir to the Lordship of Glenorchy succumb to a wound on his backside."

Meg stared at the vial. "What's in it?"

"Whale oil, houseleek and pure whisky."

"Whisky?"

"Aye. Potent, too." Alana picked up a rag and doused

it with her brew. "He'll need this applied at the turn of every hour."

Meg watched her intently. "I can see to that."

"Aye?" Alana didn't look up. "You care for our young knight, do you not?"

Meg's heart skipped a beat. "He risked his life to save me. I would never be able to live with myself if..." She couldn't say it.

Servants bearing ewers of hot water arrived, with Lady Margaret carrying a tankard, a worried crease to her brow. "I've brought the willow bark tea."

Alana took the cup. "Go ahead and tend to your duties, m'lady. Lady Meg and I have it in hand."

Lady Campbell cast a worried glance to the bed. "Very well, but I want to receive word as soon as there is any change, better or worse."

Alana bowed her head. "Aye, m'lady. You'll be the first to know, as always."

Meg reached for the tankard. "I can spoon the tea into his mouth."

"It will be difficult with him on his side, but I do not want to put him on his back."

"Mayhap if we turn his shoulders just a bit."

"Good thinking."

Meg smiled inwardly. She'd been feeling so out of place. Having the gruff older woman take note of anything she said was a small boon.

After turning the hourglass on the bedside table, Alana applied hot compresses while Meg dribbled the tea into Duncan's mouth. She released a long exhale when his Adam's apple moved. At least some of the tea was getting into him.

The matron placed a damp, folded cloth on his head. "This needs to be changed hourly as well."

"I can do that."

"'Tis late." Alana pushed a stray lock of hair under

her wimple. "You should go down to the hall for your meal."

Meg tightened her grip on the wooden spoon. "I'm not leaving him."

Alana stood and wiped her hands on her apron. "You are a headstrong lassie, are you not...ah...m'lady?" Her gaze shifted to the claw pincers that held the tankard.

Not about to allow a common woman to remark about her deformity, Meg rested the tankard on the table and faced her. "I am an earl's daughter. It is in my breeding to never give up."

The healer straightened the plaid covering Duncan. "Mm hmm."

"I may have a deformed hand, but I manage just fine and am not any lesser a person for it."

Color spread across the older woman's cheeks. "You have proven yourself thus, m'lady."

Meg had expected more of a fight. Perhaps being an earl's daughter helped—or was it because after years of being treated as a cripple by her family, Meg had finally come upon the chance to prove her worth? She picked up the tankard and resumed spooning the willow bark tea.

Carrying her basket, Alana moved in beside her. "There's nothing we can do now aside from more of the same until he wakes. Since you are unwilling to leave his side, I'll have the kitchen send up some food, m'lady."

"I thank you."

Alana carried a wooden chair from near the hearth and set it by the bed. "You should seek a bed soon."

"I cannot." Meg gratefully sat. "I owe him my life."

"I admire your strength." The matron nodded thoughtfully then pointed. "My cottage is up the hill. If he should worsen during the night, send a guard to fetch me."

Chapter Thirteen

❦

Once Alana took her leave, a barrage of visitors stopped by Duncan's chamber. Everyone expressed their worry and desire to help. Meg wished she and Duncan were back at the inn where she could be left alone to tend him, but it was fitting for his family to be concerned. After reiterating time and time again that she intended to tend Duncan through the night, Lord Campbell finally departed for his own bed.

Only an army could have removed her from Duncan's chamber. Thank the stars they hadn't resorted to that.

Meg crossed to the window and pulled aside the furs. Icy night air cut through her gown, but it refreshed her face and gave her renewed energy. She'd promised Lord Campbell she would sit with Duncan until he woke. He needed her, and she could not fail him.

She didn't tarry long at the window for fear the draft would chill the chamber. Rubbing her hands across tired eyes, she stoked the fire and returned to Duncan's side. The sand in the hourglass trickled to nothing. Dutifully, she pulled back the plaid and applied the whisky tincture.

Duncan moaned and jolted slightly to her touch.

Leaning over him, she examined his eyes. *Still closed.* "Duncan?" she whispered.

He made not a move, and she continued applying the cloth, followed by a cool compress. Three more times the hourglass drained its sand and she followed the same ritual, keeping the cloth upon his forehead cool all the while.

Often Duncan moaned, but never roused. The fourth time she turned the hourglass, her eyelids refused to stay open. *If I rest for a brief moment, my strength will return. Besides, there's naught to do but wait until the sand runs its course again.*

Meg tiptoed to the far side of the large four-poster bed. There was ample room for them both. She'd not disturb him in the slightest if she were to rest on the far side, and this time there would be no chance he'd sidle across and drape his arm over her waist.

She curled up and faced him. The candlelight flickered amber across his face, highlighting his unblemished skin, darkened by his black beard. In slumber Duncan resembled an angel, and Meg could think of nothing more beautiful than he.

His lips were moist and shimmered with the candlelight. The desire to kiss him became so strong, her entire body ached. If only she could marry a man like Duncan Campbell. He cared not about what others thought of her deformity. A man as virile and important as he would have no deference for the opinion of others. Inching across the bedclothes, Meg managed to work herself so close to him she could feel his breath upon her face.

Running her hand to his bearded chin, her breathing labored. Her blood coursed hot beneath her skin with a thundering heartbeat in her ears. Gently, she brushed a single finger over his lips—soft as satin. A yearning spread deep inside, so intense, Meg feared she might burst. Lowering her lashes, she closed the distance and kissed him.

Unable to pull away, she hovered. His mouth was warm and inviting. He smelled of cinnamon and musk, and his lips pulsed a steady rhythm. If only she could breathe life into him and take away the sweat. When she slid her hand to his chest, Duncan moaned. With the sound of his voice, not only her breasts, but her entire insides ignited into a fevered flame. Overcome with the desire to kiss him again, she smoothed her hand to his back and pulled her body flush against him.

Solid, warm male pressed into her breasts, her abdomen and her quavering thighs. Hot moisture pooled between her hips. She slid her leg across him and tugged him closer. Heaven help her, she would be damned to hell. Something hard filled the crux of her womanhood, the sacred spot alive with yearning, craving more.

Meg closed her eyes. "I wish I could keep you forever," she whispered.

She held her lips to his and savored this moment. As he'd shown her, she slid her tongue across his lips and tasted him. The bitterness of willow bark tea mixed with spicy male filled her with longing. If only he were conscious enough to kiss her back. But kissing an unconscious man must be a sin, no matter how much her insides fluttered and tingled.

Meg squeezed her eyes shut and willed herself to pull away.

Moaning, Duncan's tongue caressed her bottom lip.

Eyes flying open, Meg gasped. "Are you awake?"

A powerful arm tugged her closer. "Mm."

"I want to lie with you," Meg uttered. She hadn't meant to say it, but the words flowed from her mouth as if she were possessed. Yes, she did want him, right there and now, consequences be damned. Never in her life had she acted irresponsibly, but she wanted nothing more in this moment than to make love to Duncan Campbell. She desired to be with a man—this man—to know what it was like to be a woman loved.

Before she could speak another word, Duncan covered her mouth and claimed her with a long, languid kiss. Eyes closed, he eased Meg to her back, the weight of his chest pinning her to the mattress—not painfully, but the friction provided the pressure her breasts craved. She rocked her hips. Her entire body desired his touch, especially the powerful yearning down below.

Their mouths still joined, her hand slid under the plaid and guided his hips until he covered her. Oh glorious friction, her body was afire. When Duncan trailed kisses down her neck, Margaret opened her eyes. The plaid had slipped completely off, leaving him naked from the waist down.

He rocked his hips against her, and a smoldering need coiled between her legs. Through her gown, his manhood rubbed the spot beneath the folds that yearned the most for him.

"I've wanted you since I first looked into your eyes," he purred, unlacing her bodice. He slipped his fingers beneath her bodice and swirled them around her breast.

Arching her back, Meg cried out. With a chuckle, Duncan flicked his tongue across her nipple and suckled her. She sighed, reveling in the delectable passion coursing through her blood. She shrugged out of her sleeve and exposed her other breast for him. Like a feral cat, Duncan slid across and claimed it while pulling up her skirts.

Oh yes. She'd wanted to be exposed to him. He must quell the fire he'd kindled deep inside her body. Spreading her legs, she allowed him to tug her skirts higher until cool air caressed her womanhood.

Duncan slid his hand down and touched her there. Meg nearly erupted off the bed, her tingling spasms felt so inexplicably good. He swirled his finger around her, spreading moisture from her depths. Eyes rolling into the back of her head, Meg had never known such ecstasy. Duncan's finger slid inside. Meg churned her hips around him, wanting, needing, desperate for more friction.

When she opened her eyes, he was hovering over her, his manhood jutting from his loins like a jouster's lance. He desired her as a woman, and she'd never in her life craved a man to take her. Trembling, she reached down to grasp him, but he slid back on his haunches, just beyond her fingers. For an instant, Meg feared he didn't want her, until a sly grin spread across his lips. Dipping his chin, with one lap, he licked her—swiped his glorious tongue over her smoldering sex.

Meg collapsed against the pillows with a shudder. Duncan licked again, then swirled his tongue over her flesh. Unable to control her increasing sighs, she threaded her fingers through his hair, giving in to the urge to thrust her hips. The pressure deep within her body coiled tighter. Stars crossed her vision. A stunned gasp ripped through her throat and the world around her exploded in a maelstrom of pulsing euphoria.

When finally her breathing returned to normal, Meg opened her eyes. Duncan knelt over her, smiling. Brilliant white teeth contrasted with the dark shadow of his beard. He was still erect. Was he waiting for her to do something? Simply looking at his manhood filled her with renewed desire. She brushed her fingers over it. "I want you to show me how a man breeds."

Duncan emitted a savage growl. "I want you more than life itself." His eyes appeared glassy with the flickering of the candlelight. Slowly, his body skimmed up hers as he fluttered kisses along the way. "Your beauty surpasses that of all other women."

Meg had no recourse but to accept his words. She molded to him like clay to a potter's fingers. His manhood brushed her cleft, and her need became dire yet again.

Nuzzling into her neck, Duncan mumbled. Meg couldn't make out his words, but it didn't matter. Careful not to place her hand on his wound, she grasped his hip and encouraged him. She stopped tugging when his manhood stretched her insides to the point of tearing. But Duncan didn't stop. Slowly, he slid inside her. Meg's insides yielded with a sting, yet the exhilaration of their joining sent her body into a whirlwind of frenzy.

When Duncan stopped, she held very still, reveling in the sensation of being completely filled. As he started to rock his hips, the pinch didn't hurt quite as badly. Speeding the pace, Meg grasped him, while moisture soothed the burn. She needed him to move faster, and dictated the tempo with her hand. Without speaking, Duncan seemed to know exactly what her body craved.

Tension built. Her thighs shuddered around him. More...she had to have more of him. Duncan emitted a deep grunt, thrusting faster. Meg tossed her head from side to side, whimpering through her ecstasy. With another sudden surge, she mounted the pinnacle of passion as if she were flying, and with one glorious burst, Meg came undone around him.

His eyes wild, unfocused, Duncan bellowed loudly and pulled from her. His entire body shuddered as his seed spurted across her belly. His eyes rolled back with a satisfied exhale. "My God, you are an angel from heaven."

He reached for the cloth that had been on his forehead and cleansed her stomach. Wiped his seed from her. Meg caressed his cheek. Yes, it was best for him to spill his seed outside her womb. A bastard would bring ruination to her family, and though she relished the thought of bearing Duncan's child, she would never wish for her family to be harmed by her actions.

Duncan rolled to his side and reached out his arm. "Come here."

She crawled over to him and sank into his warm embrace, their bodies spooning as if it were the most natural thing in the world. In a heartbeat, Duncan's heavy breathing resumed. Again, he was fast asleep. Meg closed her eyes and cherished his closeness. Had she been wrong to seduce him when he was fevered? Perhaps, yet she would remember this night for the rest of her days. God had brought Duncan Campbell into her life for a reason, and she was quite certain it was to show her what could be between a man and a woman. She would never speak of this to another soul.

*

DUNCAN NUZZLED INTO THE SWEETEST SMELLING mane of silken hair, thinking he'd gone to heaven. His dream had been so vivid. Finally, he'd given in to his desires and made love to Lady Meg. All of his prior fantasies about the lass paled in comparison. A man could live a contented life in Meg's arms.

He nestled into the bed. Something soft and warm moved against him and emitted a satiated moan.

He wasn't in heaven, nor had he been dreaming. He was in his bedchamber. How the hell he'd arrived there, he had absolutely no idea.

Duncan opened his eyes. Meg curled her body against him, her hair shrouding his face. He rose up on his elbow and regarded her lovely face. Had last eve really happened? He cast his gaze down past the sleek curve of her hip. Heaven help him, her skirts were hiked up to her milky white thighs.

He jolted. Aside from his shirt, not a stitch of clothing covered him either.

What have I done?

His heart stuttered. He'd made a pact with himself never to stay the night in a woman's arms. But then circumstances had been a tad out of his control. He inhaled. Good God, she smelled like a valley of wildflowers. His cock thrummed. He slid his hips away from Meg's delicious bottom. How was he going to ferret himself out of this? He'd just ruined the daughter of an earl. As soon as Arthur Douglas discovered what had happened, he'd not only withhold payment, he'd string Duncan up by the cods.

He reached down the bed, grasped the plaid, wrapped it around his waist and staggered to the privy closet. His head swam like he'd had too much whisky—or had been bludgeoned. Duncan had no clue which. How had they come to Kilchurn? The last thing he remembered, the ship docked at Dunstaffnage Castle and he was about to arrange to borrow a pair of horses.

He sat to relieve himself, and a sharp pain shot up his backside. He leaned away from the ache. Bloody hell. Had he succumbed to a wounded arse? *I'll be the butt-end of my men's jests from now to eternity.*

After wiping his hands on a cloth, he reached for a pot of mint leaves. He popped one in his mouth and chewed. Though refreshing, it did nothing to satisfy his hunger. When he opened the door, Meg stood inches away, eyes wide as silver coins. "You're up?"

"Aye." He held out the pot. "Mint?"

She snatched a dried leaf and popped it into her mouth. "Straight back to bed with you."

"What are you on about, ordering me to the bed? My stomach's growling like a starved dog."

"You've been unconscious with the sweat. I can request some porridge for you, but you are too weak to be up and about."

Duncan gestured to his legs. "I'm standing, am I not?"

Meg's cheeks flushed scarlet, and she stamped her foot with infuriated gusto. "You were on death's doorstep b-but hours ago."

She looked adorable when she got worked up. "Aye?" He tugged her into his arms and smothered her minty mouth. His mind blanked. Sensuous woman crushed against his body, supple breasts, wanton hips. He kneaded his fingers down her spine and growled into her ear. "The things you do to me are wicked. I cannot keep my hands from you."

"Truly?" Her voice was breathless. "Do you remember what…what happened between us?"

Aye, he remembered every delectable moment. Worse, he'd also had enough presence of mind to know he shouldn't have ravished her. "Forgive me. I had no right."

"As I understand it, I was the one taking advantage of you, given your fevered state."

In no way would he allow her to take the blame for his actions. "I assure you I was conscious, and I shouldn't have allowed it to happen."

Meg backed away, clapping a hand over her mouth. "I knew you didn't want me. Not really." She turned and dashed to the sideboard.

"I didn't mean it like that, lass." He limped toward her. "Your brother will have my hide."

"Is that what you care about?" She kept her back to him. "There's no need for Arthur to know, or anyone else, for that matter."

So she wanted to keep it quiet, just as he did? Duncan liked the feisty lady more and more. "I do care about you…deeply." He sauntered up behind her and smoothed his hands over her hips. He leaned forward and buried his face in her wild locks. "You drive me mad with longing."

She sighed and leaned against him. "The hourglass

has long lost its sand. I must tend your wound, then I'll fetch you some food."

He nuzzled her neck. "We could both go back to bed and forget about the salve."

She scooted away from his grasp. "Your father trusted me to tend you." She faced him with a fiery spark to her eye. "Now haste ye to the bed afore I'm forced to call the guard."

Duncan groaned and plodded across the floor. "I'm all right now, lass."

"I'll be the judge of that, as will the healer when she returns."

A sharp pain stabbed Duncan's backside as he dropped the plaid and climbed onto the bed with his back to her. "What happened after we alighted from the galley? I cannot recall a single thing until I awoke with your blessed body in my arms."

"You were unconscious the whole time. Fevered, too." Meg gasped so loudly, he thought she'd cut herself.

Spinning, Duncan leaped off the bed and wrapped his arms around her. "What happened?"

"You...ah..." Her eyes drifted to the plaid he'd dropped. "Your bottom is bare, Sir Duncan."

"We're back to formalities now, are we?" Duncan hugged her to his chest and laughed. "I thought your ladyship wanted to tend my bum."

"But the whole time you've had the plaid draped across your waist. Except when..."

"Would you prefer it if I covered up?"

Her gaze languidly swept down his body while she chewed her bottom lip.

He could take no more. He lifted her chin with the crux of his finger. Slowly and ever so gently, he kissed her. He wanted to draw it out, savor her, show the lady exactly how much he desired her.

Wrapping her arms around his neck, Meg melted into

him. She sighed, and her eyes fluttered closed as she responded to his swirling tongue, sucking, teasing. Duncan could feel no pain with Meg in his embrace. The fever returned to his body tenfold, except this time he could have won a sparring match with an arm tied behind his back. Never in his life had he felt a yearning so powerful as the need shooting through the tip of his cock. "God help me, I want to feel your center swallow me again."

Clutching him tighter, she wrapped her leg around his hip and pushed into him. She wanted this as much as he. Duncan didn't understand it. When it came to women, he could usually exercise self-control, but when it came to Meg, he was powerless. He didn't even know if he could make it to the bed. Hiking up her skirts, he backed her to the wall. It was closer.

The door opened. Duncan snapped his head up. John quickly slipped inside and shut it. "Unhand Lady Meg this instant."

Stunned, Duncan took one step away. "Leave us, John."

"'Tis all right, Sir John, I was just about to see to Sir Duncan's wounds." Meg's voice had a high-pitched tremor, as if she'd swallowed a bird's whistle.

John bent down and picked up the plaid. "'Tis not how it appears. You're fortunate I came in when I did."

Meg blushed three times the shade of scarlet.

Duncan snatched the plaid from John's grasp and wrapped it around his waist. "Lady Meg needs to apply my ointment and then we shall break our fast."

John frowned, looking at the jar of ointment on the bedside table. "I'll do it. I'm sure the lady is in need of rest after tending you all night and fending off your advances just now."

Duncan stole a look at Meg. She cast her gaze to the floor so fast, he had no chance to smile at her. John could be such a law-abiding arse at times. She sidled toward the door. "I daresay I am tired and hungry." Her hand yanked down on the latch. "I shall request a tray brought up. You should still be abed, Sir Duncan."

Before he could say a word, she slipped out and closed the door.

John glared. "What the blazes do you think you were doing with the *Earl of Angus's* sister?"

Duncan stepped into his brother. "'Tis not what you think."

"No? Bare-arsed, you had her up against the wall, lifting her skirts. I should see you flogged."

Duncan took in a deep breath, making his chest jut out. "Aye, brother? It seems I've inherited the cods in this family."

John raised his fists. "If you weren't but one step from your sickbed, I'd lay you flat."

Rage gripped Duncan's gut. No one threatened him, especially not his little brother. Lowering his head, he barreled into John. Careening through the air, their flight jarred to a stop with a thud on the floorboards. Duncan threw a fist into John's jaw. The weasel squirmed out from under him and pulled his bloody dirk. "Put your feeble arse in the bed afore I'm forced to skewer you."

Grumbling, Duncan stood and tugged the plaid across his waist. "Do not let me ever hear you speak out against Lady Meg."

"Now I ken you're sick in the head." John jammed his dirk back into its sheath. "I said nothing of the sort."

Duncan climbed onto the bed and lay on his side. "She's delicate. Needs protection." Holy Christ, Meg's virtue shone right there atop the coverlet. Duncan scooted over the top of the stain.

"Aye, from the likes of you especially, I reckon."

"Wheesht. 'Tis not like that with her."

John yanked Duncan's plaid up. "Then what is it?

Are you fixing to visit the Earl of Angus with your hat in your hand?"

He folded his arms tight to his chest. "Shut your gob."

"Ballocks, your arse looks like shite." John slapped on the salve none too gently. "You want to see payment for nearly getting yourself killed?"

Duncan gritted his teeth—not against the pain, but because he knew John was right. "Och." He needed no lecture from his little brother. He could have scored his palm for deflowering the Earl of Angus's daughter. God damn to hell his hot-blooded urges.

John shoved the stopper onto the pot. "Keep your cock tied under your braies."

Duncan pressed his lips together and batted John's hand away.

"I mean it."

"Aye."

"I'll inform Da you're well enough to see him."

Duncan rolled to his back with a grunt. "I'll need a moment to dress."

"You should stay abed, give your wound another day to heal—come to your senses afore you resume your duties."

Remaining abed was a luxury Duncan could ill afford. "Always full of advice, are you not?"

"Aye?" John walked toward the door. "Someone needs to be where you're concerned."

Duncan sidled off the bed. "I can handle my affairs just fine."

"So says the ravisher of women."

Duncan shook his fist. "Begone with you afore I strap my sword to my belt." Even grown younger brothers could be a pain in the arse.

Flinging his hands up, John took his leave.

Duncan moved to the bowl and removed his shirt. He poured in some water and soaped up the cleansing cloth. He was madder than hell that John had found him with Meg up against the wall, his cock jutting from beneath his shirt like an oak branch. Bloody hell, Duncan knew better. And thank the stars John came in when he did. Taking the Earl of Angus's sister up against the wall like she was a commoner? He must have completely lost his mind due to the fever. A hundred times he'd told himself Lady Meg was off limits. The next thing he knew, he'd lost consciousness and awakened to the queen of the fairies in his bed. Bloody blundering idiot he was.

Chapter Fourteen

※

Meg found the stairwell and made her way to the great hall. Her face hot, her breaths came in short spurts. Completely mortified that John had burst into Duncan's chamber and found them entwined in such an unnatural state of undress, she never could face Duncan's younger brother again.

She clapped a hand to her chest. What if John revealed her indiscretion to the Lord of Glenorchy, or, God forbid, to her brother? How on earth could she have allowed it to happen? Up there in Duncan's chamber, it had seemed as if they were the only two people in the world. Had she completely lost her sense of propriety?

With one accusing glare from John, her fantasy had shattered—along with her maidenhead. Oh how she'd humiliated herself. She clutched her hands to her stomach. Not only was she exhausted, she wanted to be sick.

Standing in the hall as if dumb, a few people ate porridge at the tables, but from the sounds coming from the courtyard, it was well past time for the morning meal. Pattering from the stairwell behind her, four girls pushed past giggling and chatting all at once. Recognizing them as Duncan's sisters, Meg stepped aside. They all appeared younger than she.

One stopped and smiled. "Good morrow, Lady Meg."

She hid her claw behind her back. "Good morrow... ah..." She'd met them in such a fleeting moment, she couldn't remember a one's name.

The lass smiled as if she understood. "I'm Gyllis, Duncan's eldest sister." She pointed at the others. "That's Helen and the twins are Alice and Marion." Her brow creased. "How is our elder brother?"

By the heat in her cheeks, Meg knew she was blushing. They couldn't possibly know what happened above stairs. *Could they?* She cleared her throat. "He's awake and much stronger."

"Thank heavens," they chorused.

The younger girls pattered back toward Meg, with curiosity written across their faces. "Twins?" she said, looking between the two lovely lasses. "I can scarcely tell you apart."

Alice and Marion regarded each other and giggled. They had dun-colored locks like John, while Gyllis and Helen sported chestnut tresses. "Is Duncan the only sibling with black hair?" Meg asked.

"Aye." Gyllis grinned. "His mother died giving him birth. The rest of us are all Lady Margaret's children."

"I see."

"Come, Gyllis," Helen said.

The eldest Campbell girl turned to Meg with a friendly arch to her brow. "Have you eaten?"

Meg rubbed her stomach. "Nay, I daresay I'm famished."

Gyllis flicked her wrist toward the girls. "You go on. I'll have some porridge with Lady Meg."

"Where are they off to?" Meg asked, relieved to have someone to divert her mind from her harrowing thoughts.

"The kitchen. Cook's baking apple tarts."

Meg's stomach growled. "I daresay that sounds better than porridge."

"Aye, but Mother volunteered us to peel and core the apples." Gyllis licked her lips. "I'd rather eat the tart and let my sisters practice peeling apples."

"I miss my sisters." Meg chuckled. "Though I'm the youngest, and thus usually the lass given the brunt of the work."

Gyllis led her to the massive hearth. "In my mind 'tis payback for all the years I had to care for them."

The pot of porridge sat atop a cast-iron grill in front of the hearth. When Gyllis handed Meg a bowl, she had no choice but to grasp it with the claw while she spooned in the oats.

"Can I help you with that?" Gyllis asked.

"Nay." The familiar sensation of prickly heat crawled up Meg's neck. "I can manage on my own."

"I'm sorry."

"No need." Meg tried to smile. "I try to keep it hidden."

Gyllis picked up a bowl and served herself. "Why would you do that?"

"Some *uneducated* people might think me a witch or worse." Meg chuckled. "If only I had the nerve to chop it off."

"That's terrible. People should tend to their own ills." Gyllis cringed and led Meg to the high table. "Does it pain you much?"

"Not at all." The last thing Meg wanted to do was talk about the claw. "So what's it like having a brawny knight for a brother?"

Gyllis scrunched her nose, sliding into a chair. "Duncan?"

Meg nodded, frowning back her smile.

"He's a bit overbearing at times, but as of late, he's been away on king's business more than he's been about the keep."

"Rescuing ladies and the like?"

"Honestly, I do not ken." Gyllis shrugged. "Aside from keeping peace in the Highlands, he's never brought a lady back to Kilchurn. That's for certain."

Meg's heart skipped a beat. She liked that he hadn't brought other women to the keep. Lowering her gaze to the bowl, she spooned a bite of porridge.

"But what I cannot fathom is why you're dressed like a crofter. I would think the daughter of an earl would have an endless selection of lovely gowns."

Meg looked at her soiled dress. "Alas, there was no time to collect my trunks when I was kidnapped."

Gyllis's jaw dropped. "You were kidnapped? Och, how dreadful."

"You did not know?" She spooned a few more bites of porridge.

"Ha." The lass batted the air. "Do you think anyone around here would tell me something that *important*?"

Meg dabbed her lips. "I suppose there's no reason to keep it quiet."

"*Everything* is hush-hush, as if I'd run out to the town crier and create a scandal. I swear my parents still think me a child."

"My family as well." Meg regarded Gyllis's endearing dimples. "Pray, how old are you?"

"Nine and seven."

"Honestly?" Meg tapped Gyllis's arm. "Many a maid is wed at such an age, though not I."

"And your age, Lady Meg?"

"I'm rather embarrassed to admit..." She leaned closer so she could whisper. "Two and twenty."

Gyllis formed an *O* with her mouth. "Truly, and you are not yet married?"

Meg held up the claw. "I doubt I shall ever be."

"'Tis senseless rubbish." Gyllis twirled one of Meg's ringlets around her finger. "You are simply adorable to the eye."

Meg snapped a hand to her chest. "And you are touched in the head."

Gyllis tugged on Meg's arm. "Come. Let us go above stairs. I'm sure we can find something more fitting for an earl's daughter to wear."

&.

DUNCAN'S HAND SHOOK AS HE SCOOPED UP A BITE OF porridge the groom had brought to his chamber. He hated weakness in a man, especially in himself. His backside still felt like it had been gouged by a smithy's rasp. In all honesty, his limbs were so weakened, he doubted he'd be able to raise his sword. God forbid he'd ever admit that to anyone.

As soon as the food hit his belly, his verve mercifully began to revive. Another day or two and he'd be back to normal.

He scooped the last spoon of oats. What on earth was he to do about Lady Meg? Had he been in his right mind last eve, he never would have allowed things to go that far.

But he had.

Duncan swallowed the bite and wiped his mouth with a cloth. His attraction to Meg equaled no other. Her spirited heart-shaped face, the color of fresh cream with slightly rouged cheeks, made the cobalt of her eyes all the more striking. And her hair set his blood to boiling. Deep red locks twisted and curled in a ravishing mane, one in which he could completely lose himself.

Though he'd been semiconscious, he could still recall the sensation of having her in his arms. Her ample breasts nestled seductively against him, her skin softer than satin. His fingers twitched. He needed to hold her in his arms again, at least one more time. Oh, to run his hands through her wild locks, to kiss her succulent lips. The woman drove him to the very brink of lunacy.

With a knock, the chamber door opened. "John said you had roused." Da stepped inside.

Duncan stood too fast, and clapped his hand on the table to steady his dizzy head. "I'm much better, thank you, sir."

"'Tis good to hear. I cannot express enough how worried your mother and I have been."

Duncan gestured to the chair across the table. "Ye ken I would never succumb to a flesh wound on my arse."

"I pray not." Da sat. "Lady Meg refused to leave your side. I reckon you owe your good health to her tireless ministrations."

"Aye." Duncan picked up his tankard and watched the ale swirl within. Da could never know exactly how tireless Meg had been.

"She's grown a fondness for you."

He hid his smile behind the cup. "Oh?"

"What are your feelings for the lass?"

Of course, Da wouldn't let it rest. Duncan needed to find neutral ground, though his father would see right through him if he denied all attraction. "She's a woman with spirit, indeed. A beautiful one, truth be told."

"But her family may scorn us. I crushed the Black Douglas uprising back in '52. They're kin to the Red."

Duncan's shoulder ticked up. "Hardly. The Lord of Angus claims no family ties between the two clans."

"But the earl put his faith in you to return his sister unscathed." Da jammed his finger onto the table. "And that is exactly what we shall do."

Duncan swallowed, the tic above his eye deciding it was a good time to return. "'Tis what I've always intended."

"That is what I needed to hear." Da leaned back in the chair and stretched out his legs. "From what the lass tells me, you left the English standing on the pier in Glasgow."

"Aye, but—"

"I'll have a retinue escort her back to North Berwick on the morrow."

Duncan sat forward. "The morrow?"

"Aye," Da said with a lord-of-the-keep command to his voice. "You need to convalesce. You're too weak to ride."

In no way could Duncan allow Meg to head home without him. "I'll be right in a day or two. I negotiated with the earl. At the very least, I should have the satisfaction of returning his sister unharmed." And without her maidenhead intact—he may be forced to atone for that, but atone he would. "Please, certainly she can wait another sennight."

Da frowned and drummed his fingers. "A sennight at the most, and if I am not satisfied with your progress, John will lead the guard back to Tantallon."

"But—"

"I'll hear no more on it. I saw you nearly wobble off your feet when I entered. Your survival is more important to me than completing any task assigned to the Highland Enforcers. You are my heir."

Duncan studied his boots. "Yes, sir."

"If something were to happen to you, the lordship would pass to John. Though he's a kindhearted soul, *you* are what our clan needs. You have the strength to keep order in the Highlands. John would deliver alms to all who asked and merely shake a finger at thieves. He hasn't the stomach to govern."

Duncan had heard it before. True, John wanted to join the priesthood, but his brother had more grit than their father recognized. "John would rise to the task if forced."

"Perhaps, but you are the firstborn and my choice as heir. Think about that the next time you nearly die from a jagged cut to your arse."

After Da took his leave, Duncan swilled his ale.

John escort Lady Meg back to Tantallon Castle? Duncan would rather succumb to his wound than to say good-bye and allow someone else the privilege of delivering the lass to her brother. He had nearly recovered from his wound already. Surely he would be ready to spar with the guard come the morrow.

※

GYLLIS MUST HAVE HAD A DOZEN GOWNS SCATTERED across the bed. They were either too long or didn't provide enough room in the bust, or both. Gyllis was taller than Meg by a hand, but reed thin.

"I wish I had full bosoms like yours," Gyllis said.

Meg pressed her hand to her chest. "I do not know, at times they get in the way. Besides, I'm three years your senior. I'll bet yours have yet to completely come in."

"I hope so. I look more like a lad than a lass."

"That isn't true in the slightest." Meg stole a glance at the lass's bosoms. She was perfectly formed—had not a thing to worry about.

Gyllis dug down in her cedar chest and gasped. "This is perfect." She pulled out a deep blue kirtle and shook it out. "It will have no choice but to fit. The color matches your eyes precisely."

Meg rubbed the fine silk between her fingers. "Oh my, it is exquisite. Where on earth did you acquire this?"

"It was Mother's. She wore it before she birthed a boy and four girls." Gyllis chuckled. "She said her waistline would never be the same again, even with the new stays that are all the rage."

"Do you have a set?" Meg rubbed her ribs. "I hear some women wear them all the time rather than just to court."

141

"Mother ordered stays for all of us lassies. They arrived from Edinburgh not but a sennight ago."

"My, you are fortunate to have your mother to dote upon you."

Gyllis dropped her arms. "Has yours passed?"

"Aye. Ever so long ago."

Gyllis smiled and held the dress to Meg's shoulders. "I think we should turn you into a queen tonight. You shall wear this gown. It has a matching surcoat embroidered with gold thread." Gyllis tossed the kirtle on the bed and dug in her cedar chest again. "Here it is."

Meg clapped a hand over her mouth and gasped. "Oh my, that is lovely." She ran her fingers over the ermine at the collar. "I daresay it is a gown fit for court."

Gyllis twirled in a circle then pointed her toe to the side. "Well, Campbell land *is* the court of the Highlands, make no bones about it."

Meg admired the workmanship. "Truly, my own gowns at home are not as nice, though I am the daughter of an earl."

Gyllis held the gown to Meg's shoulders. "Aye, but you haven't your ma to dote on you."

Meg's heart squeezed. Yes, her sister Elizabeth had fulfilled the role of mother, but it wasn't the same. She glanced around Gyllis's chamber. Everything was ideal —her own chamber was stark in comparison. Meg knew the Earl of Angus's coffers were healthy, but her brother made the decisions on her allotment. All her life she had been prudent, though she did have some lovely gowns at home. Besides, all this wouldn't matter once she took up the veil.

Heat coursed across her skin, and she clapped her hands to her cheeks. Once she took up the veil, she would never again lie in Duncan's arms. A tear slipped to the corner of her eye and she blinked, swiping her hand across it.

"Are you well, Lady Meg?" Gyllis asked. "You look suddenly sad."

She forced a smile. "Aye. I was only feeling sorry for myself for a moment. 'Tis not often I miss my ma."

Gyllis grasped the claw and squeezed. Meg tensed and started to pull away, but one look at the lass's friendly smile and Meg relaxed. "We shall have so much fun this eve," Gyllis said. "I have the perfect veil we can secure with a bronze circlet. I daresay even Duncan will not recognize you."

Meg's stomach swarmed with butterflies. "Do you think he'll like the gown?"

"Of course he will." Gyllis winked. "Especially with you wearing it. He's got an eye for the pretty lassies, for certain."

Meg didn't like the sound of that. What other pretty lassies were flitting about? "Are there many around?" She tried to keep her tone neutral, though she wanted to shriek to the rafters. Heaven help her if Duncan flirted with other women whilst she was present.

"What?"

"Pretty lassies?"

"Only when we're having a grand feast. People come from throughout Argyllshire on May Day or Midsummer, ye ken, that sort of thing."

"Ah." A relived sigh whistled through Meg's lips.

Gyllis tugged on her arm. "Come, let's away to the bathhouse, and then we shall have plenty of time to dress."

Meg followed. "I ought to check on Duncan first."

"Och, you worry overmuch." Gyllis batted the air with her hand. "Alana can tend him."

Meg stopped and shook her head.

The young brunette pursed her lips. "Very well, but just a tap on the door and we'll be off."

"Thank you." Meg strode beside her. "I feel responsible for him. He was injured in the process of rescuing me."

"The way you carry on, I'd think you might fancy him."

Meg's cheeks burned. Fortunately, the passage was dimly lit, and Gyllis was in too much of a hurry to notice the blush that most certainly was coloring Meg's face.

Proceeding through a maze of stairwells and passages, Meg finally recognized the corridor outside Duncan's chamber. Her palms grew moist and her breathing quickened. Gyllis rapped upon the door and they waited. She rapped again. Still nothing.

"Perhaps he's asleep," Meg said, clasping the latch and peeking inside. But Duncan was nowhere to be found.

Chapter Fifteen

~~~

Duncan wasted no time calling his men together. He'd been abed for nearly a day—too long for any man of three and twenty. It was always sobering to have the Lord of Glenorchy sit in his chamber and tell him how he should conduct his affairs. Yes, he loved his father dearly, but Duncan was now a man. Da had handed Duncan the reins to the Highland Enforcers, an honor and a duty he would never take lightly. And every waking moment, one fact was never far from his forethought—he must strive to prove himself worthy and make his legendary father proud.

Aye, Duncan had been on many missions before, but this was the first high-level task where he'd been completely in control. He'd had a small setback with his injury, but all in all, he'd accomplished the mission successfully, at least thus far. Meg still must be returned to her brother—and then there was his indiscretion, but he'd figure a way to handle that. *Beautiful, lovely Meg.* As soon as he concluded this meeting, he'd go looking for her, since she hadn't returned to his chamber after breaking her fast earlier that morn.

Duncan's inner circle of five men sat around the table in the solar. That his father chose to stay away from the meeting reassured him. Prior to handing the lead to Duncan, Da sat at the head of the table and directed their affairs. Now Duncan filled that leather-clad chair. It was well worn, but none too comfortable, especially with the wound in his backside.

Lord Colin Campbell had earned notoriety and respect throughout Scotland, and it was expected that Duncan step into that role seamlessly. There was no question that if Duncan made a serious misstep, his father would push him aside. That was something Duncan could never allow. He'd been given trust and respect, and had every intention of holding on to it.

Guilt needled the back of his mind. Duncan pushed it aside by placing his palms on the table. "'Tis fortunate to see you all in good health."

"Aye," Robert said. "You're the one we're all worried about."

Duncan nodded thoughtfully. "Lady Meg saw Percy's man-at-arms as we were sailing from the pier in Glasgow. Did any of the rest of you run into the English?"

Sean stood and collected seven tankards from the sideboard. "Not after we crossed the Tweed."

Duncan watched him pull the stopper off the ewer and pour the ale. "Bloody hell, I was sure they wouldn't follow us west."

John reached for a tankard first. "I reckon the bastard followed you because they saw us at the farmer's barn. Only one horse went west—one horse with two riders."

Eoin leaned back in his chair. "I hope you got a good look at him."

"Nay. By the time Meg said something, he'd been swallowed up in the crowd." Duncan reached for the last cup and drank. "What about the Earl of Douglas? How did he take the news that we were taking a detour?"

John shrugged. "He was thankful we got her out,

but not so happy about our methods. What would you expect?"

"Aye, but it could have taken us a month or more if we'd dallied in Alnwick and attempted to be hired on as Percy's guardsmen."

James sat forward. "So when are we setting out to take her back? I've a few things in need of my attention in Loch Rannoch."

Duncan shrugged. "A sennight."

James ran a finger along his tankard's handle. "If you do not mind, I'll ride home in the morning, then."

"Does your business wear a green kirtle and work in the keep's laundry?" Robert asked.

James turned as red as apples. "Wheesht, the lot of you."

Everyone laughed. So did Duncan. Honestly, he loved this group of men. They'd all been fostered under Lord Glenorchy, and each one was as much a brother to him as John. He raised his tankard. "James, meet us at the inn in Callander in a sennight's time. We'll pass that way for certain."

꽃

After being refused access to Gyllis's chamber by his pernicious sister, Duncan opted to ready himself for the evening meal. At least he'd located Meg. When he couldn't find her, he'd feared the worst. It wouldn't be entirely impossible for an overzealous English spy to infiltrate Kilchurn's walls—highly unlikely, but not impossible.

What the devil was Meg doing with Gyllis? He heard the pair laughing and giggling all the way down the passageway. His sister was always the schemer, and Duncan dreaded what might happen. And then he kicked himself. Gyllis was a dear, caring and thoughtful of others, aside from her immature practical jokes.

Dressed in a clean linen shirt, a black leather doublet and a belted plaid, Duncan descended the tower stairs. As always, the great hall buzzed with servants preparing for a meal, yet a tad more excitement hung in the air. His stepmother walked in from the kitchen door. Smiling, she held out her hands. "Duncan, my dear. 'Tis wonderful to see you out of your bed so soon."

"Ma." He clasped her hands and kissed her cheek. She was the only mother he'd ever known, and he loved her dearly. "It looks as if you've prepared a grand feast this eve."

"Aye." Lady Margaret led him to the dais. "We've a noble guest in our midst. I couldn't resist a display of finery."

He pulled out his mother's chair and gestured for her to sit. "I'm sure Lady Meg will be grateful. She's had a sheltered life."

"Oh?" Ma frowned, taking her seat. "I was hoping she'd be able to give the girls a lesson or two about court. Lady Meg's an earl's daughter, after all, and living so close to Edinburgh, I would be surprised if she hasn't attended the queen as one of her ladies."

Duncan slid into his father's seat beside her. "You do dream on a large scale, Mother."

"I think not."

Hadn't Ma noticed Meg's hand? In no way would the queen allow a cripple to serve her. Duncan cringed. Until now, he hadn't considered Meg's deformity anything but a mild inconvenience, but others in Scotland would disdain her for certain.

He chose to change the subject. "I understand Gyllis absconded with the lady this morn."

"Aye, the last time I checked, all my old gowns were piled upon the bed."

"'Tis a good thing. Lady Meg has had a harrowing experience these past sennights. A day spent on women's affairs would be a pleasant diversion."

"She has eyes for you."

One corner of his mouth turned up.

Lady Margaret patted his hand. "A woman knows these things. But 'tis not uncommon for a lass to be smitten by your good looks. The question I have is: What are your feelings for her?"

Duncan froze. Exactly what *were* his feelings for Lady Meg? He'd die to protect her. Every time he closed his eyes, he saw her lovely face. He didn't even want to think about what would happen when he returned the lady to the care of her brother. Swiping a hand over his mouth, he cleared his throat. "She's a lovely lass, but a handful."

Ma chuckled and sat back. "Any woman worth her while is a handful."

Da bounded up the steps, followed by the twins. Relieved to avoid further conversation about Meg, Duncan rose from his father's chair and craned his neck to peer across the hall. Neither Gyllis nor Meg had come down yet. Blast it all. If he didn't see her soon, he would barrel up the stairwell and fetch her himself.

Duncan took his customary seat at his father's left. John pulled out the chair beside him, but Duncan grasped the armrest and glanced at his parents. "I'd like Lady Meg to sit beside me this eve."

Ma exchanged a knowing nod with Da. Holy Christmas, they were meddling. It mattered not. He'd led Lady Meg's rescue. They'd spent the greater part of a sennight together. She'd tended his wounds...they'd made love.

God on the cross, do I constantly have to remind myself of that fact?

"She can sit between us, then," John said, taking Gyllis's seat.

Lady Margaret clapped her hands. "I've arranged for the MacGregor minstrels to play after supper."

Helen and the girls at the far end of the table

squealed with delight. This would give them an opportunity to practice their dancing. Duncan had been twisted and cajoled into being a stand-in dance partner for years. Fortunately, aside from James, Duncan's men were all in attendance. They could partner with his sisters. He'd be dancing with someone of interest this night.

Thinking of Meg, he clenched his fists and again glanced toward the stairwell. *Where the devil are they? Haven't they been at it all day? How long does it take for an earl's daughter to dress?* From what Duncan had seen of Lady Meg, he doubted she would take any longer than one of his sisters. They wore similar gowns.

Just as he was ready to bound out of his seat and fetch her, a wave of blue and red silk descended into the hall. Gyllis wore red, though Duncan hardly noticed. He forgot to blink. "Merciful..."

"Father," John finished.

Duncan would have slammed his elbow into his brother's ribs if John were sitting beside him. Meg was his, at least until they returned to Tantallon. His milk-livered brother could hold his tongue.

Lady Meg had looked stunning in the chapel at Alnwick, but at the time she'd been a prisoner without a chambermaid. She stood at the bottom of the steps like a regal statue. Gyllis tugged her arm. Meg's gaze snapped to the dais and met Duncan's.

His mouth went completely dry.

If Father had leaned over and told Duncan that Meg was really the Queen of Scotland, he wouldn't have argued. Her royal blue kirtle was topped by an ornately embroidered matching surcoat, lined with sealskin fur. Her square neckline clung to her breasts as if Gyllis had painted it on.

They approached, and Meg appeared to float, gliding along the floorboards. Her rosy lips turned up in a lovely smile. Beneath her veil, ringlets of red framed her face. Duncan had never seen a woman more picturesque.

The corners of his mouth dumbly ticked up.

John hopped from his seat and nearly leaped down the stairs. "Lady Meg, you look enchanting this eve."

Blinking, Duncan jolted out of his chair. He'd been sitting there staring at the lass like a daft mute. He met Meg at the top of the dais steps and snatched her hand from John's grasp. "M'lady, indeed you are stunning to behold."

Gyllis came up from behind and smacked Duncan's shoulder. "Excuse me, but there are two lassies here."

He ventured a wink at Meg. "As always, you look beautiful, sister." He gestured to the seat at the far end of the table. Gyllis huffed and sat beside Helen.

As Duncan led Meg to her chair, she glanced over her shoulder. "Must Gyllis sit so far away?"

Duncan gestured to the padded seat. "'Tis only for the meal. Once the dancing starts, people will mill about."

"Dancing?" Her eyes sparkled with a flicker of candlelight.

Duncan couldn't keep himself from staring at her breasts. Defying nature, delectable flesh swelled above her bodice. "Aye, Lady Campbell wouldn't entertain an earl's daughter without a celebration."

Meg covered her mouth with her good hand. "I daresay it wasn't necessary to go the trouble."

Ma spread her palms gracefully. "Nonsense. My lassies adore it any time we invite the minstrels in..."

Mother continued, but Duncan didn't hear a word. Meg's skirts brushed his calf beneath the table. He slid his hand down and fingered the silk, imagining it was her bare skin. He caught a hint of lilac soap and leaned closer for a better sampling. Ah yes, lilac mixed with Meg's own desirous fragrance did unholy things to his manhood. If only he could spirit her up to his chamber so they could finish the meal without his meddlesome family about.

His gaze drifted from her breasts to her face. She smiled. Suddenly aware food and drink had been placed on the table, he lifted the ewer. "Would you care for some wine, m'lady?"

"Thank you."

She kept her crippled hand hidden under the table, as Duncan had observed before. But when she slid it onto his thigh and rubbed, stars crossed his vision. Bloody hell, how would he make it through the meal without revealing the passion in his heart? In no way could *anyone* seated at the table realize how rapidly his heart pounded or how much the sight of Lady Meg ignited a raging flame from his chest to his groin.

MEG COULDN'T HELP HERSELF. SHE RESTED THE CLAW on Duncan's thigh. Initially she'd done it because he appeared a wee bit glassy-eyed, but as soon as her fingers connected with the warm, hard muscles beneath his woolen plaid, her insides fluttered. Everything trembled. It wasn't like the shaking she'd experienced when cold or afraid. This trembling was filled with swarms of butterflies that flitted around her breast and made her blood pulse hot beneath her skin.

Duncan didn't move. She kept her hand in place and stared at her meal. The new stays constricting her waist in concert with her thundering heart made it near impossible to eat. Licking her lips, Meg opted to savor her wine.

"You are a vision of beauty, Lady Meg," Lord Glenorchy said from his large red-velvet chair at the center of the table.

She smiled politely. "I daresay Gyllis is a miracle worker."

Lady Margaret selected a chicken leg with her eating knife. "She has excellent taste. I remember when I could wear that gown, ever so long ago."

Meg tapped her hand to her chest. "I hope you do not mind that she let me borrow it."

The older woman smiled. Though threads of grey streaked through the chestnut locks peeking from under her wimple, she had a stately splendor, and kind green eyes. "Not at all. I'm happy to see it be of use after so many years."

Duncan placed his hand atop the claw and rubbed. He leaned close to Meg's ear. "You've transformed into a greater beauty than I ever could have imagined."

Meg dared glance at his smoothly shaven jaw. If only it were appropriate for her to kiss it.

Lord Glenorchy pounded the table with a solid fist. "Duncan, there will be no secrets at this table."

"Aye, Father." Duncan released his grasp and straightened. "I was just telling Lady Meg she cleans up well."

John snorted. "Bloody ravisher with a gruff tongue. I've no idea how the women continuously fawn all over you."

"Fawn?" Meg asked. "Ravisher?"

Duncan paled. "A wee bit of jealousy from my younger brother." He touched his lips to her ear. "I see no one in the hall but you, m'lady."

She cast her gaze to Lord Glenorchy. Directing his frown at Duncan, the baronet did not look happy.

Meg bit her bottom lip. The lord had made it clear he wanted no secret conversations at the table, but at her first opportunity, she'd ask Duncan why his father appeared disagreeable. Did the Highland lord not like her?

Under the table, Duncan's hand grasped the claw and pulled it back onto his lap. His color returned.

"How are you feeling, Sir Duncan?" Of course it was

only appropriate she use his title in the company of others, and it was best to keep the conversation neutral.

"Well, thank you. I plan to spar with my men on the morrow."

After nearly succumbing to the sweat? He must be daft. "So soon? Are you jesting?"

"Nay. The quicker I can resume normal activities, the better."

She cut a bit of chicken and slipped it into her mouth. "I would think you'd need a sennight of rest or more."

"I've far too many responsibilities to spend days lazing on my backside."

Lord Glenorchy tore a piece of bread from the loaf. "We'll be taking you back to the Lord of Angus soon. Duncan needs his strength. He wants to be the one to claim his prize."

Meg yanked her hand out from under Duncan's. The ravisher of women was planning to use her, and then take her back to Tantallon and collect his payment?

Knitting his brows, Duncan's gaze snapped to hers.

She shook her head and stabbed a piece of lamb with her eating knife. As soon as she could get him alone, she'd tell him exactly what she thought of his misbegotten plan. He could take his miserable money-grubbing arse and apply his own salve.

Meg had never been so relieved for a meal to end when the fiddler and pipers took their positions upon the balcony.

She turned to Duncan's brother. "Do you like to dance, Sir John?"

"Aye, m'lady." He offered his hand but looked directly at Duncan. "Would you care to stretch your legs with a high-stepping reel?"

She placed her palm in his hand. "I would love to."

Duncan scooted his chair back with a gruff grunt.

Meg didn't dare look at him. She'd heard enough at dinner. The eldest Campbell lad was a rogue. All too quickly she'd succumbed to his ruse.

Anyway, it was far safer to dance with John. The younger Campbell did nothing to make her stomach flutter with a swarm of tireless butterflies.

Chapter Sixteen

Duncan scooted his chair back in and grumbled behind his tankard of ale. *Thanks to my bloody family, Meg thinks me an utter blackguard.* Not that he wasn't. But he didn't want Meg to think poorly of him.

Laura, a serving maid, made a show of leaning forward to pick up a trencher. She hovered until Duncan glanced her way. Ample cleavage befuddled his mind.

The wench smiled. "Ye fancy a poke tonight, m'lord?" she whispered.

Bloody hell, he would immediately put an end to his womanizing. He flicked his wrist at the lass. "Begone with you." He kept his voice low, but he would have liked to bellow a string of insults to ensure no one within fifty miles of Kilchurn ever again presented him with such a vulgar proposal. He raked his fingers through his hair. A fortnight ago, he would have taken the wench up on her offer and asked if she wanted to bring a friend. Presently, Lady Meg ran amuck in his mind.

Said ginger-haired lady glared at him from the dance floor. Bloody Laura didn't leave and ran her fingers across Duncan's shoulders. *Ballocks to this.* Duncan batted the wench's hand away, stood and strode toward the dancers while the tune came to an end.

Meg smiled at John with her shameless breasts heaving against her bodice. They strained so taut, her seams could burst at any moment. Everyone in the hall could gawk at the wares she had on display.

The musicians announced a strathspey, and John led Lady Meg into the line. Oh no, that beetle-brained trickster wasn't about to dance with her yet again. Duncan hurried behind John and tapped him on the arm. "I'm cutting in."

John shot an angry glance over his shoulder. "What? No chance..."

Duncan stepped in front of him. "You had your dance. 'Tis my turn."

John looked like he could have blown smoke through his nostrils. "My word, you are an ogre of the highest order."

"Aye." Duncan gave him a shove to ensure he backed away. "That's why I'm the eldest."

Truly, Duncan loved John, but no one bar he would shower affection upon Lady Meg this eve...or any other night, if he had something to do with it.

He faced the lovely lass across the aisle.

She knitted her brows and spread her palms in question.

The music began.

Duncan sashayed forward and grasped her hands. "Lady Meg."

"What are you doing?" she snapped. "I was dancing with *Sir John*."

Locking elbows, he promenaded her in a circle. "But now you're dancing with me."

She leaned into him and kept her voice low. "With a ravisher of women."

"That was before."

"Before when?" Her eyes flashed with a spark. "Last night or this morning?"

"You do not understand." Duncan had no choice but to release her and return to his place across the aisle.

Lips thinning, she glared at him. Oh, how he'd grown to adore the lady's quick temper. Duncan's blood coursed hot beneath his skin. If only he could throw her over his shoulder and whisk her up to his chamber.

They grasped hands again. Her eyes narrowed. "I release you from your duty to see to my safety."

"What the devil...?" The woman beside Duncan locked arms and spun him away from Meg. *Now she's talking rubbish. How on earth did she come up with such nonsense?*

Their turn to take hands and promenade down the aisle, Duncan latched on to her fingers and hustled her along a fair bit faster than the tempo demanded.

Meg tried to tug from his grasp. "You're hurting me, you big lout."

At the end of the line, he gripped her hand tighter and tugged her into the nearest room—a small solar just off the great hall, where Father had sensitive dealings when hearing supplications.

Meg yanked her hand away and held up a finger. "I warn you, keep your distance."

Duncan sauntered closer, chuckling. "Or what?"

The fire in the hearth was the only light, and it cast a shadow across her trembling lips as she backed against the wall.

Duncan placed his hands either side of her and pinned her there. He bent down and nuzzled her ear. "What will you do to me, m'lady?"

She squirmed, but he pressed his thigh between her legs so she couldn't elude him. She clutched her fists beneath her chin. "I heard enough at the table. You are to collect your coin and be done with me."

"Odd." His gaze dipped to her tempting lips. "I heard nothing of the sort...just mindless prattle over a meal."

"I saw you with that serving girl. She practically made love to you on the dais."

Lady Meg's scent drove him to the brink of madness, those heaving breasts demanding he swirl his tongue over them. "She means nothing to me."

"As do I."

"That's where you're wrong." Duncan could resist no longer. He crushed his mouth over hers and forced his tongue into her mouth. Every fiber of his body needed to possess her. Seeing Meg dance with another man, even his brother, blinded him with rage. Squirming, Meg fought him. He must show how much he desired her. He slipped his arms around her shoulders and clutched her body to his. Soft breasts plied his chest.

Meg twisted her head away with a gasp. "You're suffocating me, you daft Highlander."

Duncan immediately released her. "Forgive me." For the love of God, in his fury to show his affection, he'd acted like an overbearing boar. "I only meant—"

"You only meant to ravish me and then return me to Tantallon. Your father said it—collect your tainted prize."

"That's not..." But that was exactly what he was doing. Duncan paced, pushing the heels of his hands against his temples. "'Tis not as simple as you make it out to be."

Her petite foot stomped the floor. At least she hadn't fled. "No?"

"Aye, I must return you to the Earl of Angus, but I no longer care to take his coin. I..." Could he say it? He'd only known her for a short time. How could he know if his feelings were genuine? Besides, he would be completely irresponsible if he said anything to Meg before speaking to her brother. He stood straight. "You've come to mean a great deal to me."

She blinked. "I..."

The door opened with a loud knock. "Lady Meg?

Are you well?" Gyllis slipped inside. "Mother sent me in to see if I could be of assistance." Her bloody voice sounded like a chirping harpy.

Thank God Duncan hadn't been stupid enough to raise Meg's skirts again. Duncan groaned and shot his sister his sternest, most sober look. "I needed to speak to her ladyship in private. We shall be along directly."

Gyllis wrung her hands. "Uh...very well." She craned her neck to peek around Duncan. "Does that meet with your approval, m'lady?"

Meg stepped to Duncan's side. "I believe Sir Duncan and I are finished. Let's away to your chamber." She reached for Gyllis's hand and shot Duncan a sidewise glare before the door slammed after them.

He blinked in disbelief.

Bloody Christmas, he needed to rein in his meddling family. If he didn't run into a sibling at every turn, he and Meg would never have argued. How would he ever earn her love and regain her respect with people interfering upon his every effort?

❧

Isaac had grown weary of the chase. He yearned for the comfort of his bed and his woman's arms. However, he'd made the right decision to wait out the sennight until the galley returned to Glasgow. It didn't take much coin to gain the captain's confidence. He'd not learned as much as he would have liked, but every tidbit of information brought him closer to understanding who was behind Meg Douglas's rescue.

The captain had advised the knight's name was Campbell, a powerful and feared clan in the Highlands. In addition, he had first asked to be transported to Inverary, where his uncle resided. That also happened to be the seat of the Earl of Argyll. However, this Campbell had been reasonably content to sail to Dunstaffnage, where the captain witnessed him collapse on the pier—said that as they sailed away, the lady ordered the guards about and they snapped to with urgency.

Isaac later boarded a transport with his horse and alighted on the pier at Dunstaffnage Castle. *So these are the Highlands?* He shivered. The few people he passed leered at him with sideways glances. He brushed his hand over his doublet. Perhaps he appeared a tad too English. A small village nestled outside the castle walls, and he chose to ride his horse at a walk through the muddy lane.

Finding a man loading barrels onto a cart, Isaac stopped. "Hail, friend."

The man hesitated and eyed him. "Why, you're bloody English."

"A poor minstrel looking for work," Isaac hedged. "A friend of mine was found injured on the pier. He had planned to meet me here so that I could play my...ah... flute for his family." A wooden flute was the only instrument Isaac could think of that would be easily concealed under his cloak.

"Ye mean Sir Duncan Campbell?"

"Yes, Sir Campbell. Would perchance you be able to tell me how to find his...keep?" *Wouldn't a knight in the Highlands have a keep?* Isaac crossed his fingers.

The laborer pointed toward the trees. "Ye take the path there twenty miles all the way to Kilchurn."

"I thank you."

The man stepped into Isaac's horse and grasped the bridle. "Ye best mind yer mouth around these parts. There aren't many who are as accommodating as me, and a damned mite more who would see an Englishman hanged for seeking out the Lord of Glenorchy's son." Isaac tried to back his horse, but the man held tight. "If I hear yer up to no good, I'll come after ye meself."

"Your point is well taken and understood." Isaac offered a brisk nod and dug his spurs into the horse's barrel.

Twenty bleating miles? It will be well past dark before I arrive.

§

MEG SAT BESIDE GYLLIS IN THE GREAT HALL AND swirled her spoon around in her porridge. Scarcely able to keep her eyes open, she yawned. For days Meg couldn't sleep. She'd lain awake most every night listening to Gyllis's soft snores while she replayed scenes with Duncan over in her mind. The one that bothered her most was the last time they'd been alone together.

When they'd danced, she'd been so inexplicably angry with him. And when he pulled her into the solar and crushed his mouth over hers, she thought he might ravish her right there—just as he almost had in his chamber. And her ridiculous mind couldn't decide if she wanted him to or not. Fortunately, propriety took hold and she'd forced her fists between them.

Yet when he'd stepped back, the shadows danced across his stricken face. Though the light was dim, she could not mistake the look of remorse in his eyes. After Gyllis had interrupted them, he'd kissed her hand with more tenderness than she'd ever experienced in her life. He'd held her palm and caressed it as if it were the most precious thing in the world. At that very moment, her knees had melted like snow on a spring day.

That he was a rake, Meg harbored no doubt. In his chamber, she'd wanted to make love to him and had made the decision to do it. After all, she was two and twenty, with no marriage prospects. Once she entered the nunnery and took her vows, she would have no chance of ever enjoying the caress of a lover. No, Meg would never regret giving her maidenhead to Duncan Campbell.

If only she could love such a man as he, she would be content for the rest of her days. If only he could love her as much as she did Duncan...but he was notorious among the lassies.

"You've been stirring that bowl of oats since we sat down. Are you not hungry?" Gyllis asked.

Meg blinked and shook her head. "Nay." She lifted the spoon to her lips. "I have a lot on my mind."

"A man named Sir Duncan Campbell, I'd wager."

Nearly choking on her bite, Meg coughed. "My heavens, why would you say something like that?"

"Two reasons." Gyllis grinned, looking awfully proud of herself. "First, you insisted on tending him until he came to. You like him. 'Tis clear as the nose upon your face."

Heat ignited beneath Meg's skin.

Gyllis shook her finger. "And I've never seen him look at any lass the way he gazes upon you...and he looks at lassies all the time."

"That's the problem." Meg started stirring her porridge again. "If he's watching other lassies all the time, how could he possibly want to gaze upon the likes of me?"

"Are you jesting? If only I could be half as pretty. You have natural ringlets of fire, and your face is as lovely as a cherub's statue."

Meg slid her good hand to her boiling cheek. "I look like a bairn?"

"I didn't say that, but you are a beauty, Lady Meg, whether you choose to believe it or nay."

"But..." She shouldn't have this conversation with Duncan's sister. She scooped another spoon of oats. "I'll be back at Tantallon soon. Duncan will return to Kilchurn and my adventure will be but a memory."

"I hope it doesn't end that way. I'd like it if we could remain friends always."

Helen skipped up to their table with Alice and Marion in tow. "Time for music lessons, Gyllis."

She rolled her eyes toward Meg and moaned. "Mother insists we all learn to sing and play the lute."

"A worthy pastime," Meg said.

Gyllis scooted back her chair. "Will you excuse us?"

"Of course." Meg shooed them away with a flick of her wrist. Honestly, she was glad for a bit of time to herself, especially since she'd gone two nights with little sleep. She was good company for no one.

Wandering out to the sunny courtyard, Meg stopped short. *Heaven's stars*. Before Duncan could see her, she dashed into the shadows of an alcove. He and his men were sparring, the clangs from their swords echoing off the curtain walls.

Meg's hand flew to her chest to steady her erratic heartbeat. Yes, when he'd rescued her, he'd fought and shown no mercy. He'd done what he must to save her life, but his form had been hidden beneath the robes of a priest.

However, today Duncan sparred naked from the waist up. Wielding his mammoth sword with crushing blows, every sinew in his back flexed and bulged. Even with a chill in the air, his skin glistened with sweat.

Mesmerized, Meg stood motionless in the shadows. Duncan's sword clashed with Eoin's, their blades scraping until their cross guards locked. "You're going easy on me," Duncan hissed through gritted teeth.

"Aye?" Eoin growled. "You've returned from the dead and expect to snap back in a day?"

Duncan shoved him away and crouched, both feet firmly planted apart, spreading the plaid belted low on his hips. "I'll not be treated like a milksop."

"You?" Eoin lunged. Their swords collided with a resounding racket. "I ought to run my blade across your other buttock so you have a matching pair."

Duncan pushed him away and advanced with bone-jarring force. Eoin proved a worthy opponent, deflecting the onslaught of blows as he spun away. Again their swords collided and scraped until the two knights were nose to nose.

Eoin kicked around Duncan's backside. The heir to Glenorchy howled. "That was a dirty trick."

The MacGregor heir sauntered around him. "What? Have you not had enough of Lady Meg tending your ugly arse?"

Meg clapped her hand over her mouth and tried not to laugh. Duncan's chiseled arse was anything but ugly.

"You're a bloody fat-kidneyed maggot." Duncan spun, swinging his blade in an arc. Eoin met the blow with an upward thrust. Duncan's sword flew from his hand and clattered to the cobblestones. "Ballocks, I hate miserable weakness." He trudged over and picked it up. Then, assuming his wide stance, he beckoned with his fingers and nodded to Eoin. "Come again."

Meg wanted to rush out into the courtyard and demand he stop. For heaven's sake, Eoin was right. Duncan had been half dead a few days ago. But she knew enough to stay away from sparring men. Not only could she be killed, the warriors could injure each other if their attention was drawn away.

Lord Glenorchy marched through the doors and straight past Meg. "Duncan."

Heaving, the men lowered their swords.

The lord's countenance was undeniably grave. "Come with me. I need a word."

Chapter Seventeen

❧

Duncan grabbed his shirt and followed Da into the keep. Something in the corner of his eye moved in the alcove. *Meg.* He would have stopped, but from his father's grim expression, this wasn't the time. Something was afoot. Duncan's gut twisted.

He'd seek Lady Meg out later. Besides, he needed to time to think about how best to approach her and what he'd say.

Da led him into the second-floor solar and closed the door. "'Tis good to see your strength returning."

"Aye, but it is bloody annoying. I feel like my claymore weighs seven stone."

Da took a seat at the head of the table—in Duncan's chair. "Well, I reckon you've had long enough to convalesce."

"True." Duncan pulled out a seat and gingerly slid onto the hardwood. "I must escort Lady Meg back to Tantallon."

"Indeed, she needs to be reunited with her brother, but you cannot take her."

Duncan sat forward. "I beg your pardon?"

Da didn't smile. "I've received a missive from the king. We have a new assignment." He pulled out a folded piece of vellum and held it within an inch of his nose, reading the inscription. *Good God, Da's eyesight grows worse by the day.*

"Bloody fantastic timing." Duncan sat back, wincing at the jabbing pain. "This better not be royal bravado, doing some superfluous task akin to accompanying the queen to St. Andrews."

"Nay." Da frowned. "'Tis grave."

Duncan spread his palms, waiting expectantly.

Da tossed the vellum on the table. "We're to intercept the Earl of Mar and deliver him to Laird Preston at Craigmillar Castle."

"Christ—the king's own brother? What the bloody hell for?"

Da pointed at the missive. "What we need to know is in there. He's been accused of practicing witchcraft against the king."

"You're serious?" Duncan picked up the vellum and smirked. "Seize him from Kildrummy Castle?"

Da said nothing while Duncan read. Sure enough, the missive was vague, and John Stewart, Earl of Mar, stood accused by the scrolling penmanship inscribed in the document. Duncan folded the missive and tossed it on the table. "Ye ken the fortress is near impenetrable."

"Why else would the king request our services?"

Duncan's gut muscles clenched. "God on the cross, this is bad timing." His plans to win Meg's favor would take sennights, not days.

"I recall you said the same thing when we received the order to go after Lady Douglas." Da scratched his beard. "Seems it was a MacGregor lass, was it?"

Indiscretions always had a way of coming back to him. Duncan had behaved like a rake for so long, everyone seemed to expect it of him. He crossed his arms. "Lady Meg is different."

"I'll say. She's nobility, for one." Da eyed him. "Are you telling me you're serious about the redheaded lassie?"

"I care for her."

"Aye? And you'll care for the next bonny lass who applies ointment to your arse."

Duncan swallowed his rebuttal and looked to the window. He didn't want his father meddling when it came to Lady Meg. Da could end any hope he might harbor of winning her favor. Besides, he wasn't ready to marry or do anything rash like that. He was the leader of the Highland Enforcers, a responsibility that had him away from home more often than not. What? He'd been at Kilchurn for all of a sennight? And now he'd be off again for a month, possibly more.

However, Duncan still preferred to see Meg safely home. "Have you considered what is to be done with her?"

Da retrieved the missive from the table and slid it back into his doublet. "John will take her to Tantallon."

Duncan's gut clamped harder and twisted. "John? He's one of my best men."

"Aye, but he's kin, and aside from you, he's best suited to negotiate the final payment with the Earl of Angus."

Duncan let out a heavy sigh. Leave it to his brother to be given the pleasurable detail of the journey to North Berwick with Lady Meg. He wanted to hit something. "I'd prefer to deliver Meg to her brother and then travel north to Kildrummy."

"I ken you're not daft, son." Da stood and moved to the sideboard. "The longer we postpone, the more likely the Earl will hear of this accusation and flee Scotland." Squatting so his nose was inches away from the tray, he studiously poured two drams of whisky and handed one to Duncan. "Nay, we shall leave on the morrow. You'd best tell your men."

Duncan accepted the tot and sipped. "We? Are you coming with us?"

"And not witness the look on the earl's face when

you tell him his brother's accused him of witchcraft?" Da chuckled. "I wouldn't miss that for a chest filled with silver."

"Aye? Have you and the earl been at odds?"

"Let's just say I doubt Lord Stewart could recite a witch's incantation. When he was granted the title of earl, he petitioned for grant of our lands right here on Loch Awe."

"God's teeth, he tried to take Kilchurn?"

Da raised his cup. "Aye, bloody senseless bastard."

Duncan stood. "I'll say." He adjusted his sword belt. "Well then, capturing the Earl of Mar shouldn't be as distasteful as I initially thought."

"Good on you, lad. We'll make quick work of it and be back at Kilchurn for the Easter feasts."

Duncan strode out of the solar wishing he could be half as content as his father. *Ballocks, allowing John to accompany Meg back to Tantallon? Why the hell was I the firstborn?*

❧

ISAAC SLIPPED INTO THE INN AT GLEN ORCHY. He stood for a moment to allow his eyes to adjust to the haze. A few stragglers slouched against the bar. Though it was early afternoon, they all appeared to be in their cups. He sidled up to the pot-bellied innkeeper. "A brandy, if you please."

"What?" The man leered at him beneath thick beetle brows. "Ye're English, are ye? We've whisky and ale. Which will it be?"

"Whisky." Isaac cleared his throat. "Please."

The innkeeper pulled the stopper out of a bottle and poured. "You'll taste none finer than that from the Glen Orchy still."

Isaac picked up the cup and held it to his lips. "Truly." He sipped and swirled the oaken-flavored spirit over his tongue. "I say, that is good."

Wearing a moth-eaten plaid and a linen shirt laced with a leather cord, the innkeeper looked as if the times had taken a toll. Perhaps the man was disgruntled with the lord of the land? Isaac took another sip, appraising the odd-looking fellow. "I saw a rather large herd of cattle just west of here. Do they all belong to the Lord of Glenorchy?"

The man jammed the stopper back on the whisky bottle. "Why are ye asking?"

Suspicious, just like every other Scot in this frigid country. Isaac sniffed. "Dunno...seems as if Lord Glenorchy is in the king's favor. I'd wager he carries out the king's business with a firm hand."

"Now just who do ye think ye are coming in me place talking about Lord Colin as if he were a tyrant?" The innkeeper picked up Isaac's unfinished glass. "There's nary a soul in all of Argyllshire who wouldn't take up his sword for Black Colin."

The stragglers, suddenly alert, turned to watch.

Isaac held up his hands. The last thing he needed was to cause a stir. "Pardon. My mistake. With such a grand castle, I wrongly assumed there might be some resentment on the part of the locals."

One of the men sauntered over, smoothing his hand across his dirk. "Where are ye from, Englishman? I'll wager Lord Colin will want to know."

"Aye." Another stepped behind Isaac. "Mayhap we should deliver him ourselves."

The third closed in. "Could mean a farthing or two for each of us."

Isaac's gaze darted to the door. Obviously he'd made a grave error. He'd discovered plenty about Sir Duncan Campbell and his father. They controlled everything in these parts, lived behind mighty fortress walls and ensured the local crofters were happy—if only things were as pleasant in Alnwick.

Surely his information was enough for Lord Percy. He bit his lip, but what about Lady Meg? Was she within Kilchurn's walls or had she returned to Tantallon? "I understand Sir Duncan suffered quite an unpleasant injury. Who has taken on his mantle whilst he's been recovering?"

A smelly Scot stepped within an inch of Isaac's nose, the man's breath as rancid as rotten meat. "I'd wager yer a bloody English spy."

Isaac's pulse quickened. Perhaps his last question crossed the line.

The men surrounded him. As he reached for his sword, Isaac's fingers skimmed the pommel when a fist to the jaw sent him careening backward. He stumbled over a chair and crashed to the floorboards. While scrambling to stand, a booted foot kicked his gut. Isaac snatched his dagger from his sleeve, met with a bone-jarring heel that pinned his wrist. Fingers splaying, the weapon dropped.

Bellowing, Isaac tore his throbbing arm from under the boot and sent the man toppling to his bum. All three pounced, fists pummeling Isaac's face.

The last thing he remembered was curling into a ball while he tried to protect his head in his cradled arms.

❦

RETURNING FROM A TURN IN THE CASTLE GARDENS, Meg stepped into the keep. Her eyes hadn't adjusted to the dim light when she smacked straight into Duncan's chest. His hands braced her arms. She didn't need to look at his face to know it was he. His scent filled her senses—spice laced with a hint of lemongrass. She closed her eyes and inhaled again.

"I've been all over the castle looking for you." His voice held an edge of concern.

She peered at each powerful hand gripping her then he released. "I went for a brisk walk."

He ushered her inside and into the small solar where he'd trapped her the night before. "Was it pleasant out, not too cold?"

She rubbed her outer arms where he'd touched her. "Nay. The day's quite mild for this time of year."

"I'm glad of it." He pulled out a chair and gestured for her to sit, his expression stern and commanding. "I've some news."

"Oh?" The back of Meg's neck bristled. *News* was rarely ever good, and Duncan had suddenly become too polite. She almost preferred the gruff warrior who made her sit in the rear of a Gypsy wagon.

He took a seat at the head of the table. His brow furrowed—definitely not a good sign. "My men and I have received a missive from the king. We've an urgent mission to perform."

"Oh my." She clapped a hand to her chest. "I hope 'tis nothing too dire."

"Unfortunately, I am unable to discuss any details, but we must leave at dawn." His eyes trailed away and his Adam's apple bobbed. "Though I would dearly love to see you back to Tantallon, I'm afraid John must accompany you."

A cannonball sank to the pit of Meg's stomach. Yes, she expected to say good-bye to Duncan, but only *after* they'd had a chance to make amends, and most certainly after she reached home. She covered the claw with her good hand and squeezed. What should she say? He was leaving on the morrow. She'd never see him again. Tears rimmed her eyes. She swiped a hand over her face to hide her emotion. "I suppose 'tis for the best," she finally blurted.

His eyes narrowed, and for a moment, Meg thought

he might be in pain, but he pushed his chair back and stood, facing the hearth. "You feel nothing for me, then?"

Tingles danced along her skin. "I do not recall saying that."

He snapped around. "What about my brother?"

She shrugged. "John is very nice." *But he's not you. I want you.*

"Do you have feelings for him?"

She folded her hands in her lap and stared at them. "To what are you referring? Would I thrust myself upon him and take advantage whilst he's in a fevered stupor?" Her voice became a whisper. "Nay. I would not."

Duncan stepped beside her and placed a hand on her shoulder. "Lady Meg, I—"

She jerked from under his grasp. "Stop. You owe me no apology." Pushing her chair back, she stood and slipped to the door. "We both knew this would happen. Why make it more difficult?" She jerked down on the latch and fled.

Running through the great hall, Meg could scarcely breathe. Why was she being such a mutton-heid about Duncan's news? *He doesn't love me.*

Tomorrow she would *finally* be rid of him and could focus her mind on returning home. If Arthur refused to allow her to take up the veil, she would spirit away on her own. Besides, she was ruined now. Prickly heat spread across her skin.

Pushing outside, a tear slipped from her eye and dribbled down her cheek. She didn't want to live in this cruel world. Giving herself to God, she would be cloistered in a nunnery where no one could ever break her heart again.

Chapter Eighteen

~~~

Dumbfounded, Duncan stared at the closed door. He resisted running after Meg, though every fiber of his being screamed for him to do so. She was right. Sooner or later they would have parted ways, and there was nothing he could do about it. Chasing after her now would only make matters worse.

Presently, too many things demanded his attention, the most urgent being the mission at hand. To depart on the morrow, he needed to prepare his men and supplies. Stomping around like a raging bull, Duncan barked orders whilst everyone scurried about him.

When he finally pushed into his chamber, he sat at the round table beside the hearth and cradled his head in his hands. Usually he was eager to leave on a mission, but this one filled him with trepidation. Had thoughts of Meg influenced him so much, he'd lost his fighting edge? No. Once he mounted up in the morning and felt the cold wind on his face, he'd be ready.

However, tonight he wanted to do something for Lady Meg. *But what?*

Rubbing the stubble on his chin, Duncan eyed the quill in front of him. He reached for a piece of parchment and dipped the tip into the inkwell.

'Twasn't long ago a bonny lass claimed my heart,
After meeting her gaze, I prayed we would never part.
I could nary close my eyes without picturing her bonny face.
Had we met in another time or another place,
I might have knelt before her and declared my love,
But my life's not my own,
And she must go away home,
Afore I can earn her favor.
I shall never forget her, for she is my savior, a woman I will always savor.
Forever, you will be my heavenly dove.

He sanded the parchment and reread his poem. He wasn't much for writing verse, but he'd made most of it rhyme. And now he'd written it, a weight lifted from his shoulders. He only wondered *if* he should give it to her —and when?

※

GYLLIS SHOOK MEG AWAKE. "LADY MEG, YOU'VE slept late."

Her head throbbed. This was the first good night's sleep she'd had in ages. She rolled to her back. "I'm so tired."

"Aye, but John is readying the horses to take you back to your family." Gyllis clapped her hands. "Are you excited to see the Lord of Angus after all this time?"

Yawning, Meg sat up. "I suppose. Ready to go home and resume my life."

Gyllis offered her hand and pulled Meg to her feet. "You're still set on taking up the veil?"

"Aye." Her shoulders sagged. "Now more so than ever."

"What makes you say that?"

Meg pattered to the bowl and poured in some water,

splashing her face so she didn't have to answer Gyllis's annoying question.

Without much of anything to pack, she dressed quickly, then she and Gyllis ate eggs and sausages in the kitchen.

John sauntered in and sat beside his sister. "Are you ready to ride, Lady Meg?"

"Aye." She peered around him to gain a glimpse of the courtyard through the window. "Will Sir Duncan see us off?"

John cringed. "Did he not tell you?"

"No..." Certain she didn't want to hear John's response, she bit her bottom lip.

"The men rode out at first light. They had no time to spare."

She'd missed him? Unable to breathe, she bit that lip harder so she wouldn't cry. Why on earth didn't Duncan say he wouldn't be there to say good-bye? She might have poured her heart out and made an embarrassing attempt to pledge her love. Her gut twisted. *Of course that's why Duncan didn't say good-bye—he knew I would grovel and plead, and couldn't bear the thought of it.*

"Are you all right, Lady Meg?" Gyllis asked.

She tried to smile, though her cheeks felt like two-stone weights hung from them. "Ready to ride." Meg swiped a hand across her eyes and stood. "Come, Sir John. The sooner we set out, the sooner we shall see Tantallon Castle."

Once outside, John grasped her arm. "I ken why you've had a sudden bout of melancholy, and he's not good enough for you, m'lady."

She stopped and eyed the younger brother. "I daresay you're wrong."

Isaac looked up from the moss, one eye swollen shut, his lip split, and God only knew if he had any broken bones. He'd been lucky to make it out of the inn alive. His solar plexus had ached so much, he couldn't mount his horse. He'd led the gelding into a copse of trees and collapsed on the cold, mossy turf.

Earlier that morning he'd heard the hooves of warhorses pummel the ground. A contingent of men rode with purpose, but Isaac's bleary eyes saw no woman with them. He'd led enough sorties to know something more important than the Earl of Angus's sister was afoot. Any other day, he might have tracked them, but at the moment, he could barely move.

Moments later, he received his answer as to Lady Meg's whereabouts. A procession rode past at a far slower tempo. An armored knight led a dozen sentries with her ladyship riding in the center of the retinue.

At last, the Lord of Glenorchy sees fit to provide an escort to accompany the lady home. But the big Highland warrior who protected her wasn't with them. Surely he must have been with the group that rode out earlier.

Isaac cared not for the reason. *Let the Scots ruin themselves. I've gained enough information for Lord Percy.* The Campbells of Glen Orchy were responsible for Lady Meg's rescue, and by the time Isaac reached Alnwick, she would be returned to her brother.

Lord Percy would probably dismiss him, but Isaac had enough of the bleating cold north. He'd had nothing to do but think about his future, and he wouldn't be kidnapping any more maidens for Northumberland. Fighting a battle man to man Isaac could handle, but all this backstabbing skullduggery must end.

Though he might lose his position at Alnwick, a skilled man-at-arms could find work in any town of size. He'd head home and report to Percy. If his lordship dismissed him, he'd pack up his family and move them to Shrewsbury or Carlisle.

Isaac dragged his aching body onto his horse and chuckled. *That would be a boon. Leaving the Yorkists to join the Lancastrians. It doesn't matter where I go. Each side needs fighting men.*

Chapter Nineteen

It took them a week to reach Aberdeenshire. Stopping to make camp, Duncan checked the food stores. "We'll need to hunt on the morrow."

"Hunting a man, aye," Da said. He stepped beside Duncan and looked into the saddlebag. "We've done with less."

Duncan growled. "Oatcakes and a slab of salt pork won't last long."

"We'll not hunt until we take the earl into custody. 'Tis too risky."

"Aye? Then we should not light a fire this night either." Duncan closed the saddlebag and gave it a slap. Da grasped his shoulder.

"I agree. No fire." He leaned toward Duncan's ear. "But you've been brooding since we left Glen Orchy, and I've a mind to put you on your horse and send you to your ma."

"Bloody hell." Duncan yanked his shoulder away. "I'm no wee bairn you can order about."

"No? Then you'd best stop acting like one. If you don't pull your finger out of your arse, men will die. Campbell men." Da grasped his collar. "Is that what you want?"

"I've had a lot on my mind. It does not mean I'll shirk my duties."

"It had better not. You need to remove the Douglas lassie from your thoughts. Aye, Lady Meg has a pretty face, and a feisty temper to go along with that wild mane of red tresses, too. She's best remaining with her kin."

Duncan took a step back, but Da held firm to his collar. "You're a young lad, and if you're smart, you'll have a long life like me. There are plenty of lassies to be found. In all my years, one thing is for certain. Court is never at a loss for bonny young maidens."

Duncan stretched to ensure he stood a mite taller than his father. "You needn't worry about me."

"Nay, I shouldn't. But you've no business sticking your cock where it shouldn't be." Da released his hand. "Mark me. Never cross the man who's willing to pay for your services, be him the king, an earl or a lowly sheriff."

Duncan nodded. He'd been giving himself the same lecture ever since he met Lady Meg, and he certainly didn't need to hear it from his father. "Do you not think I ken?" He reached in his saddlebag for his flagon and pulled the stopper. "I need a tot of whisky." He took a sip and handed it to Da.

The Lord of Glenorchy licked his lips and guzzled a healthy swig. "Once this business with the earl is over we'll need to pay a visit to court. I'm sure the king will want a full report."

"Aye. We'll be close enough to Edinburgh Castle to do it in person." Duncan liked that idea. They'd also be close enough to North Berwick for Duncan to take a detour to Tantallon Castle. Even if he could only see Lady Meg long enough to apologize for not saying good-bye, he had to see her one last time.

Da stepped into the clearing and raised his arms. "Come around, men. We must plan our strategy."

Duncan stepped beside him. "I shall take it from here."

Da gave him a pointed look then a nod. Yes, it was difficult for the Black Knight to let go, but he'd given Duncan the responsibility to lead the Highland Enforcers. Allowing his father to ride roughshod over him at this stage would be seen as weakness by his men. Duncan wasn't about to stand aside and allow that to happen.

❧

MEG CLOSED HER EYES AND BREATHED IN THE FRESH sea air as she rode through the gates of Tantallon Castle. It had been a long week, made longer by foul weather, but at last she was home. The family's great deerhounds barked to announce her arrival then wagged their tails and trotted beside her.

At the head of the retinue, John reined his horse to a stop and dismounted. George, the valet, burst from the keep, a grin stretched across his face. "Lady Meg! Thank the good Lord, you've finally come home."

He helped her dismount as John came up beside them. "We would have returned her much sooner if it hadn't been for Lord Percy's English sentries tailing us." John smiled at her then patted his cloak. "Oh my, I almost forgot." He pulled a missive from his inside pocket. "Duncan gave me this and asked me to deliver it to you once we arrived."

Meg stared at the parchment for a moment then raised a trembling hand to accept it. The entire journey she'd been fuming that Duncan hadn't the courtesy to say good-bye. She'd all but cursed him to rot in the bowels of hell.

Arthur must have come out, because he pulled her into an embrace. "Meg, dear. 'Tis so good to have you home."

Her brother always smelled of oiled leather and rosewater. Still trembling, she returned his hug. "And I'm ever so glad to see you." Two dogs rubbed against her on either side. "And 'tis good to see Midge and Max haven't forgotten me." She scratched Max behind the ears with the claw. She needn't be mindful of her deformity hidden within the castle curtain.

Arthur shook hands with John. "Sir, I'm surprised not to see your brother."

John bowed his head politely. "Alas, he was called away on the king's business. He very much would have liked to accompany her ladyship himself."

Arthur ushered them inside. "Come with me. I'd like a full report." He smoothed his hand over Meg's shoulder. "George, have the chambermaid draw a bath for Lady Meg." He looked her in the eye. "You must be tired after such a long journey."

"Aye." She clutched the missive behind her back, thrilled for an excuse to spirit to her chamber. "A warm bath is what I need to ease the ache from a sennight in the saddle."

"Very well. I'll send for Elizabeth and we'll sup together, just the three of us."

Meg curtsied and dipped her head toward John. "I thank you, sir, for accompanying me home. I shall always look fondly upon the House of Glenorchy."

John bowed, as was customary. "'Twas my pleasure, m'lady. One of the more pleasant duties I've been assigned."

Before she entered the stairwell, Arthur gave her a once-over with a discerning eye. Dirty from the trail, she most likely looked frightful. A bath would be heavenly—after she read Duncan's missive. She walked with stately grace until she was positive Arthur could no longer see her. Then she ran up the three flights of stairs, skipping two steps at a time.

Pushing into her chamber, she hardly noticed the

familiar trappings. She headed straight to the window embrasure and sat on the padded bench—her favorite place, hidden behind the heavy window furs.

She rarely received a missive addressed to her, and never had received one from a man.

Carefully, she examined Duncan's seal. It presented a galley with eight oars and a large sail with a boar's head. Around the edge was the Campbell motto, "Follow me." She smiled when she read it. *Aye, Sir Duncan, I would follow you anywhere.* How quickly her pent-up ire had diffused.

Taking care not to damage the seal, she ran her finger beneath it. Her hands shook as she unfolded the vellum and read.

Dearest Lady Meg,

It is with a heavy heart that I write this missive, for you must know, if possible, I would have moved heaven and earth to accompany you back to your family. I never thanked you properly for caring for me when the fever hit. Without you, I would have been left in the gutter to rot, or worse. Perhaps a man like me deserves to be cast aside. I most certainly do not deserve your kindness.

However, now I'm off on the king's business, a customary state of affairs. As the king's enforcer, I find I am rarely ever home. I'd imagine that fact would not be particularly appealing to a gentlewoman such as you. You deserve so much more than I can give.

I will never forget your smile. It brought sunshine into my heart even when snowing. I shall always remember your eyes, because they could see through to my soul. I will always laugh when I think of your temper, for it makes each day so much more fascinating. But most of all, I will remember you, Lady Meg. Whether you recognize it or not, you have a kind heart, a tireless spirit and a razor-sharp wit. These are things a man never forgets.

I can only wish you the very best this short life has to offer. And truly, it would be an honor should our paths ever cross again.

Your servant in Christ,

Sir Duncan Campbell

Postscript: I have enclosed a poem I wrote this eve. I rarely apply my pen to such whimsical arts, though tonight it seemed appropriate.

Tears streaming down her face, Meg read the endearing poem over and over until the chambermaid, Cassie, pulled aside the furs. "Your bath is ready, m'lady." She stepped in and clapped a hand over her mouth. "Whatever is wrong?"

Meg took in a stuttered breath. "I've been a miserable fool, as usual." She dabbed her face in the crook of her arm.

Cassie reached for the missive. "You've had a terrible ordeal. Here, let me take that and we'll set you to rights."

Clutching Duncan's letter for dear life, Meg shook her head. "Nay. Leave me be. I need another moment to myself."

"Are you certain?" Cassie eyed her like a mother hen, though she was near enough to Meg's age. "You look like you need to talk."

"I'm sure there will be plenty of talking, just not at this moment." Meg shooed her away. "Now begone with you. I can manage from here."

"Very well. I'll put the bell beside the bath if you should need anything."

"Thank you." Meg honestly loved Cassie, but didn't want to share a thing about Duncan with anyone. She'd spent the past week convincing herself she hated the man, only to have the wall she'd built up to protect her broken heart smashed into tiny shards. Now what was she to do? She could no longer hate Duncan Campbell, or even feign dislike.

Blast him.

Meg stowed his missive in her keepsake box and locked it. She wouldn't have any snooping servants finding it and handing it over to Arthur. Duncan's words were meant for her eyes only.

She disrobed and cast her filthy garments to the floor. Lowering herself into the warm water, she sighed. Duncan hadn't callously left her without a word. She held the soap to her nose and inhaled. *Lemongrass—like Duncan.* Her heart squeezed. Would everything continue to remind her of him? How much time would pass before her heart stopped aching so?

❧

AFTER CASSIE RETURNED TO HELP MEG DRESS, SHE descended the stairs for dinner, hair brushed and wearing a plain black gown. She figured if she were to become a nun, she may as well dress the part.

Arthur preferred to have quiet meals in his solar when family business was afoot. Both Elizabeth and he were seated at the table as Meg entered. Arthur stood and grasped her hand. "Dear Meg, you look refreshed."

"Aye, the bath was invigorating." Meg crossed to Elizabeth and kissed her cheek. "What news?"

Her sister chuckled and patted Meg's arm. "My heavens, you've been kidnapped and then rescued by a mob of Highlanders and you're asking *me* for news?"

Meg walked to the other side of the table. "You make it sound so frightful."

"Was it not?"

Both Arthur and Elizabeth looked at her expectantly.

Taking a deep breath, Meg sat. "True, the kidnapping part was terrifying. However, the rescue was exciting and fraught with unimaginable danger." She waggled her eyebrows to add shocking effect.

Eyes bulging, Elizabeth patted her chest. "My heavens." The servant came in and placed a trencher of food before her. She picked up her eating knife. "I pray Lord Percy has chosen to abandon his feud against our clan."

Arthur frowned. "I'm sure Meg's rescue inflamed his ire tenfold. He has spies all over Southern Scotland. 'Tis a matter of time before he strikes again."

Meg shuddered. "Is there anything we can do to stop him? He's completely mad."

Arthur's lips formed a thin line while he reached for the wine. "I have it in hand. You needn't worry. He'll never touch you or any of my family again." He poured for her and then himself. "I've decided 'tis time for you to marry."

Meg nearly fell off her chair. "No."

Elizabeth reached for the bread. "Meg, darling, you cannot remain a spinster your entire life."

"Why ever not? I've made the decision to give myself to God."

Arthur placed the ewer on the table. "That is a preposterous notion."

Elizabeth nibbled a bite of her bread. "I agree. You are distraught, and in no state to make such a decision."

Meg clenched her fists under the table. "I strongly, most emphatically *disagree*. In fact, on my pilgrimage to Melrose, I was planning to gain an audience with the abbot to discuss taking up the veil."

Arthur slammed his fist on the table. "Becoming a nun is out of the question. You are far too beautiful to hide behind the cloistered walls of a nunnery."

Meg's insides jumped, but with every muscle in her body taut, she maintained her composure. "You cannot stop me," she said through clenched teeth.

"Or what? You'll spirit away and end up in Lord Percy's hands?" Arthur pushed back from the table and fumed.

Meg held up the claw. "Who in their right mind would want to marry a decrepit maid?"

Elizabeth gasped. "Oh please, Meg."

Arthur leaned forward and pointed. "There a number of nobles who wish to make alliances with our house. For God's sake, Meg, *think*. You are the daughter of an earl."

She stared at her brother's accusing finger. "I will not allow you to use me as a pawn to increase our holdings."

Elizabeth's gaze softened. "Let us all relax. You said yourself you've been through a terrible ordeal. You must give it some time."

Arthur snatched up his goblet. "Agreed. We will make no decisions until you have a chance to recover from your fright."

Meg stabbed a slice of lamb with her eating knife. "I thank the good Lord for small mercies." Heaven's stars, she'd only just arrived and Arthur was already plotting her wedding to some lofty old member of the gentry. She didn't care what either of them said. She'd have none of it. No man in Scotland could match the allure of Sir Duncan Campbell. If she could not marry the dark knight, she would marry no one.

Arthur sipped and peered over the top of his goblet. "Perhaps we should attend court for the Easter celebration. Half the nobles will be in attendance for certain."

Chapter Twenty

Duncan rode over the barbican drawbridge beside his father, their horses clomping a rhythm akin to a death knell. He spat at the sour taste pervading his mouth. Together they led their men through the well-guarded gatehouse under the guise that they were meeting with the Earl of Mar regarding a lucrative wool-trading venture. As planned, they'd arrived late afternoon, not long before the evening meal.

The burly master-at-arms met them while they dismounted in Kildrummy Castle's expansive courtyard. "You're in luck. The earl has agreed to see you." The man didn't smile.

Da handed his reins to the groom. "If I know Lord John Stewart, he won't want to pass up a chance to swindle the English."

"I'll leave such dealings to his lordship." The henchman gestured to Duncan's men. "Are you planning to stay the night?"

"Aye," Duncan said. "We've been a sennight on the trail. My men would appreciate a pallet with fresh straw."

"Very well. They can bed down in the southwest tower." The big man waved his hand over his head and pointed.

Duncan bowed his head. "My thanks." Being met with cordiality made a distasteful task all the more difficult. However, the Earl of Mar stood accused. If he was indeed innocent, he could provide evidence to disprove the charges in Edinburgh. Duncan need only bring the man in, and he doubted the earl would go willingly. No one ever took kindly of being taken into custody.

He walked beside Da as the guard led them into the tower at the southeast corner. Of course the main keep had to be the furthest building from the gate, making a quick escape dubious.

Da leaned into him. "Can ye see the postern?" he whispered.

Duncan scanned the back of the courtyard. Lined with buildings, if there was a back gate, it would most likely be a part of the catacombs below. "Nay."

"Blast."

"At least we've earned an invitation to meet the earl." Duncan nudged Da's shoulder. "I only wish you would have stayed at the camp. Your eyesight grows worse by the day."

"My eyes are fine. Besides, I'm still Lord of Glenorchy, and best to negotiate with the earl."

"Very well." Duncan cupped his hand over his mouth to ensure he wouldn't be heard. "Make him an offer he cannot refuse and we'll see he's filled with whisky before he retires this night."

They climbed the winding stairwell to the second floor, where they were ushered into the solar. Smiling, the earl rose. Duncan estimated the man could be no more than five and twenty.

Da stepped forward and offered his hand. "'Tis good to see you, m'lord."

"Glenorchy." The earl accepted the hand and turned his attention to Duncan. "And who might this be?"

"Sir Duncan Campbell, m'lord."

Colin grinned. "My heir."

"Welcome. Sit." The earl gestured to the big wooden table filling the room and moved to the sideboard. "You must be parched after your travels."

"Aye." Colin sat. "A tankard of ale would go down nicely."

"Ale?" The earl lifted a glass ewer. "The brewmaster has just brought up a new flagon of whisky."

"Then whisky it is," Colin said.

Duncan sauntered to the window before he sat. Pulling aside the furs, he looked out over the back of the estate. The property sloped down a steep ravine to a river. A man carried two pails of water up the incline, along a path leading to the east tower.

"Sir Duncan, would you care for a tot?" the earl asked.

He dropped the fur curtain back across the window. "Thank you. I see you have an ample supply of fresh water from the river."

"Aye, the Snow Tower here receives fresh water on all seven floors—brought by a pulley system." The earl served the whisky with his own hand, looking pleased with himself. "Quite a work of ingenuity, I'll say."

Da sipped. "Kildrummy Castle has always been one of the better-equipped fortresses in the realm."

"Aye, and I've plans to make it even better."

Duncan hated brainless babble. His mind wandered while Da continued to stroke the earl's ego. Indeed, there was a rear gate, which he'd inspect at his first opportunity. He wanted to avoid a skirmish, especially with Da in tow. With its row of shiny black cannons, the Kildrummy gatehouse was one of the most fortified he'd ever seen. If Duncan and his men erred they'd be slaughtered, a bloodbath neatly contained within the walls.

"What is this my henchman tells me about selling wool to the English?" the earl asked.

Lord Glenorchy grinned. "Aye, last season the flies severely hurt the southern flocks."

"I can fetch four crowns per pound in Aberdeen."

"I can guarantee you six," Da lied.

"Six?" The earl licked his lips. "But transport would consume the added profits."

"Nay." Da shook his head. "If you can transfer the wool to a transport in Aberdeen, my galleys will take it from there."

Och, Da could spin a string of drivel and make it sound tempting. He'd go to hell for certain, and Duncan would be right behind him.

After the two noblemen shook hands to close the deal, Duncan and his father were escorted to their rooms to prepare for supper. Duncan thanked the groom. "Are we on the top floor?"

"Nay. The donjon has seven floors. You're on the fifth."

"My, that is impressive. I imagine his lordship gets a great deal of exercise climbing seven floors to his apartments."

"Aye, 'tis why his rooms are on the second floor."

"Indeed?" Duncan said. "I suppose that makes sense, given the secure location along the back bailey wall."

"Yes, sir. Kildrummy's walls are impenetrable."

Duncan arched his brow and made a mental note not to be quite so accommodating in the future. Kilchurn chamber locks must be inspected for sturdiness, and the grooms would be instructed not to be so free with their tongues.

Once the man left, Duncan slipped into his father's chamber. "You had quite a yarn with the earl."

"Aye, young men are easy to impress, and the earl's no different."

Duncan crossed to the window and pulled aside the

furs. Da had a view of the courtyard. "Why, do you suppose?"

"They're all eager to build upon their wealth, make their mark in the world."

"I'd wager that's why so many of them fall into ruin."

Da grasped Duncan's arm. "'Tis good ye see it now, for one day you'll be Lord of Glenorchy, and I'd turn in my grave if you were gullible enough to believe the lies I spewed today. No man in their right mind from here to Spain would agree to six crowns a pound of wool."

"Aye." Duncan nodded thoughtfully. "I'd best be off to find the postern gate."

"My guess is 'tis near the kitchens."

"Mine as well—then I'm considering asking the men to ride out on sentry duty. They'll be safer outside the walls."

Da walked toward the door with him. "But we'll need some fighting men inside."

Duncan stopped. "You think it necessary?"

"Have you learned nothing in all your years of fostering? Expect the unexpected and you'll not end up with your throat cut."

Duncan should have kept his mouth shut. He knew something could—*would*—go wrong. No plan was ironclad, but they would also raise suspicion if too many Glenorchy guards loitered near the rear gate.

Once in the passageway, he listened for footsteps in the stairwell. When certain he could slip away without drawing attention, he quietly descended the Snow Tower stairs. On the first floor, servants bustled about, preparing for the evening meal. Duncan chose to walk outside and continue on toward the northeast tower. Just as he'd predicted, there was an alleyway to the gate right alongside the kitchen. He slipped through and inspected the portcullis with its iron spikes pointing downward—designed to impale an enemy. *They probably close the blasted thing after the meal is served.* He didn't like it. The gate was two feet thick and reinforced with iron.

Scratching his chin, Duncan turned.

"Just what do you think you're doing snooping around the kitchen doors?" A giant of a man with a missing front tooth confronted him, fists on his hips.

Duncan glanced toward the kitchen entry, could smell the bread baking within. "Ah, I spent the day in the saddle. Thought I'd see if I could pinch a wee morsel of bread."

"I ought to chop off your finger for stealing."

Duncan slid his palm over his dirk. He didn't want to cause a stir, but the big oaf ought to know who the earl's guests were before he started threatening to amputate digits. Instead, Duncan held up his palms in surrender. "No harm done. I shall wait and take my meal with the earl."

The big man took a step in and grasped the collar of Duncan's surcoat, rubbing the fine leather between his fingers. "Are ye Lord Campbell?"

"Sir Campbell, Lord Glenorchy's heir." He batted the man's hand away. "And you, sir, have overstepped your station."

The man's jaw dropped, making him look rather dumb. "Apologies, m'lord. I thought ye were one of the guards milling about."

"Aye?" Duncan couldn't resist. "Every one of my men is a knight as well."

"Truth?"

"Would I dare lie to a fellow as large as you?"

"Uh."

Duncan squeezed past him. "If you do not mind, I shall be on my way." Without looking back, he strode across the courtyard. At least the brute was a simpleton. Had he a lick of sense, he would have suspected

Duncan of examining the postern gate, not trying to pinch food.

※

Duncan met his father in the great hall. As in all large castles, a number of people amassed. Most guests served the earl, many of them fighting men. Duncan had been in more precarious situations, though on this sortie something didn't sit well with him—many things, actually.

The big man who'd caught him at the back gate stood beside the man-at-arms, and together they eyed Duncan and his father as they proceeded to the dais. His visit to the rear gate would no longer be a secret.

The henchman frowned and stroked his fingers down his beard. *He suspects something.*

Across the hall, Duncan's men sat at a modest table, one far beneath their rank, as was usual when they tried not to draw attention to themselves. The henchman followed him and took his place behind the earl, serving as protector while the great man ate.

The Earl of Mar stood and beckoned them, gesturing to the two seats to his left. "Come sit beside me, Lord Colin."

A harpist appeared on the gallery and launched into a Celtic ballad. When the earl clapped his hands, servants poured from the kitchen door and proceeded to the dais. As customary, the high table was served first with a rich assortment of meats and breads.

Da peered closely at the trencher and selected a well-marbled piece of beef. "You put on a fine display, m'lord."

"My thanks." The earl lifted the ewer. "Will you have a tankard of ale?"

"Don't mind if I do." Da held up his cup to the servant. "If it is anything like your whisky, I'm sure it will be most enjoyable."

Duncan scanned the table. Only ale had been set out.

"Aye, I prefer drinking ale at night," the earl said. "Too much whisky dulls my wits."

Ballocks, another of their plans thwarted. From the corner of his eye, Duncan regarded the henchman standing behind the earl, massive arms folded, daggers lashed to every limb, a sword on one hip, a dirk on the other. The weaponry didn't surprise him, but the man had a deadly glint to his eye. No doubt, if he suspected them of skullduggery, that man would be guarding the earl's door this night.

Duncan cut a piece of meat and savored it while he mulled over their plan. The king employed the Highland Enforcers because they were swift and effective, and Duncan intended to uphold that reputation.

A light flickered at the back of Duncan's mind. *Perfect.*

"How are the deer running this season?" he asked.

The earl gestured to the henchman with his thumb. "Malcom tells me a sizeable herd has recently moved onto our lands to the east."

Duncan cut another slice of meat. "How fortunate."

"You're an avid hunter?"

"Aye." Duncan's gaze met with Da's. "Especially night sport."

The henchman snorted loudly.

Duncan grinned. "Do not tell me you haven't tried it, m'lord."

Da kicked him under the table.

Duncan reached across and topped up Da's tankard. "The beasts are easier to stun in the darkness."

The earl wiped his mouth on his sleeve. "You do not say? What guides you, moonlight?"

"And a few torches—not to mention a wager or two."

"I like the sound of that even better." The earl elbowed Da. "What say you, Glenorchy—I'd wager my henchman against your son here."

"At what odds?" Da looked appropriately amused.

Smiling on the inside, Duncan sipped his ale. Indeed, it was a hearty brew. While the lords settled on their wager, he made eye contact with Eoin across the hall. Slightly raising his chin, Duncan notified the knight there had been a change in plans.

Chapter Twenty-One

Duncan and his men saddled their mounts at the far end of the stable. Da tugged on his horse's girth a fair bit harder than necessary. "Why the blazes did you change the strategy?"

"The henchman suspected something. I felt it in my gut. Besides, there wasn't a flagon of whisky in the entire hall. The milk-livered earl doesn't like the way it makes him *feel* after he sups."

Da shook his head. "It might be all right for you to hunt at breakneck speed during the black of night, but I can barely see the path ahead in daylight."

"Did I say we'd be galloping?" Duncan beckoned the men around and lowered his voice. "We're going on the hunt, aye, but we'll not be hunting mule deer. Once we reach the herd, we'll cut the earl away whilst the others run after the beasts. With any luck, we'll be long gone before the earl's guard realizes what's happened."

"Aye, but they'll be coming after us for certain," Sean said.

Duncan pointed at Sean "the ghost's" sternum. "Not if you take care of their leader. Once that beast of a man is out of the picture, it'll be a day or two before they regroup."

Da mounted. "I hope ye ken what you're doing."

"I think 'tis bloody brilliant," Eoin said.

Duncan did too, though he would never admit it. One way or another, they'd have a fight. "At least this will take us outside the castle walls. Stay close to me, Da. I'll be your eyes."

Once everyone mounted, they gathered in the courtyard with the Earl of Mar clad in a full suit of armor.

Cumbersome. Duncan and his men wore only breastplates and helms to keep their burdens light. "Are you planning to ride into battle, m'lord?" Da asked.

"Nay, but a man can never be too careful in these times."

"Aye." Duncan rode beside them. "Especially the king's brother."

The earl held a flask to his mouth and tipped it back. He licked his lips and held it out. "Would you care for a tot?"

Da eyed him. "I thought the spirit dulled your wits."

The earl grinned. "Not when there's a hunt on."

Duncan took the flask and pretended to sip while he scanned the Kildrummy men. It appeared whisky flasks were standard fare when hunting with the Earl of Mar. He sat a little taller in his saddle. If the men were half in their cups, it certainly would make the night's work easier for him.

Duncan held back while the procession traversed the barbican. He, his father, and his five men were outnumbered three to one. Not bad odds, though he didn't like the crossbows a few of the earl's sentries carried. Erratic weapons, they could be triggered by a twitch of the finger.

Malcom, the henchman, led them to a hill, and, true to his word, a herd of deer grazed in the valley below, highlighted blue by the moonlight. He pointed north. "The best way down is the path yonder."

Duncan spurred his horse forward. "What are we

waiting for?" Indeed, this was a great vantage point, and to the south the wood sprawled as far as he could see. If he could scare the herd toward the forest, the hunting party would scatter for certain.

The pace quickened as they descended single file. Da rode behind Duncan, holding one of the torches. Next time, he'd insist the old man stay at home. Bloody hell, a mission was difficult enough without worrying about his father's failing eyesight.

At the bottom of the hill, the earl's men surged ahead, and the pace sped to a gallop. Bellowing riders charged toward the herd. Duncan had no choice but to keep stride with the others. He glanced over his shoulder. Da's torch had fallen a few lengths behind.

Galloping at the front of the mayhem, Malcom pulled his bow off his shoulder and tossed his reins in his mouth. With a roar, the henchman dug in his heels and spurred his horse faster. Following suit, Duncan charged ahead, bellowing like an idiot. But, just as he'd planned, the deer spooked and headed for the trees.

Malcom and his men drove their horses in a myriad of directions, resembling a mob of drunkards. Sean didn't miss a beat, and remained on the henchman's heels. Slowing his horse, Duncan looked over his shoulder and spotted the earl. Just as he'd instructed, his men galloped up to either side of him, gradually steering him southwest, away from Malcom and the others.

Duncan circled back. A flash illuminated the corner of his eye and fizzled. *Good, Da doused the torch as planned.* "Over here," he bellowed to ensure the old man hadn't lost the trail.

Once they hit the trees, Duncan raced in behind the earl. Eoin wasted no time and grasped the earl's reins, pulling the hoses to a stop.

"What the devil?" the earl balked.

Duncan hopped off his horse and marched ahead.

The earl reached for his sword, but Duncan latched on to the man's wrist and twisted with brute force. "In the name of King James, I hereby take you into custody for the charge of practicing witchcraft against his royal highness." He removed the earl's weapons.

The blue-black shadows of the forest made the earl's face look cadaverous. "Witchcraft? Are you completely out of your mind?"

Eoin made quick work of binding John Stewart's hands while Duncan strapped the earl's weapons to his saddle. "'Tis a question you need to pose to your brother when we reach Edinburgh."

Lord Stewart didn't even try to fight. "I cannot believe I shared the same womb with that superstitious fool."

Duncan remounted—this was by far the easiest mission he'd carried out on behalf of the king. "Come, men. Let us be on our way before one of the Kildrummy guards decides he's a hero." He scanned the faces through the darkness. Where the hell was Da? Duncan turned his horse toward the tree line—no movement flickered in the shadows.

He would not leave his father behind. *Blast. He was supposed to stay beside me.* "Eoin, carry on. I'll double back for the Lord of Glenorchy."

Duncan crept through the trees, listening. In the distance, the hunt continued. Had anyone realized the earl had disappeared? Where were Sean and Malcolm? Following his original path, Duncan trotted to the edge of the clearing where the deer had first been spotted.

"Where is the earl?" someone shouted across the glade.

Time was running out. Soon a search would be on. Duncan kept to the cliff's shadows, his gaze frantically searching through the darkness. Something moved ahead. He stopped and strained to make it out. A body hunched over a horse. Duncan blinked, but could discern no more. If he called out, they'd hear him for certain. He had no choice but to ride closer.

The shouts grew louder.

Duncan neared. "Da?" he whispered.

"Leave me," a voice strained.

It *was* him. Duncan quickly closed the distance and hopped off his mount. "Da! What happened?"

Da grunted. "Shot through the leg...blood."

Sure enough, an iron-tipped arrow from a crossbow lodged deep into Da's thigh. The Black Knight growled through his teeth, wise enough to know bellowing could see them both killed.

Duncan ran his hand below Da's leg. The horse's barrel was thick with blood. "Why did you not stay beside me?"

"Too...dark."

"Christ's bones, Da."

"Leave me. My blood's almost drained. I can feel it."

Duncan's stomach convulsed. He clenched his fist and growled. "No chance on this earth will I leave you behind." He would see his father to safety if it was his last act upon this earth.

Kildrummy scouts approached. Duncan grasped the reins of both horses and pulled them into the burn beneath the cover of a weeping willow. Da moaned. Duncan pressed his lips to his ear. "Stay quiet until the sentries pass."

God strike him dead, this was his fault. He was the most selfish lout who ever bore the Campbell name.

Duncan clutched his sword and crouched, every muscle taut. The bloody bastards rode within a stone's throw.

Da's laboring breath beside Duncan's ear sounded like the bellows of a bagpipe being emptied. Duncan's hand itched to run forward and cut them down, but fighting this close to Kildrummy Castle could bring on the earl's entire army.

"Malcom's down!" someone bellowed from across the glade.

The two scouts exchanged glances and cantered toward the noise. Duncan didn't hesitate. "Hold on, Da. I'll lead you to safety."

Grinding his teeth, Duncan trotted the horses back to the wood. Once under cover of the forest, he dug in his spurs. He would stop at the first cottage in sight. A stone the size of his helm weighed heavily in the pit of his stomach. Every muscle tense, Duncan choked on a sickly lump in his throat. He'd seen men bleed out from a deep wound to the thigh. *By God, Da will not die this night.*

&

THE VILLAGE OF HUNTLY DIDN'T VEER TOO FAR FROM the path the enforcers had opted to take. Duncan knew he'd find a farmhouse on the outskirts, and drove the horses southwest at a frenzied gait. His eyes stung with unshed tears when the smoke from a chimney spiraled light grey against the black sky. He drove the horses harder, clenching the reins in tight fists.

"We're nearly there, Da."

Father listed awkwardly over his mount's neck.

Duncan's heart wrenched. *Hang on, Father.*

He reined the horses to a skidding stop outside the cottage door. "I'll have you inside in a moment." He leapt down and pulled Da from his horse, hefting him over his shoulder. Duncan ran to the door and kicked repeatedly. "In the name of King James and all that is holy, help us!"

He reached for the latch as the door opened. A man peered out, sword in hand. Duncan had no time to deal with an armed crofter. He pushed through. "My da's suffered an arrow shot to his leg."

The man faced him, sword raised. "And who might you be?"

Duncan carefully laid Da on the table. "I am Sir Duncan Campbell, and this is my father, the Lord of Glenorchy."

Lowering his sword, the man scratched his head. "I'll be a bleating monk of Judas."

Duncan glanced to the hearth. "Stoke the fire. I need the poker flaming hot, and bring some rags."

"Aye, m'lord."

Duncan removed Da's helm and smoothed a hand over his head. "Hang on. We'll have the bleeding stanched in no time."

Da raised his lids slightly. "Nay." Even in the dim light, he looked whiter than a blanket of snow.

"I need to remove the arrow."

"Duncan." Da reached for his hand.

Blast it all, there was no time to waste. "Aye?"

Da's tongue shot out and licked dry lips. "Promise"—he drew a stuttered breath—"you'll go to Edinburgh with the earl."

A dry wedge felt like it lodged itself in Duncan's throat. "In God's name, I will see you back to Kilchurn."

"No." Da strengthened his grip. "You must finish... mission. This is your time. Delivering the earl to the king will bring"—he coughed—"favor upon you and our house."

"But—"

Da hissed through his teeth, squeezing Duncan's hand. "No matter what happens, do not delay. Promise me."

"Aye. I give my word."

Duncan tried to pull away. Da held fast. His eyes rolled back with a sticky swallow. "Tell your"—he gasped—"mother I'll always love her."

"No. You will not die here." Duncan threw a look over his shoulder. "Is that damned poker ready?"

The crofter turned it over in the fire. "Not yet, m'lord."

Duncan reached for a flagon and uncorked it. "A swig of whisky will ease your pain." His fingers trembled as he poured a dram into Da's mouth.

His Adam's apple bobbed and he coughed weakly. "You must not delay."

Duncan could have breathed flames through his nose. Da lay on the board, an inch from death, and he was worried about the mission? Duncan drew his dirk and cut away the breeks over the arrow. "Is that whisky warming your belly?"

Da uttered not a word.

Duncan's gut clenched, and he forced his gaze to shift to his father's face. For a moment he thought the worst, until Da's chest rose and fell. "Da?" he asked, but the lord didn't respond. He turned to the crofter. "Mercifully, he's unconscious."

The man nodded and held up the red-tipped poker. "'Tis ready."

Duncan straightened. "He's already lost too much blood. When I pull out the arrow, jam the poker in the wound straight away."

Chapter Twenty-Two

※

Lord Percy excused himself from the table when the groom advised his errant man-at-arms had returned. He met Isaac in the solar. "Where in God's name have you been?"

Shoulders slumped, hair unkempt, a yellowed bruise beneath his eye, Isaac looked like he'd aged twenty years. "The man's name is Sir Duncan Campbell. He's the heir to the Lordship of Glenorchy."

Isaac glanced toward the flagon of brandy on the sideboard, but Percy made no move to pour for the miserable sop. "Is that all?"

"He's the leader of a band of men called the Highland Enforcers. I believe most members are nobles. The king of Scotland uses them to maintain order in the north."

"I daresay that would be an insurmountable task." Percy stood and sauntered to the sideboard, pulling the flagon's stopper. "They mostly undertake the king's business, you say?"

"From what I could gather from the suspicious, miserable Scots around Glen Orchy. I witnessed Sir Campbell ride out with his men hours before another contingent departed Kilchurn with Lady Meg. I trailed her retinue as far as Edinburgh, and then headed south."

Lord Percy rubbed his hands. "Interesting, indeed. A man in the king's service could find himself in any manner of trouble."

Isaac looked as if he were going to drop where he stood. "True."

"Do you know why this Sir Duncan rode with such haste?"

Isaac spread his callused palms. "No m'lord. He rode north, whilst the others turned south."

Percy made a show of pouring himself a glass of brandy, then sipped loudly. "I have the fortunate opportunity to appear before King James as an emissary for King Edward." Percy chuckled. "It seems both sides are interested in strengthening their little truce. Perhaps a trip to Edinburgh could serve two purposes."

Lord Percy's gaze drifted to Isaac. The man was tenacious if nothing else. If he hadn't returned with Lady Meg, or her rescuer's head, he'd planned to dismiss the bumbling idiot. But he'd brought back a tidbit of useful information. Percy shooed him away with a flick of his wrist. "That is all. Please remove yourself, and the next time I see you, you'd better appear and *smell* a damned sight more presentable."

Isaac bowed. "As you wish, my lord."

&

DUNCAN FINALLY CAUGHT UP WITH HIS MEN NEAR Perth.

Though Da wouldn't have wanted it, Duncan had let his father sleep until dawn. Then the crofter had helped him carry his father to the horses.

The old man slipped in and out of consciousness during the arduous journey, but he uttered not a word of complaint. Hunched over astride his stallion, the

Lord of Glenorchy was too weak to sit upright. All the while, Duncan admonished himself for his bullheadedness. Over and over his mind replayed what had happened, recounting all the things he should have done to protect his father.

He'd held Da's life in his hands. Death was eminently final. His father had come too close to paying the greatest price for Duncan's bravado—his grand plan. *Night hunting? I'm an unmitigated fool.* If he would have been more attentive to Da's whereabouts, Father mightn't be struggling for his life on the back of a horse.

Duncan blamed himself. Alas, there was no other person who could be accused. Da warned against riding on a hunt at night. He'd complained about his failing vision, too. But had Duncan listened? No. He'd just barreled ahead, hell-bent on proving his own worth. His arrogance had gravely wounded his father. Duncan glanced over his shoulder. From Da's pale complexion, the baron wasn't weathering his injury well. He needed a bed, damn it, lest he succumb to his wounds altogether.

"Campbell here," Duncan hollered to avoid an arrow in the gut as he rode in behind his men.

Eoin was the first to pull up his mount and look behind. His face turned ashen. "My God."

Each man looked to Da hunched over his horse's neck and then met Duncan's gaze. His self-loathing sank with the weight of an anchor. Steeling his wits, he explained what had happened.

"Serves him right, you backstabber," the Earl of Mar said.

With a spike of rage, Duncan leapt from his horse, latched his hands on the earl's collar and pulled him to the ground. With an inhuman wail, Duncan slammed his fist into the bastard's face. The earl tried to protect himself with his bound hands, but Duncan batted them down with his left and hurled his fist into the man's face with his right.

Pulling back for another blow, someone stopped his fist midair. Duncan spun around and barreled into Eoin, tackling him before the MacGregor could utter a word. Duncan focused his ire on his best friend. All five knights pounced. Duncan struggled under the pressure of knees and hands pinning him to the ground.

Robert squeezed his fingers around Duncan's neck. "Calm yourself."

He thrashed while a man held him down by each shoulder and hip. "Let me at him, you miserable lot of sheep-biters." His body shook with his need to rip something apart.

Robert squeezed his hand tighter. "And deliver a dead man to the king? Just where do you think that'll get you?"

Duncan shuddered. His father had demanded he complete the mission, and he'd all but minced the earl's face. Grinding his teeth, he stopped struggling. "Let go."

"Will you control your ire?" Eoin asked, rubbing his jaw.

"Aye. A bloody demon came over me." With the release of their hands, Duncan sat up. He stared at the earl, who was bleeding from the nose. "Da demanded I follow through with our duty and report to the king."

"Jesus," Sean said, shoving his fingers through his thick hair.

Duncan eyed his cousins. As kin, they were best suited to take his father home. "Robert and James, find a cart and take Da back to me ma. Tell her I'll ride night and day until I make it home."

They both offered thin-lipped nods.

Duncan gestured toward the earl. "Clean him up and put him back on his horse."

"The devil will claim your soul," the earl said.

"Aye?" Duncan planted his fists on his hips. "Is that witchcraft you're using? 'Cause if it is, I'll not hesitate to bear witness to his highness."

"I've no idea to what you are referring. My miserable brother is scared to death I'll plot against him. This contrived charge is a ploy to come after me first."

Duncan watched Eoin and Sean help the earl mount. "If you are innocent, the court will release you. 'Tis why the king hired us to bring you in, else he would have ordered your death."

The earl smirked. "If you believe that, you are a greater fool than I."

AFTER DELIVERING THE EARL TO SIR SIMON PRESTON at Craigmillar, Duncan hastened to the royal lodgings at Holyrood Abbey where the king preferred to reside, a mile away from Edinburgh Castle.

Accompanied by his men, Duncan strode into the king's antechamber and addressed the chancellor with purpose. "Sir Duncan Campbell, heir to the Barony of Glenorchy, at your service." He bowed. "I've delivered the king's *package* to Craigmillar as directed."

The man frowned. "The king expected to see the Lord of Glenorchy. Has something gone awry?"

"Indeed it has." Duncan's gut twisted with guilt. "My father was struck by an arrow as we made our escape. If it pleases the king, I should like to make my report forthwith so that I may return home and see to his health."

"An arrow?"

"Aye." Duncan glanced away, wishing the man would stop asking questions.

"And he still lives?"

"The wound is grave, but with God's will, I shall see him recover."

With a skeptical frown, the chancellor ran his fingers over the medallion signifying his rank. "Wait here. I shall relay your message."

Eoin tapped Duncan's elbow. "Come, sit."

He jerked his arm away. "I'd rather be on my way."

"I ken, but we've no choice but to wait."

They sat in chairs upholstered with ornate embroidery, reflective of scenes from God's creation of the world. Duncan leaned forward and rested his elbows on his knees. His head pounded.

The men knew to be quiet. They most likely were stunned as well. Colin Campbell had fostered them all, turned them from pimple-faced adolescents into the most elite fighting men in Scotland. Black Colin of Rome was their hero, a man who could never succumb to an arrow wound.

Duncan replayed the night hunt over and over in his head. How could he have prevented Da from being shot? How did he lose sight of him during the hunt? He'd always been such a strong leader, Duncan had never considered that aging might have weakened Da in any way.

Why did I not realize he'd fallen behind sooner?

When the door to the king's chamber opened, Duncan scarcely remembered where he was. Duncan looked up and wiped a hand down the beard that had grown in since leaving Kilchurn nearly two weeks ago.

"Duncan Campbell, Lord of Glenorchy," bellowed the page.

Duncan gulped. "My father still lives. I am Sir Duncan Campbell, son of the said Lord of Glenorchy." He resisted the powerful urge to slam his fist into the young man's face. The slight of tongue should not go unpunished, but now was not the time for a fistfight. Flanked by Eoin and Sean, Duncan proceeded into King James's chamber. His majesty sat upon a wide throne, clad in black velvet, his head topped with an ermine bonnet.

As customary, Duncan knelt and bowed his head. "The Earl of Mar has been delivered to Craigmillar, sire."

"But not without heavy losses, I understand." The king's reedy voice grated with an accusing tone.

"Aye. My father was hit by a stray arrow from a crossbow. We led the earl out of Kildrummy by enticing him to partake in a sport of night hunting. Unfortunately, all did not go as planned."

"Hunting at night?" The king rubbed his hands and chuckled. "An ingenious challenge—however, 'tis a wonder not more were killed."

Duncan's shoulder twitched. "I suppose it did confuse the earl's guard enough for us to spirit him away without them any the wiser."

The king spread his palms. "I am impressed with your ingenuity, especially to your king."

Duncan bowed his head. "Forgive me, sire."

"Rise." The king reclined in his throne and crossed his legs at the knees. "The Earl of Angus tells me he's pleased with the return of his sister."

Duncan stood, but couldn't meet the king's gaze. If the Earl of Angus knew Duncan had lain with Meg, he wouldn't be so bloody happy. "Thank you, sire." God knew Duncan's failings, and one day he'd burn in hell.

"I'd like you to dine with me tonight. It would be amusing to hear the details of your recent pursuits."

Duncan bowed deeply. "I thank your highness for your generous invitation, but I must away home. I've a father to attend and a mother to console."

"But 'tis nearly time for the evening meal—surely you cannot take your leave until the morrow."

"Forgive me." Keeping his head bowed, Duncan took a step back. "I gave my word that I would ride night and day until I returned to Kilchurn. Please excuse my impertinence, sire."

"Very well." The king's gaze traveled from Duncan's head to his feet. "Perhaps some other time."

"I would enjoy that very much."

The king's frown was decidedly forbidding as he flicked his wrist and waved Duncan away.

Now he'd disappointed the king on top of it all. Duncan ground his back molars. It couldn't be helped. The king could not be so crass that he expected Duncan to ignore his duty to clan and family.

After a final bow, Duncan led Eoin and Sean back to the antechamber. But the page's next announcement stopped him dead. "The Earl of Northumberland from Alnwick, England."

Heart hammering in his chest, Duncan looked up to see Lord Percy's pinched face. The man puffed out his chest and strode straight past him, too filled with his own importance to give Duncan a glance.

What the hell is that bastard doing in Scotland?

꙳

MEG PULLED HER CLOAK SNUG AROUND HER shoulders and headed for the castle garden. When she stepped outside, Midge and Max bounded up to her, rubbing their scruffy coats against her legs.

"Och, ye wee beasties, would you like to help me?"

In the past, she'd spent some time in the gardener's workshop, but her days tending Duncan made her realize the importance of herbal lore. Also, any nun worth her salt would need a good understanding of the healing arts.

Though spring was near, the trees were still barren of leaves. Only brown, skeletal stalks of last summer's harvest sprouted from the lines of planting boxes. As usual, the path to the workshop was so soggy, Meg had to hold up her skirts to avoid getting them muddy.

Hubert, the old gardener, sat hunched on a stool, snipping the roots from a clump of a dried plant. He wore layers of woolens with a navy plaid draped across his shoulders.

Standing in the entrance, Meg cleared her throat.

Hubert glanced up with his kind, rheumy eyes. "Lady Meg? What brings you out to the garden on this chilly day?"

She stepped inside. A peat fire smoldered in a brazier at the center of the room. Meg waved her hand to clear the haze of smoke. "Two more sennights and we shall pass the vernal equinox."

"That we will." He held up the clump of roots. "'Tis why I'm preparing this avens for planting."

"Avens? 'Tis an important herb, no?"

"In my opinion, the most important." He snipped thoughtfully. "The Benedictines call it 'the blessed herb.'"

Meg's attention piqued. "Aside from flavoring ale and preserving linen, does it have healing properties?" She pulled another stool from beneath the table and sat.

"Aye, avens is used for a great many remedies. It can keep a wound from bleeding out, and some say 'tis more effective than St. John's wort for dressing deep cuts and preventing them from turning putrid." He held the clump to the light and examined his work. "And a tincture can be made from boiling its roots—administer it for the ague, sore throat, headache and chills."

"All that? My heavens, no wonder they call it blessed."

Quietly, Meg watched Hubert work. She doubted the Gypsy salve contained avens. If it had, Duncan wouldn't have succumbed to the sweat. But she wouldn't mention it to Hubert. If anyone at Tantallon were to discover exactly how familiar she'd become with Sir Duncan, she'd be locked in her chamber for life. "So, when will you plant your avens?"

"Ye must be wary and not sow too early, lest a frost kill the shoots. But ye do no' want to leave it too late, either."

"May Day, then?"

"Aye, mid-April at the earliest, but keep in mind ye need a healthy crop by midsummer."

Meg hung on his every word. "What medicinal herbs should a castle garden never be without?"

"Well." Hubert scratched his chin and looked to the rafters. "I've quite a list, but ye'd never find me without avens, of course...St. John's wort, mallow, comfrey, feverfew—especially when there are bairns about."

"For the colic?"

"Aye." He rubbed his head as if trying to access the recesses of his memory. "Valerian, common house leek and hollyhock."

Meg repeated each word as he said them. As soon as she returned to her chamber, she'd write them down. "Now I need you to tell me what ailments each herb cures."

Hubert sputtered a guffaw. "I haven't all day to laze about and give ye a lesson."

"No?" Meg straightened and raised her chin. "I disagree, and I believe Lord Arthur would as well. Now, let us start with valerian."

With an audible sigh, Hubert launched into a recitation of the herb, how best to grow it, and its proven as well as unproven uses. Meg's head swooned with information. Hubert's lessons would take a great many days to relate. Next time she'd bring a quill and parchment. Over the years, gardeners might store all their knowledge in their heads, but she wanted a record to which she could refer.

When he finished with valerian, Hubert inhaled

deeply, as if he'd never strung so many words together at once in his life.

Meg patted his shoulder. "My thanks. Perhaps I can come back on the morrow with a bit of parchment. I want to be sure to note every detail."

He stared with his mouth agape. "The morrow, m'lady?" He removed his bonnet and scratched his thinning hair. "I dunna ken—"

"I'm most certain Lord Arthur will approve." She offered a consoling smile. "If we cover one herb per day, it should not be too taxing. Besides, you cannot expect to keep such vast knowledge in your head for an eternity. What if you were to forget something?"

"Ah, m'lady, I never forget."

"Are you certain?" she asked. He twisted his mouth with hesitation. Meg held up a finger and stood. "Everyone forgets something." She moved to the doorway. "I shall see you midmorning on the morrow and let us talk about mallow."

She didn't wait for him to answer—she abruptly turned and collided with Arthur. Sputtering, he grasped her shoulders and pulled her back along the path. "The valet told me he'd seen you head for the gardens. Whatever are you doing out here in Hubert's cold workshop?"

She tugged her arm from his grasp. "I've realized I need to know a fair bit more about herbal remedies if I'm to bec—"

"Become?"

Why must her brother always tie her stomach in knots? "Merciful mercy, Arthur, it matters not. Wife or nun, I need to know more about healing."

"Now that's my Meg. Always worried about caring for others." He stopped and faced her. "'Tis good to see you focusing on something useful."

Meg exhaled. If Arthur would have forbidden her from seeing Hubert again, she might have lost all control and slapped him across the face. How dare he interfere with something that would be so trivial to an earl, anyway? Then she recalled the valet had told Arthur of her whereabouts. "Were you looking for me?"

"Ah yes." His expression grew dark. "News has arrived that Lord Colin Campbell was gravely injured by an arrow. Since you spent a sennight at Kilchurn, I thought you'd want to be aware."

Meg clasped her hands to her mouth. "Oh my heavens, that is awful. It only seems like yesterday when I last saw him." She steadied herself on the stone fence. "Will he survive?"

"I know not."

"If only there were something I could do."

"Lord Colin is at home resting, surrounded by his family. 'Tis the best thing for a man when he's injured."

Duncan must be sick with worry. "How did it happen?" Meg's voice grew softer while her eyes welled with tears. If only she could reach out to him. She hugged her shoulders and rested her chin upon her chest.

"Word is something went awry when they captured the Earl of Mar and took him into custody."

"The king's brother? Why ever would they capture him?" *That must have been the secret mission Duncan spoke of.*

Arthur continued to amble along as if this news were commonplace. "He's been accused of using witchcraft against the king."

"Honestly? How dreadful." Meg's hands trembled. Truly, news of Mar was grave, but she could not control the pounding of her heart. Trying to breathe normally, if it weren't for Arthur looking at her with an apprising stare, she may have swooned. If only she could rush to Kilchurn. Duncan would need someone to talk to—he probably felt responsible. Even if he had only tepid feelings for her, she wished she could do something for him...and Lord Campbell, who had been so kind to her.

Meg had no idea how long she'd been silent when they'd arrived at the castle steps. Arthur placed a hand on her shoulder. "You seem deep in thought."

"Aye, just shocked by the news. Sir Duncan would be troubled, I am quite certain."

"Aye, and he'd have a great many details to attend as well. A wound like that can take months to heal, if ever." Arthur still appeared to be completely unaffected. "I must away to France but plan to return before Easter. Thank heavens 'tis late this year."

Meg nodded and hung her head.

He lifted her chin with the crux of his finger. "I've ordered the tailor to attend you. I believe new gowns are in order for our visit to court."

Meg's jaw dropped. She'd just learned Duncan suffered in the midst of turmoil, and she was supposed to while away her time on courtly gowns? Heat shot through her skin like a streak of lightning. She wanted to strangle Arthur for his indifference. But she could not. If she showed too much emotion, he'd suspect something for certain.

Chapter Twenty-Three

※

Lord Percy rode a bay gelding beside the king, who was mounted on a black Galloway stallion. Riding through King James's vast private hunting grounds, they had more privacy to discuss delicate matters. Now filling the role as King Edward's emissary, there was much to discuss.

The king glanced over his shoulder. "The guard is out of earshot."

Percy smiled. The meeting he'd had with King James a sennight prior had proceeded well. He had assured the king of Edward's desire to maintain peace and foster cooperation along the borders. That was no easy feat with the sheep-stealing clans north of the border. Though Lord Percy would manage his end of the bargain and see to it that no thievery was ever blamed on the English side. "Your message must be grave, indeed."

"Let us say 'tis sensitive."

"Whatever England can do to support your endeavors is certainly in our best interests to strengthen our truce."

Ambling in his saddle, the king gave Percy a deprecating glance. "Alas, my brother has used witchcraft against me."

"No." Percy did his best to look surprised, though all of Edinburgh was abuzz with the news. "If you do not mind my inquisition, what manner of witchcraft has he used?"

"Incantations." The king sighed. "Reported directly from within his own ranks."

"'Tis an abomination for one of an exalted rank as the Earl of Mar to employ such heresy."

"So very true. Though a trial will sully my name. It could grow into a farcical charade, ruinous not only for me, but for all of Scotland."

Percy shook his head. "'Tis grave, indeed. If only I could be of assistance to you, sire."

The king cued his horse to a canter and Percy followed suit, ensuring he did not make the mistake of pulling ahead of the royal's mount. Together they rode up a steep incline, and the king reined his horse to a stop at the crest. He gazed out over the city of Edinburgh, his face hard, as if he were about to ride into battle. "If the problem can be extinguished outside of court, a very handsome reward could be arranged."

Lord Percy licked his lips. "A task best undertaken by someone other than a Scot, I'd surmise."

"Precisely."

Dabbing the spittle from the corners of his mouth, Percy curbed his desire to grin. "What is the extent of such a payment?"

"Land, gold." The king looked him directly in the eye. "Only if there is no scandal."

Lord Percy bowed his head. "Of course, all suspicion would be drawn away from you, sire." He rubbed his fingers together as if he already held the king's gold sovereigns in his hands. "Perhaps if the earl were transferred to a suite of rooms for his comfort during his incarceration, a suitable disposition could occur."

"Hmm." The king stroked his beard. "Under the pretense of making my brother more comfortable?

That could be just the thing to draw away untoward suspicion."

Percy picked up his reins and turned his horse back toward the path. "I shall see it done. If you would be so kind as to notify Craigmillar Castle of the transfer."

"I shall send a missive to Sir Preston forthwith." The king slapped his crop against the stallion's rump, and together the two men cantered back to Holyrood without a single deer spotted. Percy chuckled to himself. He much preferred human prey.

&

Duncan arrived at Kilchurn Castle weary, unshaven and dispirited. He'd made the three-day journey only stopping when necessary to rest his horse. It was quiet when he strode through the great hall—too quiet.

He doubted he'd ever forgive himself for his lack of judgment at Kildrummy. That the king had shown little remorse for his father's wound also ratcheted up his ire. Colin Campbell had given his life to Scotland, had quashed the Douglas uprising and had been a hero in no less than three crusades. *And the king wanted me to stay and dine with him?*

Duncan stopped by his chamber to remove his weapons, and then proceeded to the lord's rooms. He stood outside Da's door for a moment, not sure what to expect. Ten days had passed since the incident at Kildrummy. With luck, the Lord of Glenorchy might be sitting up—he hoped. Holding on to that hope, when he finally opened the door, a lump formed in Duncan's throat.

Da lay on his back, the duvet pulled up to his chin. Ma sat on a chair beside him, holding his hand. She glanced up. Her anguished eyes were rimmed by red. Walking inside, Duncan met her gaze, and then saw

Da's ashen face—even paler than it had been when Duncan had last seen him in Perth. His eyes were closed. "Is he sleeping?"

"Aye," she whispered. She gently released Da's hand and stood, gesturing to the settee over by the hearth. "He's been asking for you."

Duncan followed her and sat. "How is he?"

Ma shook her head and drew a hand over her mouth. "I'm afraid mortification of the leg has set in." She gasped and choked back a stuttered breath. "The wound has gone putrid and the skin on his leg has turned from pale to brown. The physician says 'tis only a matter of time." Her shoulders shook.

"Och, Ma, there must be something we can do." Duncan pulled her into an embrace. "He's strong as an ox with the heart of a lion."

Her breath stuttered, as if she were trying to hold in her tears. "Aye. If anyone can overcome this, 'tis your da." Sighing, she dabbed her eyes with a kerchief.

"Duncan?" Da called from the bed. The weakness in his voice made him sound one hundred years of age.

Ma patted Duncan's cheek. "Go to him. I'll leave you alone for a moment."

After helping her up and seeing her to the door, Duncan moved to the chair beside Da's bed. "The king sends his regards." It sounded pathetic, but Colin Campbell wouldn't want his eldest son weeping over him like a milksop.

Da reached out his hand. "And the earl?"

Duncan grasped it between his palms. His hands were ice cold. Duncan never remembered his father's hands being so cold. "Delivered to Sir Preston at Craigmillar."

"Very good." Da licked his lips and offered a faint smile. "I am proud of you."

"Nay." Duncan shook his head. "I never should have

taken the risk." He'd thought of little else the past several days.

"Why? Because I'm an old man and cannot see beyond my own nose?"

"There were other ways to ferret him out."

"But yours was the least risky of all."

Duncan gaped at Da's ashen face—nearly as white as the bed linens. "How can you say that when you lie abed?"

"Because you were right before we set out. I should have stayed behind."

Duncan pursed his lips. True, he'd asked his father not to go, but that did not make his decision right. He alone was responsible for this ill state of affairs. "What news while I've been away?" Another stupid question, but Duncan needed the conversation to go elsewhere.

"Mother says she kens spring is on its way because the hens are laying."

"Are they?" Idle talk helped him steel his nerves.

Da panted, seemingly unable to draw in enough air. "Aye, and Gyllis is teaching Marion and Alice the latest court dances."

"Have they been up to give you a demonstration?"

"Earlier today, in fact." Da closed his eyes. "Whilst Helen played her lute."

"It must have been quite a spectacle. I'm sorry I missed it." Any other day, Duncan would have made every excuse to avoid such a performance.

Da let out a long exhale, followed by several shallow breaths. "I could listen to Helen for hours. She's as proficient as her mother." He coughed and grimaced as if he were in a great deal of pain.

Duncan tightened his grip around Da's hand. "What can I do to ease your burden?"

"We have built a fine force of men." Da completely passed over Duncan's question.

"Aye, none better."

"Stay in the king's good graces. Every good deed will be rewarded, and our coffers will grow."

Duncan nodded.

"Do not let them grow soft."

"Never."

"You are their leader now. Never forget that they look up to you."

Duncan had been their leader for a while now, but there was no need to remind his father of it. "They're all good men. You've trained them well."

"I wasn't talking about the enforcers. I was talking about the entire clan."

Duncan blinked. When did the conversation move to the clan? But the change of topic wasn't what bothered him. "Do not talk like that. You'll preside over many gatherings to come."

Coughing again, a bead of sweat rolled down Da's temple. "I can no longer feel my leg."

Duncan reached for a cloth and dabbed his father's forehead. "It'll come good."

Da snatched Duncan's wrist and held it firm, his eyes turning dark. "I am a warrior and an old man. I do not want to live out the remainder of my life as an invalid."

Duncan nodded once, then tossed the rag aside with a trembling hand. Clenching every muscle in his body, he'd never show weakness in front of his father.

"Promise me you'll take care of your stepmother."

"Of course I will."

"And find husbands for your sisters." Dad erupted in a coughing fit. "Blast it, I should have married Gyllis off by now."

Duncan wanted to take his father by the shoulders and shake him. Tell him he would be there to see his daughters wed, but he tightened his fists and resisted his urge to burst out and bellow. "The lasses will be fine."

"They are all beautiful creatures—each and every one in their own way."

"Aye, bonny like Ma."

Da grinned. "Your mother is the bonniest of them all."

Duncan sat beside him for hours. Sometimes in silence, and when Da would drift off, Duncan allowed himself to admire the man who'd fought for Christendom. Colin Campbell was the greatest hero in Scotland. A greater father a man could not have. He could spend his life trying to be half the man Da was and still wouldn't succeed. But one thing was for certain. He vowed to strive to be as strong, as good-hearted, as brave, and as honorable as the man lying in that bed.

As the night progressed, the family came in. The girls sat on the bed beside Da, all telling him fantastical stories—all painting on smiles and putting on courageous faces for him. That was how he wanted it. When John entered, he said not a word to Duncan—just sat in a chair and stared, as if he'd already passed judgment. John's silence spoke volumes about Duncan's guilt. He wouldn't blame his younger brother for hating him. Duncan hated himself.

In the wee hours before dawn, Duncan and Ma maintained a vigil beside the bed. Da opened his eyes and smiled at Ma. "I'll always love you, Margaret," he whispered.

Then, with one last exhale, the Lord took him away.

All of Argyllshire attended the funeral. Duncan imagined there were as many people in attendance as there were at the annual Beltane gathering at Dunstaffnage Castle. The church at Kilmartin was brimming with people, and even more clansmen and women stood outside, having come to pay their respects to the great legend.

Duncan sat on one side of Ma, with John on her other. Iain had arrived with their uncle, the Earl of Argyll, and they filled the pew to John's left. Iain had grown taller and had filled out since Duncan had last seen his youngest brother. He'd be a fine addition to the enforcers when he completed his fostering with Argyll.

Lady Margaret had been a pillar of strength until the mass began, and then her wailing resounded off the walls with an eerie poignancy, making gooseflesh rise across Duncan's skin. The love she harbored for Da was immeasurable, and the depth of her pain drove a spike into Duncan's own heart. If only he could have been the one to take the arrow.

Gyllis and her sisters sat to his right, all weeping and covering their faces with white kerchiefs. Duncan's spirits sank. Aye, he would have given anything to be the man in the marble sarcophagus. The death mask had been ordered and would stand as a monument to the great knight for eternity.

Duncan sat numbly and listened to the Latin mass. Life had a beginning and an end—birth, death and rebirth. That was the way of it. He was now the Lord of Glenorchy, and it was his responsibility to beget an heir who would one day preside over his own funeral. Closing his eyes, a picture of fiery red hair fluttering in the breeze captured his mind. Then Lady Meg's angelic face smiled at him. He recounted their fleeting time together and how gruff he'd been with her at first. Most likely, she'd never forget his boorishness. He'd erred in so many ways.

The priest swung the brass thurible, sending clouds of incense wafting throughout the nave. Duncan inhaled deeply, the heady aroma clearing his mind. As baron, there was much to do. He straightened and caressed Ma's wimple. He would protect and defend his family and his clan until he took his last breath, just as Da had and his father before him. They were Campbells and proud—leaders of the great nation of Scotland.

Now was the time to take the reins and lead. And by God, he would own up to that duty.

Chapter Twenty-Four

Sitting beside the hearth in his chamber, Duncan swirled the whisky in his goblet and stared at the amber liquid. His chest completely hollow, he doubted he possessed a soul. He needed to be alone. Behind closed doors, he could allow himself to come to grips with his loss. The tic above his eye twitched mercilessly—punishing him, no doubt.

A knock resounded at the door. Duncan ignored it, but the door opened. John walked in and sat in the chair across from him. "You must move into the lord's rooms."

Duncan said nothing.

John leaned forward. "Mercy, brother. Are you so filled with your own remorse you cannot see the others who suffer around you?"

Heat flaring up the back of his neck, Duncan threw the goblet at the hearth. Shards of pottery scattered with a racket. "You think I do not carry the burden of Mother's loss? You think I don't know the pain each one of our sisters is feeling this night? If you do, you're sorely mistaken."

"You carry on as if Da's death is your fault."

"It is." Duncan stood and kicked at the shards. "I thought we'd have a better chance of absconding with the earl and avoiding bloodshed if we coaxed him out of Kildrummy at night."

John crossed his ankles. "How many were killed by doing it your way?"

"One of ours and one of theirs."

"How many would have died if you'd tried to squeeze through the narrow passage at the rear?"

Duncan shrugged. "I've been playing it over and over in my head. But there's no way to have known. We could have all slipped out without injury."

"Aye, you could have, else some bastard could have lowered the portcullis and crushed you whilst the guard cornered you in the passage. Worse, some could have been caught and enjoyed the hospitality of the Kildrummy dungeon."

Duncan shook his head and sank back into his chair.

"Do not tell me I'm wrong. I discussed it with Eoin." John smoothed his hands over the armrests. "You made the right choice at the time, and I'll wager if Da were alive he'd say the same."

Duncan knew that wasn't true. Da had voiced his concern.

John stood and walked to the sideboard. He pulled the stopper out of the flagon and poured a single tot of whisky. Returning, he placed the spirit on the table beside Duncan. "I'm leaving."

Duncan sat back. "What the devil?"

John turned toward the hearth and stared at the fire. "All my life I've wanted to take the cloth. With all that's happened, I figure now's the time. I'm off to Ardchattan Priory on the morrow."

"Are you out of your mind?" Duncan snatched the whisky and tossed back a healthy swig. "I need you. The enforcers need you more now than ever before."

John spun around and spread his palms. "The Highland Enforcers was Da's dream. And now your dream.

I'm not a warrior like the pair of you. I've no stomach for killing."

"What are you saying? You're as fine a fighter as any of the men."

"Technically, aye, but my heart's not in it. I'd rather save lives than take them."

Duncan slammed the goblet on the table. "Save lives? Jesus, John, that's exactly what we're doing. Aye, we fight the battles that need fighting, but in the end, we're making the Highlands lawful, safer for women and children."

John rested a calming hand on Duncan's shoulder. "I ken, brother. All I'm saying is 'tis not right for me."

Duncan slouched further in his chair. "Have you told Ma?"

"Aye. She gave me her blessing."

"Well, I guess that's it, then."

"I hope one day you'll understand."

Duncan flicked his wrist dismissively. "Go on with you. Leave when the family's in the midst of a crisis and we need you the most."

"I didn't—"

Duncan sliced his hand through the air. "Enough. You've been talking about becoming a priest your whole life. This time I'll not stop you."

Duncan stared at the fire while John's footsteps crossed the room. When the door closed, Duncan cradled his head in his hands. When he needed John to stand beside him, the boil-brained maggot up and left. After Duncan returned from Edinburgh, John had made his feelings clear. He considered it deplorable that Duncan had completed the mission and met with the king. John bloody thought it was unforgivable to ask his cousins to return Da to Kilchurn, but Duncan had made a vow to a dying man—their father, no less.

The leaping flames mesmerized him. He took another sip of whisky. It was pathetic that his only comfort was the spirit. He longed for the gentle touch of a woman. But he abhorred the idea of spending the night with a passionless wench who cared more about a few coins than she did for him.

He emitted a rueful laugh. Ever since he'd met Lady Meg, he hadn't thought about wenching. Before, he'd had an insatiable lust for any pretty, buxom lass wearing a kirtle. He'd made great sport of wooing women until they swooned into his outstretched arms. And he'd always been ever so eager to oblige them.

Now the thought of swiving any lass aside from Meg held little interest. Worse, he never should have stolen her virtue in the first place. As the flames danced, he pictured her hair, and the way the wind picked it up when they'd ridden together, sending the mane of curls sailing into his face. She smelled of sweet honeysuckle and roses. Her smile had given him an airy lightness, as if he'd walked outside on a glorious summer's day. Now he'd never feel that kind of joy again.

Duncan rubbed his fingers along his arm and dreamt of running his hand from her breast, down the curve of her waist and up the arc of her hip. If only he could talk to the Lord of Angus and ask for Meg's hand, but that wouldn't be right. He'd rescued the lass. The earl would consider his suit impertinent and an abuse of their business transaction. *Would he not?*

Another tap at the door sounded. Duncan snapped from his trance and groaned. "Come."

Her dressing gown belted tightly around her body, Lady Margaret stepped inside and quietly closed the door.

Duncan stood, crossed the floor and took up her hand. "Mother, I thought you'd be abed by this hour."

"I couldn't sleep."

"Nor could I." He led her to the chair opposite his. "Would you like a tot of whisky to calm you?"

"Aye, a wee portion, please."

Duncan poured her a goblet, thinking a full cup would ease her woes. "You spoke to John?"

"Many times in the past, but I agree with him. 'Tis time he followed his own dreams. If he remains here, you'd soon have him carrying out another mission for the king."

"But I need him. The men need him."

She took the goblet from him and sipped. "Aye, but think of your brother. All his life he's lived in your shadow. 'Tis time he came into his own." Mother set the drink on the table and dabbed her lips with her finger. "John has always been a gentler soul. I must admit, I am happy for him. He shall make a fine priest."

Duncan nodded and stared at her for a moment. Though his birthmother had died giving him life, he'd always recognized Lady Margaret as his ma. She'd acted as mother to him in every way. "And how are you holding up?" he asked.

"Still numb, I suppose."

"If only I would have listened to him…"

"You mustn't blame yourself. Your father chose his path long before you were born." She smiled sadly. "I remember when Colin was called away for his third crusade. It was early December. You were but a bairn in arms, and I was left alone to provide Christmas cheer to the castle, when all I wanted to do was hide in my chamber and wallow in misery."

"What did you do?"

"Do you remember Mistress Effie?"

Duncan's tension eased when he recalled the nursemaid. "Aye, she was very old when I was but a lad."

"She was indeed, and outspoken." Ma raised her goblet. "On Christmas morn, she reminded me of my duty as lady of the keep. She also told me that I set the tone for the clan. If I was sad, my mood would affect the others. As their leader, all eyes were on me to provide a stoic example of strength."

Duncan regarded his mother with reverence. Indeed, she was hewn of strong Highland stock, and he'd always admired her for it. "What did you do? Surely you could not mask your heavy heart forever."

"Nay, but I could sit tall and conduct the business of Glenorchy lands fairly, with honesty and respect for all who pay us fealty. For the feast, I donned my best gown, trod down the stairwell and opened my arms." Mother spread her arms wide. "I welcomed all to the feast, and after, I danced until my feet could take no more." She rested her elbows on the armrests, her smile a bit happier. "From that day, I knew I could manage your father's affairs until he returned."

"You are truly a remarkable woman." He meant the compliment from the depths of his heart.

"And you are an even more remarkable man, Duncan. 'Tis time for you to take up your father's mantle and wear it with pride. 'Tis what I and the clan expects. Moreover, 'tis what you were bred for."

🙦

With the door cracked open a mere fraction, Isaac hid in the privy closet while the groom prepared a bath for the Earl of Mar. Of all the unsavory tasks Lord Percy had assigned him, this was by far the most reprehensible. Isaac had been trained to be a warrior, not an assassin.

The sound of water being poured into the washbasin rushed through the air, sending prickles up Isaac's spine.

"The water's nice and hot, m'lord."

Isaac recognized the groom's voice from their earlier conversation.

"Thank you. A bath brings a semblance of comfort to ease my troubles."

The earl didn't sound like someone who would incant a spell of witchcraft. But then, who was Isaac to judge? Perhaps the earl had made abominable threats against Scotland's king. Isaac smoothed his sweaty palm over his dagger's pommel. Yes, that was it. This man was a traitor against Scotland. He had committed unforgivable acts against the king. Any man committing abominable crimes must be dispatched swiftly.

Isaac held on to this thought and focused on the black hole of hatred forming in his heart. He would carry out his duty and rid the earth of a barbaric tyrant.

He visualized the plan in his head and listened. The groom had been instructed to leave the earl alone and close the door loudly.

Fingers slightly trembling, Isaac waited. His breath rushed in his ears as if it were a gale. The water sloshed. "'Tis warm indeed," the earl said.

Some rustling resounded from the chamber. "Oh dear, I must have forgotten the soap. I shall fetch it forthwith," the groom said.

"Take your time."

Footsteps clapped the floorboards.

Hinges creaked then the door slammed. Isaac's insides jolted. He sucked in a deep breath to steady his hands. One thought filled his mind: *Finish him*.

Pulling his dagger, he cradled it firmly in his hand so the blade pointed downward for the most powerful and deadly strike. Without a sound, he pulled the privy door open and stepped inside.

The earl had his back to him, dribbling water with his hands while he reclined.

With his eyes wide and his heart pummeling his chest, power surged through Isaac's limbs. In three strides, he reached the basin.

The earl's gaze shifted to Isaac, and his eyes flashed with horror.

Before the man could gasp, Isaac slashed the dagger across John Stewart's throat.

With gurgling croaks, the Earl of Mar uttered his last audible words. *"Jesus Christ."*

Blood turned the bathwater red. As the man's face faded from a healthy pale to blue, a lump the size of a cannonball formed in Isaac's gut. He ran to the privy closet and vomited over and over until there was nothing left. Worse, he had to walk past the earl's corpse again to exit the chamber.

My God, I've allowed the Earl of Northumberland to turn me into a monster.

Chapter Twenty-Five

※

Meg was afraid to move for fear of being skewered by a straight pin. She huffed impatiently. Why on earth was Arthur spending coin on these fancy dresses? She wanted nothing to do with court or the pompous men who all slathered themselves with entirely too much scented oil. Even the tailor pinning her into the latest contraption smelled like he'd doused himself with lavender oil that morning in an attempt to cover up the sickly odor of male sweat. Meg lifted her nose and tried to inhale air less permeated by the man's stench. She coughed. Unfortunately, there would be no getting away from Master Tailor until he'd managed to prick her at least a dozen more times.

Elizabeth sat at Meg's table beside the hearth. Out of the corner of her eye, Meg watched her sister study the herbology notes she'd taken.

Elizabeth held up the parchment. "What is this?"

"I've been studying with Hubert."

"The old gardener?"

"Aye, he kens a great deal about the healing arts."

Elizabeth tossed the parchment on the table and huffed. "You, my dear, are incorrigible."

"Why?" Meg lowered her arms.

"Up," Master Tailor garbled with pins filling his mouth.

"I think you take pleasure in torturing your victims." Meg rolled her eyes to the ceiling frieze and lifted her aching arms. She turned her attention to Elizabeth. "Every woman should have a sound knowledge of herbal remedies."

"A general understanding, aye, but herbology is for healers and gardeners like Hubert."

"I disagree. There is not always a healer on hand." Oh, how Meg would have loved to tell Elizabeth about Duncan's arse, but she bit her bottom lip.

Elizabeth stood and eyed the tailor's work. "As a future lady of a keep, you'll need to have a healer in your employ. A crofter's wife usually suits." Elizabeth pulled on one of Meg's sleeves with a critical eye. "These must extend at least three inches past her ladyship's fingertips."

"Yes, m'lady," the tailor said in a clipped tone.

Elizabeth had never been overly practical. But she'd married an earl. Practicality wasn't necessary, nor was it expected from a countess. Meg sighed and looked at Master Tailor's weathered face as he fastened yet another pin. "I cannot hold my arms up any longer."

"A moment." He took a step back and eyed the garment as if it were his greatest masterpiece. "Lower slowly. I shall attend the skirts whilst you rest."

Elizabeth resumed her seat by the table. "Have you heard about the Earl of Mar?"

Meg rubbed the outside of her arms. "That he's been charged with witchcraft against the king?"

"Worse." Elizabeth drummed her fingers atop the table. "Word came this morn that he'd been murdered in his bath."

Gasping, Meg clapped a hand over her mouth. "Do they know who did it?"

Elizabeth shrugged, as if murder were a minor affair.

"Some are blaming King James—after all, he's the one who had the earl arrested—but Arthur said there is already a long list of suspects."

Meg turned her head away. Duncan had brought the earl from Kildrummy to Edinburgh. Had he anything to do with the murder? Surely not, especially after his father had been badly injured. She hadn't received news from Kilchurn. Not that she expected to. Duncan would be too busy to think about her.

She chewed her thumbnail. If only she could find a way to see him.

Would Duncan attend court for the Easter plays? She glanced at the top of Master Tailor's bonnet while her heart fluttered. Perhaps being fitted for new gowns was not such a bad idea. If only she could see Duncan once more before Arthur married her off.

Is there any way to ensure he'll be there? I must give that notion some thought. Sending him a missive would be uncouth. Hmm...

THE LORD OF NORTHUMBERLAND WAITED WHILE THE valet announced his arrival. Today he would take his nooning in private audience with King James.

After he was escorted into the king's inner chamber, they exchanged pleasantries until a meal of boiled pheasant and turnips was served.

The king raised his goblet. "I prefer to drink watered wine to avoid dulling my wits so early in the day."

Percy raised his goblet in kind. "Smart of you, your grace."

When at last the servants exited the chamber and closed the door, the king frowned. "You said all suspicion for my brother's death would be drawn away from me."

"I assure you, sire, presently no one knows what to

think. There are as many murder suspects as there are monks in Holyrood Abbey."

"There is practically anarchy on the streets of Edinburgh, and the chief suspect is me." The king picked up his eating knife and waved it under Henry Percy's nose. "I told you I would only make payment if a scandal is avoided. You said you would draw suspicion away from me, damn you."

Percy shifted away from the accusing blade. The sooner he left Scotland, the better. He couldn't care less if the sniveling Scottish king was led to the gallows on the morrow. However, as emissary to King Edward, he must play his part. "'Tis precisely why I deemed your idea for a private audience fortuitous. I've found the perfect pawn, but I must commandeer a Scottish contingent of men to arrest him. If English involvement is suspected, my plan will not work."

The king stroked his fingers down his beard. "Aye, all Englishmen are suspect this side of the border. An English army would be suspicious indeed. How many men do you need?"

"A retinue of twenty fighting men, led by your most skilled man-at-arms."

"Very well." The king thumped his fist on the table. "You'll have your men, but I want none of my subjects killed."

"We shall do our best on that account, though I'll not be able to keep your men from defending themselves."

The king grasped Lord Percy's shoulder. "If you, sir, make a mockery out of me, it will not only mean the end of the truce between Scotland and England, I will personally see that your line is removed from the earldom once and for all."

Percy lowered his eating knife. Months ago he vowed he would murder anyone who threatened to take away his title, and the King of Scotland wasn't so regal he was absolved of that oath. He licked his lips and regarded the king's long neck. If anything went wrong with his plan, it would be an easy throat to cut.

The king reached for his goblet. "Now tell me, what is the name of the unfortunate bastard to whom you are referring?"

Chapter Twenty-Six

✦

In the courtyard, Duncan sparred with Eoin, thrusting his sword in short jabs. Wearing his partner down, he advanced with each strike. Duncan's chest still tight with remorse, he drew on the inner demons. It was as if his father's soul had taken over Duncan's body, driving him to fight like never before.

He spun with a sideways strike. Eoin's blade clattered to the cobblestones. Panting, the MacGregor man gaped in disbelief. "Are you possessed by the devil?"

Duncan lowered his weapon and waited for Eoin to pick up his sword. "You're growing soft."

Eoin stooped for his blade. "Bloody hell."

"The king's riders," hollered a sentry from atop the guard tower.

Duncan looked at Eoin and then his other men. They all shrugged. "Open the gate." After sheathing his sword, he removed his helm and wiped his face with a drying cloth. It wasn't unusual to receive messengers from the king, though it didn't happen often. Duncan figured it was merely a formal proclamation until twenty mounted sentries all wearing royal tunics emblazoned with the lion rampant, rode into the Kilchurn outer bailey.

The man-at-arms dismounted and strode to him with purpose, followed by a half-dozen other guards.

Duncan planted his fists on his hips. "What is the meaning of this?"

The guards surrounded him while the leader unrolled a piece of vellum. "By order of his majesty, King James of Scotland, you are hereby accused of murdering the Earl of Mar and Lord Colin Campbell of Glenorchy.

Duncan's insides turned to ice. All six men latched on to his arms. "This is preposterous."

The man-at-arms made quick work of removing Duncan's weapons.

Eoin sidled up to the soldier. "You know these charges are contrived. Even the king saw Duncan leave for Kilchurn after he'd delivered the earl to Craigmillar."

The king's man shrugged. "That is not for me to determine."

Eoin drew his sword. "I'll not stand to see my lord wrongly accused."

"No!" Duncan struggled beneath the sentries' grasp. "We fight for Scotland, and uphold the laws of this land. Fear not. I will stand absolved of these false charges."

The man-at-arms whipped a hemp rope around Duncan's wrists.

Lady Margaret rushed out from the keep. "Remove your hands from my son!"

The worry on his stepmother's face hit Duncan in the gut. Regardless that the charges were contrived, it tore him apart to see Lady Margaret so visibly upset. He tried to reach for her, but the guards wrestled him away.

She took the missive from the man-at-arms and read whilst the guards led Duncan to a mule. She crumpled the vellum and glared at the king's man. "These charges are completely false. My son has been by my side since he delivered the earl into Sir Preston's hands."

"Aye?" said the man-at-arms. "Of course the accused's mother would perjure herself to see her son released."

"Mother, go back inside and tend to the girls. There has been a misunderstanding, which should be easily resolved."

Lady Margaret stood stoically. Eoin moved to her side and placed a protective arm around her shoulders. "We shall follow and come to your aid, m'lord."

Forced to mount a mule, hands bound, and being led like a common criminal, Duncan gazed at his closest friend. Their brief eye contact communicated more than a thousand words. Eoin would not only follow, he would use their Edinburgh resources to delve to the bottom of this charade.

True, the Campbells of Glenorchy had a great many enemies. That happened when tasked with the unsavory mission of bringing order to a land as rugged as the Highlands.

Who has the king's ear? Or does the king himself need a scapegoat? On the charge of killing my father, I would gladly plead guilty if it would bring him back to the family...but the charges of murdering the Earl of Mar? I smell a rat bigger than Kilchurn Castle itself.

❦

ISAAC STOOD ON THE EDINBURGH CASTLE battlements beside Lord Percy while the king's procession made its way up the winding cobbled road to the gaol. A cold wind blew in off the firth and cut to the bone. It didn't seem to matter how many layers he piled on—in Scotland, Isaac always felt cold.

Percy pointed. "There he is. He's not looking so cocky now his hands are bound." He smirked. "They chose a fine ass for him to ride, as well."

Isaac watched the figure of Lord Glenorchy ride a

mule—not an ass—along the path to the taunts and jibes of the crowd. The large man wore no cloak and clutched his elbows to his sides, hunched over against the gale.

"Burn him!" screeched a woman across the path.

The Lord of Glenorchy's jaw hardened. Looking straight ahead, he raised his chin and straightened in the saddle, as if he were carrying the pennant for the once great king, Robert the Bruce. Then the baronet turned his head. Isaac's heart slammed against his chest. At first he thought Duncan Campbell looked directly at him, but it was the man standing beside him who was the recipient of a glare filled with alarm. While the horse neared, the man didn't avert his gaze—rather, he narrowed his eyes and set his jaw. By the time the mule walked past, Lord Glenorchy's stare had darkened to unmistakable hatred.

Lord Percy examined his fingernails. "I daresay, that man is capable of anything, undoubtedly murder. We're doing Scotland a service by delivering him to her gallows."

Heat rushed up the back of Isaac's neck in concert with the tightening in his chest. "You mean to tell me you feel no sense of guilt?"

"Why ever should I?"

Isaac clenched his fists at his sides. "The man is innocent."

"That same man stole into my home, kidnapped my prisoner and killed three of my guards. He may not be hanged for his crimes against me, but he will receive his just punishment."

Isaac fidgeted with his sword belt. The damned thing seemed to have become ill-fitting overnight. When he closed his eyes, he saw the back of the Earl of Mar's head. The man had been peaceful, ladling water over himself in the bath, and then Isaac had run the blade across his neck—killing in the name of the

Earl of Northumberland. Would he meet a similar end?

"Come," Lord Percy said. "I've important emissary work to attend."

Isaac watched the rear of the procession disappear behind St. Margaret's Chapel. The thickness in his throat refused to ease. "I shall be along shortly."

He had no place to go, but presently the thought of following the Earl of Northumberland anywhere sickened him. Needing to think, to clear his mind and seek absolution for committing murder, Isaac strode along the battlements that overlooked the firth. If only he could leave this hellacious place and return to his family, one day he might forget his wretched past and the abominable deeds he'd committed in the name of the Lord of Northumberland.

DUNCAN HAD BEEN CHAINED TO THE WALL FOR THREE days. He only knew this because a ray of light shone through a crack in the mortar near the ceiling of the dungeon. Aside from a filthy scrapper bringing around a cup of water once a day, he'd had no sustenance.

His arms hung from manacles, and two days ago his hands had gone numb. At first he tried to move his fingers to revive the feeling, but now he no longer cared. His mind was a blur, unable to focus on anything except his raging hunger. Even his vision blurred. Worse, he'd heard naught except the moans from the prisoner alongside him. None of his men had made contact.

Duncan shifted his weight, and the trembling resumed in his thighs. If he hadn't been chained to the wall, his legs would have given out by now. He moved every now and again to redistribute his weight, but he'd lost control of his muscles. He'd even tried to hang from his arms, but that only served to worsen the pins and needles driving through his fingertips.

When the iron door creaked open, Duncan opened his eyes and forced himself to raise his head. A man dressed in the black robes of a headsman, ushered in two guards. The executioner sucked in his gaunt cheeks, making his cadaverous face appear even more skeletal.

The man sauntered forward. "I'm surprised you're still conscious."

Duncan's arid tongue tapped the roof of his mouth, but he said nothing.

"You must know why I'm here." The man's breath stank of rotting teeth.

Duncan met his sallow gaze. "I do not suppose the king has seen fit to grant me a pardon." He coughed, barely recognizing his own voice due to the grating rasp. "The last time he asked me to dine, I couldn't stay."

"Oh?" The man's putrid breath hit Duncan in the back of the throat and made him gag. "Why?"

"I had a funeral to attend."

"Ah." The bastard chuckled. "Not unlike the one you'll be attending soon. Except you'll be the guest of honor."

"I am innocent of the charges. Dozens of people can vouch for me."

"Hmm." The man stroked his pointed beard. "That should not be necessary. My duty is to make you confess."

Duncan's gut dropped to his toes. "I'll die first."

"That has been known to happen. Confess and I'll see to it you meet a swift end. Surely you'd prefer a beheading over sennights in irons."

Duncan met the man's black stare. "I prefer justice."

The executioner's sickening laughter swelled throughout the chamber. "Tell me you murdered your father because you couldn't wait for his riches to pass to you."

"Never."

"Tell me you murdered the Earl of Mar whilst he lingered in a bath, and you staged it to cast a dark shadow over the king."

"How could I kill someone in Edinburgh when I was in Glen Orchy?"

"Do you deny your brutish handling of the earl whilst he was in your custody?"

Duncan hissed. *Christ.*

The villain jabbed a finger into Duncan's sternum. "Why, Sir Preston reported Mar had a black eye when you delivered him to Craigmillar."

Duncan would admit truths only. "The earl laughed at my father when he was hunched over a horse, close to death—any man would have done the same."

The man drew back his fist and slammed it into Duncan's jaw before he had a chance to flinch. Shoving his tongue to the corner of his mouth, the iron taste of blood turned his empty stomach. Still, this was only the beginning.

The black-robed scoundrel gestured to the guards. "Take him to *my* chamber."

Duncan tried to rub his arms when they released them from the manacles, but his relief was short-lived. Shoved into a chamber equipped with every torture device he'd ever seen, and a few Duncan didn't recognize, he wished they'd left him chained to the wall.

They stripped away his doublet and shirt, and cast them to the damp, earthen floor. They tied his arms to an iron loop protruding from the wall. With all the contraptions in the room, they planned to whip him?

The vile man stepped so close, his black woolen mantle scratched Duncan's flesh. He flinched when the maniac ran his fingernail across an old knife scar at his flank. "You're not a stranger to pain, I see."

The bastard dug into another scar, slowly drawing his jagged nail across it. The deliberate, deep scratch brought the memory of every wound to the forefront of Duncan's mind. Each scar stung and throbbed as if it had been sliced open.

Duncan closed his eyes and conjured a picture of Meg. Those blue eyes that captivated his heart. When they'd first met, all she need do was raise her lids and his heart belonged to Meg Douglas. The porcelain face framed by curls of fire—curls that wouldn't stop, wild like a lion's mane.

Rustling came from behind. Duncan didn't turn his head, but ground his teeth, every muscle clenched taut. He'd been whipped before. He could take it.

Something hissed through the air. Duncan steeled himself for the impact—but it didn't come. Excruciating pain seared across all his exposed flesh. His gaze shot to his shoulder. Burning droplets of molten lead sizzled on his skin, filling the room with the stench of burning flesh.

His head shuddered against the unbearable pain. His eyes watered. Grinding his teeth, he growled and held in his urge to bellow.

"The whip would have been too kind for the likes of you," the executioner said, holding the handle of a metal sprinkler in his palm. It looked like the one the priest used to scatter holy water, yet this instrument served a far more sinister purpose.

The man then pushed his dirty fingernail under a droplet of the cooling lead and levered it up. "Confess."

Duncan arched his spine as the blood trickled from his shoulder and down his back. With each blistering tear of the skin, the bastard demanded a confession. Duncan lost track of time, his mind overcome with pain and exhaustion, his extremities trembling out of control. The only things keeping him sane were the moments when he'd close his eyes and focus on Lady Meg.

When they brought in a beast of a man holding a whip with three thick tongues, Duncan's insides gave way. He retched as thick yellow bile burned his throat and spewed to the ground.

"Confess!" roared the black-robed villain.

A strike of the lash hit Duncan with such force, his head slammed into the post. Stars crossed his vision, and his eyes rolled back while freshly carved welts stung as though his entire back had just been branded.

"Confess!"

Duncan tried to picture Meg, but saw only flashes of light. "I..."

Everything faded into blackness.

Chapter Twenty-Seven

"A gentleman has come to call, m'lady," Cassie said from the doorway. The early-morning sun shone through the window, illuminating the lassie's face.

Meg's heart skipped more than a beat. She tried to steady her breathing whilst she set her quill in the holder. "Who is this gentleman?"

"He's an Englishman. He asked to speak to Arthur, but when the guard said he was out, the man demanded to speak to you—said it was a matter of grave importance."

Meg's heart went from fluttering with elation to a tremulous palpitation. "Englishman? Is he armed? Did he come with a contingent of soldiers?"

"He's alone, m'lady. Shall I send him away?"

"Nay." Meg stood, cradling her hands against her stomach. "Call my guard. See to it this man bears no arms and have him escorted to Arthur's solar. I shall meet with him there."

"Yes, m'lady."

Meg adjusted her wimple. *An Englishman calling to see Arthur, and then asks to see me? The man must be completely daft walking through the gates of Tantallon alone.*

She met Tormond outside the solar. "Is he within?"

The guard wore a hauberk with a sword strapped to

his back and another at his hip, in addition to dirks and daggers lashed to his every extremity. "Aye, m'lady."

She rubbed the outside of her shoulder. "He is disarmed?"

"Aye, and I shall be beside you the whole time."

"Very well."

She reached for the latch, but the guard's hand grasped it first. "You do not have to meet with him."

"He said he had a message of dire importance, did he not?"

"Aye."

"Then I shall hear what he has to say." She nodded for him to open the door.

She stood in the doorway and gasped. *That same scar.* "You?"

Isaac shoved back his chair and stood. "My lady, forgive my intrusion, but I have grave news."

She crossed her arms and stepped inside. "It had best be grave indeed, or you'll see yourself thrown in the dungeon and left to rot."

He held up his hands. "Understood, but I must speak to you in private."

Tormond moved forward, hand on the hilt of his claymore. "You shall never have a private audience with her ladyship."

Isaac looked to Meg, his brows slanted outward. "I beg of you, Lord Campbell is in dire need of assistance from your house."

"Lord Campbell? Has he recovered from the arrow wound?"

"Arrow wound?" Isaac's scar stretched with his confounded stare. "Ah...I was referring to Lord *Duncan* Campbell."

Meg gaped at him. "The Black Knight has perished?"

"Sennights ago."

She stumbled forward, grasping the back of a chair for support.

Duncan is in trouble? His father dead? Meg nearly swooned.

Tormond advanced and seized Isaac. Her mind raced—this could be a plot to spirit her back to Alnwick. Isaac's gaze did not waver. Something in his stricken expression made her trust the man. "Release him."

"M'lady?"

"Do it, I say, and leave us."

Tormond's brows drew together. "I cannot."

"Remain outside the door. If Sir Isaac should raise a finger, I shall call you in."

"But—"

"Leave us." She pointed. "Now."

The guard stepped away from Isaac. "If you do anything improper, anything at all, you will not leave this chamber alive."

Meg watched Tormond take his leave, and then turned to Isaac. "Sit."

He obliged, and folded his hands atop the table in a gesture demonstrating his surrender.

Meg chose to remain standing. "Sir Duncan, I mean Lord Campbell is in peril?"

"Yes. Lord Percy has conspired with King James to accuse him of murdering the *Earl of Mar*." Isaac repeated the late earl's name, as if the man's ghost sent a cold shiver across his back.

Meg again clutched the back of the chair. "My God."

"It gets worse." Isaac pushed the heels of his hands against his eyes and shook his head. "They're also accusing Lord Campbell of murdering his father."

Meg's stomach turned over with a sickening squelch. "He would never raise a hand against his da. He respected him as much as the king—more so."

Clutching her arms across her stomach, she paced. What could she do...and why was Isaac at Tantallon bearing witness against his lord? "Why did you come here, of all places?"

"I thought the Lord of Angus might help, especially considering the fact that Lord Campbell rescued you from the clutches of a tyrant."

"But you're loyal to Northumberland. You followed us after Duncan rescued me from Alnwick. I saw you on the pier in Glasgow." She slammed her hand on the table. "You kidnapped me!" Meg desperately wanted to trust this man, but could she? Was this a ploy to entice her from Tantallon's fortress?

"I can no longer live under the yoke of lies and tyranny. I'm the one..." Isaac swiped a hand across his mouth, as if he'd almost revealed a key confidence.

"You're the one?"

His face paled, and there was something damning in his eyes she'd not noticed during her stay in England. They expressed something greater than fear. She cocked her head to the side. "Do you know who killed the Earl of Mar?"

Isaac's jaw dropped, but those eyes remained filled with horror.

Meg suspected he did, but when he looked away, she opted not to push him. At the moment, the more important matter was Duncan. She chose to rephrase. "How do you know Lord Campbell is innocent?"

Isaac's gaze returned to his folded hands. "Because he was in Glen Orchy when the murder occurred."

Meg could feign a calm demeanor no longer. Fists clenching, she paced like a caged animal. "Where is he now?"

"In the gaol at Edinburgh Castle."

Dear Lord, help. Duncan could succumb to any number of heinous deeds. "How can we spirit him out?"

"I was hoping your brother could petition the king.

A strong word from the Earl of Angus would be considered with utmost solemnity."

Meg could scarcely breathe. "Arthur is in France and is not expected to return for a fortnight."

Isaac's shoulders dropped. "By then it will be too late."

Meg placed both her hands on the table and leaned forward. Isaac had seen the claw, and at this point, she cared not. "I will go in Arthur's stead. We must leave immediately."

"But, my lady, the king will not see you, and the queen is at Dunfirmline."

"Oh?" She stamped her foot. "Then we shall find another way."

Meg marched to the door and flung it wide. "Tormond, we ride to Edinburgh within the hour. Ready the guard."

Isaac sprang from the table. "It will draw suspicion if you ride into Edinburgh with an army of men."

She raised her chin in defiance. "I will not put myself in a position to be kidnapped by Lord Percy again."

"Very well—tie my hands if you like, but bring only a few good soldiers. Smart men who know how to blend into the shadows if need be."

She glanced at Tormond. The fear in Isaac's eyes had made her trust him. "Do it. I shall meet you in the courtyard in the turn of an hourglass."

After dashing up to her chamber, the first thing Meg packed in her satchel was her new assortment of herbal remedies, including a vial of avens oil that she'd made under Hubert's tutelage. She'd already learned that when it came to Duncan Campbell, a woman needed to be close by with a potent remedy.

It was nearly dark when Edinburgh Castle loomed on the horizon. Meg wasted no time and spurred her horse to a brisk canter. Duncan's soul called to her, needed her. Nothing would stand in her way—not even the iron bars of the castle gaol.

Her guard had no choice but to match her pace. Isaac, too, rode beside her. He'd said little along their journey. Meg suspected he was deep in thought. Lord Percy must have done something abominable indeed to make his loyal man-at-arms turn traitor. And she gave thanks to God that he had.

Meg had visited Edinburgh Castle enough to know exactly where the dungeon was situated. Without slowing her horse, she drove the mare straight up the cobblestones past St. Margaret's Chapel and to the prison gate. "I shall go in alone."

"I cannot allow that, m'lady," Tormond said from behind.

Yes, her guard would always be tenacious. Though Meg was the daughter of a peer, the man thought he had complete authority over her. She ignored him and spurred her mare faster.

Outside the ugly black doors, Meg didn't wait for assistance. She quickly dismounted and pulled the latch. It didn't budge.

"Allow me." Tormond heaved on the door, and it slowly opened.

"My thanks." Inside she was met by guards with their battleaxes held across the passageway. "I demand to have an audience with Lord Campbell immediately."

"And who might you be?"

"I am Lady Douglas, daughter of the Earl of Angus." She poured forth the words with such authority that no one would dare question her power to march into the gaol.

The guard looked at her as if he'd never seen a woman before. "I cannot allow a woman—"

She pushed his battleaxe aside. "Take me to the baronet forthwith, and I'll not hear another word of dissension from *anyone*." She glanced at Tormond and spread her palms out to her sides. "Besides, what harm could a mere woman possibly do?"

She marched down the dank stairs, her mouth growing dry, the stench of human excrement burning her eyes. Meg wasn't about to allow them pause. If she showed a modicum of weakness, they might toss her into the courtyard and ban her from ever approaching the gaol again.

She tipped up her chin, hoping she looked important and in control, though her fingers shook like a nervous dog. In no way could she allow the guards to sense her fear. She would see Duncan this day, and she would do anything to ensure her success. Tormond followed closely behind.

At the bottom of the stairs, the stench nearly overcame her. She pulled the collar of her cloak over her nose and turned full circle.

"This way, m'lady."

The guard led her down a dank passage lit by a sole torch on the wall. The further they went, the colder it became. They stopped outside a cell, shut off by iron bars. When Meg's eyes adjusted to the dim light, she gasped. A man lay curled in the middle of the tiny room, wearing only a pair of woolen chausses.

Duncan. "Open this gate immediately." She wrapped her fingers around the bars and squinted. To her horror, the flesh on Duncan's back oozed with blood.

Her guard stepped beside her. "Lady Meg, 'tis not proper."

She gave Tormond a solid whack on the shoulder. "I will see the prisoner now, and fetch my satchel. It has a vial of avens oil to soothe his wounds."

Tormond scratched his beard. "He won't be needing any remedies where he's going."

"Pardon?" Meg clenched her fists and faced him. "This man is innocent of all charges, and I will see him released. Hurry."

The hinges creaked as the king's guard opened the door. "If he survives," the sentry mumbled under his breath.

There was no time to argue with the oaf. Meg dashed forward and dropped to her knees. Afraid to embrace him, she grasped Duncan's filthy hands. "Duncan, can you hear me?"

His eyes opened and closed. "Lady Meg?" His voice rasped hoarsely and he grimaced. "Now I ken I've lost my mind. I'm even imagining her in the cell with me."

Meg shook his hand and held it to her lips. "Duncan, 'tis me. I'm here."

This time his eyes opened and focused. "Lady Meg? What? Why?"

She cared not if it was dirty, Meg cradled his hand to her cheek. "Hush. What matters is that I'm here and I know you are innocent." She lightly touched his shoulder. "What did they do to you?"

Duncan hissed. "Singed off my flesh, then lashed me until I lost consciousness." He licked his lips, but no spittle formed.

"Bring water," Meg screeched. "Quickly."

"Ye are an angel"—he sucked in a ragged breath—"sent from heaven."

"I do not know about that, but I shall do what I can to see you released."

Tormond entered with her satchel and a cup of water, followed by a guard carrying his battleaxe as if Duncan were going to jump up and give them a good fight.

"I should never have allowed you in here," the guard said.

Meg grasped the satchel and pulled out the oil. "Your treatment of Lord Campbell is deplorable." She pulled out the stopper. "I will have words with the king as soon as I've tended his wounds."

As gently as she could, she spread the oil on each weeping welt. "Am I hurting you?"

"Nay..." Duncan's voice trailed off.

Of course he was hurting. She'd never seen a man bludgeoned thus. She helped him drink the water, wishing she had some food to give him.

Conscious of the guards surrounding her, she leaned forward and pressed her lips to Duncan's ear. "Hold on, my love, for I *will* see you a free man, so help me God." Tenderly, she pressed her lips to his temple and closed her eyes. Her heart twisted. If only she could take him into her arms, and lead him to a soft bed where she could properly nurse him back to health. "I thank you, Duncan, for your touching prose. You are truly a gift from heaven."

Meg stood and faced the miserable guardsman. "Sir Campbell is a peer of the Kingdom of Scotland and you have discarded him in this cell like a common criminal."

"But—"

She shook her finger. "I'll hear no excuses. Your treatment of his person is unforgivable. Ensure he has a pallet of straw, food and watered wine at once. Clearly you've tortured him within a hair's breadth of his life and left this valiant knight to starve."

The man threw a worried glance to Tormond.

"I shall gain an audience with the king at once." Meg eyed him. What could she do to ensure the guard followed her orders? She boldly stepped toward him. "If you see to Lord Campbell's comfort, I will do everything in my power to ensure you keep your position in the king's guard."

"Y-yes, m'lady."

She held up a finger. "But if Lord Campbell reports any further mistreatment, I shall make it my personal goal to see that not only you, but the entire prison guard is replaced."

"Yes, m'lady."

She bent down and smoothed her hand over Duncan's head. "Hold on. I shall see you soon, my love." Then she nodded to the king's guard and headed out. When at last they reached fresh air, she faced him. "The Lord of Glenorchy will not die. For it is your head I will call for if his health should take a turn for the worse."

Meg turned to Tormond. "Come." She had no idea how she'd gain an audience with the king, but she would find a way.

Chapter Twenty-Eight

It was an answer to prayer when Meg spotted Eoin MacGregor across the bustling courtyard. She dashed into the mass of people, shoving though. "Excuse me, pardon me."

She'd thought she'd nearly made it when she ploughed straight into a barrow laden with pig carcasses. The claw sank into thick, clammy flesh.

A laborer strong-armed the cart to a stop. "Bloody hell, watch where yer going, wench."

Meg caught her foot on her hem and her ankle twisted. "Apologies."

"If these pigs had fallen and had been covered with dirt, the cook would have had me head."

She cringed and transferred her weight to her throbbing ankle, peering through the throng. Had she missed Eoin?

The laborer grasped her arm far too firmly. "I ought to give ye a good thrashing, running into me barrow as if it were nothing. I'll tell you, the king prefers me pork over all others."

Meg tried to wrench away. "Fortunately, sir, there was no harm done."

He pulled his hand back as if he were going to deliver a slap. Meg flinched and turned her head, but the blow never came.

"Unhand her now, or you'll feel the cold iron of my dirk."

Meg jerked her arm free. "Sir Eoin!"

He kept his dirk flush against the man's neck. "Lady Meg. We seem to meet in the most peculiar circumstances."

"*M'lady?*" The laborer wrung his hands. "Apologies."

She gave the man an exasperated look. "You may release him, Sir Eoin. Aside from a vile temper, I believe he's committed no crime." Fortunately, the pain in her ankle had eased.

The man bowed and grasped the handles of his cart. "Thank you, m'lady. Forgive my disrespect."

Meg waved him on. "I do hope there will be ample roast pork on the king's table this eve, given your import to deliver it." She stepped toward Sir Eoin. "We must meet with the king immediately. They've nearly tortured Lord Duncan to his death."

Eoin gestured to Sir Sean and Sir Robert, who had come up behind him. "We've been trying to gain an audience with the king for days."

"'Tis nearly time for the evening meal," Robert said. "I say we march into the great hall and plead our case."

Eoin ran his fingers across his chin. "'Tis a risk. He may take offense to our brazenness."

Sean pounded his fist into his palm. "We've been waiting to gain an audience for three bloody days. As Lady Meg said, we've no more time to waste."

Meg placed her hand on Eoin's arm. "I would think three knights all in line to inherit titles would pique the king's attention." She stood a wee bit taller. "Besides, you'll have an earl's daughter standing beside you."

Eoin shook his head. "I daresay you should stay away. We all could be seized by the guard and thrown into the dungeon merely for our association with Lord Campbell."

"Aye, that would be smart of the king." She grasped his forearm. "He'll end up with half the gentry in his gaol, and anarchy will run rampant throughout Scotland."

"If you come with us, will you promise to stand aside where you'll be free from harm should a skirmish break out?" Eoin asked.

"Aye." *I'll no sooner stand aside than I would stay away.*

Robert leaned in. "Lady Meg, we thought you were at Tantallon. How did you know Duncan was imprisoned here?"

"You will not believe it." She scanned the scene for Isaac, but he was nowhere to be seen. *Odd.* "Lord Percy's man-at-arms came to call—said he could no longer tolerate the earl's tyranny."

Eoin and the other knights exchanged glances. "Percy?" He looked to Meg. "Do you think he has had a hand in these false charges?"

"Though Sir Isaac did not specifically state thus, I have no doubt that somehow Lord Percy is at the root of our woes."

Sean planted his fists on his hips. "It seems he will never let go of the rift he had with your father."

"That man is a hater," Meg agreed. "I fear it appears he will never leave my clan alone, or anyone who comes to our aid."

With Tormond remaining in the shadows, Meg followed Duncan's Highland Enforcers into the great hall. She'd dined here with her brother many times, but presently the enormous chamber seemed foreign. As usual, the king sat in the center of the table upon the dais. Meg took in a quick inhale. Lord Percy sat to the right of the king, and behind the earl stood none other than Isaac.

Gooseflesh rose upon her skin.

Percy's man-at-arms met her gaze with a quick nod and then glanced away. *What on earth is Isaac playing at? He has turned traitor, but for whom?*

At the dais, Sir Eoin was stopped by two guards who blocked the steps with their battleaxes. "Sire," Eoin boomed, raising his voice above the throng. "I am Sir Eoin MacGregor, firstborn son of the great MacGregor chieftain, and with me I have Sir Sean MacDougall and Sir Robert of Struan, both heirs to vast land holdings in the Highlands. We all supported Lord Colin Campbell and now bear arms for his son, Lord Duncan Campbell, and we request a word."

Chewing, the king spread his arms. "Can it not wait until after I've supped?"

Lord Percy eyed the knights, but his gaze stopped dead when met with Lady Meg's. A fire burned in her stomach. Behind her back, she tapped her pincers.

"And who is this lovely lass?"

Meg shifted her gaze to the king. He was staring directly at her. Of course he would have no recollection of an earl's fifth sister.

"Lady Douglas, sister to the Earl of Angus," Eoin said.

Heat scorched her cheeks. She bowed her head and curtsied. "Your highness. I also had the unfortunate incidence of being one of the Earl of Northumberland's unwilling guests."

Percy's eyes flashed wide. "'Tis an outright falsehood."

"Oh?" Emboldened by the earl's lie, Meg stepped forward, gesturing toward Duncan's men. "And these gallant knights, the king's very own Highland Enforcers, came to my rescue." She glared at Lord Percy. "Though you had us followed all the way to Glen Orchy."

Percy emitted a nervous chuckle. "I daresay the woman is daft. She has a deformity that proves it."

Sir Eoin caught Meg's arm and pulled her behind

him before she could utter another word. "I can vouch for her ladyship. She was abducted from Melrose Abbey by Lord Percy's men."

The king assessed the Earl of Northumberland. "You kidnapped the Lord of Angus's sister?"

"I-I can explain." Percy tugged on his ruffled collar.

"Seize him." His royal highness motioned to the guardsmen.

Lord Percy's chair clattered, toppling over as he stood. "She lies! You Scottish heathens are conspiring against me."

Isaac drew his sword and shielded the earl. Together they fled out the side door whilst the king's sentries gave chase. The stairs now left unguarded, Meg hastened to climb to the dais. "Sire, this has all been a ruse. Lord Campbell is innocent."

The king's small eyes darted across the scene. "So say you?" Running his fingers down his chin, he spoke slowly, as if his mind was calculating. "Who then killed my *beloved* brother?"

Eoin stepped beside her and pointed to the side door. "I suggest you ask Henry Percy. That trickster is behind this deception for certain."

Meg balled her fists and dipped into her deepest curtsy. "I beg of you, your most merciful highness, release Lord Campbell. He's nearly succumbed to your... ah...the torture inflicted upon him."

The king's gaze darted to the side exit. "Hmm." He drummed his fingers on his goblet, as if the life of one of his nobles were as unimportant as that of a dog. He then looked to each man standing before him. Certainly three brawny Highland knights armed to the teeth must give him pause, especially now that his guardsmen were off chasing after the earl. "You are aware Lord Campbell is also accused of killing his father?"

Sean slammed his palms on the table and leaned forward. "If you believe that, you never witnessed the love

Duncan had"—he gestured wide—"we *all* had for the late Lord of Glenorchy. Each one of us would gladly lay down our lives for the baron, and most assuredly Duncan Campbell would give his right arm to see his father again preside over Glen Orchy lands."

The king frowned at Sean's aggressive stance.

Robert pulled Sean back into line. "Well put."

"Agreed," Eoin said.

The king leaned forward and regarded a man clad in black velvet toward the end of the table. "Lord Chancellor, has the prisoner confessed?"

The man cleared his throat and dabbed his mouth with his sleeve. "Last I heard, not as yet, sire. He lost consciousness before the executioner could extract the truth."

"Are you mad?" The words slipped out before Meg had a chance to think. But the ire burning up the back of her neck compelled her to hold forth. "Lord Campbell is on the verge of death itself, and yet he still maintains his innocence. Is that not enough? Must you kill a man if he does not speak as you wish?"

The king narrowed his eyes and gave her a belittling glance. "You are boldly outspoken for a woman." He smirked. "But I'd expect no less from a *Douglas* lass."

She curtsied. *Oh dear, I've made a mess of things now.* "Forgive my display of exuberance, sire."

He pounded his fist on the table. "I shall consider your plea once Lord Campbell's interrogation is complete." He waved a dismissive hand. "Now begone and leave me to dine in peace."

Eoin led them to one of the low tables, far away from the king's ear. Meg's fingers trembled. She couldn't believe that after Lord Percy had fled the dais, the king still clung to the accusations of Duncan's guilt.

Sean grabbed a ewer of ale and four tankards from a passing servant while they all climbed over and sat upon the benches. Meg leaned forward and kept her voice low. "Duncan will not last much longer."

"Aye," Eoin said, sliding a tankard in front of her.

A servant placed a bowl of pottage and four pewter plates on the table. Meg held her tongue until the man moved on. "What are we going to do about it?"

"We?" He looked at her as if she were daft, then gestured to Tormond, who obediently stood behind her. "I'd say you'd best take your guard and head back to Tantallon at first light. Leave the dirty work to we knights."

Meg's gut clenched. "Have you completely lost your mind? I will not tuck my tail and head home whilst Duncan suffers."

Robert raised his tankard. "This is no place for a lady. Eoin's right. There's nothing you can do for him now. And if we spring him, there'll be no stopping. If found within Edinburgh's walls, you could be arrested for conspiring against the king."

Hogwash.

The men leaned their heads together as if she weren't sitting beside them. Over the rumble of the crowd, she struggled to make out their mumblings. Feigning interest in her ale, she leaned a tad closer. *Tonight?*

Meg reached for a bit of bread and doused it in a bowl of pottage. "If I must start back to Tantallon on the morrow, I'd best locate my rooms." She turned to Tormond. "Come."

Chapter Twenty-Nine

Duncan had no idea if it was night or day. The cell they'd put him in after his last bout of torture had no cracks in the walls. But his aching body lay on a fresh pallet of hay. Thanks to Lady Meg, he'd eaten his first solid food since he'd been imprisoned. The oil that still soothed his wounds was proof Lady Meg's visit had not been his imagination running amuck.

In a few short months, he'd had too many regrets. He'd failed in so many ways. Aye, he was responsible for Da's death, and moreover, he never should have allowed John to return Lady Meg to Tantallon. He should have insisted that she remain at Kilchurn until his return. If only she'd been there, things would have been different, and somehow he would have found a way to approach her brother and ask for the lady's hand.

Now all was lost. He was about to meet his end. The king had no intention of releasing him—his men must have failed in their attempt to plead his case by now. The executioner would torture him until he confessed or died. Duncan thought the latter more probable. He would never confess to a crime he did not commit. What good would that do, aside from spare him a few moments of misery? Worse, confessing would smear his name throughout Scotland. His lands could be forfeit to the king, and his sisters ruined. No, he would never confess.

Duncan's mind homed in on that thought. Who did kill the Earl of Mar? Surely the king wouldn't be dimwitted enough to order a murder. But then, he'd arrested his brother on the charges of witchcraft. *Bah*. In all his life, Duncan had never seen a true act of witchcraft. Aye, some odd things happened, like a tapestry falling from a wall, or the creaks in the castle at night... but witchcraft? And though the earl seemed a wee bit eccentric, he didn't appear to be a sickly worshiper of Satan.

Duncan moved and the raw skin on his back tortured him, as if a thousand dull knives carved his flesh. If only he could hold Lady Meg in his arms one more time before he met his end, yet it was not to be.

A grunt echoed in the outer passage. Through the cobwebs of his mind, the sound reminded him of a man being run through. Instinctively, Duncan raised his head.

Footsteps pattered, as if running.

"Halt," a deep voice roared.

Iron clanged. Duncan had heard the hiss and collision of swords too often not to mistake the sound. He pushed himself to his knees, grinding his teeth against the searing pain. The hinges of the door creaked and a blinding torch pushed inside.

"Duncan, are you in here?"

He raised his hand to shield the light, and tried to peer around it. "Eoin?"

"Aye," his friend said.

A wave of relief washed over him. "Have you seen the king?"

Eoin approached. "He plans to wait until after your interrogation to decide your innocence."

"Bloody hell."

"Aye, my thoughts exactly." Eoin knelt beside him. "Och, you look like shite."

Sean stepped into the light. "Lady Meg said you wouldn't last through another bout of torture."

Duncan shoved the hair from his face. "Och aye, she was right."

"Can you walk?" Eoin asked.

"Bloody oath I can." Duncan tried to stand on wobbly legs.

Sean dashed beside him and grabbed him under the arm. "Steady."

Duncan leaned into the knight and steadied his legs. "I'm right as rain." He looked between the two men. "What's the plan?"

"Robert's waiting with the horses," Eoin said. "We'll slip out of here and ride like hell."

"Och." Duncan grinned, his chapped lips splitting open. "The usual."

"Can you run?" Sean asked.

"For freedom? I'll beat you to the door." Duncan swallowed against his urge to puke. Bloody Christmas, his legs wobbled.

"Make haste." Eoin dashed to the gate and beckoned. "They'll find the dead guards soon."

&

Meg hated to trick anyone, but it had to be done. Before she'd "retired" for the night, she'd given Tormond a tot of whisky laced with valerian essence. According to Hubert, the dosage she'd administered would ensure her personal guard would sleep soundly at least until midmorning. She prayed he would not hate her for the rest of his life, but she was desperate. In no way could she return to Tantallon whilst Duncan suffered in the bowels of Edinburgh Castle's dungeon.

She had absolutely no intention of remaining in her

chamber through the night, especially after she'd overheard Duncan's men. They knew as well as she that Duncan wouldn't survive more torture. Meg couldn't even think about what would happen if they broke him and he confessed. Yes, Duncan Campbell was the toughest man she'd ever met, but everyone could be broken...or killed.

Wearing a white wimple to ensure she would look like a chambermaid, Meg placed her ear against the door and listened for any sign of movement. All was quiet in her wing of the tower. Sliding her hand to the latch, she cracked open the door and slipped her head out. *No one.* Wishing she could have pinched a change of men's clothing, she tiptoed through the dark passageway.

After she pattered down the stairwell, she hugged the shadows and made her way to the stables. The light was dim, though a group of soldiers stood at the near entrance. Slipping around the back, she tiptoed to her horse's stall and quickly saddled the mare. Before leading her out, Meg listened. All was quiet.

Slipping back the way she came, she picked up Tormond's bow and quiver of arrows, thanking the good Lord her guard left them in her path, and that Arthur had taught her to use them ever so long ago. Meg tied her mount outside the St. Margaret's Chapel.

Once inside, Meg moved to a narrow window. If the men were planning to help Duncan escape, they might need someone watching their backs. She'd enjoyed archery as a lass, though sometimes the claw could be a bother. She'd learned to shoot left-handed, and pulled back the string with the claw. She loaded an arrow in her bow and waited.

An eerie calm hung over the courtyard. The clammy shiver coursing across Meg's skin reinforced why midnight was called the "witching time." Everything was so quiet, her heartbeat was like a thundering drum.

Clouds, illuminated by the moon, sailed past. A cold breeze blew her wimple back and made her entire body shudder. Had she missed them? She was sure she overheard Eoin say midnight.

Meg cast her gaze back through the dim chapel. A moonbeam reflected off the bronze cross sitting atop the altar. *Dear Lord, please watch over your servant, Duncan, this night. Keep him safe. Keep all the men safe.*

Horse hooves clattered on the cobblestones. Meg snapped her head around and tightened her grip on her bow.

A deep voice echoed off the curtain walls. The hoofbeats sped. Around the bend, the first knight galloped into view, furiously slapping his reins against the black steed's neck. Meg recognized Eoin's helm, then Sean and Robert. Hunched over his horse's neck, Duncan kept pace. Seeing him in such obvious misery made her stomach squelch.

Next, a foot soldier followed, running with a pike in his hand. Unable to keep pace, he climbed to the top of the bend. Up there, he'd have a clean line to all four men once they rounded the next corner. The man stopped at the top and took aim.

Meg snarled and pulled back the bowstring as far as it would go. Grinding her teeth, she let the arrow fly. Hitting the man in the leg, he dropped his weapon and fell to his knees. Meg snatched another arrow and trained it on the cobbled road leading from the gaol, sucking in stuttered breaths. The enforcers' hoofbeats faded. No one else followed. She threw her weapons over her shoulder and raced to her horse.

Galloping faster than she'd ever ridden in her life, she headed for the gate. The shadows of the men darted through the barbican. Voices bellowed from atop the wall-walk, but with the wind rushing in her ears and the metallic beat of shod hooves, Meg couldn't make out their words.

A wrenching groan reverberated from the gatehouse. That noise meant one thing. The guards were closing the portcullis. Determined, Meg rounded the last bend and darted straight into the darkness of the gatehouse. The dim light beyond was narrowing by the descent of the black, iron-toothed portcullis.

The downward-thrusting barbs would skewer anyone who got caught beneath them. Meg's heart flew to her throat. If she ducked and pushed her mount hard enough, she might make it through.

Closing her eyes, she slammed her crop into the horse's rump, hissing like a snake. The horse beneath her surged forward. The chains above creaked under the weight of the deadly gate.

Meg dared open her eyes. The cobbled road stretched endlessly into the black night. She glanced back as the portcullis slammed to the ground with an earthshaking boom.

§

DUNCAN'S GUT ROILED FROM THE JOSTLING MOTION. Earlier, he'd eaten his first meal in days, and now it churned in his gut. It was all he could do to sit in the saddle and spur his horse forward. With every jarring gallop, he grunted. His wounds punished him. When his eyes rolled back, he shook his head. If he lost his wits and passed out, he'd be a dead man.

"We'll ride hard until we reach the River Almond, then we'll slow to a steady trot," Eoin called over his shoulder.

"Aye? And what of the horses?" Duncan asked.

Eoin's teeth flashed white in the darkness. "Fresh mounts await at the inn in Callander."

Duncan's pain eased a bit. Of course Eoin would have a solid plan to ensure a successful escape. For the first time in days, hope of freedom filled his chest. He couldn't about facing the king's army until he and his men were safely behind Kilchurn's walls.

Once home, he would figure out a way to prove his innocence and earn a pardon. He focused upon one driving thought—when he arrived home, he would regain his good name, and then he'd be free to seek Lady Meg's hand. If she would still have him.

Duncan followed his men across the bridge, then they slowed to a trot. God on the cross, trotting jarred his wounds worse than the smooth gait of a gallop. When stars crossed his vision, Duncan shoved his heels downward to steady his body. He didn't have enough strength to post with the horse's movement, but he must stay the course. After they changed horses, they'd ride until they reached Kilchurn—he had all night and a whole day to endure this miserable motion. He'd best steel his mind to it now.

"A rider approaches!" Sean called over his shoulder.

Duncan stole a backward glance. *Will they not allow a tortured man a moment of respite?* The heathen was bearing down on them like a ghost in a windstorm. Something white flapped, as if he were wearing a pennant. "Did you see any others?"

"Only the one."

Eoin pointed. "There's a bend up ahead. Let's ambush him there."

Robert and Sean drew their swords. A warning tickled at the back of Duncan's mind. He couldn't quite put his finger on it. "Let's see what the bastard wants before we kill him."

"You're serious?" Eoin asked. "He's likely to have a go at one of us."

Duncan strengthened his grip on his reins. "Only one rider after the notorious Highland Enforcers? Either he's out to get himself killed, or he could help us."

"How?" Robert asked.

Hoofbeats pummeled the earth before Duncan

could answer. Each man moved into the shadows and waited as the galloping horse approached.

Duncan watched him sail past, but it wasn't a man. Dark skirts billowed behind, while her wimple flapped in the wind. He'd only seen one woman in his entire life who could ride like hellfire. *Lady Meg*.

Sean and Eoin took the lead, spurring their horses to a gallop beside her. Duncan clenched his teeth and took up the rear. "'Tis Lady Meg," he bellowed, praying to God they heard him before anyone laid a hand on her.

She shrieked when Sean reached in and tugged on her reins.

"Stop, you bloody bastards!" Duncan forgot his pain and urged his horse ahead.

When he pulled beside Sean, they'd started to slow.

The whites of Sean's eyes were as big and round as silver shillings. "We've caught Lady Meg."

"That's what I've been hollering about." Duncan reined his horse to halt. Catching his breath, he leaned forward and steadied himself on his mount's withers. Wincing as the pain returned with vengeance, he bellowed like a dying bull.

"Duncan!" Meg leapt from her horse and rushed to his side. "I've a tonic for your pain."

His agonizing wounds no longer mattered. He swung his leg over his horse's rump and slid down, pulling her into an embrace. "What are you doing out here, lass? You could have been killed."

"Me?" She placed her hand on his cheek. "You would have been struck by a lance if I had not been in the chapel with my bow."

Eoin stepped beside them. "Lady Meg, I told you to return to Tantallon."

Duncan thumped MacGregor's shoulder with a quick backhand. "Did you not hear? She covered us whilst we escaped."

Meg gazed up at him. "I couldn't run to home. Not with so much at stake."

Duncan smoothed his hand over her wimple and cradled her to his chest.

"But what of your guard?" It didn't appear Eoin would let things rest. "I gave him instructions—"

A grimacing smile stretched Meg's face. "Methinks Tormond will be sleeping rather late. Forgive me, but I gave him a tonic that was sure to put him to sleep."

Duncan staggered a bit while he led her to her mount. "Did you purchase a potion?"

"Nay. Ever since I returned to Tantallon, I've been studying healing arts with the gardener."

"Ah, m'lady, you are always full of surprises." He grasped her hand and bowed over it. A lovely fragrance of rose blossoms filled his senses and he pressed his lips to the back of it. If only he could cradle her in his arms throughout the duration of the night.

"We've no time for niceties," Robert said. "The king's men will be following for certain."

Duncan nodded and gave Meg a leg up. "We've no choice but to take you with us."

"'Tis what I want."

"Your brother will be in a rage when he discovers you missing." Duncan hobbled back to his horse and mounted, choking back his urge to bellow. "But we cannot worry about that now. Lead on, Sir Eoin."

Chapter Thirty

It was early morning when Isaac awaited Lord Percy's retinue on the north side of the Melrose city gates. He'd arrived ahead of the king's sentry, but not by far. The rider had given a proclamation to the town crier, who announced the Earl of Northumberland was accused of murdering the Earl of Mar and that every effort should be made to apprehend the criminal.

Thank God I moved my wife and babe to her parents' home in Carlisle.

Lord Percy had sent Isaac ahead on the off chance something of this nature would happen. Riders paid to deliver missives from the king could speed ahead faster than any army. They had posts established. When a horse tired, they'd pass their messages to another rider who'd proved his speed. News traveled fast in the lowlands of Scotland, just as it did in Northern England.

No man could be on the run for long without everyone the wiser.

As Lord Percy approached, he held up his hand and commanded his retinue to come to a halt.

Isaac rode up beside him. "They've barricaded the city gates—you've already been accused of murder."

Lord Percy smirked. "Well then, if they'd only

known, they could have seized you and this whole mess would have been resolved."

Isaac clamped his lips together. He'd best keep his mouth shut, else his employer would not hesitate to hand him over to the Melrose sheriff. An earl had a much better chance of obtaining a pardon than did a lowly man-at-arms.

"King James sold us out already?" Lord Percy scratched his beard. "Miserable, backstabbing Scottish bastard."

"We shall need to stick to the byways." Isaac pointed. "We can follow the river to the east and give Melrose and Dryburgh a wide berth."

Percy frowned. "The horses are spent."

"We'd best not stop until we reach the cover of Thornielaw Wood."

Percy shook his head. "No."

"Are you mad?" Isaac immediately wished those words hadn't spewed from his mouth. "I beg your pardon, my lord. But do you wish to be caught?"

"I assure you, I am quite sane." Lord Percy drew his sword and slammed Isaac in the chest with the flat side.

With no time for Isaac to deflect the blow, his breastplate caught it full force. He squeezed his knees in an attempt to remain mounted, but his horse whinnied and reared. Crashing to the ground with a thud, Isaac lay on his back and tried to catch his breath. With each gasp, his world spun.

"If you ever disrespect me again, I'll use the sharp edge to take off your head." Then Percy laid the rein across his steed's neck and turned northward. "They're expecting us to cross the border. We shall disappoint them."

Meg had never been so happy to see anything as she was when they rode out of the forest and Kilchurn Castle loomed against the moonlit sky. The keep cast a serene shadow on Loch Awe, and if she had not seen it before, she would have thought the place enchanted.

Aside from a few breaks and a brief rest to change horses, they'd ridden nonstop. Everything ached. Her eyelids refused to stay open, and her head bobbed forward in rhythm with her horse's steady gait.

But Meg had no intention of sleeping. Not until she set Duncan to rights. She thought it fortunate they had arrived at night. It would be easy to slip into the keep and spirit Duncan up to his chamber without alerting his mother and sisters.

Once inside the inner bailey, Sean and Eoin helped Duncan dismount. Grimacing, his teeth reflected white in the moonlight. And though it was dark, Meg could tell his face had taken on an ashen pallor.

Meg took charge. "Take him to his chamber. Robert, fetch the bath and buckets of hot water."

"Aye, m'lady."

No one questioned her directives. They were all most likely too tired to balk. She didn't care. If anyone had said a word, she would've issued a quick retort.

Meg clung tight to her medicine bundle and followed the men up the dark stairwell. Duncan's strained grunts echoed through the tower. Just as bad, the sickly pall from the gaol clung to him and wafted to her nose. So strong the odor, she had to turn her head to the side.

The men stepped into the passageway on the third landing and headed straight to Duncan's chamber. Meg thanked her stars she'd been there before. Once they cleared the door, she rushed past them and pulled the duvet down to expose the linens. "He'll need to be bathed."

Eoin helped Duncan hobble to the edge of the bed. "You don't mean for him to sit in a tub?"

"I can cleanse him here, but I'll need fresh linens."

"I'll fetch them," Sean said.

Meg set her bundle on the table. "Thank you." She then set to striking the flint to light the candle on the bedside table.

The men helped Duncan climb onto the bed and lie on his side. He moaned when his head met the pillow.

Eoin wiped his hands on his chausses. "What can I do?"

"Light the fire, then help Robert with the water buckets." Meg glanced to the bowl and ewer. Soap sat beside them atop a folded drying cloth. "Once I have the water and the linens, I'll have all I need to tend him. You men should seek your rest."

Eoin placed a hand on Meg's shoulder. "You need to sleep as well."

"I shall, once I've tended to Duncan's needs."

"I could fetch the healer." Eoin struck the flint.

Duncan pushed up on his elbow. "I would have no other hands care for me but those of Lady Meg."

Heart fluttering, she snapped her gaze to the bed. He flopped back onto his side with a whooshing exhale. The effort seemed to be the last Duncan could muster.

"The water." Flicking her hands, Meg shooed Eoin away. "Make haste."

Once the men had left, she opened her bundle and pulled out the avens oil. Meg's hands trembled. The whole time they were riding, all she could think about was getting Duncan into his chamber and applying her healing salve. But now that she was alone, so many emotions coursed through her. She looked at his broad-shouldered form resting on the bed with his back to her. All she wanted to do was wrap him in her arms and hold him for eternity.

But he was hurting. He'd been half conscious the past several miles—rode the entire distance in the cold without a shirt. She crossed the floor and placed the bundle on the table then caressed his shoulder. "Are you awake, my love?"

"Mm."

At least he was conscious at some level. The door burst open. Eoin and the others entered with water, linens and a trencher of bread and chicken. "I thought you could use some food." He pulled a flask from the back of his chausses. "I've brought a flagon of whisky as well."

"My thanks to you all." Meg faced them. "Now off with you."

"Are you sure you no longer need us?"

"Quite certain."

"Get the bloody hell out," Duncan brayed like a wounded bull.

Meg wasn't sure if he knew what he was saying. She bent over him. His eyes were closed. She clasped her palms and bowed her head to Duncan's men. "I've no doubt everyone will be in better spirits on the morrow."

"Aye," Sean said. "Duncan always turns into a swollen-headed ogre when he hasn't had enough sleep."

They all seemed reluctant to leave, so Meg spread her arms wide and led them to the door. "Everything will be fine. I've brought some powerful essences with me. I'll have Lord Duncan set to rights in no time."

When she finally closed the door, Meg sighed. She'd cleanse Duncan first. *No use wasting the salve when I'd just turn around and wipe it off.*

She stood back and looked at his tattered woolen chausses. They were hardly worth saving. "I shall unfasten your belt and then cut off your hose."

Duncan's only response was deep breathing. Meg relaxed. He needed to sleep, and she could care for him whilst he did so. After removing his boots, she picked up the shears and made quick work of removing his chausses and braies. Holding the smelly garments at arm's length, she carried them to the hearth and tossed them on the fire.

She dipped the cloth into the bucket of tepid water and lathered it with soap scented with lemongrass. Humming a ballad, she worked the lather over Duncan's skin, ever so careful to avoid his injuries. Her breasts grew heavy and her throat thickened to the point where she could no longer hum. Though he'd been starved, his body still maintained its well-muscled tone. Every inch of him was sculpted by the chiseled muscle beneath.

Reverently, she lifted his arm and smoothed the cloth down the underside until she met the apex where his hair thickened. Meg swirled the cloth a wee bit more vigorously then wrung it out in the bucket. Once freshly lathered, she reached over him to cleanse his chest. Her breathing stuttered while she ran the cloth down the bands of muscles on his abdomen. Meg could have sworn they rippled at her touch.

Her fingers began to quaver again when she reached the black curls surrounding his sex. Their coupling was still fresh in her memory. She may be condemned to hell, but her womanhood grew hot with a yearning so powerful she had to clench her muscles to fight it back.

As if his sex were as fragile as a porcelain figurine, she cradled it, smoothing the cloth in languid strokes. He lengthened in the palm of her hand. Meg cast her gaze to Duncan's face. His eyes remained closed, his breathing steady.

Emitting a stuttered sigh, Meg continued the bath, cleaning between his thighs and carefully running the edge of the cloth through his toes. She reached under him, and once she had Duncan as clean as possible without moving him, she shifted to his head and ran a soapy cloth through his hair. She then repeated every movement to remove the soap.

Duncan shivered a bit.

"Are you cold?"

As she expected, he made no reply. Meg methodically swirled the drying cloth over his skin until his tremors ceased.

"I must apply the avens oil." She reached for the vial and poured some on her fingers. "It might hurt a bit, but I can see yesterday's application has done some good." Meg had no idea why she kept talking, other than it soothed her to do so. She hadn't lied when she said his wounds looked better. They'd scabbed over and were not as angry red as they'd been in the gaol.

When she touched her fingers to Duncan's back, he jolted, a hiss slipping through his lips.

"Are you all right, my love?" Meg gasped. She needed to stop calling him "love."

Duncan relaxed into the pillow. "Mm."

Truly, he was awake at some level. She continued with her work. "Your skin looks like it was scalded. What did they burn you with?"

"Lead."

Meg's heart skipped a beat when Duncan uttered the word. She'd heard of the use of molten metal to extract a confession, but to see the practice actually used seemed as archaic as crucifying someone. *God forbid.*

Smoothing her fingers down his back, she gently rubbed in the salve. When she hit a hard spot, she leaned in for another look. A farthing-sized piece of lead still clung to his back. She scraped it with her fingernail, but decided not to pull it off. With luck, the lead would slough away in time like a scab, and to remove it at this stage would only serve to cause him more pain.

When certain every wound was properly dressed, Meg moved to the basin and washed her hands. She stood there for a moment, pushing suds through her fingers and regarding Duncan's naked form through shuttered lashes. Odd, but she cared not what his men would think when they discovered she'd stripped him bare. He no longer smelled of the dungeon, and his wounds would soon heal.

If Duncan shunned her, she would at least be content in the knowledge that she'd helped him recover from an abominable ordeal. The food on the table caught her eye. She shoved a bite of chicken in her mouth and washed it down with a swig of whisky straight from the flagon. She clapped her hand over her mouth and coughed. Her eyes watered with the flame burning her throat. *How can men drink this?*

Meg walked to the foot of the bed and leaned on the bedpost. Duncan had to be the most beautiful man in all of Scotland. His long legs weren't slender, but sculpted with solid muscle and peppered by bold black hair. If she weren't so completely exhausted, she would like nothing more than to stand and gaze upon his magnificence all night, but her legs could hardly withstand more punishment.

Gyllis's chamber was one floor above. She should slip up there to sleep. Meg tiptoed across the floor.

"Stay."

She stopped and scanned the room. No one besides Duncan could have uttered a word. She returned to his side. "Are you awake?"

"Aye, lass," he slurred.

She swiftly crossed to where she could see his face. "Are you in much pain? I could give you some valerian. 'Tis what I gave to Tormond to make him sleep."

He smiled, but his eyes remained closed. "Nay. Come here and rest in me arms."

"I really should..."

"Pl...ease."

How could she resist the deep tenor of his voice? "Are you chilled?"

"Mm."

After bolting the door, Meg pulled the duvet over his shoulders then crossed to the other side of the bed as if she were Duncan's wife. Her hands started to tremble again. She removed her wimple, unlaced her gown and slid it from her shoulders. The heavy wool whooshed to the floor. Wearing only her shift, she climbed under the bedclothes and slid across the chilly linens until her body spooned into Duncan's warm chest.

With a satisfied moan, he slid his hand over the dip in her waist and placed his open palm on her abdomen. "I shall never let you go. Not ever again."

Chapter Thirty-One

❦

Once Meg crawled into bed with him, Duncan gave in to his exhaustion and slipped into heavenly sleep. With his woman in his arms, the pain eased. When he woke, a sliver of light shone through a crack in the window furs.

Though his head throbbed, he'd never felt so alive. Meg slept cradled against his body the entire night, and he'd been more than content to have her there. Her red tresses tickled his face. Duncan drew in a deep inhale, blessed with the heavenly bouquet of wildflowers. Meg's sweet scent could make him swoon. Yes he, the leader of the Highland Enforcers, could go weak at the knees simply by being too close to Lady Meg.

He tugged her closer. The pillow-soft cheeks of her bottom cradled his rigid cock. He didn't know when he'd become erect, but by the searing heat in his groin, he could have been as hard as his sword all night.

His hand smoothed up her belly and found a pliable breast. A wicked nipple jutted through her linen shift, and he swirled his fingers around it. He nuzzled into her neck and flicked his tongue from the base of her nape up to her ear. "Are you awake, my love?"

Meg shifted her lovely bottom against him, the slightest moan escaping her lips.

"I want to ravish you."

She brushed her hand over the fingers toying with her breast. "Aye, Duncan."

He loved how her lilting voice spoke his name. But then she rolled to face him and rose up on her elbow. "What are you saying? Should you be so vigorous whilst you're healing?"

He grinned at the concern expressed in her eyes. "To be depraved of your love would injure me far more than any mortal blow."

Her next breath stuttered as she stared into his eyes and cupped his cheek in her hand. "Love?"

"Aye. I know now that I love you. I cannot bear to think of living without you, Lady Meg."

She slid her arm around his back and tugged.

Duncan winced.

She quickly released. "I want to wrap you in my arms, but I'm afraid I'll cause you pain."

He grasped her fingers and guided them to his hip. "Put your hands on me. You know where."

With a nervous chuckle, she swirled her fingers across his abdomen, her knuckles lightly brushing the tip of his manhood. Duncan moaned with pleasure. "Your mere touch will make me come undone."

Her tongue shot out and tapped her top lip. "Is that so bad?"

"Nay, but I want this time to last." He tugged her shift up. "And first I want to feast my eyes upon your exquisite beauty."

She emitted another of her nervous chuckles. "I'm not all that much to look at, I say."

Ignoring her, he encouraged her to lift up while he tugged the gown over her head. Meg's eyes narrowed with a flash of fear, and he fluttered kisses along her jaw-line to calm her. After he eased her back onto the mattress, he gradually pulled back to his knees.

"My God, you are exquisite."

Meg crossed her hands over her body.

"Nay." Duncan grasped her wrists and gently tugged her hands to her sides. "You're more beautiful to gaze upon than a marble statue." He leaned over her and kissed her mouth fully, swirling her tongue with his, igniting a desire he never knew existed within.

She closed her eyes and smoothed her hand over his stubbled jaw, ever so careful to avoid touching his back. Languidly, he trailed kisses down the length of her neck until his mouth met with an erect nipple.

Her full breasts were velvety soft, tipped by rosebuds. Her skin was the color of unblemished porcelain. So many women used lime to make their complexions like Meg's, but not a one could come close to her loveliness.

Duncan gave in to his passion and caressed her while he suckled her breasts. Rising to his haunches, he smoothed his fingers down the curve of her waist, drinking in her womanly shape. Meg's hips flared seductively, framing a nest of red curls.

Ever so lightly, he flicked his thumb between her legs while he stretched out beside her. His cock pushed into her hip—so rigid, he wouldn't last much longer. "Open your legs for me," he whispered.

She complied and reached for his swollen member. When her fingers wrapped around it, seed leaked from the tip.

Kissing her neck, Duncan slipped his finger inside her and swirled while she stroked him. Without thought, his hips thrust. She milked him with a steady movement. His breathing sped. His mind could think of nothing but claiming her. "I can wait no longer."

"Make love to me."

He needed no more encouragement. Climbing between her legs, he hovered over her. "You are so fine to me."

Her tongue flicked out and smoothed across her top

lip. She cast her gaze down and grasped him. Then her crystal blue eyes met his, and she guided his manhood to her opening. Duncan could scarcely breathe for the emotion swirling through his entire body. *This is what it is like to truly love a woman.*

He shuddered as he gradually filled her. Meg moved her hands to his buttocks and grasped him firmly. Then she showed him what she wanted. His cock slipped so deep, it touched her womb. Arching her back, Meg closed her eyes and sighed—the most blissful sound he'd ever heard.

A gasp caught in the back of her throat. The hands on his buttocks became more insistent. Duncan's heart raced as he thrust his hips. She swirled her mons to increase the friction. Duncan tipped his hips forward to hit the spot he knew would drive her mad, but he could hold on no longer. His eyes rolling to the back of his head, he gave in to his basal desire. Like a blast from a cannon, his seed shot deep within her womb.

Crying out, Meg came undone around him and gasped for breath. Duncan took his weight on his elbows and collapsed above her. "My God, you are decadent."

She swirled her palms on his buttocks. "As are you."

He covered her mouth and kissed her, taking his time. But as their mouths became more impassioned, he again grew rigid inside her.

※

THREE TIMES THEY MADE LOVE UNTIL DUNCAN'S hunger reminded him they needed to eat. "Are you hungry, my love?"

"Aye. There's some chicken and bread on the table."

He grinned. "How fortunate. We have no need to leave this chamber."

"And I must again tend your wounds."

As Meg spoke, Duncan was reminded of the needling pain in his back. At least the morning's activities had given him relief.

Meg climbed out of bed and reached for her shift, but Duncan grasped her wrist and tugged it away. "Are you cold?"

"A wee bit."

He pulled the plaid from the foot of the bed and draped it over her shoulders. "This will keep you warm, but do not close it all the way. I want to gaze upon you whilst we eat."

"Very well." She arched her brows while her gaze meandered down his body. "Only if I can watch you as well."

"Agreed." He chuckled and led her to the table. Definitely not a fancy display. He held up the flagon. "It looks like we've only whisky to drink."

"Aye, well, Eoin brought up the food when we arrived last night."

Duncan poured two modest tots and took the seat opposite Meg. The smell from the chicken made his mouth water. They'd had little to eat on their mad dash from Edinburgh—oatcakes and some bully beef. But rather than savagely dig in, he held the trencher up to Meg. "M'lady." She tore off a leg and devoured it while he cut off half the breast. "I see I'm not the only one famished."

"Apologies." Meg clapped a hand over her mouth. "I could eat that whole chicken myself."

Duncan chuckled. "When did you last have a good meal?"

Meg tore off a piece of bread. "Goodness, it must have been before I left Tantallon. Once I reached Edinburgh Castle, I was too busy worrying about you to think of eating."

He washed a bite down with a swig of whisky. "We

shall have to see that you're well fed. You need your strength to keep up with the likes of me."

An adorable blush rouged her cheeks, and she looked down, as if suddenly shy. "Aye."

He reached out and covered her hand with his palm. "I haven't asked you about Arthur. Where has he been through all this?"

"He has business dealings in France."

"Ah, that explains it." Duncan cast his gaze toward the hearth. *The Earl of Angus has no idea she's here.* He bit his bottom lip.

"What?"

"Aside from proving my innocence to the king, I'll also need to mend fences with your brother."

Meg stopped chewing and folded her hands in her lap. Clearly the mention of her brother concerned her. Duncan wanted this to be a happy occasion, so he tore off the other leg and handed it to her. "Not to worry—we've plenty of time to sort out the ire of kings and earls. And presently, we've nothing to enjoy but each other."

She accepted the leg and ate it—like a lady this time. "I'd like that."

"Aye." Since he was unable to sit back, he rested his elbows on the table and studied her. Never before had he been completely smitten, but he would not complain if he were forced to sit in that spot and stare at Lady Meg for hour upon hour. He reached out and spun a curly lock around his finger. "You are so fine to me."

❧

MEG SIPPED HER WHISKY AND COUGHED. "IT WOULD be nice to have some watered wine."

Duncan stood. "I shall call for some."

"Nay." She didn't want their time to be interrupted

any more than he did, but she would stop sipping whisky this instant, lest she fall into her cups. "We can wait until the evening meal."

"Very well."

She stood and gestured to the bed. "Now, let me apply my salve and bandages."

He lay face down, as he'd done several times for her now. "I think this new concoction is the best yet."

"Truly? When I returned to Tantallon, I began studying the healing arts with the gardener."

"A gardener?"

"Aye, he's the most knowledgeable healer I know."

"I'd reckon so, if he taught you to concoct that potion."

"'Tis avens oil. Hubert says 'tis the most important herb in a garden."

She dribbled some of the oil on Duncan's back and tenderly rubbed it in. "I wish we could stay here in your chamber forever." Honestly, since they'd eaten, she'd been worried about how they'd face everyone. Now there would be no question that she was ruined. What would Duncan's family think when she descended the tower stairs?

"Aye." His voice sounded dreamy—the avens oil must indeed be working a miracle. "But too many folks are relying on us."

"You perhaps, but no one cares overmuch about me."

Duncan rolled to his side and grasped her wrist. "I never want to hear you say that." He sat up then pulled her into a tight embrace. "*I* care. I will always care."

"But what will everyone think when we leave this chamber?"

"I am the master of these lands. They will think whatever I want them to think."

If only she could believe him. "'Tis easy for you to say."

"It is—"

When the ram's horn sounded to announce the evening meal, Meg's stomach squelched. *What will Lady Margaret say?*

Chapter Thirty-Two

Once Meg had wrapped Duncan with linen bandages, they dressed. After he helped her reaffix her wimple, they headed down the tower stairs. Her nervousness grew with every footfall. What would everyone think of her now? Duncan had said a number of endearing words, but never once had he mentioned marriage. Meg wanted nothing more than to stay with Duncan, but without a contract of marriage, her brother would interfere for certain.

Before they rounded the last bend, Meg took in a deep breath to steady her wits. Duncan glanced at her with a half-cocked grin. "Everything will be all right, lass."

She emitted a nervous chuckle, but there was no time for a rebuttal. Stepping into the great hall, benches scraped across the floorboards. Everyone stood, clapping and singing the pibroch of the Campbells.

Duncan puffed out his chest and tightened his grip on Meg's arm while they strode through the center aisle. When they reached the dais, he held up his palms and requested silence. "Friends, family, Campbells, I am happy to say I am back with you once again. I suffered greatly at the hands of the king. Lady

Meg assisted in my escape and brought with her a salve that has worked wonders to bring me from the very edge of death. Though I stood wrongfully accused, I fear this ordeal has not yet come to pass. On the morrow, we must prepare for battle." He scanned the hall, all faces gaping at him expectantly. "But tonight we celebrate!"

The hall erupted in a raucous applause. Duncan resumed his grasp on Meg's elbow and led her to the seat beside his.

Once situated, Meg looked to her right. Lady Margaret nodded politely. "'Tis quite a stir you've caused around the keep."

Meg clapped her hand to her cheek. "Gracious, I was afraid to come down." She bit her bottom lip. "But I worked so hard to care for Duncan's wounds."

Lady Margaret raised her eyebrows knowingly, as if she had a peephole through to Duncan's chamber. It was a look that said, *I am well aware of what you've been up to, so do not bother trying to pull the wool over my eyes.*

"Ale?" Duncan asked.

Meg rapidly nodded. "Please."

"Duncan, we must talk," Lady Margaret said.

"Aye, Mother." He raised his tankard. "I've a great many plans to discuss with you."

The lady gave him a smug nod.

Meg wished she could pull Duncan back up to his chamber for a quiet meal. The world had been so perfect when they were alone and shut away. She glanced across the table. The Highland Enforcers all grinned at her the same way Lady Margaret had.

I'll be burn in the fires of hell for certain. Meg hid behind her tankard. *And now that everyone knows I'm ruined, what will become of me?*

Duncan carved a slice of pork and set it on her plate. "You must eat. The chicken we had was hardly enough to sustain you."

She looked at the piece of meat and her stomach squelched.

At the far end of the table, Gyllis waved and grinned. At least *her* smile was more innocent and welcoming than the others.

Lady Margaret leaned close. "You might want to sleep with Gyllis tonight."

"I'd love to spend time with Gyllis again. She's so friendly."

"Yes, she is." Lady Margaret rested her eating knife on the table. "Where, pray tell, is the Earl of Angus? Is he aware of your presence here?"

Meg could have crawled under the table. "He's in France on business." Couldn't the lady let sensitive matters rest until after the meal, and in a more private setting?

"I see." Lady Margaret frowned. "And what of your marriage prospects? Or are you still thinking of taking up the veil?"

Meg pushed her piece of meat around her pewter plate with her knife. Honestly, she had no answer for Duncan's mother. She dipped her chin and turned so that only Lady Margaret could hear. "I've not discussed my future with Arthur since I returned from Alnwick." That wasn't the complete truth, but after all, Arthur hadn't announced her engagement. She forced a smile. "With any luck, my brother is concerned with too many other affairs to worry about me."

Duncan leaned forward. "Come now, speak up so we can all hear."

Lady Margaret reached for the bread. "I'm ever so glad to see you in acceptable health, son." She gave Meg that knowing smile again. "Locked in your chamber all day, I've been worried you've been on the brink of death."

"After being whipped and splashed with molten lead, followed by two days of hard riding, I believe a day of rest was not unwarranted." He gestured across to his men. "I'd wager you all slept late."

"Aye, past matins," Eoin said.

Lady Margaret cut her pork. "That may be, but we've more to worry about than the king's men."

Duncan gave her a stern look. "Aye, and I shall meet with you in my solar at first light. Does that meet with your approval, m'lady?"

Under the table, he grasped Meg's claw then touched his lips to her ear. "Do not let Ma worry you. Deep down she's an angel. I shall set her straight on the morrow."

※

THE NEXT MORNING, DUNCAN ROSE IN A FOUL MOOD. His meddling mother had insisted Meg sleep with Gyllis, proffering the miserable excuse that the lassies got along so well. Never mind there were a half-dozen guest rooms in the main keep. Giggling, Gyllis took Meg up to her chamber shortly after the evening meal. *Blast meddlesome women.*

He splashed water on his face and gingerly ran a razorblade over the morning's beard. His back itched and needled him. If he'd had his way, Lady Meg would be near enough to apply her ointment. After he'd dressed, a rap came at the door. Hoping it was Meg, he strode across the floor and opened it wide. His stomach sank. "Mother."

She pushed past him. "We need to talk." Ma had a maddening way of pretending she was in charge. She waltzed to the table and sat in *his* chair.

Duncan combed his fingers through his hair. The best way to handle Lady Margaret when she had a hair up her arse was to face it head-on. He sauntered over and took the seat across from her.

She frowned, which made her cheeks wrinkle against her grey wimple. "I'll go straight to the point."

"Please do."

"What are your intentions with Lady Meg?"

"I—"

"I allowed your indiscretion to pass the first time she remained in your chamber and tended you, because your father convinced me you were unconscious and the headstrong lass would see it no other way. But when I learned you had been spirited into the castle yet again with unimaginable wounds."

Duncan opened his mouth to speak, but Mother held forth, gesturing with wide arms.

"And the pair of you locked the chamber door. No one knew if you were dead or alive."

"But—"

She shook her finger. "I had no doubt that you were conscious, and I can only imagine what went on in here." She stood and paced. "Lady Meg is the daughter of an earl. She's not some tart you brought home from the Taynuilt alehouse."

He cringed. "You knew about that?"

She shook a threatening finger. "I know *everything* that happens in this keep." She resumed her seat. "Now, as I see it, we have a grave problem."

Duncan gulped back his response and resigned to let her talk.

"First of all, it appears Lady Meg's brother has no idea she's here. You must spirit her back to Tantallon forthwith before he returns from France. That is the only way we can cover up this mess without ruining the lass's reputation, and to remain in the earl's good graces."

Duncan stared at Ma's careworn face. "You've got it all figured out, I see."

"Aye, well, someone must watch out for your reputation if you refuse to do so. For all that is holy, you were nearly killed in the Edinburgh dungeons." She covered her mouth and blinked rapidly. "I couldn't have borne it if I were to lose you, too."

"Ah, Mother. My incarceration was a misunderstanding, and I did not confess. But I'm afraid your plan for Lady Meg will not work."

She dropped her hand and feigned an exasperated expression. "Pardon me?"

"I love her."

She clapped her hands over her mouth. "Duncan, there are rules of etiquette which must be followed. You simply cannot ride off with a noblewoman and send a missive to her family telling them you've planned to wed."

"But that's exactly what I must do...and forthwith."

"You cannot be serious."

"I cannot take her back to North Berwick, especially not with the king's men in pursuit. I shall send the Earl of Angus a missive at once."

Lady Margaret sighed and sat back. "An alliance with the earl would do our family well—if he doesn't have *your head* first."

"Oh ye of little faith, Mother. I swear, no one will take my head."

"I'm not happy about this state of affairs." Mother watched him while he collected a piece of parchment, a quill and ink. "How are you feeling this morning?"

Duncan dipped his quill. *Now she asks?* "I'd be better with a fresh application of Lady Meg's avens oil, but otherwise I am well."

"I can apply the oil for you."

Duncan glared from his writing with an arched brow.

"Never mind." She stood and moved toward the door.

Duncan shook the quill. "I will appoint Lady Meg

with her private chamber. Since she will be remaining here, she will require her own quarters."

"Absolutely not. I do believe Gyllis and Lady Meg would prefer to share. They've grown such a fondness for one another." Mother opened the door. "I shall send Alana to tend you."

Duncan scrawled with a bold hand. Why must his mother meddle so?

§

DUNCAN SENT THE MESSENGER ON HIS WAY WITH TWO missives. One was addressed to King James, explaining his innocence and requesting a pardon. The second was for the Earl of Angus, and it proved much more difficult to write. Duncan ruined three sheets of parchment before he was satisfied with the contents.

He then met with his men in the solar. The six of them stood, staring at a map on the table.

"I doubt they'll come by sea." Duncan scratched his chin. "They'd most likely ride by way of Callander."

Robert pointed. "Aye, but the king could commandeer the army at Dumbarton Castle and sail from there."

Duncan knew he was right. They could expect an attack from east or west. "We must post lookouts at all inroads. There's no getting around it."

"I'll see it done, m'lord," Sean said.

"My thanks. If fortune smiles upon us, the king will receive my missive before his men set out." Duncan turned to Eoin. "After what you said about Lord Percy slipping away when you and Lady Meg gave testimony, I'm in hopes the king will grant me a pardon forthwith."

"One never knows," Archie said from across the table. He was always the questioner of the group. "I reckon the accusation of the Earl of Mar using witchcraft was contrived in the first place."

"It matters not. We must now do what we can to regain the king's good graces and continue our work in the Highlands."

"Hear, hear," Eoin said.

Duncan rolled up the map. "And in the interim, I need to reclaim my fighting legs. I'm afraid the king's hospitality sapped me of my strength."

Eoin slapped him on the back. "We'll see you set to rights."

Duncan's knees buckled, and he braced his hands on the table. Showing weakness to his men would be a great folly. One he doubted he would ever live down. He hissed through his gritted teeth. "I'll remember this when we're sparring, friend."

Chapter Thirty-Three

❧

Taking advantage of the sunshine, Meg strolled through the garden with Gyllis. After a few days of good food and care, Duncan was back to managing his affairs. Daffodils and tulips happily danced around them with the promise of more days of favorable weather.

"Do you think you will marry Duncan, or are you still intent on taking up the veil?" Gyllis asked.

Meg looked away and shrugged. She'd asked herself that same question a hundred times, but Duncan had yet to pose the question, and since his mother had insisted she stay with Gyllis, Meg hadn't seen much of him. True, he had a great many things to organize and very little time. It seemed whenever he came around, Lady Margaret was nearby. "Marrying your brother isn't up to me."

"Aye, but I'm sure you have an opinion."

"Well." She smiled at Gyllis's sweetly expressive face. "We shall see in time—how about you? Are you courting a handsome lad?"

"Not formally."

"Formally? That does sound intriguing. Pray, do tell."

Gyllis giggled and pulled Meg behind a tall hedge.

"You mustn't tell a soul, but I've noticed Sir Sean Mac-Dougall look my way many times as of late."

Meg whistled. "Oh my, he's in line to inherit the lairdship, is he not?"

"Aye."

After they'd fled the burning barn, Meg recalled Sean riding into their party as if he'd come from nowhere. "He's quite adept on the trail. Duncan said he's like a ghost."

"Honestly?" Gyllis clapped her hands over her heart. "And he's so skilled with a sword. I've watched him spar from the upper chamber window."

"Have you now?" Meg knew exactly how giddy Gyllis must be feeling on the inside. The same fluttering sensation tickled her insides every time she saw Duncan wielding his claymore. "Perhaps I could say something to Sir Sean."

"Oh, would you?" Gyllis waved her palms in front of her face and shook her head. "But you mustn't. It wouldn't be proper."

"I could make it sound innocent..." Meg tapped a finger to her lips. "Perhaps encourage him to dance with you the next time minstrels come to play."

Gyllis twirled in a circle. "Aye, I could dance with him all night." Laughing, she spun around the corner of the hedge, straight into Duncan's arms.

He grasped Gyllis's shoulders. "With whom would you like to dance?"

Gyllis gasped like she'd been skewered. "N-no one." She grimaced over her shoulder and winked at Meg.

Clasping a hand over her own racing heart, Meg winked back. Duncan had obviously been sparring. His tresses were damp and pushed away from his face, sweeping his collar. The laces on his shirt were spread open, giving her a view of a hard, masculine chest that glistened in the sunlight.

Duncan released his hold on Gyllis and bowed.

"Lady Meg, please do the honor of dining with me in my solar this evening. We've a great many things to discuss." He sounded unusually formal.

"Very well." She curtsied. "Do you need your dressing changed?" she asked, trying to keep the longing from her voice.

He looked at Gyllis and frowned. "Mother has seen to it the healer has been tending me."

Meg had thought that might have been the reason she'd not seen Duncan more. *Mothers could be meddlesome*. She wanted to comment about her disappointment, but anything of the like with Gyllis present would have been untoward. "Until supper, then?"

He again bowed. "Ladies."

Gyllis giggled as he took his leave. "I do not believe I've ever seen my brother so serious."

Meg cringed. Hopefully whatever he needed a private audience for was not grave. Wincing with the trepidation crawling up her spine, she hid her misgivings by wrapping her arm around Gyllis's shoulder and leading her toward the stables. "In my opinion, Sir Sean is an accomplished horseman. Do you like to ride?"

&

TROTTING THROUGH THE GLEN ORCHY WOOD WITH Gyllis did nothing to settle Meg's nerves. By the time the ram's horn announced the evening meal, Meg had herself convinced that Duncan would use the healer to tend his wounds from here on out, her avens oil had caused a rash and he'd decided to take her back to Tantallon at his first opportunity.

She clutched the claw against her midriff and squeezed. If only she weren't a cripple, she might find happiness in this life. She stood outside the solar door wondering if Duncan was already within. Meg stared at the latch, deliberating as to whether to turn tail and lock herself in Gyllis's room, or collect her wits and continue on with it.

Should she knock?

Meg slapped her cheeks to clear her head. She wasn't one to dally and she most certainly wouldn't start now. With a deep inhale, she grasped the latch and pushed open the door. Then she gasped.

Duncan snapped his gaze to her and quickly stood. Meg had never seen a man look so magnificent. He wore a forest-green plaid emboldened with a hint of yellow in Highland style, gathered around his waist and pulled over his left shoulder, held by a large brooch with an amethyst center. Beneath, he wore a quilted black doublet atop a ruffled linen shirt.

His black hair was combed away from his face and touched his shoulders in thick waves. He'd shaved since Meg had seen him that morning. His chin almost glistened, and when he looked at her, his eyes turned dark, as if telling her to step inside and lock the door behind her.

She did exactly that.

"Lady Meg, you look lovely this evening." He approached and raised her hand to his lips. "Thank you for meeting me. I've no idea what I would have done if you hadn't come."

Meg allowed him to lead her to a seat. Then she noticed the lavish display of food upon the table. "Will the family be dining with us?"

"Not this eve." He chuckled. "This night my desire is for you not to want for anything."

So much extravagance when he's planning to send me back to Tantallon on the morrow? Meg sat in the chair he held and looked closer at the dishes spread on the table. Pheasant stuffed with sweetmeats, apple pottage with currants and aromatic spices, lamb shanks, stewed dates, and a trencher of hearty bread.

He reached for a glass bottle with a wide, flat bottom. "This wine is from our finest vintage." Duncan poured for Meg and then for himself. He held up his goblet. "To us."

Meg lifted hers and arched a brow. "Us?"

"Yes, I wanted to enjoy a delicious meal with you before I..."

She couldn't breathe. "Yes?"

"Before we partake in the most scrumptious dessert."

The delicious scent of cloves wafted from the apples. "You mean there's more?"

Duncan brushed his fingers across the back of her hand. "Aye, so much more, but first we must eat. I want this evening to be perfect."

Meg's hand trembled as she sipped her wine. The more Duncan talked, the more confused she became. She studied him, sitting back in his chair. Did the healer have a better salve? "How is your back feeling?"

"'Tis coming good, thanks to your avens oil." He cut the leg quarter of the pheasant. "You prefer the dark meat, as I recall?"

"Thank you." She held up her pewter plate. "Has the healer been applying my avens oil? I have scarcely seen you in days."

"Apologies for that, there was much to be addressed. And yes, my prying mother instructed Alana to apply your salve, though I daresay your hands are far gentler."

"You mean my hand." Meg held up the claw. "This one isn't of much use." When Duncan frowned, she clasped it in her lap. Why must she draw attention to her deformity? He was well aware she was impure—never would be an acceptable match, especially for a man as virile as Duncan Campbell.

He sat like a statue and stared. "I disagree. Both of your hands are gentle. I hardly notice the crippled one, except when you mention it. Honestly, Lady Meg, it is functional. You can pick up objects and hold them. I've yet to see where it has caused you to live a lesser life."

Meg's jaw dropped. No one had ever spoken about the claw in such explicit terms. And then he'd just babbled on about it as if the blasted thing caused no consternation. If she had been formed normally, Arthur may have married her off by now, but no. When callers came, they smiled at her face, took one look at the claw and dashed for the nearest escape. Before she left for Melrose, Arthur had started corresponding with older suitors. Meg took a healthy swig of wine and wiped her mouth. "My, that is good." *Leave it to Duncan to charm me with delicious wine so that I cannot fixate on that which irritates me.*

He smiled as if he had just read her thoughts. "It seems you have become good friends with Gyllis?"

"Aye." *Should I mention her interest in Sean?* Duncan was still grinning, and Meg chose to save that conversation for another day. "She's ever so pleasant."

He took a bite of pheasant. "You're both spirited."

Meg turned her attention to her food as well. "Scottish lassies need to be spirited to keep up with the likes of lads like you."

"Like me?" His smile turned devilishly rakish. "Whatever do you mean?"

She scooped the stewed apples with her spoon, forcing her racing heartbeat to steady. "Ye ken what I mean."

He must have, because he picked up a lamb shank and tore the meat from it with his healthy white teeth. Chewing, he rubbed his fingers together to dispel the grease. "I haven't thanked you properly for coming to my aid in the gaol. There are no words to express how much your kindness meant to me." He smoothed his fingertips over the table's grainy wood. "I thought I'd never breathe the air of Kilchurn again."

Meg set her spoon down. "When I heard of your incarceration, I could think of nothing else."

"But why did you not return to Tantallon as Eoin proposed? Your presence here could be ruinous for your reputation."

Meg's mouth went dry. Did he not know how much she loved him? She'd given him her virtue. Yes, he had a reputation for womanizing, but she'd always sensed they shared something deeper. Was Duncan so shallow he was ignorant of the love she bore for him? Did he harbor no such feelings for her?

How on earth could he talk about ruining my reputation, when he himself has taken my maidenhead? Suddenly unable to sit a moment longer, Meg shoved back her chair and raced for the door. Tears rimmed her eyes as she reached for the latch.

Duncan's hand squeezed around her arm. "Wait." He pulled her so close, she could smell spicy cloves on his breath. "Forgive my impertinence." His eyelids lowered as his gaze shifted to her lips. "Perhaps the reason you could not return home is the same as why I do not want you to go."

Meg's heart thrummed in her chest and a flash of heat ignited deep inside her loins. Duncan lowered his mouth to hers and gently kissed her. Unable to resist, Meg welcomed his mouth, her hands growing a mind of their own and sliding around his shoulders. How much she'd craved his touch.

Duncan tapped his forehead to hers. "Again I must ask your forgiveness."

"It appears I am powerless to resist you, even when you're planning to send me away."

He straightened. "Pardon?"

She tried to step aside but his arms remained clamped around her, his chest ever so warm against her aching breasts. "I cannot remain here, especially since you have ruined me."

"Is that what you think?" He groaned and clasped her hands between his palms. "I am making a mess of this."

"Of what, exactly, m'lord?" *Please embrace me again. Please.*

Then he chuckled. Meg had no doubt he'd gone mad when he dropped to his knee. "Since we first met, I have been unable to look at any other woman aside from you."

"But..."

He held her tightly and drew her hands to his heart. "What I'm trying to say is I cannot imagine my life without you, Lady Meg. I love you and I want to marry you."

Her entire body went completely numb, her mouth dry, then gooseflesh sprang up upon her skin. Had she heard him correctly? "M-me?"

"If you will have me."

"I..." Meg glanced to the claw, which was covered by his large hand, then her gaze returned to his eyes and her stomach spun in a circle and flipped upside down. "You could love a woman like me?"

"You mean a woman who's not afraid to stand up against English tyrants, who is bold enough to ride in the back of a Gypsy wagon?" Still kneeling, he kissed her hands. "A woman who would risk everything to visit me in the bowels of the Edinburgh dungeon, just to apply a new salve she's concocted—and then risk complete and utter ruination by administering a potion to her guard and following a band of knights into the Highlands?"

She cupped his cheek with her hand. "I do not sound so awful, when you put like that."

He pulled her onto his knee and wrapped his arms around her waist. "Awful? You are an angel, Meg. You're *my* angel."

Gazing into his intense eyes, Meg saw only pure determination and something else. He did love her. Truly. Flitting fairies took up residence in her breast. If Duncan didn't have his hand around her waist, she might float to the ceiling. She ran her palm across his smooth jaw. His tongue slipped out, inviting her to kiss him. Ever so slowly, Meg moved closer, watching his eyes until her lips met his welcoming mouth. Filled with warmth and happiness, she molded into him like a river molds around a solid rock that will stand proud through the ages of time.

"Please," he gasped. "Will you marry me?"

Her limbs weightless, she thanked heavens for Duncan's strong hands. "Aye. There's no place I would rather be than by your side." Throwing her arms around his neck, Meg kissed him, swirling her tongue with his in blissful union.

In one movement, Duncan stood. Cradling Meg in his arms, he carried her back to the table. Resting her in her chair, he gently kissed her forehead and knelt beside her. "We must drink to our engagement."

Holding her hand with his left, he raised his goblet with his right. "May we enjoy a lifetime of happiness together and, God willing, our children will grow into fine Campbells."

With tears rimming her eyes, Meg raised her goblet and tapped it to Duncan's—so overcome with emotion, she couldn't speak. After she sipped, he kissed her, the fruity bouquet of wine deliciously swirling in their mouths as they sealed their love.

Meg set her goblet on the table and giggled. "I do not suppose I would have made a good nun."

"I cannot imagine your loveliness ever being covered up by a nun's habit." He reached into his sporran. "But there's more."

Meg glanced at his hand and gasped. Duncan held up a ring of gold, set with ruby the size of a hazelnut.

He took her right hand and slid it onto her ring finger. "With this ring, I pledge my love and my betrothal. I pray you never remove it."

She held it up to the candle and the stone flickered with red. "'Tis the most beautiful stone I've ever seen."

"It reminds me of your hair of fire." He rubbed a lock between his fingers. "Do you like it?"

"Aye." She grinned. "But you indulge me."

He nuzzled into her tresses. "I intend to spend the rest of my life ensuring you are pampered, my love."

Closing her eyes and surrendering to his touch, Meg prayed this moment would last forever.

Chapter Thirty-Four

※

Duncan went about his affairs with renewed zeal. His only frustration was Mother. Though she was ecstatic with the news of his betrothal, it seemed to make her all the more intent on ensuring Meg's virtue remained safe from further tarnish. Or so she thought.

At the very least, Lady Margaret did everything in her power to keep the couple separated, especially after the evening meal. She'd even gone to the extent of posting a guard outside Gyllis's chamber at night. When Duncan confronted her about it, she had expostulated that if he wanted the marriage to be carried out with the Earl of Angus's blessing, Duncan had best behave chivalrously and with the utmost respect for the lady's reputation.

But today, Duncan had devised a plan that even his stepmother begrudgingly agreed to allow—not that she had the capacity to order him around in any way. Mother always managed to dictate her desires through the use of other means, like his sisters. *Ballocks to my Meg sleeping in Gyllis's room with a guard posted outside the door, and ballocks to a chaperone.*

Basket in hand, he paced in the great hall, awaiting Lady Meg to appear from the stairwell. When lightly tapping feet echoed from above, he knew it was she, merely by his thundering heartbeat. She wore a blue gown, the neckline scooped low from shoulder to shoulder, low enough he could see the dark shadow of her cleavage. He almost moaned with his need to touch her silken flesh. Her hair had been combed back and braided around her crown, and, to Duncan's delight, was devoid of a veil.

He held his hands out to her. "You look lovely." He allowed himself a brief dip of his eyes to drink in the lusciousness of her breasts.

A blush spread across her cheeks. "Thank you. Your mother lent me the gown…like all the others."

He offered his elbow. "At least you're putting them to good use."

She looped her dainty hand through it. "Once you've received word from Arthur, I shall send for my things. Then I will not be such a burden to everyone."

"You could never be an encumbrance." He gestured ahead and led her to the gate. "The skiff is awaiting our departure."

She glanced up at him, her blue eyes sparkling in the sunlight. "Excellent, and who will be our chaperone today?"

He glanced over his shoulder for any eavesdropping family members then lowered his voice. "It shall be only the two of us."

She grinned like a lass who'd just found a gold sovereign. "How did you manage that?"

"Mother may think she's lord of this castle, but I assure you, she is quite mistaken."

Meg skipped beside him. "I was beginning to wonder."

"Pardon?" He chuckled with an exasperated expression while they walked around the corner of the castle and down to the private dock. "Cook prepared a basket with tasty morsels for us."

"A picnic away from the castle grounds?"

He placed one foot in the boat to steady it, and then offered Meg his hand. "Aye, in a place where we can be sure to avoid prying ears and eyes."

She put her claw in his palm, something she'd never done before, and then lifted her skirts with the other hand. "'Tis a perfect day for a boating adventure."

Once she was settled, he climbed in, sat facing her and picked up the oars. "I believe spring is finally upon us."

Meg folded her hands in her lap and drew in a deep breath. "'Tis so peaceful out here. At Tantallon we're on the edge of the Firth of Forth with forceful waves crashing against the rocks endlessly."

"Aye, but that's a different sort of beauty."

"I suppose it is." She cast her gaze to the far shore and pointed. "Look at the mule deer."

Duncan followed her finger. Sure enough, a small herd of does grazed with fawns beside them—a sure sign that spring had arrived at last.

Meg laughed and covered her mouth with her hand while Duncan continued to pull the oars. The water shimmered in the sun behind her and made her hair look alive like a flame.

Her smile caused his heartbeat to stutter. "How long do you think it will take before we receive a reply from Arthur?" she asked.

His shoulder ticked up. "A fortnight, mayhap two."

"That long?"

Duncan chuckled. "'Tis not really all that far off. Are you anxious, lass?"

"Aye." She sighed. "I dearly love Gyllis, but I feel as if I am imposing, sleeping in her chamber every night. I honestly do not understand it, especially since Kilchurn is so well appointed with bedchambers."

He regarded her lovely blue eyes, focused upon him as if the thought of another month with his sister would drive her to insanity. "And here you thought you wanted to take up the veil."

She rolled her eyes and looked to the cloudless sky. "Alas, this is somewhat different than taking an oath of chastity and staying in a dormitory of nuns."

"I could appoint you to a chamber and station the guard outside." He pulled harder on the oars to speed their pace. "Mother would most likely not balk too much."

"And hurt Gyllis's feelings?" Meg shook her head. "I think not."

Duncan puzzled. "Very well, then—shall we leave things as they are?"

"I suppose we must, at least until we hear from Arthur."

As Kilchurn Castle grew smaller in the distance, Duncan rowed the skiff to an island in the center of Loch Awe.

"Look at this place," Meg said. "'Tis lovely. What do you call it?"

"Innis Chonain. When we were boys, John and I used to paddle out here and play King of the Island."

Meg got a faraway look in her eyes. "Do you miss him?"

Duncan rowed until the boat stopped on a sand bank. "Aye, the milksop." He hopped into the knee-deep water then tugged the skiff onto the beach so that Meg could stay dry. He offered his hand. "M'lady."

"Thank you." She picked up the basket and allowed him to assist her. "Kilchurn looks so far away."

"Aye, 'tis why I brought you here." He pulled her into his embrace. Her scent flooded his senses and he closed his eyes, nuzzling into her hair. "I wanted you all to myself."

She lifted her chin and he kissed her. Pulling away, she chuckled. "I imagine Lady Margaret is upon the battlements with a spyglass."

He took the basket and led her into the wood. "I thought of that, too. There's a clearing ahead with a wee pond."

※

Meg gasped when the trail opened to a spectacular oasis. True to Duncan's word, a small pond sat in the center of a clearing, the ground covered by moss. Ferns sprouted everywhere, dotted by yellow primrose, and from the trees hung drapes of green moss—the trees themselves showing a hint of budding leaves. On one side was an outcropping of rocks so picturesque, Meg imagined mermaids sunning themselves beside the dark blue water. Hand in hand, they stood. The only sound was the call of a warbler overhead. "'Tis so peaceful."

Duncan set the basket on the ground. "Are you hungry, lass?"

She was about to say yes when she looked into his eyes. He stared at her with a hunger that had nothing to do with the need for food. She'd seen that look countless times, but now knew him well enough to know what he desired. Every fiber of her body had been craving for his touch, craving intimacy. She waggled her shoulders. "Hungry for you."

A deep chuckle rumbled from his throat and his eyes turned dark as obsidian. "Come here." He drew her into his powerful arms. Before she could blink, his mouth covered hers with an unexpected wildness to his fervor. He all but consumed her in a rush of frantic kisses.

Hard and long, Duncan molded his body to hers. Meg matched his passion, allowing her own suppressed yearnings to boil to the surface. Afire, she ground her hips to his while his hands slid down her back and grasped her buttocks.

His lips trailed down her neck and atop the breasts that peeked above her scooped neckline. "Thank God you wore a gown with easy access." With a flick of his finger, he loosed her laces and exposed her nipple. Licking, he swirled his tongue in an erotic dance.

Meg's breasts swelled and her thighs quavered. Duncan tugged her laces more. With trembling fingers, she helped him loosen them, then shrugged out of her gown. "I've lain awake each night with wanting for you."

"You too?" He pulled the plaid from the basket and spread it beside the pool and then turned to her. "I have but one request."

"Aye?"

He faced her, eyes still dark. "To gaze upon you completely naked."

She crossed her arms and brushed her hands along her shoulders. "'Tis not too cold?'

He pulled her into his arms and kissed her as if he could swallow her whole. "I shall keep you warm."

She inhaled his scent laced with cloves. Her insides turned molten. "Only if you strip bare as well."

Chuckling, he unbuckled his belt and let his weapons fall. "I'm only too happy to oblige, m'lady." He pulled the plaid from his waist and dropped it. Wearing his shirt, hose and boots, he stepped forward. "Now you."

Meg uncrossed her arms and held them above her head. Duncan tugged her shift up and cast it aside. A cool breeze made the gooseflesh stand proud upon her skin. She felt chilled, yet afire while he slid his warm fingers down her sides and then slipped a hand between her legs. She parted slightly, and he teased her with his finger before he knelt to untie her garters. His nose only an inch from her sex, he closed his eyes and inhaled. "Merely the scent of you can bring me to my knees."

Meg shuddered. She knew exactly what he meant.

After he'd removed her hose and slippers, Meg grasped his shoulders and pulled him up. His manhood strained against his shirt. Aye, he wanted her as much as she did him. Duncan didn't wait. He yanked off his shirt and boots, but Meg held up her palm. "I shall remove your hose." She knelt and untied the flashes, slowly smoothing his stockings down his muscular calves.

As soon as his feet were free, he pulled her into his arms and crushed his mouth over hers. His body warmed her, his manhood brushed her abdomen, but she desperately needed him lower. Meg wrapped her leg around his and ground her mons into him.

Duncan groaned. "I can hold back no longer."

"Me also." Meg's breathless words came whispered and fast.

Taking her hand, Duncan led her to the plaid. He sat and looked up at her with a gleam in his eye. "Straddle me."

"We can do that?"

His eyes grew wide. Then he looked left then right. "Who will stop us?"

She complied, and his sex sat between the apex of her legs as if it were meant to be there. Kissing him, she rocked her hips so he slid up and down the place that craved him most.

Duncan drew in a stuttered breath. "My God, my seed is about to erupt."

She placed her lips against his ear. "Take me, Duncan."

"I want you to ride me." He lay back and grasped her hips. No words needed. He lifted her up. Taking his manhood in her hand, she guided it into her core. With a moan, Duncan's eyes rolled back, and then he stared at her as if she were the only woman in the world.

With his urging hands, Meg moved along his shaft until his manhood brushed a place that begged for more. If she stopped, she'd die. Faster and faster, Meg rocked her hips, craving friction, the tension coiling tighter and tighter inside her body. A shrill cry caught in the back of her throat, and the heavens opened with blessed, shattering release.

Duncan roared and drove his hips faster, plunging into her as his eyes lost their focus. "God's teeth, woman. You will send me mad before we are married."

Meg collapsed atop his body. "'Tis exactly why I want word from Arthur so quickly. Nights without you in my arms are torture."

He smoothed his hands up her breasts and kneaded her, the friction building again. How could he turn her into such a wanton with his mere touch? "I want you in my bed forever."

Drawing in a ragged breath, Meg covered him with her body and captured his mouth with a kiss. She then tasted his skin—the saltiness of his powerful neck, his smooth jaw, his eyes, his brow. Never in her life would she gain her fill of Duncan Campbell.

"You are so fine to me, Lady Meg." He rolled her to her side. Drawing the plaid across their bodies, he faced her. "So what do you think of my Highlands?"

She grinned with a low chuckle. "All this fresh Highland air grows fine-looking men, I'll say."

"Aye, but the Lowland lassies are not to be rivaled."

"I do not know. Your sisters are beautiful."

Duncan smiled and reclined on his back. "They are lovely. And now that Da is gone, 'tis up to me to find them husbands."

Oh how wonderful it was when a window opened. Meg rose up on her elbow. "You know, Gyllis quite fancies Sir Sean."

"Sir Sean?" Duncan blinked twice and grimaced. "That flea-bitten son of a dog?"

Meg rested her head on his chest and smoothed her

hand through his downy-soft hair. "Pardon? He will be the next MacDougall chieftain—"

"Do you not think I ken? None of my men will *ever* marry one of my sisters. 'Tis…'tis…"

Meg gazed at his face. "What?"

The corners of his mouth drew downward as if he were entirely baffled. "They're practically as close as siblings. Besides, Sir Sean did not earn the moniker 'Lusty Laddie' for naught." Duncan eyed her with an air of distaste. "He has an affinity for the lassies."

A laugh spewed from her lips, and she clapped her fingers over her mouth to stanch it. She wanted this to be a serious conversation. "And you were a monk before you met me?"

"That is entirely different."

Gyllis was right. Duncan could be bullheaded when it came to his sisters. "Hmm." Meg trailed her fingers down his well-muscled abdomen, not quite ready to change the subject. "Pity. Gyllis is the only lass I've seen him eyeing since I've been here. A match between them would solve one of your problems."

"He'd better keep his lusty eyes from my sister." Duncan sat up. "Enough. There is no way would I allow Sean MacDougall to court Gyllis. We shan't speak of it again." He glanced over his shoulder. "Now where's that damned basket? I'm famished."

Meg swallowed her urge to giggle. Perhaps Duncan needed a little time to consider her suggestion. Thank heavens she'd mentioned it away from the keep and Gyllis. "I do hope you've brought some watered wine. I'm ever so thirsty."

Duncan set two tankards on the plaid, held up a flagon, swirled it and sniffed. "Me thinks 'tis ale."

"That will do." Meg craned her neck and peered at the basket. "What other surprises did Cook prepare for us?"

Chapter Thirty-Five

Duncan sat in the laird's seat at the high table with his family and Lady Meg by his side. A lone messenger wearing the king's colors marched up the aisle, and the hall grew silent.

Duncan stood and met the man at the dais steps. "What news?"

He reached inside his cloak. "I've a missive from the king."

Meg gasped behind him.

Trepidation raising his hackles, Duncan accepted the parchment and slid his thumb under the seal of King James.

"What does it say?" Lady Margaret asked before he could unfold it.

Duncan ignored her and read. A weight lifted from his shoulders. He handed the missive to Meg. "Thank God."

"What is it?" Mother stood and rushed to him.

"I've received a pardon." He grinned and thrust up his fists in triumph. "Both charges against me have been rescinded," he bellowed for all to hear.

The entire hall erupted in cheers. Clansmen and women pounded the hilts of their daggers on the tables. The pipers on the balcony launched into a round of the pibroch of the Campbells whilst every soul stood and sang.

A tear streamed down Meg's porcelain cheek, and he drew her into his arms. "I am a man truly blessed."

🐾

"The view is spectacular from here," Gyllis said, staring out over Loch Awe.

"Aye, it surely is." Meg wasn't looking at the lake, but rather stared at the men sparring in the courtyard. "The battlements give an ideal vantage point to a great many things." With a sigh, she leaned through a crenel notch.

"Och, not there, silly," Gyllis said.

"No?" Meg waved her over. "On that I disagree."

Gyllis slid into the notch beside her and rested her chin on her palms. "Oh yes, I see what you mean."

Meg fanned her face. "Unfortunate the knights have forgotten their shirts."

"Mm…" By her lack of ability to speak, Gyllis must have spotted Sir Sean MacDougall sparring with Sir Robert Robinson. Formidable opponents they made, but Meg's eyes strayed to the black-haired knight clashing swords with Sir Eoin.

She could never tire of watching Duncan with or without his clothing. But today he gave her a special treat. He wore his plaid belted low across his hips and sparred with his back to her. His sturdy waist flared until it met with powerful shoulders.

Even from the top of the wall-walk, she could see his muscles ripple beneath his glistening skin. And Duncan was nearly a head taller than all the other men in the courtyard. Meg doubted a one of them could best him. He advanced on Eoin, swinging his sword in his right hand and brandishing a targe in his left. Eoin deflected Duncan's most savage blows. Meg bit her bottom lip. Their war play was not barbaric, but so fluid, it looked like a dance.

The two men circled, weapons held high, awaiting the next strike. Eoin lunged in. Duncan scooted aside, and it was on yet again.

"He's incredibly beautiful," Gyllis said.

Meg blinked, as if popping out of a trance. "Aye."

"And faster than a fox."

Meg sighed.

"And his chestnut hair glistens with streaks of copper when the sunlight hits it just right."

Meg glanced to her future sister-in-law and smacked her shoulder. "You're not watching Duncan, are you?"

"Nay, silly. What lassie would want to watch her brother spar?"

Meg recalled watching Arthur with the guard and cringed. "Most certainly not I. My brother needs an army in front as well as behind him."

Gyllis leaned into her. "Do you think you'll hear from Lord Douglas soon?"

"I hope so. Nearly two fortnights have passed since Duncan sent the missive to Arthur. Soon it will be an entire month."

A sword clattered to the cobblestones. Both women peered through the crenel notch to watch Sir Sean retrieve it, then he turned and grinned up at them.

"Isn't he dashing?" Gyllis rose up on her toes and waved with a smile full of sunshine.

Meg chuckled. The lass was smitten indeed.

When Sean resumed sparring, Gyllis sighed. "You'd think the men wouldn't need to practice so hard since Duncan received the pardon from the king."

"Aye, they no longer have the king's ire to worry about, but these are trying times. The men can never let their guards down, especially with the work the Highland Enforcers carry out for the king." Meg leaned out until she dared not go any farther. Craning her neck, she could no longer see Duncan.

Gyllis sighed and sat in the crenel. "I wish every day could be as dreamy as this."

"I'll say. Perhaps we could practice dancing in the courtyard after the men finish sparring. Beltane is coming. We can brush up on our May Day dances."

Gyllis clapped her hands. "I think you have a splendid idea."

"And what, pray tell, is that?" Duncan's deep voice rumbled behind them.

Meg quickly straightened. "We were talking about practicing the May Day dances in the courtyard later." She curtsied. "Will you come?"

"I've far too many things to attend. Besides, my days as a practice partner are over."

Meg shot a glance at Gyllis. "Perhaps we'll have to ask Sir Sean to join us."

Gyllis nodded like a woodpecker hammering a tree. "Aye."

"Och, are all women schemers? I'll see to it Sir Sean has his hands full this afternoon as well."

"Why, you're no fun at all." Meg grasped his elbow. "What brought you up here? Are you finished sparring already?"

He gave her a sideways look, one that made butterflies swarm throughout her insides. "We must talk."

"Oh? Is that why you cut short today's practice?"

"Aye." He placed a hand upon Meg's shoulder and looked at his sister. "Gyllis, would you please excuse us?"

Meg pointed toward the courtyard. "Go find Sir Sean to see if he'll partner with us for dancing practice."

Duncan frowned. "You'd best leave him alone and report to your mother. I'm sure she'll have something for you to tend to."

Gyllis headed toward the stairwell. "I like Lady Meg's suggestion better."

"Insufferable women. Now that John's gone you're all ganging up on me."

Meg chuckled. "Is the poor lord of the keep being bullied by a mob of lassies?"

"Wheesht, woman, and come with me." He led her down a flight of stairs into a small chamber where the guards upon the wall kept their weapons. He bolted the door.

Meg's stomach squelched. "What you came to discuss must be very grave indeed, m'lord."

He slid his fingers to the back of her neck, his gaze lowering to her mouth. "It is. Most grave." He brushed his lips across hers ever so slightly. "Of utmost urgency."

Moaning, Meg welcomed him while he deepened the pressure, his lips hot and demanding. Her breathing quickened. Her body instantly alive with need for him.

Growling, Duncan pulled his lips away. "When I saw you watching down below, I could not wait another moment."

Meg pressed her body against his and swirled her hips. "If only..."

Duncan covered her mouth and lifted her by the waist, setting her on the bench behind them. "Let me between your legs."

Her insides ready to erupt, she complied and pulled his mouth down to hers. Frantically kissing her, he tugged up her skirts until the air cooled her sex. But it wasn't enough to quell her insatiable yearning. She tugged on his belt.

Duncan raised his kilt. Meg glanced down. His manhood jutted between them, demanding not to be ignored.

Her breath stuttered as she slid her hips closer to him. "I want you."

"You've nearly brought me undone." His words came out in short bursts with urgency.

Meg slid her fingers down and helped coax him toward her. "I can wait no longer."

With one long thrust, Duncan entered her, a shuddering moan rolling from his throat.

Sweet release came fast for them both.

Panting, Meg clung to him. She opened her eyes and looked at the assortment of weapons surrounding them, and then to her bare knees. "This is an armory?"

Duncan cringed. "'Tis worse than the larder." The place of their last tryst.

Meg rested her head upon his chest. "And the embrasure in your mother's chamber."

He held up a finger. "But that was a stroke of genius. Mother would never have thought to look for us there."

Meg couldn't help but laugh. "If we do not receive word from Arthur in the next sennight, we will need to wed immediately."

Duncan kissed her temple. "Perhaps I should send another missive."

"Heavens, by the time we receive word, our firstborn will be walking."

He grasped her shoulders and held her at arm's length. "Are you with child?"

"I think not." Meg counted back. So many things had happened, she couldn't recall the last time she'd seen her courses.

"Are you certain?"

"Yes. No. Possibly." Heat prickled her skin. Ah yes, it had been at least six sennights since her last show. "Perhaps I'm late."

Before Duncan had the chance to respond, the ram's horn blew three times. Their eyes met, and Meg's shoulders tensed. She didn't need Duncan to tell her three blares was not a good sign. "An attack?"

"Mayhap." Duncan stepped back and adjusted his

belt. "Unknown riders approach, that is a certainty." He helped Meg hop down from the table and smooth her skirts. "Find my mother and the lasses. Lock yourselves in my solar until I come for you."

Meg flung her arms around him. "Duncan, no. I cannot hide whilst you face some unknown enemy."

He gave her a firm squeeze. "Do as I say. I'll not see you hurt. Quickly now."

Her heart racing, Meg descended the tower steps, but stopped at a narrow window—one used by the archers. Clutching her hand to her chest, she gasped. The approaching army carried none other than the Douglas pennant. "My God, Arthur. What are you thinking?"

Meg turned and fled up to the battlements. She would not be locked within a chamber whilst her brother led an attack on her betrothed.

Chapter Thirty-Six

❧

Standing beside Eoin upon the battlements, Duncan watched the Earl of Angus's great army surround Kilchurn Castle's walls. The retinue progressed slowly, led by teams of oxen pulling two impressive Portuguese cannons. The earl's men wore the Douglas tunics, emblazoned with the blue and red seal of the Earl of Angus.

A squire carried the earl's pennant while it fluttered in the wind.

Duncan wanted to hit something. "No wonder it took the earl so long to respond to my missive. It would have taken a great deal of time for the teams of oxen to drag those cannons into the Highlands."

Eoin slapped his hand against the stone wall. "Bloody oath. The bastard has no sense of humor, has he?"

"It appears not."

"So he's planning to use the big guns to blast through our walls though his sister is within?"

Duncan ground his fist into his palm. "Not if I can help it."

Eoin stepped back. "You've a plan?"

"Aye." Duncan headed toward the stairwell.

His friend hurried alongside him. "Oh no, you're

not walking away without a word. Besides, if your plan does not work, you'll need alternative tactics."

Duncan stopped. "I'll go out alone and talk to him."

"What? Have you lost your mind? He's toting two cannons that can blast your miserable arse all the way to Inverary."

Duncan placed a hand on Eoin's shoulder and squeezed. "This is one fight I'd prefer to avoid. He is Lady Meg's brother. If nothing else, I owe it to her to attempt a parley."

Eoin spread his palms to his sides. "What if he fights?"

"Post the archers over the gatehouse. If it comes to blows, have them kill everyone surrounding me *except* the earl. I'll not have Arthur Douglas's blood on my hands." Duncan eyed him. "Then we'll show him what it means to fight in the Highlands."

"But you could be killed out there by yourself."

Duncan started down the steps. "I'm not intending to fight." He regarded Eoin over his shoulder. "Have you not been my friend long enough to trust me?"

"Aye, but this is madness. Talk to him from atop the battlements—or by messenger."

"Nay. I must do this my way." Duncan pointed his thumb behind. "Go, don your armor. Organize the men."

Duncan's squire, Jamie MacGregor, met him in his chamber. The smart lad already had his coat of arms laid out. "I came as soon as I heard the ram's horn."

"Good lad." Duncan slipped into a pair of chausses and a quilted doublet. While Jamie went to work fastening buckles, Duncan recounted the points he needed to make to the Earl of Angus. That the man had arrived with an entire army befuddled him. Why go to such great expense before he tried to talk? Had Duncan's missive not been clear? Did the king have something to do with it? Had the king issued a pardon in hopes that the Campbells would let their guard down?

"All set, m'lord." Jamie said.

Duncan blinked. "My thanks. Head up to the battlements with your bow."

"Aye, m'lord." Jamie started toward the door and turned. "Do you reckon they'll blast those big cannons at us?"

"They might. Make sure you run for cover if they do."

The lad blanched and headed out.

Duncan grabbed a black cloth and his helm, then hastened to the guardhouse. "Bring me a poleax," he shouted.

A guard stepped forward straight away. "You can have this one, m'lord."

Duncan took it and affixed the black cloth. Amused by the confusion written on the man's face, Duncan chuckled. "Have your weapons at the ready in case my plan does not work. If the Red Douglas lives up to his reputation, he might start swinging before the first word is uttered."

At Duncan's nod, the guard opened the gate. Lord Campbell marched through, bearing the black flag of parley, suspended from the poleax.

The gate closed behind him with a boom that reverberated through his bones. Duncan eyed the procession. A man-at-arms stood at the front of a V formation, flanked by impressive-looking sentries, all armed with pikes and swords. Duncan held the flag high so it would be seen by all. "I request a word with the Earl of Angus."

The man-at-arms glanced up to the battlements. "Tell your archers to stand down first."

Duncan didn't like the blatant lack of trust, but gave the signal to Eoin above. The archers would stand out of sight and that was all.

The earl's men sidestepped their horses and opened a pathway for Duncan to proceed.

Bloody rat's bane, they're acting as if I would singlehandedly skewer them all.

Mounted on a grey steed, Arthur pushed back the visor on his helm. "You had better speak quickly, Glenorchy. If you've laid so much as a finger upon my sister, so help me, I'll blast you and your kin to hell."

Duncan held up his palm and bowed deeply—something he'd been reluctant to do when he'd met the earl months ago. "Hear me, m'lord. Lady Douglas has done me a great and honorable service and I am in her debt."

"Stop this madness!" Meg's shrill voice pierced through the tension in the air. She raced up beside him. "What on earth are you thinking, Arthur?"

Duncan grasped her hand. "Meg. You could be hurt."

She pulled her hand away.

Arthur hopped down from his horse and marched up to Duncan, craning his neck. "You dare call my sister familiar?"

Duncan again bowed. Ballocks, he could be an imbecile. "Forgive me—"

"I love him." Meg pushed between them.

Arthur drew his sword. "You rutting bastard!"

Duncan ushered Meg behind him. "Before you choose to wield your weapon, I beg you, come inside and sit with me like a gentleman. Hear me out."

Arthur eyed him, as if the puny, beef-witted codpiece would have a chance in hell of fighting Duncan. God's teeth, the man's posturing rivaled all other milksops.

Meg shoved between them. "Please, Arthur. Listen to reason."

The earl glared at Duncan and lowered his sword. "Ready yourselves for battle, men!" He grabbed Meg by the arm and yanked her beside him. "I'll have words with you next."

Duncan eyed Eoin upon the battlements and gave the nod for the archers to resume their places. Though the earl had proved himself adept at posturing, anything could happen whilst they were engaged within the walls of Kilchurn.

Duncan led Arthur to the antechamber behind the dais. There he'd be far away from the earl's men and those cannons.

He stopped outside the door and grasped Meg's hand. "Lady Douglas, please wait here."

Her gaze shot to Arthur. "But I cannot allow him to—"

Duncan squeezed her hand and frowned. "This is business to be conducted between men. Please—"

"For God's sake, Meg, go sit at the high table and await my return," Arthur snapped.

She flashed Duncan one last worried look before he ushered the earl into the chamber and closed the door. "Can I offer you a tot of whisky?"

Arthur took a seat at the head of the table—Duncan's seat. "Do you plan to dull my wits before I run you through?"

Duncan chose not to sit. They could do away with bloody pretense now they were behind closed doors. He had no doubt he could take the Earl of Angus right there in that room if it came to blows. But he didn't want that—only because Meg would be devastated. He crossed his arms over the top of his cold breastplate. "Why the elaborate show of weaponry and men?"

Arthur removed his helm and stretched his neck. "Are you serious? What did you expect? My sister administered a potion to her guardsman so that she could flee to the Highlands with a convict? Do you know how that looks at court?"

Duncan dropped his arms. "My men advised her to

return to Tantallon with her guard. I did not steal her away."

"Nonetheless, I am the laughing stock of the gentry." Arthur slammed his fist on the table. "And then there's your goddamned missive."

"Aye?"

"You blubbering fool. It lacks propriety. No man keeps a highborn woman within his castle and sends a missive. Why on earth did you not return her to Tantallon and approach me, as is proper? It was one thing when your father was lord. He was older and married." Arthur looked him from head to toe. "But you...Christ, you look like a pirate."

Duncan swallowed his groan and took a seat. "After she'd come with us, it seemed the most practical course of action. Besides..."

"What?"

He drew in a deep breath. *Time to show my hand.* "You could have refused me. And that would have suited neither me nor Lady Meg."

"Suited you? What about *my* wishes? Were you aware I was in France arranging Lady Meg's betrothal?"

"Nay." Duncan's gut clenched. "Was Lady Meg aware?"

"Of course not." Arthur pushed his chair back and paced. "I did not want to raise the poor lassie's hopes, but I planned to tell her as soon as I returned to Scotland."

"And what of this Frenchman's suit?"

"Withdrawn." Arthur stamped his foot. "Because I received a missive from Tantallon of Lady Douglas's imminent ruination."

Duncan placed his palms on the table. This needn't be difficult. "If she marries me, she will not be ruined, and our houses will be all the more powerful."

"So you say." The earl moved to the sideboard and poured himself a tot of whisky. "And how was your stay in the Edinburgh dungeon? How can I allow my sister to marry a man who was accused of killing the Earl of Mar?"

Duncan had enough. He pushed back his chair and stood, towering over Arthur by a head. "I am innocent. I've received a pardon from the king."

"After you refused to confess."

"After the king had me tortured to within an inch of my life—yet I still professed my innocence. Good God, I was the one who captured Mar from Kildrummy by the king's orders. If I wanted to kill him, I could have done it whilst we were on the trail."

"Aye? By my account, I hear you practically did." Arthur tossed back his whisky, his eyes darting toward the door. Was he a wee bit nervous about facing down a larger man—a trained killer? "What about the accusation that you killed your own father during this unfortunate sequence of events?"

The words cut Duncan with the force of a bullwhip. Clenching his fists, he took a moment to steel his grit. "True, my father was killed in the skirmish, but aside from my mother, no soul was more devastated than I." Duncan relayed the story of what happened to Da, and by the time he'd finished, every muscle in his body clenched taut to help him maintain a steady voice.

Arthur poured two tots this time, and handed one to Duncan. "I respected your father. He was a good man."

Duncan accepted the cup. "None better."

"And Meg, she likes it here?"

"Aye. She's formed quite a friendship with my sister." Duncan sipped thoughtfully. "Forgive my frankness, m'lord, but I love her. I want to marry her more than I've ever wanted anything in my life."

The earl sucked in a deep breath. "But she has such a grotesque deformity."

"'Tis but a wee flaw that in no way detracts from her beauty or her exuberance."

Arthur chuckled. "She does have enthusiasm to spare."

"It would be my greatest honor to marry Lady Douglas." Duncan held up his cup. "Shall we drink to it?"

"Not until we've agreed to terms." Arthur stroked his fingers down his beard.

Duncan gestured toward the table. "Then let us begin."

The earl's posture relaxed as he moved to his seat. "The men will be unhappy if they've come all this way without a fight."

"Perhaps we can remedy that with some sport?"

※

MEG WRUNG HER HANDS AND PACED ACROSS THE DAIS. She'd never seen Arthur look so angry. Duncan either, for that matter. Yes, he was most likely upset that she hadn't joined the women in the solar, but surely he understood she couldn't possibly hide—not when her *brother* intended to wage war.

How could Arthur drive his army into the Highlands without first trying to speak to Duncan? Besides, Duncan is highborn and a knight. I doubt Arthur could find a better match if he looked for years.

They had been locked inside the antechamber for ages. The only reason she'd known they hadn't killed each other was that she'd heard no struggling within.

What have they got to talk about that would take so long? I love Duncan. He loves me. Arthur should be elated to have me off his hands at long last. Duncan is a good match. Certainly, he's wealthy. Aye, he's known for being the king's henchman in the Highlands, but that should only serve to further impress my brother.

Meg's heart nearly burst out of her chest when the

latch clicked. She spun around to see Duncan and Arthur smiling broadly, their noses red. They'd had more than a tot. She didn't care. Their grins were infectious. Her gaze darted between them. "Well?"

Arthur cleared his throat. "I have given my consent for you to marry Lord Campbell."

Meg sighed with a huge breath. Flinging her arms wide, she couldn't decide whom to hug first. Duncan made the decision for her by properly stepping back and gesturing toward her brother. She flung her arms around his armored neck, which was none too welcoming. "Thank you, Arthur. Thank you!"

"You shall be Duncan's worry from here on out." He held her at arm's length. "What were you thinking, racing into the Highlands after a band of knights?"

Meg guffawed. "Do you forget so easily that these were the same men who rescued me from the clutches of the Earl of Northumberland?"

Arthur shuddered. "Another bastard I've yet to deal with."

With a broad grin, Duncan grasped Meg's hands. "On the morrow we shall celebrate our betrothal with Highland games for the warriors, followed by a feast to rival all others."

Meg's heart leapt. "And dancing?"

"Of course. No feast would be complete without minstrels and high-stepping reels."

Chapter Thirty-Seven

※

Meg and Gyllis sat upon a plaid and watched as the men laid out the rope for the tug o' war. Duncan and his Highland Enforcers were matched against Arthur and his best men. The Highlanders wore plaids belted around their hips, while the Lowlanders wore linen shirts tucked into their chausses. Meg leaned into Gyllis so no one else could hear. "Poor Arthur has not a chance."

"Hmm." Gyllis drummed her fingers against her lips. "Though it looks like his men have some impressive muscle."

"Aye, but I've seen both sides spar, and the Douglas guard could learn a few things from the Campbells."

Fortunately, the sun made an appearance for the day's events, and families milled about the castle foregrounds with an air of excitement that came with spring. Meg leaned forward when Duncan and Arthur faced each other and shook hands. Leading their men, they stooped to pick up the rope. She clasped Gyllis's arm. "It begins!"

Arthur tugged first, catching Duncan off guard, but the larger man dug in his heels, using brute force to haul the rope back. At the rear of the Campbell party, Sean bellowed the command to heave.

Meg's heart hammered. She desperately wanted Duncan to win, but only after the Douglas side made a good show of strength. The rope suspended taut between the two teams. Meg folded her hands beneath her chin and prayed for a tie. But her whisperings were fleeting words whisked away by the wind.

Duncan and his men heaved to the cadence of Sean's booming voice. In the blink of an eye, Arthur and the Douglas guard were dragged into the muddy bog.

Meg covered her mouth and tried not to laugh. Arthur had fallen on his face. He looked like a wet dog. Duncan planted his hands on his hips and chortled. Meg almost died. No one should ever laugh at a Douglas earl.

Arthur and his men ran straight for Duncan and tugged him into the bog. Bellowing their war cries, the entire contingent of men was soon covered in mud, wrestling in the muck, fists flying.

Gyllis stood clasping her hands to her head. "Make them stop!"

Meg shook her head. "You want to be pulled into that mayhem?"

From the top of the wall-walk, the bagpipes launched into a sobering Highland rendition of "Hey Tuttie Tatie." Lady Margaret stood beside them like a queen, her red veil flapping in the wind. Meg pointed. "Your mother is a smart woman."

"I'll say."

The men stopped their bandy and stood at attention. Every soul in Scotland was familiar with the tune, made famous when Robert the Bruce's troops marched into the Battle of Bannockburn.

After the tune ended, Duncan and Arthur walked arm in arm toward Meg. She'd never seen her brother in such high spirits. He grinned at her. "I'd like to join with your enforcers and go after that pox-marked maggot, Northumberland."

Duncan swiped a hand across his muddy face. "And break the truce?"

"I doubt even the king would agree the truce applies to that slimy snake."

Meg shuddered. "I want no more to do with Lord Percy. Leave him to wallow in his own misery, I say."

%

AFTER CHANGING INTO A CLEAN PLAID AND DOUBLET, Duncan headed to the great hall. As usual, Gyllis had absconded with Lady Meg so they could dress for the feast. Duncan chuckled, wondering what sort of elegant gown Meg would don this eve. If only he would later be able to spirit her up to his chamber and rip it from her deliciously seductive body.

When he rounded the stairwell, it pleased him to see the ladies already upon the dais. Meg looked his way. A radiant smile lit up her face. She stood and moved to the steps—floated, actually. Never in his life would he grow tired of watching her. This eve, she wore a burgundy gown, edged with gold trim. Unfortunately, this one had a high-necked collar. It did make her look regal, though Duncan preferred a lower-cut bodice. Alas, Mother undoubtedly had something to do with the dress selection, especially since her brother was in attendance.

Duncan crossed the floor quickly and took Meg's hands in his palms. "You look stunning, as always." She did. Her hair was pulled away from her face by a conical hennin and her tresses had been tamed and brushed down her back. She turned and the fiery red locks swept across her buttocks. Duncan's loins stirred to life. He glanced at Arthur, who was already seated at the high table beside Lady Margaret. He watched Duncan with hawk-like eyes.

Duncan faced the hall and raised his arms. "Welcome, friends and family. Let us feast and make merry!"

"The entire keep smells divine," Meg said, walking with him to the chieftain's chair. "Your mother has outdone herself."

She sat in the chair beside his, and he regarded her with renewed concern. "Soon it will be your duty to appoint the feasts."

She grimaced. "I couldn't displace Lady Margaret, and she enjoys it so."

"Perhaps she could entertain more of a consulting role."

Meg gestured toward his seat. "That is something you may consider discussing with her. I'll stand for no hard feelings in my new home."

Duncan made a mental note to speak to Mother. The transition of bringing in a new lady of the keep might be difficult for her. She'd overseen the keep for years—even overseen the building of it so long ago. Duncan was about to sit when he stopped dead. Gyllis was sitting beside Sean, batting her damned eyelashes. "What the devil?"

Meg tugged on his hand. "Sit. I made the seating arrangements."

"You?" Duncan plopped in his chair. "Mayhap I should rethink moving Mother into a conciliatory role."

She thwacked his shoulder. "Pardon me?"

He held up a finger. "I'll allow it this *once*."

Meg grinned like she'd just won a battle with the English.

"But I'll not allow them to dance."

Meg reached for the ewer and poured the wine. "No? Come, Duncan. What harm is there in dancing?"

Arthur leaned forward. "Are you a dancer, Glenorchy?"

Duncan glared across the table at Sean. "Not when it comes to sisters."

The earl chuckled. "I ken exactly what you mean."

The minstrels climbed upon the balcony and began to play a light assortment of music suitable for dining. Duncan relaxed and passed a trencher of assorted meats to Arthur.

The earl stabbed a lamb shank with his eating knife. "You'll need this wedding to be over soon so I can head back to North Berwick."

"My thoughts as well." Duncan glanced to Meg. "What say you? On the morrow?"

The ram's horn sounded.

The music stopped.

Everything went silent.

The horn blew twice more.

A lead ball sank to the pit of Duncan's stomach.

Chapter Thirty-Eight

⚜

Duncan held his breath and moved to the front of the dais while footsteps clattered from the stairwell. The sentry raced across the floor of the great hall. "The pennant of Northumberland, m'lord."

"Curses." He'd been ill at ease ever since Arthur mentioned that Lord Percy hadn't crossed the border. "God's teeth, will my every nemesis show his face before the day's end?" Duncan eyed the guard. "How far out are they?"

"The spy reported four miles, m'lord."

Arthur hastened beside Duncan. "Their numbers?"

The sentry looked between them. "He estimated fifty cavalry and a hundred foot soldiers armed with pikes and battleaxes."

"Bloody hell." Duncan raked his fingers through his hair and frowned at Arthur. "It looks like your men will have their fight after all."

"How fortuitous." Arthur ground his fist into his palm. "I've had a taste for revenge since the bastard abducted Meg. Better yet, now he's the one breaking the truce."

Meg stepped in and grasped his arm. "The cannons are outside our walls."

Duncan looked to Arthur. "Can your men wheel

them within the bailey quickly? We've an hour, two at best."

Arthur marched down the steps. "Consider it done."

Duncan scanned the faces of the womenfolk at the high table, every one of them in his care. "Haste to the lady's solar at once and lock yourselves inside." He grasped Meg's shoulders. "I mean it this time. This is not your brother come to posture for your virtue. This is a madman who wants nothing but vengeance."

Meg nodded, her eyes rimming red. "Come with us. Please. I would die if something happened to you."

He grasped her hands between his palms and kissed her fingers. "You know I cannot. Go now. The battle will soon be over."

A tear slid down her cheek. Duncan couldn't help himself. In an open display of affection, he surrounded her in his arms. "It will be all right, lass." He pressed his lips to her forehead and closed his eyes, inhaling her scent. Her honeyed fragrance calmed his thundering heart. "I'll fetch you as soon as I can. Now take my mother and sisters and show them the strong Lady Meg I've grown to love."

Her body trembled while she drew in a breath. "Be careful—you have six women relying on you."

Duncan swallowed hard and forced himself to step back. Gyllis, Helen, Marion, Alice and Mother all stared at him with fear in their eyes. "Go with Lady Meg. Hurry, now."

He gazed out over the stunned crowd. "To arms!"

After again donning his coat of armor, Duncan met Arthur upon the battlements. He figured it was close to midnight when Lord Percy's torches flickered between the forest trees.

"You think he'll wait until first light?" Arthur asked.

"If he has any sense, he'll rest his men before launching an attack."

Eoin stepped beside Duncan. "They'll not stop. Mark me."

Duncan climbed up on the wall and spread his arms to address the men. "We will not light the battlement cauldrons until they are upon us. Archers, lie in wait behind the merlon notches. Once they are in formation, we shall fire and show no mercy!"

True to Eoin's word, the Earl of Northumberland's troops marched up the path to Kilchurn. Surrounded by water on three sides, Duncan had the advantage. *What tricks does the bastard have up his sleeve?*

Ominous clouds sailed overhead as Percy's men filed into formation.

"Light the fires!" Duncan bellowed. "Archers ready!" He glanced at Arthur—the earl gave a sharp nod. "Fire!"

The battle was on. By the shrieks of pain wailing from below, several archers had hit their marks. "Give no quarter! Reload!" Duncan bellowed. "Fire at will!"

The entire fortress shuddered with a booming thud.

"The battering ram," Arthur said.

"Is the tar ready?" Duncan hollered.

James gave a thumbs-up from the kettle. "Nearly there."

Duncan turned to Arthur. "Can you line up a cannon with the portcullis?"

"And blast a hole through the gate? That would only invite them inside."

"Nay. The gate may be three foot thick, but it will not last forever. Once the bastards break through, I aim to blast them to hell."

Arthur clapped Duncan's shoulder. "I like the way you think." He beckoned his man-at-arms. "Take a crew to the bailey and line the cannon up with the portcullis. When the gate is breeched, send them to Satan."

"Right away, m'lord."

Duncan leaned close to Arthur and kept his voice low. "When the time comes, it would do me a great honor if you would remain on the battlements and lead the archers, m'lord." In no way could Duncan allow the Earl of Angus, Meg's brother, to take up a sword.

Arthur looked at him with narrowed eyes, but then nodded. "If that is your wish."

※

Meg walked to the window embrasure and pulled away the furs. "'Tis nearly light." Another blasting thud came from the battering ram. Meg nearly jumped out of her skin every time it hit the portcullis.

The only one still awake, Lady Margaret joined her. "I cannot believe we haven't stopped them yet. Duncan is every bit the knight his father was."

"Aye. But we're wearing them down. Can you not tell from the shrieks outside our walls?"

Lady Margaret ran her fingers along the stone. "I built this keep with my own hands. Colin was away fighting in the Crusades, and all the while I worked with the master mason to see this castle to completion. I do not take lightly the evil forces down below trying to breech our walls."

Meg fingered the eating knife in her pocket. "Nor do I." She looked back to Gyllis and the others, all huddled together in the corner. They'd probably worried themselves into a stupor. Meg hated being locked inside where she couldn't see what was happening. Listening to the battle rage had to be worse than watching it from the wall-walk.

A tap came at the door.

Lady Margaret gasped. "Who is it?"

"Sir Isaac."

Meg gaped at Duncan's mother. "How did he slip inside?"

Who? she mouthed.

Meg headed to the door. "He's the one who came to

Tantallon to tell me about Duncan." She grasped the latch. "Are you alone?"

"Yes. Hurry."

Meg hesitated. "How did you slip inside?"

"The water intake. Please." His English accent sounded strained. "Open the door."

Lady Margaret grimaced, her brows pinched together. "Can you trust him?"

"He risked everything to warn me." Meg bit her lip. *But he was standing beside Lord Percy when I approached the king with Sir Eoin and the others.* Could she risk opening the door?

Chapter Thirty-Nine

※

Not long after dawn, the great portcullis splintered. Swords drawn, Duncan and his men raced down the tower stairs. "No one will attack Kilchurn and live! This is what we've been trained for. Fight for your kin and your lives!"

After two more savage blows with the battering ram, the gate gave way. Duncan barreled into the guardhouse. "What are you waiting for? Fire the cannon now!"

The bumbling sentry held the torch to the slow match. With an earsplitting blast, the cannon shot its black powder and hurled a lead ball through the gaping hole in the gate. The enormous black gun recoiled all the way to the edge of the courtyard.

Duncan marched forward, peering through the foul, sulfur-tasting smoke and surveyed the carnage. At least a dozen men lay dead or writhing on the ground. Behind them, Lord Percy's troops rallied. Braying their battle cry, the pikemen advanced.

Duncan's men were already in formation. "They have only one small gap in which to enter. Do not let a one past you." He pointed. "Robert, send your best men up to guard the solar door."

Northumberland's pikemen shoved their weapons

through the gatehouse. With a swing of his blade, Duncan hacked the nearest spear in half, lunged in and pulled the soldier into the courtyard. The man reached for his dagger. Grinding his teeth, Duncan struck with lightning speed, plunging his sword into the swine's belly for the kill.

On and on, the men fought, clashing iron with iron until blood made the ground slick and red. Duncan circled with a brute of a man brandishing a short sword. The bastard laughed and beckoned him forward, but Duncan was too well practiced to fall for his ploy. He eyed the weak spot in the man's armor: he wore only a leather collar—a deadly mistake. When the soldier lunged, Duncan darted aside, aiming his blade at the man's neck. Hitting his mark, the sword sliced off the collar, but the blow wasn't enough to kill the beast.

Duncan crouched, ready for another bout.

Above, the ram's horn blared. *What in Christ's name?* Duncan kept his eyes on his opponent and circled.

"Stop!"

He would never mistake Meg's voice. But taking his eyes off the warrior now would be a deadly mistake.

"Stand down," a man bellowed.

The Englishman backed away and lowered his weapon.

Duncan's gaze shot to Meg. A scar-faced man in Highland dress had his sword angled up at Meg's throat. Duncan's chest tightened. He looked to Eoin, then to Sean. They each gave a nod. The first mistake this bastard made would be his last.

"We've captured her!" the scar-faced man shouted with an English accent.

"I am unharmed, Duncan," Meg said in a steady voice.

Flanked by a dozen cavalrymen, the Lord of Northumberland rode a black steed into the inner bailey. "Well, well. The wayward priest and his crippled accomplice." He snickered. "How charming. Lady Meg fell in love with the knight who rescued her from my clutches."

Duncan's gaze shot from Northumberland to Meg and her villainous captor. "Do you think you can win by doing this? You'd risk breaking the truce to pursue your own feud?"

"*Your* king has all but ruined the fragile little truce." Lord Percy ran his reins through his gauntleted fingers. "I couldn't resist, knowing I've got you both in one place. I shall kill two at once."

The Englishman with Meg moved closer. Duncan gripped his sword and nodded to Eoin, but before he could make a move, an arrow flew from the battlements.

Lord Percy grunted, his face blanched and his torso fell against his horse's neck. An arrow lodged at the junction of his armband and his breastplate.

"Release my sister at once," Arthur shouted from above.

The Englishman winked at Duncan. "Ever so happy to oblige." He pushed Meg into Duncan and advanced toward the earl, brandishing his sword.

"Retreat!" Percy commanded, spinning his horse in place. Behind the thunder of hoofbeats, the remaining pikemen raced from the courtyard.

Duncan pointed to the plaid-wearing Englishman, now chasing after Northumberland and swinging his sword over his head. "Seize him!"

Eoin and Robert made quick work of disarming the scarred man.

Duncan pulled Meg in a tight embrace. "Are you all right, my love?"

She smiled—how could she appear so calm when she'd just been held captive? "Aye, but you must release Isaac. 'Twas his plan to trick Lord Percy into the inner bailey and have Arthur shoot him."

Duncan regarded the Englishman wearing a plaid belted beneath a breastplate, standing perfectly still in Robert's grasp. Sauntering toward them, a hint of recognition tickled Duncan's mind. "Was it now?"

Isaac offered a sheepish grin. "Aye. Lord Percy wouldn't have stopped until he saw both you and Arthur dead."

Duncan stroked his chin. "You're the one who followed us from Alnwick, are you not?"

"Yes, but when Lord Percy commanded me to kill the Earl of Mar, I'd had enough."

Meg gaped. "That was you?"

"Acting upon my master's orders." Isaac bowed his head. "I vow I will never stoop so low again."

Meg grasped Duncan's hands. "Please, my love. You are alive because of Isaac's assistance."

"Release him." Duncan pointed toward the stables. "Highland Enforcers, after Northumberland! No one wages war on the Campbells and rides away."

Arthur dashed from the tower. "But what of the truce?"

Duncan sheathed his sword. "Are you satisfied he will leave you alone?"

"I will petition the king." He gestured to Isaac. "With this man's confession that Lord Percy ordered Mar's death, we can ruin the man with a direct complaint to King Edward in England. The bloody earl was Edward's emissary to Scotland. He's a traitor of the worst sort." Arthur spat on the ground. "I'd love to see his title stripped for good."

"I daresay that would be more painful to him than death," Isaac said.

Duncan nodded, weighing Arthur's words carefully.

Meg clamped her fingers atop the armor on his arm. "We do have a feast to resume."

"And a wedding on the morrow." Lady Margaret stepped into the courtyard.

Duncan looked to Arthur. "You shall ride for Edinburgh immediately following the wedding?"

The earl nodded. "Bloody oath I will."

Duncan eyed Isaac. "What are we to do with you?"

The Englishman removed his helm. "After I returned to Alnwick, I moved my family to Carlisle. I would like leave to fetch them, and pledge my fealty to you, m'lord."

Duncan frowned. Could he trust this man? He'd murdered the Earl of Mar—but then couldn't rest when Duncan had been blamed. "That is a bold request."

Meg stepped forward. "I believe Sir Isaac has shown his true loyalty. He risked his life to make amends for his evil deeds."

Duncan gave the Englishman a once-over. The sturdily built man could be of use, especially on missions that took them south of the Scottish border. "Fetch your family, but you will need to prove your worth one hundred fold."

Isaac again bowed. "Thank you, my lord. You will not be disappointed."

"I had better not be." Duncan faced the crowd of bedraggled warriors. "You all have fought well. Let us resume our meal and then seek our beds. For tomorrow there will be a wedding and a great gathering to celebrate our victory!"

※

THE NEXT MORNING MEG AWOKE TO A CRISP BREEZE blowing from the loch. Gyllis still slept beside her, snoring ever so lightly. Butterflies flitted throughout her insides. Today she would marry the man of her dreams. She slid out of bed and sat in the window embrasure. The sun reflected in an angle over the loch, making the ripples on the water shimmer as if the water were alive.

Green sprouted everywhere. Even the trees were

showing their first hints of mossy green in a promise to enliven Argyllshire with the vibrant colors of spring and summer.

Meg drew her knees up and wrapped her arms around them. On one side she wished the ceremony would come quickly, but on the other, she wanted to savor every moment. She never again would be a bride, and this day topped her list for the most important in her two and twenty years.

She closed her eyes and inhaled the cool morning air. Calm spread from her chest to her limbs and out the tips of her fingers. Her mind cleared and took her to a place where she was one with nature, almost like floating as a downy feather on the wind.

After she'd reached the pinnacle of calm, the chamber door flew open and in strode Lady Margaret, carrying a voluminous red gown, followed by chambermaids with buckets of steaming water and a groom carrying a wooden tub.

"Put it in front of the hearth." Lady Margaret pointed. "You must wake, Gyllis."

"Already?" Gyllis asked with a sleepy voice.

The chambermaids emptied their buckets into the tub and filed in a procession out the door.

Lady Margaret smiled brilliantly. "'Tis good to see you awake, Meg. Are you excited for your wedding day?"

Meg stood and wiped her hands across her face. "Yes, thank you. I had a refreshing night's sleep, and am ready to take my vows." Though these were vows she'd never allowed herself to dream she'd be uttering.

"We've much to do before you'll be ready to stand before the priest." Lady Margaret flicked her wrists. "First into the bath with you, then we need to pluck your eyebrows, rouge your cheeks and lips, then file your nails." She crossed the room and fingered a lock of

Meg's hair. "And I shall send up my own chambermaid to attend your lovely tresses."

"Aye, with hair like that, she scarcely needs a headpiece," Gyllis said.

"Sacrilege!" Lady Margaret strode to the bed and picked up the gown she'd brought in. The velvet overdress was the most brilliant shade of red Meg had ever seen, trimmed with sealskin. "I daresay this is still in fashion after all these years."

Meg smoothed her hand over the velvet, woven with thread of gold. "'Tis exquisite."

The lady's gaze softened. "It was my very own wedding dress."

Meg clutched her fists under her chin. "Oh my, I cannot wear such an important family heirloom."

"And why ever not? You are marrying into the family." Lady Margaret picked up Meg's hand and held it to the dress. "Besides, it matches the ring Duncan gave you."

Meg sighed. "Aye, it does."

"Ooh," Gyllis said. "Mother, you think of everything."

"Yes I do, and there is no time to waste. Off with your shift. I shall call in the chambermaid at once." The matron sounded as giddy as a wee lassie.

Meg complied and slipped into the warm water. She grinned. Soon Lady Margaret would run out of reasons to keep her from Duncan's arms.

WEARING THE CEREMONIAL ARMOR PASSED DOWN from his father, Duncan paced at the back of the chapel. His inner circle of men all stood patiently, as if this were just another humdrum day. Duncan thumped Eoin on the shoulder. "Say something, would you?"

The knight cleared his throat. "The salmon will be running up the Orchy soon."

Duncan should have hit him harder. "Fishing?"

"Aye." Eoin spread his palms to his sides. "Would you rather I challenged you to a wrestling match? You might look a bit unsightly for your bride with a black eye."

Duncan paced in a circle. "Bloody miserable hell, where is she?"

As if he'd uttered the secret password, the chapel door opened and Lady Margaret slipped inside, followed by Duncan's sisters. "Oh good, you're ready," Mother said.

He looked to the rafters. "I've been ready since the cock crowed at first light."

Mother smiled in her serene way and patted Duncan's cheek. "A prize as lovely as Lady Meg is worth the wait." She flicked her wrists toward the altar. "You'd best take your place."

He'd bloody waited long enough. Mother led the girls to the pew at the front of the chapel. Duncan followed and stood at the rail. He stared at the door thinking it would never open, but then a sliver of sunlight spread into a glowing ray. Through that light, Meg appeared like an apparition sent from heaven. The sunshine first caught the ringlets of hair peeking from under her veil. It wasn't until Meg stepped farther into the chapel that he could see her face. Her radiant smile ignited the embers of his heart.

Meg looked more regal than the Queen of Scotland, more beautiful than a meadow nymph, and, best of all, this day she would be his.

Arthur escorted her down the aisle of the small chapel.

Meg reached out her hands to Duncan, blessing him with such luminous beauty, his heart thrummed in his chest. "You are stunning, my love."

Her eyes sparkled. "As are you."

While the priest chanted the Latin mass, Duncan recalled the first time she'd unveiled her striking cobalt eyes to him. He'd done his best to act like a priest, but she'd seen right though his ruse. From the outset, Meg could gaze into his soul and find the truth. And from that blessed moment in the Alnwick chapel, this remarkable woman had won his heart forever.

Epilogue
EIGHT MONTHS LATER

Having recently returned from the borders, where he and his men were patrolling for English spies, Duncan paced in front of the hearth. The shrieks coming from the adjoining lady's chamber had his wits on the ragged edge. God's bones, he'd rather be fighting an army of MacDonald rogues than listening to Meg suffer through labor.

"I can see the head," Alana's matronly voice resounded through the walls. "Bear down with your next pain."

"I cannot bear to breathe anymore, let alone withstand the pain to push him out!" Meg sounded on the brink of hysterical.

"'Tis nearly over," Mother soothed. "You shall hold your bairn in your arms soon."

"The pain is killing me!" After a few sharp gasps, Meg cried out in such agony, Duncan was convinced he'd lose her.

He could take no more. He marched to the door and stopped, holding his hand above the latch. He mustn't go in there. It was bad luck...and work only for womenfolk. But Jesus, he needed to do *something*. Raking his fingers through his hair, he stared at the sideboard against the far wall. Aye, he could use a stiff drink.

Shrieks and gasps clawed through the walls, creeping up Duncan's skin. His hands shook as he uncorked the flagon and filled a goblet.

He held it to his lips.

Meg screamed.

Whisky sloshed down the front of his shirt.

"Keep pushing," Alana yelled.

Duncan picked up the flagon and guzzled.

Something clapped. A wee voice cried. *A darling wee voice indeed.*

Meg laughed.

Duncan did too.

"'Tis a girl!" Mother said with elation.

Duncan set the flagon down. *A girl?* He could have crowed from the rafters.

When the door between the chambers opened, Ma walked over, holding a bundle. "Say hello to your daughter."

Duncan grinned and hastened across the room. "Elizabeth. Meg wanted to name a girl after her sister."

Mother placed the bairn in his arms. With red fuzz atop her dainty head, she gurgled.

After taking one look at the darling face, Duncan was completely enraptured. "She's the most beautiful bairn I've ever seen." He then looked up. "How is Meg?"

Ma smiled. "She's—"

A shrill cry screeched from Meg's chamber.

Ma grimaced with a look of terror.

"Hold on," Alana bellowed. "There's another wee bairn coming!"

The door slammed in Duncan's face as Meg launched into another bout of nerve-fraying screams. Duncan started for the sideboard and looked down. Elizabeth's face turned bright red...and then she started crying. Duncan froze. What in God's name was he to do with a bairn in his arms? And she didn't look quite so adorable with her face all scrunched up and a high-pitched cry rattling about inside his ears.

"Push, push, push!" Alana cried.

Duncan tried to soothe and bounce the bairn, but Elizabeth cried louder.

"I cannot," Meg shrieked.

"Just once more. You can, m'lady. You. Can!"

After an earsplitting howl, Duncan could take no more. He burst into the chamber to see Alana hold up a gory mass of bloody gook and smack it on the behind. The matron had the audacity to grin while bairn number two cried loudly, sucking in frantic gasps.

The matron continued to grin as if it were the happiest day of all. "You have a son as well, m'lord."

"Praises be." Ma beamed as if Meg weren't lying sprawled across the bed in a pool of blood.

Duncan's jaw dropped. "But—"

"Let me hold Elizabeth." Meg reached up.

Duncan held out the bairn as if he were handling a basket of fragile eggs. "Are you well, my love?"

"I've never been better," Meg hummed, as if she hadn't been screaming bloody murder for hour upon hour.

Duncan sat beside her and brushed a lock of damp hair from Meg's forehead.

Alana dunked the boy in the basin, splashing water over him and wiping him down. The wee lad carried on with boisterous cries. Duncan didn't blame him. The water was most likely ice cold.

Ma spread a plaid over Meg's lap and hid the mess. Though Meg's hair was mussed in a tangled mane, she looked like an angel when she glanced up with a radiant smile.

Duncan's heart melted.

Then Alana placed the lad in Meg's other arm. "You must make the bond soon."

Meg looked from one of her breasts to the next. "Both at once?"

"Aye."

"And what name have you chosen for the lad?" Mother asked.

"Colin," Duncan said without hesitation. "He shall be named for the founder and patriarch of our clan. The legendary knight who fought in the Crusades. His name will be revered by our family forever."

As Elizabeth and Colin began to nurse, Duncan kissed Meg's forehead. "You have given me the greatest gift a man could ever hope for. I love you and our children from the depths of my heart, and I always will."

Author's Note

I hope you enjoyed *A Highland Knight's Desire*. Though Duncan Campbell, the Second Lord of Glenorchy did exist, and he did marry Lady Meg (Margaret Douglas), their stories are rather obscure. Duncan was a poet and became the Second Lord of Glenorchy after his father's death (the date of Colin Campbell's death is a point of contention and is listed differently in the records, with some quoting 1475. The official family record, the Black Book of Taymouth, records his death as being 1480, though no cause is mentioned). Duncan, in subsequent years, did a great deal of building and acquired lands, further increasing the Campbell dynasty.

Aside from Lady Meg being the daughter of the Fourth Earl of Angus (George Douglas), little is known about her life. The Earls of Angus were called the Red Douglases, and at this point in history, kept themselves apart from the Black Douglas renegades who had fallen out of favor with King James III.

Though many of the characters in this book were styled after real people, nearly all of the events involving Meg and Duncan are fictional.

In the coming series, Lord Duncan will continue to rule as the patriarch over the Campbell dynasty. Leg-

AUTHOR'S NOTE

ends, both factual and imagined, will be laced with sweeping tales of romance. I hope you will join me for the ride.

Also by Amy Jarecki

Highland Defender

The Valiant Highlander
The Fearless Highlander
The Highlander's Iron Will

Highland Force:

Captured by the Pirate Laird
The Highland Henchman
Beauty and the Barbarian
Return of the Highland Laird

Guardian of Scotland

Rise of a Legend
In the Kingdom's Name
The Time Traveler's Christmas

Highland Dynasty

Knight in Highland Armor
A Highland Knight's Desire
A Highland Knight to Remember
Highland Knight of Rapture
Highland Knight of Dreams

Devilish Dukes

The Duke's Fallen Angel
The Duke's Untamed Desire

ICE
Hunt for Evil
Body Shot
Mach One

Celtic Fire
Rescued by the Celtic Warrior
Deceived by the Celtic Spy

Lords of the Highlands series:
The Highland Duke
The Highland Commander
The Highland Guardian
The Highland Chieftain
The Highland Renegade
The Highland Earl
The Highland Rogue
The Highland Laird

The Chihuahua Affair
Virtue: A Cruise Dancer Romance
Boy Man Chief

About the Author

A descendant of an ancient Lowland clan, Amy adores Scotland. Though she now resides in southwest Utah, she received her MBA from Heriot-Watt University in Edinburgh. Winning multiple writing awards, she found her niche in the genre of Scottish historical romance. Amy loves hearing from her readers and can be contacted through her website at www.  amyjarecki.com. Visit her web site & sign up to receive newsletter updates of new releases and giveaways exclusive to newsletter followers.